Another
WOMAN'S
HUSBAND

By Gill Paul

Women and Children First
The Affair
No Place for a Lady
The Secret Wife
Another Woman's Husband

Another
WOMAN'S
HUSBAND

GILL PAUL

REVIEW

First published in Great Britain in 2017
by HEADLINE REVIEW
An imprint of HEADLINE PUBLISHING GROUP

1

Cataloguing in Publication Data is available from the British Library

ISBN 978 1 4722 5044 5 (Hardback)
ISBN 978 1 4722 5045 2 (Trade paperback)

Typeset in Adobe Caslon Pro by
Palimpsest Book Production Ltd, Falkirk, Stirlingshire

Printed and Bound in the United States of America

HEADLINE PUBLISHING GROUP
An Hachette UK Company
Carmelite House
50 Victoria Embankment
London EC4Y 0DZ

www.headline.co.uk
www.hachette.co.uk

For Amazing Lor,
who helped so much with this novel.
You will never be forgotten.

Chapter 1

Paris, 31 August 1997

RACHEL RESTED HER HEAD ON ALEX'S SHOULDER and slid a hand onto his thigh. His arm was curled around her in a way that was not entirely comfortable given the taxi's safety belt and the tightness of her silk cheongsam dress, but she didn't give a fig. Through the window, the lights of Paris blurred against the night sky. She inhaled the scent of him, and mused that she was exquisitely happy. Her heart was full to the brim with happiness. How many moments in life could you say that about?

Earlier that evening, back in their stylishly stark hotel room, while Rachel was applying scarlet lipstick and checking her reflection in a gold compact mirror, Alex had begun to speak, then stopped.

'Darling, there was something I was going to ask you tonight, but I don't know . . . maybe in the restaurant . . .'

He seemed flustered and uncertain, quite unlike himself.

She raised an eyebrow and smiled. 'Cat got your tongue?'

He turned to look out of the window, then faced her again. 'No, I'll do it later . . .'

She regarded him with affection. 'For goodness' sake, spit it out. You've started now.'

He paced around, one hand fumbling in his trouser pocket. 'The thing is . . . Oh God, Rachel, do you think we should get married? I mean, will you marry me? Please?'

It was such a surprise that she stared at him, open-mouthed. 'Do you mean it?' He had a habit of winding her up, but surely he wouldn't joke about such a momentous subject?

'Of course.' He produced a tiny dark blue jewellery box and handed it to her.

She felt like bursting into tears. At thirty-eight, with the carnage of several disastrous relationships behind her, she had thought this moment would never come. The man she was desperately in love with was asking her to spend her life with him. It was so overwhelming she couldn't find words.

'Are you going to open it?' Alex asked.

Inside there was an antique diamond ring: two decent-sized stones nestled in a marcasite setting on a rose-gold band. It was beautiful.

She blurted the first thing that came into her head: 'I want to have babies. Are you up for that?'

How unromantic I must sound, she thought, biting her lip. As if negotiating a business deal.

'Of course,' he agreed. 'Me too.'

'What if we have to make our children the high-tech way, in a tube at a fertility clinic?'

'Whatever it takes,' he promised. His hand was shaking as he slipped the ring onto her finger, and she realised how nervous he was. This clearly meant a lot. She looped her arms round his waist and clung to him. They had always felt right for each other: her head at the perfect height for his shoulder, hip bone touching hip bone.

'Time for a spot of baby-making practice before dinner, Mrs Greene?' he asked, his voice a little husky. He started to unfasten the shoulder buttons of her dress.

'Whoever said I would take your name?' She kissed him. 'I think you should take mine.'

He pulled her down onto the bed. Fortunately the restaurant held their dinner reservation.

Thinking back as she sat in the taxi, Rachel realised she hadn't actually said yes, but they were engaged all the same. She examined the ring on her finger, turning her hand this way and that. It was the most extraordinary compliment a man could pay you. She and Alex had been living together for eighteen months, but he'd never mentioned marriage before and she'd got the impression he was an independent type who might never settle down. It seemed she'd been wrong.

They were driving along a tree-lined road beside the Seine. On the opposite bank, the iconic shape of the Eiffel Tower was glowing against the dark sky like an arty postcard. The taxi was heading down into a concrete underpass, had just entered it when suddenly the driver swerved and braked hard. Rachel was thrown forward, the seat belt cutting into her collarbone, then her head jerked back.

'What the . . .?' she heard Alex exclaim, as the taxi driver swore in French.

Rachel looked through the windscreen and saw that the road ahead was blocked by motorbikes parked at odd angles. Strobe-style lights were flashing and her first thought was that it might be some kind of theatrical event.

'*Un accident*,' the driver explained. He switched off the meter.

Alex unclicked his seat belt and opened the door. 'I'll see what's happening,' he said, his TV producer's instinct for a story kicking in.

Rachel reached over too late to restrain him. She didn't want him to seem like a voyeur when people could be injured. She watched him walk towards the crowd, and as her eyes adjusted to the rapid flashes she saw they were photographers and the strobe effects were coming from their cameras. Maybe it was a celebrity who had crashed. Alex was talking to a man in a leather jacket holding a crash helmet.

The taxi driver got out as well, leaving Rachel on her own. She opened her door, leaned her head out to get a better view and was stunned by the noise of the cameras. It echoed round the tunnel like the rat-tat-tat of machine-gun fire. In the background, a car horn blared and there was a choking smell of smoke and petrol.

She saw Alex hurrying towards her, his eyes wide with shock, his expression urgent. He waited till he was close before speaking, so she could hear over the din.

'Jesus Christ, Rachel,' he said. 'It's Princess Diana!'

Chapter 2

Burrland, near Middleburg, Virginia, July 1911

MARY KIRK PERCHED ON HER NARROW BED, flicking through a fashion magazine. Half a dozen other girls were lazing around, four of them in tennis whites from a recent doubles match, a couple fanning themselves and moaning about the sweltering heat. They were sharing a guest cottage at Miss Charlotte Noland's summer camp for girls, and there was no ceiling fan so the air sat thick and damp, smelling of sweaty tennis shoes and laundry starch.

The door opened and Miss Katherine Noland, Charlotte's sister, came in, leading a slim girl with dark hair and a strong bone structure, who gazed around as if getting the measure of them. Mary looked back. The newcomer wasn't pretty but she was striking; her dress was plain but well-cut; she wasn't tall but she held herself like a tall person.

'This is Bessiewallis Warfield,' Miss Katherine said. 'She's joining us today and I'd like y'all to make her welcome.'

'Wallis,' the girl said, in a voice that was surprisingly deep for a fifteen-year-old. 'Everyone calls me Wallis.'

The other girls went up to introduce themselves, one by one, and when it was Mary's turn she smiled and asked, 'Isn't Wallace a boy's name?'

A pair of deep-cornflower-blue eyes met hers with amusement. 'I'm named after my grandfather,' Wallis said. 'What about you? Are you named after the Blessed Virgin?'

Mary chuckled. 'No, nothing like that. My name represents a complete failure of imagination on the part of my parents.'

Wallis smiled and her eyes sparkled. 'You look like Mary Pickford, although your hair is darker: more auburn than strawberry blonde. There are worse namesakes to have.'

Mary flushed at the compliment. She'd never been to the movies, but Mary Pickford's face was in all the magazines and she was breathtakingly beautiful.

Miss Katherine led Wallis to a bed in the corner and asked the girls to show her around before they met on the lawn for a picnic later. Mary showed her where to hang her frocks and fold away her undergarments, and stood watching as she unpacked.

'Where do your folks live?' she asked.

'My mom lives in Baltimore, but my pa died when I was a baby.' Wallis's tone was matter-of-fact.

Mary was aghast. How awful not to have a father! 'What did he die of?' she asked, then wished she could bite back the tactless words.

Wallis didn't seem to mind. 'TB,' she replied. 'But Mom got remarried to a man called Mr Rasin and he's kind. He got me Bully, my French bulldog, and an aquarium of tropical fish.'

'Do you have brothers and sisters?'

'No, just me. What about you?'

'I'm the middle of three sisters: Buckie is the older and Anne the younger.'

'Darn it!' Wallis exclaimed. 'I wish at least one of us had brothers so they could introduce us to their friends. I go to an all-girls' school and now an all-girls' summer camp, and I don't know how in the heck I'm ever gonna meet boys at this rate. Is there anywhere round here we can find some?'

Mary was secretly thrilled at the bad language. She would have been roundly scolded for saying 'heck' or 'darn' at home. This girl seemed more fun than the others at camp, who tended to be prissy. 'I've only been here a day longer than you so I haven't gotten started on hunting for boys yet. But I hear we will be invited for tea by local families and some of them must have sons.'

'What else are we going to do for the next two months?' Wallis grinned. 'There's only so much horse-riding, swimming and tennis a gal can stand.'

The picnic was laid out on trestle tables on the sloping lawn between the white porticoed plantation house and the tranquil blue lake that snaked for a couple of miles, meandering into bays and inlets. All around as far as the eye could see were green fields separated by rows of trees in full leaf. The air was still, and the insects sounded drowsy in the warmth of the afternoon.

The girls wandered over to inspect the spread of cold veal chops with their stems enclosed in ruffled paper, potato salad, baked ham and pickles, and a range of fancy cakes, with lemonade, tea and coffee to drink. The Noland sisters supervised as they wandered round conversing with each other. It was an art to balance food and drink, to eat delicately and avoid speaking with your mouth full. Mary noticed that Wallis managed it by scarcely eating at all.

They strolled down to the water together, their faces angled to catch a slight breeze.

'Tell me, who is your ideal beau?' Wallis asked.

Mary had an answer on the tip of her tongue. 'Prince Edward of England. I'm *crazy* about him. Just imagine: the girl who marries him gets to be a queen some day.'

'Not bad.' Wallis cocked her head appreciatively. 'But would you know what to do if he came round that corner?' She pointed to a headland. 'How is your curtseying?'

Mary bobbed a curtsey and giggled. 'I think I would faint clean away.'

'Don't worry. I would do the talking. I'd tell him you are the most wonderful girl in the world, and lend him some smelling salts to revive you as he cradled you in his arms.'

They laughed. Miss Charlotte was calling for them all to mingle, but Mary and Wallis drifted further from the group, engrossed in their budding friendship.

'Do you ever wonder what it's like to kiss a boy?' Wallis asked. 'I can't decide whether you are supposed to keep your lips closed or to part them just a little. I've practised on my hand and I'm not sure which feels better. You try.'

Mary kissed the back of her own hand, once with lips closed and the next time open. 'I don't know. I guess you just go along with whatever the boy is doing.'

Wallis threw her head back and cackled. 'Mary Kirk, that attitude is going to land you in a whole heap of trouble!'

Mary blushed. 'Of course, I wouldn't kiss a boy anyhow until we were engaged.'

'My grandma used to say, "Never let a man kiss your hand or he'll never marry you." That, and "Never marry a Yankee."'

'I certainly would never dream of such a thing,' Mary drawled in her best Southern belle accent.

'What would you not dream of?' Miss Charlotte asked, coming up behind them. 'Are you two going to join our party or are you setting up a private society?'

'Sorry, Miss Charlotte,' Mary said straight away.

'Don't worry. It's good to see you making friends.' She smiled from one to the other.

Mary felt proud to be friends with Wallis. She was unquestionably the smartest, most sophisticated and most interesting girl in the entire place.

A local family named the Tabbs invited a group of girls, including Wallis and Mary, for Sunday supper, and when they arrived in the Nolands' horse-drawn coach they were helped to step down by the two Tabb brothers, Lloyd and Prosser. At seventeen, Lloyd was the more handsome and suave of the pair; Prosser, at fifteen, had the gawkiness of youth. Straight away, Wallis was engaging Lloyd in conversation, apparently hanging on his every word. Prosser offered to fetch Mary a glass of cool cherryade.

'Why, thank you,' she said. She was pleased not to be left on her own but unsure how to talk to boys. What were they interested in? If only Wallis and Lloyd were closer, she could have listened to them; it seemed Wallis had no trouble at all finding a topic.

'Have your family lived here long?' she asked Prosser. 'What kind of farming do they do? Are you keen to work on a farm one day?' She was boring herself, while listening to laughter from the direction of Wallis and Lloyd. What on earth were they laughing about?

She was relieved when Prosser suggested they stroll across to join the others but baffled when she heard the subject of their conversation.

Lloyd told them: 'Miss Warfield and I are arguing over Ty Cobb and Nap Lajoie. She thinks Ty's stats were cheated last season and that Nap should have won best batsman outright.'

'I agree.' Prosser said. 'Did you hear about the St Louis game? There's no question he got a perfect eight-for-eight.'

Mary felt as if she had alighted in a country where they spoke a different language. It took her a while to realise they were talking about baseball, and she gawped at Wallis's fluency with the terminology. How did she have the first clue?

'I read about it in the newspapers,' Wallis explained later. 'All boys like baseball so I knew it would come in handy.'

Lloyd and Prosser asked to take them rowing the following day and, without consulting Mary, Wallis agreed that they would meet at 2.30 p.m., just after luncheon. She had already worked out their alibi, and told the Miss Nolands that they were going berry-picking.

'Let me give you some baskets,' Miss Katherine beamed. 'We'll have cook make pie for supper.'

On the way to the spot where they had agreed to meet the Tabbs, they picked a few handfuls of huckleberries, planning to find more on the way back.

The boys were already waiting and helped them into a wooden rowboat. As Mary lay back in the stern, trailing her fingers in the water, she felt as though she had been transported into a new and glamorous world. It didn't matter that Wallis was more confident; Mary could be the quiet one, simply laughing at the boys' ham-fisted jokes. She was thrilled that she appeared to have her first-ever beau. Prosser was sweet and considerate and she liked watching the muscles of his arms as he pulled on the oars.

It was the first of many meetings between the four over the long, lazy days of summer. The Miss Nolands never questioned Wallis's excuses for their absences and seemed happy to encourage the friendship.

One afternoon, while the four of them were picnicking, Wallis and Lloyd wandered off into the woods together. Prosser lay on his side, propped up on his elbow, gazing at Mary as she reclined on the grass.

'You're the purtiest girl I ever did see,' he said. 'I'm one lucky boy.'

'Thank you.' She smiled.

'I sure got the purtier of the two of you, no question about it,' he said.

'You're very kind,' she replied. 'But Wallis is pretty too.'

'Not like you.' He leaned closer, his eyes all soft and melting. 'Can I kiss you? Just a little kiss?'

Mary sat bolt upright. 'Absolutely not! You scoundrel! What kind of girl do you think I am?'

He shrugged, shamefaced. 'Your friend lets Lloyd kiss her all the time.'

Mary coloured. 'I don't believe you. What a black lie!'

As they walked back to camp after their dates, Wallis and Mary usually swapped stories about what the boys had said or done. It was on the tip of Mary's tongue to tell Wallis what Prosser had reported. Surely she would be outraged that he had made up such a scandalous falsehood?

But for some reason she didn't mention it. Deep down, she suspected it might be true.

Chapter 3

Baltimore, autumn 1912

IN THE FALL OF 1912, WALLIS AND MARY ARRIVED at Oldfields boarding school in Baltimore to begin the final two years of their education among fifty-six of Maryland's finest daughters. They were delighted to find they were sharing a room, and that Miss Rosalie Noland, another sister from the family who ran the summer camp, would be their tutor. Wallis had developed a crush on the Nolands' thirty-five-year old brother, Philip, and he had long since supplanted Lloyd Tabb in her affections, but Mary still corresponded with Prosser, in an exchange of letters that was sweetly innocent. He wrote to her about the harvest, or the welfare of the farm animals, and she replied telling him of a new hat she had purchased, or a romantic novel she had read.

Wallis and Mary's room had floral wallpaper, two iron-framed beds and a washstand with a Delft-pattern jug and ewer. On the door there was a sign printed with the school motto: 'Gentleness and Courtesy are Expected at All Times', and they soon realised this was posted on every door throughout the sprawling mid-nineteenth-century building, prompting some hilarity.

'Allow me to gently pass you the cream for your coffee,' Wallis joked at breakfast.

'May I courteously offer you some butter?' Mary riposted.

Wallis's quick sense of humour soon made her popular amongst the other girls. She was a talented mimic who could capture the Scottish burr of the headmistress, Nan McCulloch, to perfection: 'No talking after lights out, girrrls. And no drrreaming about boys.' She could do a decent English accent too. One of the girls, Eleanor Jessop, was from England. Her family were visiting Baltimore for a year because of her father's business interests and she was attending the school as a day pupil rather than a boarder. Wallis listened carefully to her accent, asking her to repeat phrases such as 'My father can't row boats', until she had mastered the unfamiliar vowel sounds.

Sometimes, if Mary came upon Wallis chatting head to head or strolling in the grounds with another girl, she felt a quick stab of jealousy, but deep down she knew there was no need. Wallis would always wave her across to join them and make it clear that Mary was her *best* friend, her chosen one.

'What's it like to have sisters?' Wallis asked one day.

Mary considered. 'They can be annoying. They borrow clothes and books without asking, and my older sister Buckie is patronising. But I guess they have their uses.'

'Am I like a sister to you?' Wallis asked. 'Are you as close to me as you are to Buckie and Anne?'

Mary shook her head firmly. 'We're much closer. I could never tell them half the things we talk about.'

'We can be honorary sisters then,' Wallis said, taking Mary's hand. 'Sisters who chose one another rather than ones we got stuck with because of the family we were born into. I like that idea. I don't have enough relatives. There's just Mom, Mr Rasin, Aunt Bessie, Uncle Sol and a few cousins – hardly any of us.'

'Of course I'll be your honorary sister.' Mary beamed with pleasure. 'I'd love to.'

~

Wallis wasn't a rebellious pupil. Her grades were perfectly good, the teachers liked her and she didn't get scolded any more than the next girl. What separated her from the herd, Mary thought, was that she had more imagination. She was always thinking of new projects and had the gumption to make them happen. Wallis was the one who smuggled in some cod liver oil and saw to it that they both held their noses and swallowed a spoonful every morning because she had read a magazine article that said it could help you lose weight. (Not that Wallis needed it: she was slender as a rake while Mary had a tendency towards plumpness.) Wallis was the one who got hold of some household bleach and applied it to the freckles on Mary's nose, causing it to become red and sore, then invented a ridiculous story involving a tennis racquet and a suddenly opening door to explain the disfigurement to Miss Noland. Wallis was the one who asked Eleanor Jessop to give them a list of places one might meet Prince Edward if one happened to be in England, just so that Mary might have a chance of bumping into her idol one day.

'He's studying at Oxford University,' Eleanor told them, 'and he plays in the polo club there. According to the newspapers he simply *loves* polo.'

'There you are!' Wallis winked at Mary. 'You just have to become an expert on polo, turn up at a game – are they called games? – and let him catch sight of your beauty. I do feel for poor Prosser, though. You're going to give him his first lesson in heartache.'

'Oh goodness, it's not like that.' Mary blushed. 'We're both too young for it to be serious.'

'My mom always said you should take puppy love seriously. She told me: "If you step on a puppy's tail, it hurts just as much as if you step on a dog's."'

Mary couldn't tell if Wallis was joking or not, but she began to feel bad that she might be leading Prosser on. She wrote to him trying tactfully to explain that she enjoyed his friendship but that was all. Unfortunately, she was caught by Miss McCulloch as she slipped out of school to mail her letter. Writing to boys was strictly forbidden and Miss McCulloch decided to raise the subject at their devotions the following morning.

'You are all young women of good breeding. When you are wed one day, your husband will want to be assured that he is the one and only . . .' She gazed around the room, her hawk eyes resting on one girl after another. 'I suspect you do not appreciate the seriousness of corresponding with a young man who is not a relative. It is an act that could have the most *profound* repercussions, and should *never* be undertaken lightly.' She paused for effect. 'Now it has come to my attention that one Oldfields girl has been writing to a boy she met at summer camp. I ask you all, if there are any others engaged in a similarly foolish correspondence, to confess now so that we may repair the situation before it is too late.'

Wallis was the first to raise her hand and, lent courage by her example, more followed, until all but two of the pupils had their hands in the air. Miss McCulloch's face flushed and for a moment it seemed she might burst into tears, but she regained her composure.

'I want to speak to each girl who raised her hand. In private. In my study.'

They queued to go in, one by one, and emerged several minutes later with downcast eyes. After her turn, Wallis made a beeline for Mary and described her private conversation with the head.

'She wanted to know to whom I have been writing,' she grinned, 'and you should have seen her face when I told her it was none other than the Miss Nolands' brother. She muttered, "He should know better," so I guess she will put a stop to it.' She shrugged. 'But I don't care. He's too old for me anyhow.'

The scandalous disclosure that all but two of the pupils were writing to boys provided the subject for several weeks' worth of entertaining chatter. Letters were passed around for comment and photographs shown in secret. Girls who had not been particular friends now had something in common. It rather livened up the winter of 1912–13 at Oldfields.

When, on 4 April 1913, Miss Rosalie Noland came to their classroom during an English history lesson and asked Wallis to accompany her to Miss McCulloch's office, Mary's first thought was to wonder what her friend had done now. Which rule had she transgressed? She couldn't think of anything in particular, but the school had so many rules it was hard to get through a day without breaking a few.

Ten minutes later, Miss Noland returned and asked Mary to come with her.

'What is it about?' Mary whispered as they walked down the corridor.

'Your friend needs you,' Miss Noland replied, and her tone was gentle. That was odd.

Mary followed her to the bedroom the girls shared, where she found Wallis shoving some clothes into a leather weekend bag and sobbing hard, her eyes red and her face shiny with tears.

Mary ran to her, threw an arm round her, pulled her in for a hug. 'My God, what happened?' she asked.

'Mr Rasin d-died,' Wallis stuttered. Her breath was ragged, her chest shuddering.

'No!'

'H-how can I have lost two fathers by the age of seventeen?' Wallis wailed. 'What is *wrong* with me?'

She clung to Mary and wept with abandon, her skinny frame shaking, tears soaking the shoulder of Mary's dress.

Mary didn't know what to say. Wallis must be terrified. Who would support her and her mother now? Without Mr Rasin paying the fees, would she even be able to continue her schooling? Mary felt a pain in her chest, a tightness as if the grief were hers too, and she hugged Wallis even harder.

'I'll be your friend for life,' she promised. 'Your honorary sister. Always and forever, until the very end of time.'

Chapter 4

Paris, 31 August 1997

RACHEL GOT OUT OF THE TAXI AND LOOKED AT the throng of photographers with huge black cameras in their hands and extra ones slung around their jackets. She could hardly see the crashed car because the tunnel was only dimly illuminated by some strip lights set high on either side, and the flashbulbs created a flickering glare around the scene.

'Are you sure it's Diana?' She almost had to shout to be heard over the noise.

Alex seemed in a hurry to return to the scene. 'I caught a glimpse of a blonde head. There's a doctor tending her.'

'Is she badly hurt?'

'I don't know. One of the photographers heard her speaking.'

Rachel felt a wave of disgust. 'Imagine what it must be like for her trapped in the middle of that.' The men swarming round the car were like a SWAT team on a military assault, their cameras like weapons.

Alex shook his head, pulling his hand from her grip. 'I'm going to see if I can help. They might need a translator.'

His French was fluent, so that made sense. More people were arriving every minute, making their way towards the wrecked car, jostling for a view. Where were the police? Someone should move them on.

A burst of rage engulfed her and she marched up to the nearest photographers. '*Laisse la tranquille!*' she yelled, standing in front of them.

One shouted back at her in rapid French, clearly swearing, and lifted his camera to shoot over her head.

'*Arrête!*' She held up her palm. Poor Diana. Rachel was no monarchist; in the seventies she had been a punk, with the 'God Save the Queen' T-shirt and short bleached-blonde hair to prove it, but at the same time she couldn't help being fascinated by the glamorous princess who had breathed life into the moribund monarchy. The royal wedding had been every little girl's fairy tale come true.

Unable to think of more phrases in French, she began to lambast the photographers in English. 'She's injured. This is obscene. Stop it!'

She pushed past them, trying to block the intrusive lenses, and that was when she caught sight of Diana. She was in a strange position, kneeling in the well between the front and back seats, almost facing backwards. She must have spun round with the force of the collision. There was an oxygen mask covering her face but the hairstyle was undoubtedly hers. What was she thinking as she knelt there, so vulnerable?

'You *bastards!*' Rachel screamed at the pack. '*Arrête!*'

She couldn't see any of the other passengers or the driver, but got a fleeting impression of an arm, the back of a head, some legs that seemed at the wrong angle to the body, a dark glimmer that could only be blood. The front left side of the car was a twisted mass of buckled and torn metal. She turned away, not wanting to see more, sick from the smell of petrol and the sheer horror of it all. Sirens heralded the arrival of the first police cars and, looking towards the tunnel entrance,

Rachel saw they were closing off the perimeter. An ambulance with lights flashing drove up the other side of the carriageway and screeched to a halt. She watched the crew leap out and push their way through the crowd. Some photographers seemed reluctant to stand aside and she screamed: 'For God's sake, move!' A few bystanders joined her in remonstrating with them.

Someone – the police, she imagined – switched on bright arc lights that illuminated the scene in an eerie glow. It was a grim, claustrophobic place, with a harsh row of rectangular concrete pillars separating the two carriageways. The walls were made of dimpled textured concrete, the ceiling blackened with decades of exhaust fumes.

She could see Alex near the car and wondered if he was speaking to the princess. Perhaps it would be comforting for her to hear an English accent. He was used to dealing with celebrities in his job. Too many people tiptoed round in awe of their fame, but Alex gave honest opinions, and they seemed to appreciate it.

The police were rounding up photographers, sending them to wait at the end of the tunnel. One man was arguing, reluctant to hand over his camera. Rachel walked back to their taxi, where the driver was behind the wheel once more. She hoped Alex would join her because she didn't want the police to get the impression he was part of the press pack.

At that moment, she saw him approaching, his expression grim. He opened the door and climbed in.

'She's still in the wreckage,' he reported. 'They're cutting the roof off.'

The taxi driver interrupted to ask, '*Que se passe-t-il?*' and Alex translated for him.

'Who else is in the car?' Rachel asked. 'Oh God, it's not her sons, is it?'

Alex squeezed her knee. 'No, it's Dodi Al-Fayed, a bodyguard and their driver. Dodi and the driver are dead.'

During the summer, the papers had been full of the news that the Princess was dating Al-Fayed, son of the Egyptian owner of Harrods department store. Rachel was shocked to hear he was dead. She was about to ask Alex how he knew, but couldn't face hearing any grisly details.

Cars and motorbikes were starting to move out of the tunnel. A policeman came over and Alex got out to talk to him, leaving his door open. Rachel could hear the officer asking for their names, writing them in a notebook. Alex explained that they were on holiday but flying home the next day, and he gave the name and address of their hotel. The policeman asked if they would stop in at the Criminal Brigade headquarters on quai des Orfèvres before they left, insisting they must give statements even though they had not seen the crash itself.

Their driver made a U-turn and headed out of the tunnel the way they had come. Rachel glanced at her watch: nearly one in the morning. They had been there over half an hour. The ambulance was still in the same spot so she guessed Diana had not yet been freed from the wreck. She must be petrified.

'Did you translate for the Princess? How was she?'

Alex shook his head. 'The doctor knew enough English. It looks as if she has a head wound, maybe a broken leg.'

'And a broken heart too, if it was serious with Dodi. She'll be very shocked.'

They sat in silence holding hands the rest of the way to the hotel, and when they got to their room, Alex flicked on the television set. Every channel was showing pictures of the ambulance taking Diana to the Pitié-Salpêtrière Hospital, where, the commentator assured viewers, a team of top specialists was waiting to take over her care. Rachel kicked off her heels, which had been pinching all evening, and listened from the bathroom as she wiped off her make-up, brushed her teeth and changed into a 1930s satin robe.

When she returned to the bedroom, Alex was holding a small silver-coloured object. He stretched out his hand to show her. 'This fell out of the car while the doctor was trying to move Diana. No one else noticed, so I picked it up.'

Rachel took it from him. It was a tiny heart with the Roman numeral XVII engraved on one side. Seventeen. It was heavy and had a whitish tinge that made her think it was platinum rather than silver.

'Do you think it's hers?'

Alex shrugged. 'There weren't any other women in the car.'

Rachel turned it over. The back was engraved with the initial J. 'You'd better give it to the police when we go to the station tomorrow,' she said, and he nodded.

'Yeah, will do.'

On screen, the ambulance was shown pulling into the hospital grounds, and Rachel lay back on her pillow and closed her eyes, the scent of petrol still in her nostrils. What a strange night it had been: first the proposal and now this. She felt shell-shocked by it all.

Chapter 5

Paris, 31 August 1997

'RACHEL, WAKE UP!'
She came round slowly from the blankness of deep sleep. Alex was rubbing her shoulder.

'She's dead,' he blurted, the words catching in his throat. In the background she could hear a murmur of French words emanating from the television set, their tone sombre, factual.

Who was dead? She glanced at the clock by the bedside: 6 a.m. The events of a few hours earlier flashed into her brain and she rolled over to face him.

'Do you mean Diana?'

He nodded without taking his eyes off the screen.

She felt a jolt of unreality and pulled herself to a sitting position. 'How is that possible? You said she was talking in the car.'

A press conference was being held. A man identified on the screen as 'Sir Michael Jay, Ambassadeur du Royaume-Uni en France' spoke in English: 'The death of the Princess of Wales fills us all with deep shock and deep grief.' His words translated into French scrolled along the bottom of the screen. A doctor explained that she had suffered catastrophic internal injuries, and that although they had resuscitated her at the scene and operated as soon as she reached the hospital, there was nothing that could be done.

'I can't believe it.' Alex's voice sounded wobbly. Rachel noticed he was still dressed, hadn't got into bed.

'Poor woman,' she murmured. 'All those photographers were taking her picture as she was dying. It was grotesque.'

Someone on the television was speaking in French now, and Alex listened. 'Her bodyguard is alive but seriously injured. I was right about the other two, the driver and Dodi Al-Fayed. They're both dead.'

Scrolling headlines confirmed his words.

'Oh my God, her boys!' Rachel exclaimed, the implications beginning to sink in. 'I wonder if anyone has told them yet?' She couldn't remember what ages they were; in their early teens, perhaps.

Alex was only half listening, still focused on the television. 'The news anchor says they've informed Prince Charles and the Queen, but the boys will be told in the morning.' The words caught in his throat again. His own mother had died when he was twelve, and there must be echoes for him of that traumatic time.

Rachel put an arm round him, stroked his back, and he turned to her, stricken. 'I don't understand why they couldn't save her. What the hell were they doing?'

She shook her head, uncomprehending. A woman a couple of years younger than her; a mother. She supposed these tragedies happened all the time, but not to such globally famous people. Her parents' generation always said they could remember what they were doing when they heard the news that President John F. Kennedy had been shot; this was clearly destined to become the touchstone moment for her generation – and she had been there.

'Did you hear what she said in the car? Did she know how badly she was injured?'

'I didn't hear myself,' Alex replied, 'but one of the photographers told me she turned to look at Dodi and exclaimed, "Oh my God." Then she said, "Leave me alone," when one of them tried to help her. That's all I know.'

'She wasn't bleeding, was she?'

'A tiny trickle of blood on her forehead. Nothing on her clothes that I could see.'

He had been close enough to reach out and touch the Princess had he wanted to, and he had seen enough of the other occupants of the car to know that two of them were dead. Rachel wondered if he was in shock.

She got out of bed, filled the kettle with water from the bathroom tap and set it to boil. There were PG Tips tea bags and sachets of Nescafé along with cartons of long-life milk on a tray. She put tea bags in two of the cups and waited for the kettle to boil, watching the images on the television with a sense of unreality. There was the tunnel, still closed to traffic but with a street-cleaning truck already at work inside; the exterior of the hospital swarming with media types; archive footage of Balmoral, where the royals were staying.

'They're saying the paparazzi caused it,' Alex told her. 'They chased the Princess's Mercedes from the Ritz Hotel, where she and Dodi had dinner. Perhaps one of them cut in front and the driver swerved to avoid him.'

Rachel stirred milk into one of the cups of tea, noticing that her hand was trembling, then passed it to Alex.

'Those cameras with the big long lenses were like guns. The photographers were feral. Lawless.' She gave an involuntary shudder and her own tea slopped into its saucer.

'It's not a very tasteful way to earn a living, that's for sure.'

They watched the screen in silence, sipping the tea, which had a slight metallic taste. It was hard to accept that the iconic presence was gone for ever: Di in her flak jacket in an African village; in an evening gown at the ballet; or in those mumsy two-pieces she wore for the meet-and-greets that were part of modern royalty. If only they had got it wrong: a case of mistaken identity. If only she wasn't dead.

Out loud, Rachel said: 'I wish it wasn't true. I wish some nurse in the mortuary would suddenly notice her eyelashes flutter, or a tiny gasp for breath, and rush her back up to a ward where doctors manage to revive her.'

Alex shook his head. 'The doctors will have tried absolutely everything known to medical science. The eyes of the world were on them. To have saved her would have been a major coup. No, the only thing that concerns me is how slow they were in getting her to hospital. It must have been at least two hours after the accident. That could have made the difference between life and death.'

Rachel felt goose bumps prick her skin. If only they could turn back the clock, do things differently. If only.

~

They had planned to spend the day wandering round Montparnasse but both felt dazed from lack of sleep. Instead, they had *café au lait* in a street café. Alex ate an omelette but Rachel didn't feel like food. When he had finished, they went straight to the Criminal Brigade headquarters to give their statements.

After half an hour sitting in a crowded waiting room that smelled of stale garlic, Rachel was taken to a windowless interview room. There was barely space to squeeze round the table and chairs set in the middle. She let the young female police officer take a photocopy of her passport and write down the name of the restaurant where they had dined, the bar where they had danced cheek-to-cheek after dinner and the hotel where they had stayed. The woman spoke only rudimentary English but Rachel refused her offer of waiting till later when a translator might be available and answered in school French. She had only seen the Princess from a distance, she said, because the photographers were in the way. She wanted to express how sickening it was to watch them snapping away, but the best she could do was, '*Les photographes étaient horribles.*'

Her interview was soon over, but when she got back to the waiting room, Alex was nowhere to be seen. She sat down to wait, flicking through her guidebook. A smiling Frenchman leaned across and asked: 'May I read your skirt?' She was wearing a fifties swing skirt with a pattern of old French newspaper extracts set over illustrations of Paris's tourist attractions. It had seemed appropriate for a visit to the city but now it felt twee. She smiled politely and returned to the guidebook.

Alex took ages – at least another hour – and when he emerged he was pale and tense. 'Let's get out of here,' he whispered, taking her hand, pulling her to her feet.

'How did it go?' she asked once they were out in the warm sunshine.

'Awful! The officer was quite hostile. I had to mark on a chart exactly where I was standing and try and tell them where each of the photographers was. He showed me pictures of the seven men they've arrested, but I only recognised a couple. It wasn't them I was focusing on.'

'Of course not.' She slipped an arm through his. 'Did you give them the little heart?'

He cleared his throat. 'I didn't like to. They seemed antagonistic, and the last thing I want is to be charged with tampering with a crime scene.'

Rachel was worried. 'What if you can be seen picking it up in the CCTV footage?'

'I dunno.' He looked sideways at her. 'I guess I've got time to come up with an excuse. Amnesia, dementia, something like that.'

'I'll vouch for it,' she said in an attempt at humour.

He pulled the heart from his pocket. 'Can you keep it in your bag?' he asked. 'I'm scared I might lose it.'

She zipped it into the loose-change compartment of her purse.

Back at the hotel, the aloof receptionist informed them that because they hadn't checked out before noon, they would be charged for an extra day's stay.

'In that case, I'm going to get some kip,' Alex announced. 'OK with you? I'm beat.'

Rachel agreed. It seemed a shame when they had five hours left in Paris before they had to head for the airport, but she felt dizzy with exhaustion.

Alex switched on the TV as soon as they got into the room, and they saw Prince Charles and Diana's two sisters arriving at the hospital. Rachel blinked back tears as she tried to imagine how she would feel if her own sister died.

'Charles is the last person Diana would want there,' Alex commented, stepping out of his trousers. He pulled back the sheet and within seconds of lying down he was asleep.

Rachel studied him for a minute: his sandy hair tousled on the pillow, his strong back, the curve of his calf. Then she retrieved the remote control from beneath his arm and stopped to watch as Mohamed Al-Fayed emerged from the hospital with bowed head. The poor man. The news broadcasts were almost exclusively about Diana, while Dodi and the driver were relegated to afterthoughts. She gave a little shiver and clicked off the TV.

Chapter 6

Baltimore, October 1914

'Miss Mary, it's for you,' the housekeeper called and Mary leapt from her seat in the morning room, clutching a large white envelope to her chest as she ran into the hallway.

'Hi, Wallie,' she trilled down the mouthpiece in the top of the candlestick-style transmitter, holding the cylindrical receiver to her ear. 'Has your mail arrived?' She bit her lip.

'It sure has,' came the deep voice, 'and I'm holding a Bachelors' Cotillion invitation right here in my hand!' Wallis could barely contain her excitement. 'I assume you got one too?'

'Yes!' Mary giggled in delight. 'Oh, thank God!' She had been worried Wallis might not receive the prestigious invitation because her mother was not wealthy, and they lived in an apartment in a less salubrious part of town. But the extended Warfield family had connections in the right places and Wallis *would* go to the ball. It would have meant social death to be excluded.

'We have so much to discuss. Shall I come over?'

'Yes, but *hurry*! There are only six weeks to go!'

Mary was still in her morning housecoat with curling papers in her hair, but there was no need to get dressed for a visit from Wallis, who spent so much time in the Kirk household she practically lived there. At least once a week she stayed over, and the girls spent several hours together each day.

When Wallis arrived, they scurried up to Mary's bedroom to talk in peace, away from her sisters' interruptions. First they examined each other's invitations, then dived into the most important topic of the day: what they were going to wear. Because of the war raging in Europe, each debutante had been asked to sign a pledge that they would not indulge in the usual 'rivalry of elegance' and 'extravagance in entertaining' that season. Both Wallis and Mary had signed, but it made the clothing choice even more tricky: they could not look too fancy, but they still wanted to be '*très chic*', as Wallis put it.

'Mother is taking me to Fuechsl's tomorrow,' Mary said. 'I wanted to go today in case all the best frocks sell out, but she's having tea with a friend. Will you come and help me choose? We can look for one for you too . . .' Her voice trailed off. Wallis's mother would never be able to afford the prices at the town's most fashionable shop.

'Of course I'll come with you, but I've already decided what I want to wear. Look at this.' Wallis reached into a pocket and produced a picture torn from a magazine. 'It's Irene Castle in *Watch Your Step* on Broadway. Look how pretty her dress is!'

It had a satin bodice and a chiffon skirt that fell to just below the knee, with bands of satin and pearl-encrusted embroidery looping around.

'It's divine,' Mary breathed. 'A dream of a frock. But if you got one like this, what would you wear on your shoulders?'

'There could be chiffon over the shoulders, like so.' Wallis swept her hands to demonstrate. 'I'll get Mother's dressmaker to make it up in white.' A shadow passed across her face. 'First I'll have to persuade Uncle Sol to part with the money. I'll give it my best Southern charm, and emphasise how important it is for the family name that I shine on my society debut. Heavens to Betsy! I might even meet a rich husband there and that would get me off his hands.'

Mary laughed. They'd often talked about the qualities they wanted in a future husband. Mary hoped for someone kind, who shared her interest in reading and music so they could swap books and go to concerts together. Wallis had always been clear that she wanted a wealthy husband, and Mary could understand why. Uncle Sol, her late father's brother, doled out money inconsistently, sometimes leaving Wallis and her mother in near penury, then stepping in just before the rent was due or the coal merchant was about to stop supplying them. A rich husband would give her the financial security she craved. Of course, it went without saying that their future spouses must be handsome and charming, with impeccable dress sense and a fine line in repartee.

After they had exhausted the subject of their outfits, down to the last accessory, they discussed who they would take along. Each debutante could invite two or three partners, usually family members. Wallis had already decided upon her cousin Henry and the husband of her cousin Lelia.

'I will tell Henry that if no one else asks, he must dance every dance with me,' she insisted. 'I couldn't bear to be a wallflower, not with everyone watching.'

'For goodness' sake, you would never be a wallflower,' Mary protested. 'I've never known a girl have so many admirers. Carter Osburn would dance every single dance with you given the chance.'

They discussed which boys of their acquaintance could be guaranteed to ask them for dances and which might need a nudge. Their invited guests must be briefed to step in if there seemed to be even a remote possibility of them having to sit out a number.

'This will be the most important evening of our lives so far,' Wallis said dramatically. 'Possibly the most important ever.'

~

The evening of 7 December came, and all their careful plans went like clockwork. They arrived at the Lyric Theatre on the arms of their escorts, clutching their bouquets. Wallis looked ravishing, and when Mary went over to greet her, she noticed she was wearing a hint of rouge on each cheek, something that was considered a little 'fast'.

'You look beautiful, Miss Warfield,' she beamed.

'You too, kiddo. Let the fun begin!'

The first impression inside the theatre was of a profusion of flowers; boxes of each girl's favourite bloom arranged next to each other merged into one long, lush scented garland. The seats had been removed to create a dance floor and the stage was decorated as a magical forest bower where supper would be served. The band struck up the first number and for the next few hours Wallis and Mary scarcely saw each other as they were whirled round the floor by a succession of partners. They danced the one-step, the foxtrot and the German waltz to songs like 'When You Wore a Tulip', 'Land of My Best Girl' and 'Tsin-Tsin'. The final song, 'Parfum d'Amour', was played just after eleven, but that still wasn't the end of the evening. A young crowd, including Wallis and Mary, jumped into automobiles and drove to the Baltimore Country Club, where they danced till dawn was streaking the sky as if with a giant brushstroke of orangey-pink paint.

The following afternoon, Wallis lay on Mary's bed as they dissected the evening.

'I danced three dances with Carter Osburn,' Wallis said, making a face. 'I'm lucky to have any toes left.'

Mary smiled. 'He's so sweet on you, he would be your beau in a heartbeat.'

Wallis wrinkled her nose. 'I like his car . . .' Carter drove a Packard. 'But he's a little on the short side, don't you think? And he never stops talking.'

'What about Arthur Stump? He's tall and silent. I rode in his Ford to the country club and thought he was a good driver.'

'Yeah, Arthur's nice. But I'm not sure he has much gumption. He's what my mother would call "a big drink of water".'

'You sound disappointed, Wallie. Was the evening not as magical as you expected?'

Wallis tilted her head to one side and considered. 'I guess I wanted to fall in love and there wasn't anyone to fall in love with. Don't you agree? They're all nice boys, but none of them is *it*.'

Mary laughed. 'We're only eighteen; I don't think we qualify as old maids yet.'

~

Over the social season, from December through April, they attended at least one ball, dinner party, luncheon or tea dance every week, and both Mary and Wallis collected a coterie of male admirers: Tony Biddle, Reggie Hutchison, Bryan Dancy, Harvey Rowland and many more. Sometimes the girls invited a couple of boys to Mary's house after dinner to have a cool drink and a chat. Wallis was in her element on such occasions, and Mary enjoyed them too. She had become more confident about talking to boys now she spent more time in their company, and she tried to follow Wallis's lead and ask them about sports, cars, or what career they intended to pursue. Mary's parents left them unchaperoned in the living room, but if they got too noisy, or if the boys stayed past curfew time, her father would bang on the ceiling with his shoe.

It was traditional for each debutante's family to throw a coming-out party for her. Mary's mother hosted a stylish luncheon at the Baltimore Country Club, but although Wallis pleaded with Uncle Sol, he refused to pay for an event in her honour.

'I can't sanction the expenditure in wartime,' he said, and would not be moved, even by his niece's tears.

Wallis and Mary seldom thought about the war. Europe was a long way away, so Uncle Sol's argument that it was 'no time for festivities' carried little weight.

'It's not even America's war,' Wallis grumbled. 'He really is insufferable.'

'It doesn't matter,' Mary reassured her. 'You're the most popular debutante even without throwing a party, and everyone agrees you are the best dressed. Millicent Beacham was positively green with envy over your cloth-of-gold gown.'

'Millicent?' Wallis raised one eyebrow with a wicked glint. 'I wouldn't rate her taste in fashion, would you? That gown with all the layers made her look like a prize cabbage at a country show.'

Mary laughed so hard she choked and Wallis had to pat her on the back until she stopped spluttering.

In the summer of 1915, as the girls were making plans for the start of a new social season, Wallis's paternal grandmother had a fall, and a few weeks later she passed away. The family went into formal mourning, which meant that Wallis would have to wear black and would not be allowed to socialise for six months. She was bitterly disappointed to think of all the balls and dinners taking place without her.

'I'll tell you every last detail,' Mary promised. 'But it won't be the same without you. It's going to be a very tedious winter.'

Later that day, after Wallis had gone home, Mary overheard her parents talking to her elder sister Buckie in the dining room. She paused at the door to listen.

'I hope Mary will make some new friends this winter,' Buckie was saying. 'Wallis is clearly not a suitable companion.'

'I agree,' her mother said. 'It could even affect our chances of marrying her into a good family. What do you think, Henry?'

'Quite,' her father muttered, his usual response when he did not want to be drawn into a discussion.

Mary burst into the room in a temper. 'How dare you say such things about poor Wallis! It's not her fault her father and her stepfather died. She and her mother don't have much money but the family are perfectly respectable.'

'The *family* might be,' Buckie said, 'but Wallis herself is just a bit . . . disreputable. I hear she flirts with all the boys and strings them along like pet pooches. It's not fair to treat anyone like that.'

'That's not true!' Mary shouted, her fists clenched by her side. For the first time since childhood she felt the urge to punch her sister, hard.

'Darling, she wears rouge,' her mother said. 'Nice girls don't wear make-up. You know that. It sends out all the wrong signals.'

'It's only because she has especially pale cheeks. You hardly notice it.'

Her mother sniffed, clearly thinking otherwise. 'We can't stop you seeing her, of course, but I hope you will treat this season as a chance to make new friends. Perhaps some of them will have eligible brothers. Wouldn't that be lovely?'

Mary stood with her hands on her hips and declared passionately: 'I will never abandon Wallis. Never.'

Then she turned and stomped from the room, slamming the door hard behind her.

Chapter 7

Baltimore, April 1916

Dearest Mary,
    You're not going to believe this, but IT has happened. You know what I mean by IT? I've fallen head over heels in love.

Mary gasped as she read the beginning of the letter. Wallis had only left a week earlier to visit her cousin Corinne in Pensacola, Florida. How could she have fallen in love already?

I know you won't believe me. I can't believe it myself as I've only known him for thirty-six hours, but I knew straight away when he arrived for luncheon yesterday. He walked into Corinne's living room and I felt giddy and more <u>alive</u> than I've ever felt before. They say your heart skips a beat, but mine skipped so many beats it's a wonder I didn't collapse.

Mary read the letter quickly, feeling a stab in her own heart. I can't be jealous of Wallie, she thought. One of us had to fall in love first, and I always knew it would be her.

I guess I'd better tell you all about him so you can see that I haven't clean lost my mind. His name is Earl Winfield

Spencer, and he's a pilot who flies Curtiss N-91 planes out of the airbase here. It's unbelievably brave and clever of him because everyone says they are devilish tricky to control. He's tanned and lean, with dark hair and a moustache, and intense eyes I just want to sink into. You know I've always liked older men, don't you? Well, he's twelve years older, which seems to me exactly the right amount. He's mature and worldly but still young in his outlook.

So he was over thirty? That seemed impossibly old to Mary.

We talked all through luncheon and afterwards he asked if he could call for me the following afternoon. Trying to appear nonchalant, I claimed I didn't know what plans my cousins had for me but he said he didn't care so long as those plans included him! So he returned the following afternoon (wearing his elegant white Navy uniform with gold stripes on the shoulders) and he stayed for dinner and we talked non-stop. He says he is going to teach me to play golf. Now, you and I know that I have not the slightest smidgen of interest in the game, but what a clever excuse to spend time together without a chaperone! I can't wait to see him again. He only left half an hour ago and I should be trying to sleep but I simply had to tell you . . .

It's one of her crushes, Mary thought. Like Philip Noland. Wallis couldn't be properly in love with someone she had only met twice. But then, they had always agreed that they believed in love at first sight. Her mother said that was what it had been like for her and her father.

You will know instantly when IT happens to you, Wallis finished her letter. *It's as different from merely liking a boy as peaches are from pickles.*

Mary felt critical. How could Wallis be so sure? Was love really so cut and dried? Buckie was sitting in a chair on the other side of the morning room working on some embroidery.

'Do you think it's possible to be in love with someone you've only met twice?' Mary asked.

Buckie looked up. 'Oh Lord, is Wallis in love? Who is it this time?'

'He's a pilot at Pensacola.'

Buckie gave a little grunt. 'I can't see Wallis as a Navy wife. She would hate it. They get moved round the country and have to live on military bases, in identical little houses. And there are lots of rules to follow, even for the wives. Wallis is not a rules type of girl, is she?'

Mary shrugged. 'I suppose she could be for the right man.'

Buckie shook her head. 'I would never marry an airman. Those machines are death traps. I heard the fuel tank is right behind the pilot's head, so if they crash and the fuel ignites, they don't stand a chance. Most die outright, but if they live, they're horribly disfigured from the burns.'

Mary shuddered. 'I hope she doesn't have her heart broken by marrying someone who makes her a widow.'

'She would find another man soon enough, if I know Wallis.' Buckie returned to her needlework with pursed lips.

All day Mary pictured Wallis on a golf course in the Florida sunshine, with a tanned officer standing behind her, leaning over to adjust her grip on the club. She wrote back with pretended enthusiasm – *How incredibly glamorous he sounds!* – but felt as if she had a stone lodged in her heart. All day she was moody and out of sorts, unable to force herself to join the talk at dinner and pleading a headache afterwards so she could retire to her bedroom.

I must be a wicked person, she berated herself. Poor Wallie had a horrible winter so it's only fair she has a bit of fun now.

Lying fully clothed on her silk bedspread, she mulled it over and realised she was not jealous because Wallis was happy; on the contrary, she was glad of that. It was just that she was scared she was going to lose her. She would no longer be Wallis's closest friend in the world, and that would be hard to take. But Wallis was due back in just over three weeks, and maybe she would have gotten over her airman by then.

~

Wallis wrote that she was extending her stay an extra couple of weeks so she could spend more time with her beloved 'Win'. When that period was nearly up, she decided to stay another two weeks, then one last week. With each delay, Mary felt her friend slipping further away. It was impossible to express herself in letters, impossible to say how sad she felt at the distance between them. She had many other girlfriends in Baltimore, and had been spending time with her old schoolfriend Renée du Pont, but none of them had Wallis's sparkle.

In early June, Wallis finally returned and she telephoned Mary straight away to ask if she might come over.

'I've got so much to tell you,' she gushed. 'Things I couldn't put into letters.'

Within an hour they were sitting in the rocker on the back porch of the Kirks' house sipping lemonade from tall glasses. Wallis's skin was golden from the Florida sun and she was more animated than Mary had ever seen her, with a permanent smile on her face and joy lighting up her eyes.

'I've had the time of my life, Mary. I never thought I would meet someone who had all the qualities I'm looking for in one package.'

'Is Win wealthy?' Mary asked. 'That was always your top priority.'

Wallis nodded. 'Officers get paid plenty, and he's bound to get promoted over the years. The Navy would provide a house for us on the base, and you get to choose your own decor. All the women are friends with each other, and there are parties at the San Carlos Hotel at weekends, with dancing and lots of liquor . . .'

Mary interrupted. 'You talk as if you are planning to marry him.'

Wallis put a cautioning finger to her lips, with a mischievous glint in her eyes, then whispered: 'He asked me a couple of weeks ago.'

Mary gasped, dismayed. 'But you've hardly known each other any time!'

'I know, but I've never been so sure of anything.'

'What did he say? Tell me everything. Did you say yes straight away?'

Wallis giggled. 'I told him he has to come and meet my mother, Aunt Bessie, Uncle Sol and you, and that if all of you approve he is in with a chance. You will approve, won't you, Mary dearest?'

'I'm sure I will. If you love him, I am bound to love him too.'

During the two weeks before Win arrived in Baltimore on leave, Wallis talked about him constantly, as if relaying every single memory from their time together stopped her missing him so badly. She told Mary that they used to walk along the beach in Pensacola picking up seashells, that they went to the movies and sat in the back seat holding hands, that they would slip out of the San Carlos Hotel to sit in his Ford and kiss.

'Lips open or closed?' Mary asked, and Wallis grinned.

'Definitely open.'

Mary wore a smile that increasingly had to be forced as Wallis told her about Win's background. 'He was born in

Chicago and graduated from Annapolis Naval Academy. He was serving in the Atlantic when he got interested in flying. All his superior officers tried to talk him out of it, but he knew it was the job for him. It's hard to become a flyer, but as soon as he started, everyone said he was a natural.'

'Isn't it terribly dangerous?'

'It is. Two men at his base died in a crash while I was there. I worry every time he takes to the air, but he says he knows his plane so well he could get out of any fix. He checks every last nut and bolt before he takes off.'

'What if America joins the war?' Mary asked. There had been talk of it since the Germans sank the passenger ship *Lusitania* the previous year. 'He might have to go and fight in France.'

Wallis shivered. 'I would support him all the way but I hope it doesn't come to that.' She switched mood. 'Oh, I can't wait for you to meet him. I know you're going to *adore* him.'

'Perhaps he will have a friend for me,' Mary suggested lightly. She had plenty of beaus that summer but all of them casual. She would have loved to describe them to Wallis but couldn't get a word in. Besides, they sounded dull in comparison to Win; none of them were pilots.

'Wouldn't that be fun?' Wallis laughed. 'I'll definitely ask.'

Two weeks later, Win arrived, and after the couple had made a tour of the Warfield relatives, Mary was invited to meet them at the Baltimore Country Club, where they sat on a back veranda looking towards the golf course, arm in arm, like visiting royalty.

'Miss Kirk,' Win said, rising to greet her, 'I do declare you are every bit as pretty as Wallis told me. What stunning auburn hair! Pray sit down.' He pulled out a chair for her. 'Can I offer you a cocktail?'

'Iced tea would be perfect. Hello, Wallie.'

Win called the waiter to place the order, requesting a bourbon on the rocks for himself, and began talking about his impressions of Baltimore. 'How fresh the summer air is compared to Pensacola. There you can always detect a hint of jet fuel in the breeze. But down south we have dolphins playing in the Gulf at sunset, which is a sight I never tire of.'

Mary watched him and could see right away what had appealed to Wallis. He was head and shoulders above the local boys, with their stilted conversation and gawky self-consciousness. Win was a man of the world, with laughing eyes that had little creases in the corners. Wallis was softer around him than Mary had ever seen her: girlish and winsome.

They told her they had met Uncle Sol that morning and he had given his permission for them to wed. Mary wasn't surprised. She imagined he would be glad it was no longer his responsibility to subsidise Wallis.

'What a distinguished gent,' Win said. 'So refined. We're planning to get hitched as soon as possible, probably in the fall.'

'You will be my bridesmaid, won't you, Mary?' Wallis pleaded.

'Of course! I'd love to.'

They chatted about plans for the wedding, and Mary noticed that they caught eyes often, and that Win kept touching Wallis's arm, her fingers, her hair, as if he couldn't keep his hands off her. The thought made her blush and she fanned herself to cool her cheeks.

'Will you move to Pensacola straight after the wedding?' she asked, and Wallis said yes, adding that Mary had an open invitation.

When she got home that evening, her mother asked what Wallis's husband-to-be was like and all Mary could think to say was that he was 'very charming'. She had not got a sense of his character beneath the polished veneer, but perhaps that was because she had not spent any time on her own with him. There was no question he was deeply enamoured of Wallis. Why then did Mary feel a reservation? Probably because she didn't want to lose her friend.

That night as she lay in bed waiting for sleep, she felt a tear sliding down her cheek, then another. So Wallis was definitely getting married, the first of their season's debutantes to tie the knot. She was going to Pensacola in a few months' time and she wouldn't be back. It felt like the end of Mary's girlhood.

The wedding took place in Baltimore Christ Church on 8 November, just seven months after Wallis and Win had met. The bride wore a gown of white panne velvet decorated with seed pearls and carried a bouquet of white orchids and lilies of the valley. Mary and the five other bridesmaids were dressed in orchid-coloured gowns with wide blue velvet girdles. The vast church was full of the sweet, almost overpowering scent of white roses and chrysanthemums, stacked around the altar and filling every available niche. Win wore his full naval dress uniform, as did his ushers and his brother Dumaresque.

The reception was riotous, with dinner and dancing for a lively crowd. The Spencers and Warfields got on swimmingly, to Wallis's immense relief. Mary enjoyed the day but felt an underlying sense of loss. She watched Win help himself to his new wife's uneaten dessert then claim her hand for the first dance, and she sensed that her friendship with Wallis would never be as close again.

When the couple left to get into the car that would whisk them away from the reception, everyone showered them in white rose petals. Wallis turned her back and tossed her bouquet over her head in Mary's direction. It was a good throw and all Mary had to do was raise her hands to catch it.

She sniffed the heady scent of the lilies of the valley and smiled her gratitude.

Wallis blew her a kiss and called, 'You next,' before climbing into the car, making sure her long train was completely inside before Win slammed the door.

That was it; she was gone. Wallis had moved on, leaving her old life behind, and Mary felt bereft.

Chapter 8

Brighton, 1 September 1997

RACHEL OWNED A SHOP CALLED FORGOTTEN DREAMS in Brighton's North Laines, just fifteen minutes' walk from her flat. It sold antique clothes dating from the 1900s through to the 1950s, alongside shoes, handbags, hats, belts, a selection of old jewellery and a few trinkets. She was passionate about the artistry of these decades and always dressed in period style, so she was a walking advert for her own wares. Old clothes were her passion. Sometimes she felt she could sense ghosts in the fabric that gave a hint of lives lived long ago, and she enjoyed speculating about previous owners, inventing back stories for them: 'the jilted bride', 'the scarlet woman', 'the grumpy spinster'.

In the shop's early days, customers used to complain about the prices she charged for what they deemed 'second-hand', but now they had accepted that she was selling wearable antiques rather than jumble. Forgotten Dreams had been open for almost ten years and it had been touch and go at first, with hefty bank loans and scary credit-card debt, but for the last few years she had been running in profit. She'd had to be a workaholic, controlling every aspect of the business, to get where she was, and only recently had she hired a part-time member of staff, an artist friend called Nicola. It was a mixed blessing: Nicola was a bit scatty and too generous with discounts, but it was only thanks to her presence that Rachel had been able to take the weekend off to go to Paris with Alex.

As she walked to the shop on the Monday morning after the crash, dressed in a tight pencil skirt and a short-sleeved blouse with a polka-dot pattern, her mind was still full of images of the wrecked car. She couldn't help wondering what Diana had been thinking as she lay trapped inside. Did she have any idea she was dying? She must have been able to hear the photographers, must have known exactly what those dazzling flashes and loud explosions meant. It was awful to think these were the last sounds she heard.

Rachel rounded the corner into the North Laines, and even from afar she could see that something looked amiss in her shop window. The Lucien Lelong halter-neck dress in pale lilac satin that had been hanging to one side was missing, as was the Edwardian hand-painted parasol, while the rest of the display simply looked messy. Had Nicola left it like that? She quickened her pace. When she reached the shop she could see that everything in the window was upturned, lying in a jumbled heap, and the cream backcloth had been torn down.

Heart pounding, she took out her key and turned it in the lock then pushed on the door: it opened an inch, then stuck. Peering through the gap, Rachel saw that the chain was fastened on the inside.

'Who's there?' she called, hammering on the door. 'Nicola, is that you?'

There was no answer. Rachel tried to slip her hand through the gap to dislodge the chain but it was designed precisely to prevent that happening and all she did was scrape her knuckles. Inside, she could see clothes strewn all over the floor and that was when she realised there had been a break-in.

'I'm calling the police,' she shouted, and pulled her mobile phone from her handbag. Her voice was shaky as she dictated the address and told the operator, 'I think they must still be inside because the chain is on the door and there's no other way out.' But as she spoke, she remembered the bathroom window that gave onto an alley at the back.

The police operator told her to wait until a squad car arrived, but Rachel couldn't bear the suspense. She hurried round into the alley and saw that, as she had guessed, the bathroom window was wide open. It was ten feet above the ground but the intruder had pulled across one of the industrial bins that lined the alley and must have climbed on that.

Rachel hitched up her pencil skirt, took off her stiletto heels and hauled herself with difficulty onto the bin. It stank of waste that had fermented in the weekend heat: a sour, stale, cloying smell. The window was made of security glass but someone had managed to drill through it – she could see drill holes – and remove a section just big enough to slip a hand through and unfasten the locks inside. The burglar had come prepared; it seemed to be a professional job.

Rachel knew she should wait, but she was desperate to inspect the damage. 'The police will be here any moment,' she called, just in case there was anyone inside. After giving them time to escape out the front, she clambered through the window, a shard of glass embedding itself in her left shin. When she bent to pull it out, blood trickled down her leg. She had been carrying her shoes in one hand but now she put them back on, adjusted her skirt and crept into the shop, heart thumping in her chest.

At first it was unrecognisable. Nothing was where it had been when she left on Friday afternoon. Clothing rails were overturned and garments scattered. Display cabinets were smashed, their shelves empty. A favourite art deco lamp was broken, the sylph-like girl in her flapper dress detached from the stand and lying on her side. Rachel was about to pick her up when she remembered she wasn't supposed to touch anything.

For several minutes she tiptoed round, breathing hard, just looking. It was clear that all the jewellery had gone, along with the more expensive evening coats and gowns. The burglar did not seem to have been interested in the embroidered cardigans, lace blouses and fifties patterned skirts. He had left behind the glass perfume bottles and chain-mail evening bags, and most of the leather gloves and high-heeled slingback shoes.

It was the wanton destruction that upset Rachel most. She had worked hard to create an atmospheric interior, with mood lighting, strings of beads and fans hanging on the walls, shawls and feather boas draped around a coat-stand, but they had all been ripped down. A silver-framed art nouveau mirror had been smashed: seven years' bad luck. Her precious lair had been violated. She knew it couldn't be personal but she felt as though it was.

She dialled Alex's mobile, hoping for some words of sympathy, but it went straight to answer machine; he had gone to London for a meeting and must still be there. It wasn't news she wanted to leave in a message so she hung up, and at that moment a police car rolled up outside. Rachel made her way to the door, trying not to tread on anything, and unfastened the chain to let the two officers in.

~

'Are you insured?' the policewoman asked, notebook at the ready. She didn't seem old enough to be qualified; her plump, pretty face could have been that of a sixteen-year-old school-leaver, but her expression was compassionate.

Rachel nodded. She had generous insurance cover.

'That's good,' the policewoman said. 'At least you can make a claim. It's still upsetting, though, isn't it?'

'Did the alarm go off?' the older male officer asked, peering around.

Rachel suddenly realised she hadn't seen the light flashing outside the way it normally did when the alarm was tripped. She went to the unit and frowned when she saw a green light.

'Doesn't look as though it was switched on,' the policeman concluded. 'Were you the last person here?'

Her throat tightened. 'My employee, Nicola, was here on Saturday.'

'Any cash on the premises?'

'No, we always bank it at the end of the day.' Her bank, just two blocks away, had a drop box.

'We'll need to speak to Nicola.' The policeman was businesslike. For him, it was just another job.

Rachel dialled Nicola's number and could tell from the sleep-slurred voice that she had wakened her. 'We've had a break-in at the shop,' she said, trying to keep her tone calm, 'and the police want to talk to you. Any chance you can pop over?'

'Oh no!' Nicola screeched, sounding near-hysterical.

'It's not the end of the world,' Rachel soothed. 'These things happen.'

'Oh God, you're going to kill me,' Nicola cried. 'I was running late when I closed up on Saturday and didn't have time to get the takings to the bank. There was over two grand in the cash register.'

Rachel rushed to the counter and looked in the register. It was empty. The money was gone.

◡

Nicola couldn't stop crying as she spoke to the officers, her words almost incomprehensible through her sobs. 'I'm sorry, I thought I had set the alarm but, looking back, I can't remember if it made that ticking noise. Normally you've only got two minutes to leave after activating it. I was in a mad rush to get out.'

The officers glanced at one another. 'Could you show us how you set it?' the policeman asked.

Nicola demonstrated and the alarm worked perfectly, the ticking starting straight away and continuing until Rachel keyed in the code to stop it.

She couldn't bring herself to meet Nicola's eye. The wording of her insurance policy was crystal clear: the alarm had to be activated when the shop was empty.

'Could the burglars have disabled the alarm?' she asked the officers.

'No wires are cut,' the policeman said, 'so they could only disable it if they knew your code. You don't leave the number written down anywhere, do you?'

Rachel shook her head. 'I don't suppose . . .' She bit her lip. 'Listen, I'm only a small business and I don't know if . . .' She hesitated, wondering if she dared ask them to falsify the evidence. 'Is there anything else that could have happened to the alarm? Any way you can cut me some slack here?'

The policeman frowned, about to reprimand her, but the young female officer spoke first. 'I completely understand. It's a very distressing experience, but I suggest you are honest with your insurers and hope they are supportive. If you've paid your premiums on time, you might be fine.'

They asked her to go through the stock, work out exactly what had been taken then get the full list to them as soon as she could.

Nicola's face was shiny with tears, her eyes pleading for forgiveness. 'Let me help,' she pleaded. 'It's my fault after all.'

'No, don't worry,' Rachel replied, trying to keep her tone light and non-accusatory. 'I can't do anything till the shop's been dusted for prints, then I'd rather clear up on my own.' Applying herself to the absorbing but mindless task of a stock-take would stop her from crying. She needed to stay focused.

While the fingerprint expert covered every surface in dark-grey dust, she checked the fine print of her insurance policy and found she had been right: they would probably not pay up. Her stomach twisted. Now she just had to work out how much she had lost.

Rachel was glad when the fingerprint woman left so she could sort through the remaining stock. She arranged it into piles – undamaged, needing a clean, broken but fixable, broken beyond repair – and checked it off on a list. It wasn't long before she realised that all her most valuable stock had been taken: the designer-name dresses for which she could charge over a hundred pounds each; the ball gowns and wedding dresses, the full-length coats – all gone. There wasn't a scrap of jewellery left either; most of it had been costume jewellery but it was good quality. The burglar had known what he – or she – was doing. All in all, she reckoned she had lost over seventeen thousand pounds' worth of goods, on top of the two thousand cash. And the problem with her business was that she couldn't just go to a wholesaler and restock. It had taken years of pains-taking hunting in a wide range of outlets to build the kind of collection she'd had. It couldn't be re-created overnight.

Mid afternoon, she looked up as the shop door opened and was overjoyed to see Alex, his briefcase in one hand, his brow creased in a frown of sympathy. She leapt up and ran to throw her arms around him.

'How did you . . .?'

'Nicola rang to tell me and I caught the first train. You poor thing.' He kissed her forehead, stroked her hair. 'How bad is it?'

'It's pretty bad.' She had a lump in her throat as she spoke. 'I've lost all my best stuff.'

'I'm so sorry. Nicola's in pieces. Seems to think it's all her fault.'

'Actually, it *was* all her fault.' Rachel clung to him, the familiar shape, the scent making her feel a little calmer.

'Don't be too hard on her. Everyone makes mistakes,' he said, head on one side. He had known Nicola much longer than she had: they'd been at art college together, had even shared a flat for a while; Rachel and Alex had met each other at her birthday party eighteen months earlier. 'Will you be all right though?' he continued.

'The insurance won't pay out because the alarm wasn't on. It's going to be tight.' There was an iron band of worry circling her chest.

'You'll be fine,' he soothed. 'You're a brilliant businesswoman.' He looked around. 'Let me help you clear up. Do you have a brush and shovel?'

He got to work sweeping the tiny shards of broken glass from the floor and wiping the dark-grey fingerprint dust from surfaces. While he was busy, Rachel totted up the figures, her stomach doing somersaults. The rent would have come out of her account that day and she had VAT to pay by the 14th while it looked as though she would lose at least a week's takings, possibly more. On that basis she didn't know how she was going to stay afloat. Everything she had worked for over the last ten years could be lost because of Nicola's one careless moment.

Alex spotted her expression and asked, with concern in his eyes: 'Do you need some money to tide you over? I can help.'

She shook her head and turned away so he wouldn't see the tears welling. It was her business, her problem. It didn't seem right to take his money, even though they were going to be married. She had always valued her financial independence and didn't want to rely on a man for money.

'Thanks, but I'll be fine.'

'Just let me know.' He noticed something on her leg and pointed: 'Darling, you're injured.' She looked down and saw a trickle of dried blood, like a worm, on her calf.

Alex crouched to examine it, his touch gentle. 'It's not deep,' he pronounced. 'I'll give it a clean.'

She closed her eyes as he dabbed at the cut – more of a scratch, really – with a paper towel soaked in warm water.

'Have you heard the Diana news today?' he asked. 'They're saying the driver Henri Paul was drunk. He had three times the legal alcohol limit in his blood.'

Rachel was surprised. 'Why did they allow a drunk man to drive her? Surely her security people should have stopped it?'

'Get this,' Alex continued. 'American website Executive Intelligence Review thinks the crash wasn't an accident. They're saying she was killed deliberately, possibly by secret services.'

'That doesn't make sense. Why would they?'

Alex seemed energised, his eyes lit up. 'Because she knew something they didn't want to be revealed? I'm not sure yet, but I'm going to try and get a commission to make a documentary about the crash. Who better than me, since I was actually there?'

Rachel was alarmed. 'Don't you think you should keep a low profile? They might identify you as the person who picked up that platinum heart.'

'Nah,' he blustered. 'CCTV won't be clear enough. All they'll make out is that I bent over. If they ask, I was fastening my shoelace.'

'Is it not too tabloidy for you?' she persisted. Alex had a reputation for making high-quality arts and historical documentaries.

He threw the paper towel into a rubbish bag and stood up. 'This story is going to run and run, in the broadsheets as well as the tabloids. Tony Blair tapped into the mood when he called Diana "the People's Princess". I know it's cheesy, but there's a story to be told and I want to be the first to break it.'

Rachel felt uneasy. It seemed exploitative and she opened her mouth to tell him so, but stopped. This was his career. He didn't interfere in the way she ran her business, so maybe she should leave him to it.

By late afternoon, the shop was clean and tidy again but it looked bare, like a warehouse. Empty hangers swung from rails, and there was nothing to put in the glass-less display cabinets. She would have to redesign the decor since so many items that hung on the walls had been lost, and she would need more stock before she could reopen for business. Before leaving, she set the alarm, but it was like closing the stable door after the horse had bolted. Alex put an arm round her, as if sensing what she was thinking.

As they walked back to the flat together, Rachel tried to force herself into a positive mindset. She had built the business from scratch before and she could do it again. It would mean hard graft, penny-pinching and determination but she would manage. Having her own clothes shop had been a childhood dream and she was not about to let it go without a fight.

Chapter 9

London, 2 September 1997

IRST THING NEXT MORNING, RACHEL STARTED telephoning her usual suppliers to try and replenish her stock. She bought from a mixture of auction houses, antique markets and private individuals and relied on word-of-mouth tip-offs about forthcoming sales, so it made sense to get the news out that she was on a buying spree. The feedback was disheartening: there were several sales coming up in a few months' time, but she needed stock long before then or she wouldn't survive.

As she worked down her contacts list, she came upon the name Susie Hargreaves. At the beginning of the year Susie had inherited her family estate near Chichester, which had room after room of wardrobes, cupboards and chests full of period clothing. She had approached Rachel at an auction and invited her to the house to look through it and select items she thought she could sell. They agreed to split the proceeds fifty/fifty and the first batch of a dozen garments had sold quickly. From Susie's excitement on being handed an envelope containing five hundred pounds, Rachel realised that money was tight.

'I had no idea what the running costs of the house would prove to be, and how many repairs were needed. I'm afraid I'm on an economy drive,' Susie had confessed. 'I'm selling everything I can.'

Since then, Rachel had sold three more batches of Susie's family heirlooms and liked to think they had become friends of sorts. She was sure Susie would agree to her picking up more stock once she heard about the break-in. Mentally crossing her fingers, she dialled the number, pen poised over her Filofax.

When Susie picked up the phone, Rachel asked whether they could make a date for her to look through more of the clothes.

There was a pause. 'I do want to . . .' Susie paused. 'But I'm not sure if I'm up to it. I'm a bit of a wreck this week.'

Rachel heard a muffled sound down the phone and realised Susie was crying. 'I'm terribly sorry,' she said quickly. 'I didn't mean to intrude.'

'I still can't believe it,' Susie sobbed. 'I can't seem to pull myself together. The funeral's on Saturday and I have to go, but it doesn't seem real. How can Duch be gone? She was so full of life.'

Rachel felt awkward. Susie seemed to have lost a friend and was assuming Rachel knew who she was talking about. 'I'm sure it will take a while to get used to. Was she your age?' She reckoned Susie was in her late thirties, similar to her.

'A couple of years younger. And there are the two boys. It's such a tragedy. I'm scared I'm going to make an awful fool of myself at the funeral because I simply can't stop crying.'

'That's expected at funerals,' Rachel soothed. 'No one will mind.'

'But it's going to be on national television. The whole world will be watching. I'll have to find a seat behind a pillar or something.' She blew her nose hard.

Rachel was stunned as realisation dawned. 'Are you talking about Diana? You were friends with her?'

'Yes, I'm sure I told you. We've known each other since childhood. She was like a sister to me.'

Rachel hesitated, then told Susie that she had been in the Alma Tunnel the previous Saturday and had tried to fend off the photographers crowded round the car.

'Oh my God! Did you speak to her? How did she look?' Susie wanted all the details, and Rachel told her what little she could.

'I spoke to her only a couple of weeks before,' Susie said, her voice strained. 'While she was on holiday in Greece.' She burst into a fresh fit of crying. 'She was happy at least. She'd had a wonderful summer.'

'It's just awful,' Rachel agreed. 'I haven't been able to get it out of my mind and we never even met. It's extraordinary the effect her death has had around the world. I'm sure some good must come of it.'

'I wish I could believe that, but I'm afraid I don't think the world is a just place.'

They agreed that Susie would call Rachel about sorting more clothes for sale once the funeral was out of the way.

Rachel hung up the phone and it rang almost immediately. Alex was on the line in buoyant mood.

'You know it normally takes weeks of preparation before I can get a new project off the ground? Weeks of making up budgets, writing shooting scripts, attending endless meetings? Not this time. As soon as I went to Clive this morning and said, "You will not believe what happened to me at the weekend . . . and I have a hunch there's more to this crash than meets the eye", I got a commission straight away. He said the media has been bowled over by a tidal wave of Diana fever and there are only so many times the archive footage can be rerun.'

'That's brilliant, darling,' Rachel said, trying to sound enthusiastic. It was good news for him, even though she remained dubious about the subject.

'It means I'll have to spend the rest of the week in London putting a team in place. I'll come back on the last train tonight and leave early in the morning. You don't mind, do you?'

He sounded wired, like an over-stimulated child. 'Of course not,' Rachel said. 'Congratulations! I'm sure you'll make a great job of it.'

~

Rachel submitted the paperwork for her insurance claim, just in case they would make an exception. She had the glass in the bathroom window replaced and security bars added so no thief would get in that way again, and even got quotes on installing CCTV, but they were prohibitively expensive; she would just have to make doubly sure the alarm was switched on every time she left the shop.

There were a couple of dreary, hopeless auctions to attend, then she spent the rest of the week redecorating the shop window and interior with items brought from her flat. She even reluctantly put some of her own clothes up for sale, so there would be enough stock for her to open the shop on Saturday. It was usually her busiest day, although Diana's funeral was bound to affect trade.

On Thursday evening, Alex rang from London and urged her to come and see the flowers outside Kensington Palace. 'It's historic,' he said. 'Every day the sea of tributes is stretching further out from the back entrance and along two approach paths. The smell makes you reel.'

'A good time to be a florist, then.'

'Christ, yeah! I spoke to one in Victoria station who told me she's had to order huge shipments from abroad because everyone arriving in London for the funeral is picking up a bouquet as they pass through.'

'Have you talked to any of the Diana fans?'

He chuckled. 'I've got the crew doing vox pops outside Kensington and Buckingham palaces. Nothing original. They all say she was a beautiful person, it's shocking that the Queen hasn't spoken to the nation yet, and they can't understand why the flag isn't flying at half-mast over the palace. And they keep repeating that they can't believe it.'

'Who would have predicted this reaction? I knew her face sold magazines, but this is unprecedented.'

Rachel felt incredibly sorry for Diana and the two boys who had lost their mother, but there was something about the avalanche of unleashed emotion that made her uncomfortable. It didn't feel genuine. All the same, she agreed to join Alex on Friday evening. She could spend the day visiting charity shops in well-heeled areas like Hampstead, Kensington and Putney, where she had sometimes found bargains donated by wealthy locals. After that she'd meet Alex and pay her own respects to the woman whose last moments she had witnessed in the Alma Tunnel.

Chapter 10

Baltimore, December 1916

*W*ALLIS HAD PROMISED TO WRITE TO MARY FROM HER honeymoon in order to share the inside scoop on 'marital relations', a subject of which both girls had only the vaguest understanding. No letters arrived, though, until just before Christmas, by which time Wallis had taken up residence in her new house on the Pensacola military base.

The sunshine is glorious for December, she wrote, *and there are climbing roses and oleanders in full bloom.*

I have so many social engagements, my diary is bursting at the seams. All the officers' wives want to introduce themselves and I am accepting every invitation. And why not?

Our house is small but very homely and my only complaint is the grim brown furniture. I'm having it whitewashed and putting cheerful drapes in the windows and then it will be perfect. We have a maid and a cook, so there is little for me to do except shop and chat to my new friends – and you know me, that's never a hardship! Married life is simply peachy.

Mary felt a familiar prick of jealousy at the talk of new friends, but shrugged it off. Wallis made friends wherever she went; besides, Mary had Renée du Pont. She replied by return, describing the events of the Baltimore social season, the (wholly unremarkable) beaus she was seeing, and how much she missed Wallis. *Nothing is the same without you*, she wrote.

There was a gap of several weeks before another letter arrived, and in this one Wallis invited Mary to visit. *Perhaps we can find a dashing pilot for you*, she chirruped. Mary thought that sounded wildly exciting. They set a date for a week in March 1917, and it couldn't come soon enough for Mary. As she gazed out of the window on the train heading south, she felt a welling of excitement. Perhaps her life was about to change just as Wallis's had. Perhaps she too would find her great love.

~

The Wallis who met her at Pensacola station looked thinner than Mary had ever seen her and talked nineteen to the dozen. There was a frenetic quality to the energy with which she pointed out landmarks, waving an arm towards the airbase, where a plane circled overhead like a bird of prey. She listed all the social engagements she had booked for the week of Mary's stay, and began describing the characters they would meet.

'George is always horsing around and playing practical jokes, while his wife Edna is a complete prude with no sense of humour. You wonder how *that* marriage works behind closed doors . . . And you need to watch Scott because he cheats at poker.' She laughed. 'If you're going to be a cheater, try not to drop your cards.'

Wallis's bungalow had a veranda in front that opened onto a sunny living room, with three bedrooms and two bathrooms leading off it. Down some steps were the dining room and kitchen. It was compact but neat and functional.

'It's lovely!' Mary cried. 'A real home of your own. How does it feel to be married? Are you enjoying it?'

'My goodness, I never have time to stop and think,' Wallis said. 'Life is so hectic. Let me call the maid to bring us a cool drink.'

She seemed jumpy, and Mary wondered if it was because of the growing likelihood that America would enter the war in Europe. Would Win have to go and fight? She didn't like to raise the subject, but it wasn't long before Wallis did.

'Win's positively hankering to go to France. He thinks war is inevitable now that German submarines are sinking our ships willy-nilly. I don't want him to go, of course, but the tales of our pilots in the Lafayette Escadrille are so exciting, don't you think?'

Mary had read about the daring feats of the American pilots who had volunteered to fly as part of France's air corps: their mid-air fire fights and split-second escapes were riveting. 'Don't they have a high fatality rate?' she asked.

Wallis ignored the question. 'Did you know they have pet lion cubs named Whiskey and Soda at their base? All the airmen I've met have a great sense of humour.'

'But what would you do if he went?' Mary persisted.

Wallis smoothed a crease on her skirt. 'If they won't let me sneak along in his suitcase, I'll just have to wait it out with the other wives. I'd be so proud of him.'

Her tone did not convince Mary, and she was trying to think of a response when suddenly a loud gong sounded. Wallis jumped from her seat and ran to the window.

'What in the heck is that?' Mary asked.

Wallis pulled a face. 'It's the crash gong. They sound it when someone has crashed. Oh Lord, I hope it's not Win.'

She rushed out onto the veranda and craned up the street. Mary joined her and saw that several other wives had emerged onto their verandas as well.

'Do you know what's happened?' Wallis called to the woman next door.

'Not yet. It takes a while. We're not allowed to call the base in case they have to contact relatives.' The woman peered at the sky, tight-lipped.

'I'm sure it's fine,' Wallis told Mary in an attempt at breeziness. 'Worst comes to worst, I'll be the base's youngest widow. Only twenty years old!'

'Oh, Wallie!' Mary put an arm round her and gave her a squeeze. 'Aren't you under a lot of strain worrying about him?'

'Not at all. He knows what he's doing.' The words sounded light-hearted but her expression told a different story.

They went back indoors, but Mary could tell Wallis was still on edge until her neighbour popped her head round the door an hour later. 'Just to let you know it was a cadet who crashed. He's OK; plane's a write-off. They shouldn't let them up so early in training. Such a waste of money.'

Win was in a lousy mood when he came back for dinner, slamming the door and barely acknowledging Mary's presence. He walked straight through to the dining room and came back with a tumbler full of an amber-coloured drink.

'That's not . . .' Wallis began, then bit back her words. Mary had never known her so timid.

'It's consommé,' Win told her in a sarcastic tone. 'Can't I have a drink of consommé of an evening?' He turned to Mary. 'We pilots aren't allowed to drink liquor when we're flying the next day, so thank goodness I have a wife who checks up on me.' He took a defiant swallow.

Over dinner he kept topping up his glass with a liquid of the same hue and it soon became clear to Mary that it must be alcohol, because his words were slurred and his face flushed. His mood deteriorated, and no matter what topic of conversation Wallis raised, it seemed to irritate him.

After the entrée, he drained his glass and glared at Mary. 'Aren't you glad you came to witness our marital harmony?' he asked. 'I suppose you two witches have been cackling away all afternoon as she told you our secrets.' He imitated a cackle, with an ugly expression on his face.

Wallis tried to make light of it. 'Yes, dear, we've been stirring up potions in a witches' cauldron . . .' but her words were interrupted by Win hurling his empty glass into the corner of the dining room, where it shattered on the floor.

'See if you can invent a spell to clear that up,' he snapped. 'I'm off to bed.'

The maid hurried in with a brush and dustpan as Win stormed out.

'He's under a lot of pressure,' Wallis said by way of explanation, and Mary thought it wisest not to comment.

Poor Wallis, she thought. She's married a drinker. She knew from listening to relatives' gossip that no good would come of that.

The next evening they dined at another couple's house and Win was on best behaviour, but Mary noted that he poured himself a large 'consommé' as soon as they got home. On Saturday night at the San Carlos Hotel, he frequently disappeared outside to get some air and seemed a little unsteady on his feet when he returned. And at home, when he'd had a drink, he was rude to Wallis.

'You're losing your looks already,' he told her one evening. 'Is that a wrinkle I spy?'

'It's a laughter line,' she said wryly. 'Because life with you is such a barrel of laughs.'

Another time he told her that she had a man's hands. Mary knew Wallis was sensitive about her rather large, square hands, which she always tried to hide in photographs, and thought it was cruel of Win to point them out.

She wished she could talk to Wallis about Win's drinking and coax her to open up about her new life, but whenever she broached the subject, Wallis found a way to duck out of it.

'Win might be temperamental,' she said, 'but he's a dear. I do love him. I'm just sorry we haven't been able to find a handsome pilot for you. But don't worry; I'll make it my mission.'

On the last evening of her stay, as Wallis lay on the bed watching her pack, Mary asked her about marital relations. 'Is it nice? Does it hurt the first time?'

Wallis screwed up her nose. 'When it's your turn, try to stop them going south of the Mason–Dixon line. It's messy and unpleasant.'

Mary was surprised. 'But don't you want children? You'd be a great mother.'

Wallis shuddered. 'There's plenty of time for that. I'm in no rush.'

Mary was quiet on the way home. She didn't open the novel she'd brought with her but gazed out of the window at the fields of yellow corn swaying in the breeze. Instead of feeling jealous that Wallis had been first to get a husband, she now felt desperately worried for her. How could she live with that awful man?

Back in Baltimore, when her sister Anne asked her what Win was like, Mary replied, 'He's a louse.'

Chapter 11

Baltimore, April 1917

MARY SHIVERED WITH ALARM WHEN HER FATHER told them over dinner on 6 April 1917 that America was at war with Germany. What would it mean for them all? Would her friends' brothers have to go and fight overseas? How about Win? She rushed upstairs to write to Wallis, asking if Win was being sent to France. If so, she suggested, Wallis should come for a prolonged stay in Baltimore so she didn't get lonely.

It was some weeks before a reply arrived, and Mary was surprised to see a Boston address on the envelope. She tore it open.

Win is bitterly disappointed not to be shipped to France, Wallis wrote. *Instead we are in Boston, where he has been asked to organise the air station.*

A suspicion entered Mary's mind that Win's superiors knew of his drinking and had decided not to trust him in battle. A desk job would keep him out of the way.

Wallis continued:

I am on my own during the days but entertain myself by taking a streetcar down to Middlesex Superior Court, where I have become addicted to a rather lurid murder trial. I sit in

*the public gallery weighing up the evidence and I must admit
I will be furious if the jury do not find this poor man innocent. I strongly believe he's been framed by his neighbour. At
any rate, it's an entertaining way to spend a summer!*

At the end of the letter, she mentioned that she would be
visiting Baltimore for a couple of weeks in August. Mary looked
forward to it, and was disappointed when Wallis told her they
couldn't spend much time together.

I'm dated up, she apologised. *It proved impossible to see everyone
in such a short visit and instead I'm missing out on what I wanted
most, which was plenty of time with you, dearest Mary. You'll have
to visit us in Boston!*

But no sooner had she returned to Boston than she wrote
that Win was being transferred to San Diego and they were
setting off on the long train journey across to the West Coast.
It seemed she got further away with every move, both physically
and emotionally. Mary was saddened by the news. She had
other friends – plenty of them – but none with Wallis's verve,
or her wry humour.

Sometimes a letter revived the spark of their friendship.
When Mary wrote with descriptions of three beaus she was
spending time with, Wallis replied: *Let me advise you in your
choice between Squinty Sid, the Lanky Lothario and the Case of
the Unpleasant Odour: stay single!* Her letters told how much
she loved the lush plants, the light and the heat of California,
and said that she was starting to make friends among a very
glamorous set, a crowd who sometimes mixed in movie circles.
Mary noted that she never mentioned Win any more, not even
in passing. She did not like to ask about her marriage in a
letter; besides, she suspected Wallis was too proud to tell her.

One summer evening she was at the Baltimore Country
Club with a group of friends when she heard someone speaking

in a foreign accent and turned to see a tall and extremely handsome man in military uniform. His chestnut-brown hair was receding, giving him a widow's peak, and he was clean-shaven. He saw Mary watching and his eyes crinkled in a smile.

She turned away quickly, but seconds later he appeared at her side.

'Jacques Raffray,' he said, extending his hand. 'Please take pity and make a little conversation with me. I know so few people here.'

Close up, his eyes were hazel and very warm. Mary shook his hand and it was warm too. 'What brings you to Baltimore?' she asked. 'You are clearly not from these parts.'

'Very true.' He smiled. 'I am French, and have been sent here to train American pilots to fly the death machines we call aeroplanes. But before we talk of such serious matters I must fetch you a drink, because it is very warm this evening, is it not?'

Mary was grateful for the offer, and as she sipped the root beer he brought, she asked about conditions in war-torn France.

'You know that both sides have dug trenches, with what is called "no-man's-land" in the middle?' Mary nodded. 'It means huge areas of our countryside have turned to mud, with bodies rotting in it because neither side dares to fetch their dead. It's hell for the soldiers, yet a mile or so behind the front line life goes on. Farmers grow their crops, bartenders serve drinks and pretty girls flirt with soldiers during their precious time off.'

Mary blushed at this and suddenly he reached out and brushed her cheek with the side of his finger. 'My God, you are beautiful.'

She was startled by his touch and for a moment she gazed into his eyes, spellbound, before remembering herself. 'I hope your family are safely away from the front line, Mr Raffray.'

He kept his eyes fixed on her as he replied. 'My father is in Rome; he's a scientist. I grew up with him there because my mother died soon after I was born, but I attended school and military college in France. Part of the time I stayed with my Aunt Minnie, who's an artist. She lives a very bohemian life with lots of unconventional friends. You'd like her.'

Mary was flattered that he thought she would like someone bohemian. She wasn't entirely sure what the word meant, but imagined someone bold and artistic.

Jacques asked about her family, and she told him the Kirks were silversmiths, owners of a company dating back to 1817. He asked how she liked to spend her time and she replied that she loved reading and music.

'I could tell you were an *intellectuelle*,' he said. 'You have intelligent green eyes.'

'My goodness, you are a flatterer.' She laughed, then decided to try the kind of bold line she had often heard Wallis using. 'Anyone would think you were trying to seduce me.'

He chortled out loud. 'Ah, you have spirit as well. I think you are my ideal woman. Of *course* I am trying to seduce you.'

Before the end of the evening, they had agreed that he would call on her the following day and he would also purchase tickets to take her to the Baltimore Symphony Orchestra, who were playing Strauss at the weekend.

In bed that night, Mary felt as if she was glowing all over. She replayed their conversation in her head, remembering the way he'd looked at her as if she were the most fascinating creature who ever lived. She thought of Wallis's words that you knew instantly when you were in love because it was as different from liking a boy as peaches from pickles.

I guess I must be in love, she decided as she drifted off to sleep.

~

Jacques appeared the next day holding a bunch of roses in a pale shade of yellow. When Mary accepted them, a delicious cloud of scent enveloped her. She introduced him to her mother, who was soon charmed by his impeccable manners and general affability.

'What kind of plane do you fly?' her mother asked.

'I trained in the Blériot XI,' he told them, 'which we pilots call *Le Tuer* – "The Killer" – because its mechanics are not very stable. We've switched to the Nieuport design now. It's got one and a half wings on each side – the lower ones being much smaller and narrower – and that makes it more agile and safer in the air. I'm over here to train American pilots to fly Nieuports.'

'What kind of things went wrong with the Blériot?' Mary questioned.

'Pfft . . .' He sighed, as if the problems were too many to mention, before saying, 'It was not uncommon for one of the wings to break off. Thank God that never happened to me. But I did have one stall in mid air and I had to climb out onto the wing to restart the propeller.' Both women gasped out loud, and he smiled. 'I wouldn't like to do that too many times. You are only born with so much luck.'

'We read in the papers about someone called the Red Baron and his Flying Circus. They seem very fearsome. Do the Germans have better planes than you?'

Jacques' face darkened briefly and Mary wished her mother had not asked such a tactless question.

'They fly Fokkers. In my opinion, Herr Richthofen, whom you call the Red Baron, and his colleagues are successful not because of the technology of the planes but because of their *tactiques*. They fly in formation, choose a victim and separate him from his squadron, then swoop from above and chase to the kill . . . I have lost many friends to them so I can't think of it as a "circus". But Richthofen will not see out the end of the war. We will get him. You can be sure of that.'

'I'm sorry we reminded you of sad times, Mr Raffray,' Mary said. She wanted to wrap her arms around him and give him a hug.

'Ah, not at all.' He smiled. 'I'm happy to be here in America, doing work that is useful to the war effort. And I am delighted to have met you – both of you.'

On the evening of their date at the Symphony, Jacques presented Mary with some French perfume. Called Black Narcissus, it was in an elegant glass bottle with a lady in a ball gown on a black and gold pastille. She was overwhelmed by the gift, and clasped her hand to her mouth.

'Allow me.' Smiling, he removed the stopper and touched it to her wrist. The scent was rich and exotic, like nothing she had ever smelled before.

'I love it,' she breathed, stumbling over the words and almost saying 'I love you' instead.

~

Mary wrote a long letter to Wallis telling her about Jacques. She said she was delighted that both of them had fallen in love with aviators because he and Win would have lots in common when they met. But she was disturbed by the reply that came from Wallis two weeks later. *Whatever you do, don't marry an airman*, she wrote. *Win's brother Dumaresque just died in the air over France and he is distraught. It's patently ridiculous for a grown man to take off into the clouds in a tin can, and I fear it attracts those who have a warped, suicidal character.*

She's writing of her own experience, Mary thought. Jacques was not like that. He was motivated by patriotism and just wanted to save his country from being overrun by the Kaiser.

By this time she was seeing Jacques most evenings and sometimes during the day as well. She felt as though she was floating on air as they listened to French music on his phonograph, sat arm in arm at concerts, and kissed with ardour – lips slightly ajar – whenever her parents left them alone in the drawing room.

The morning when Jacques asked whether he might petition her father for her hand in marriage was like a dream. She said yes straight away, almost before he had finished his sentence, making them both laugh.

He knocked on the door of her father's study and Mary hurried into the morning room to tell her mother, Anne and Buckie the news.

'He's a very charming man,' her mother said straight away, 'and I can see why you have fallen for him, but I worry that he is not wealthy enough to keep you in the style you deserve.'

'He'll make money after the war,' Mary insisted. 'He's very clever.'

'Will he not want you to go back and live in France?'

Mary shook her head. 'No. He wants us to live in New York. I would be close enough to visit often, Mama. Or you can come to me.'

'You're just copying Wallis,' Buckie remarked in a cynical tone. 'She married an aviator so you feel you have to as well.'

'That's nonsense!' Mary rebuked. 'You know you like him. Why can't you be happy for me?'

Jacques managed to persuade Mr Kirk that he would take good care of his precious middle daughter and the wedding was planned for the following summer. They needed plenty of time to make it a society event worthy of the family name.

~

Mary asked Wallis to be her matron of honour and was over-joyed when she said yes, but closer to the time, Wallis announced she could not be part of the pre-wedding celebrations. She had other commitments that kept her in San Diego so she would not arrive till two days beforehand. That meant Mary had to find a gown for her that matched those of the rest of the wedding party and get the dressmaker to adjust it to Wallis's measurements. Wallis arrived in time for a final fitting, where-upon she immediately rejected the gown Mary had chosen, preferring to wear one of her own instead. She seemed distracted and unhappy. Mary did not have any time alone with her, so was not able to ask what was wrong.

When Wallis was introduced to Jacques, he bowed with old-fashioned courtesy, exclaiming how delighted he was that she had been able to come, and saying she would always be welcome in his and Mary's home.

Wallis barely replied. She was acting very strangely altogether.

Just before the ceremony, as they stood in the church porch waiting for the music to strike up, Wallis whispered one piece of advice to Mary: 'Remember not to let him south of the Mason–Dixon line, kiddo.'

I'm not you, Mary thought. Jacques drove her into such a frenzy with his kisses that she couldn't wait for that aspect of their marriage.

She smiled and took her first step down the aisle.

Chapter 12

London, 5 September 1997

THE SMELL HIT RACHEL SOON AFTER THEY EMERGED from the tube station and crossed the road into Kensington Gardens: warm, sweet and biological, like the compost heap in her dad's garden. She turned to Alex with a question in her eyes and he nodded. 'That's it.'

When they were still some way off, she could see the outline of the vast expanse of floral tributes and hear the rustle of cellophane wrappers fluttering in the breeze; they sounded like a Greek chorus whispering in a tragedy.

Alex led her down the main approach to the palace, shadowy in the gathering dusk, carrying Rachel's holdall, which she had filled with charity-shop finds.

'I can't believe how empty it is,' he said. 'Earlier this place was heaving, but now the hard-core fans have gone to stake a claim for their places to watch the funeral.'

Rachel was stunned into silence as she absorbed the sight of thousands upon thousands of wilting bouquets, hand-drawn cards, balloons, photographs, candles and teddy bears. Only a few souls stood around the vast memorial: a blonde woman who was sobbing quietly while a friend tried to comfort her; a bespectacled Chinese man, who was stooping to peer at the cards; a family with two small children, who were squawking their boredom. A banshee sound filled the air and Rachel turned to see a bearded man in baggy shorts and knee-length socks blowing into a didgeridoo. The mournful tones seemed oddly appropriate.

She wandered round, reading some of the cards: *We miss you, Di*; *Always in our hearts*; *We will love you forever.* People had written poems, or cut pictures out of newspapers and put them in heart-shaped frames attached to heart-shaped helium balloons, straining on the end of their ribbons. That ubiquitous symbol of love, always red, was so overused as to be meaningless. She and Alex didn't buy each other Valentine's cards or pay a premium for a meal out on 14 February. He was romantic in other ways, often leaving her little notes in the form of skilful hand-drawn animal cartoons, a legacy of his art-school education.

'Isn't it strange how people seem to think they own a piece of her?' she remarked. 'She's *their* princess, they're on first-name terms, and they love her, even though they never met her and were never likely to had she lived. They might not have *liked* her in person.'

'Shhh!' he cautioned. 'That's heresy.'

As they walked to Kensington High Street in search of a restaurant, Alex described the video footage of Diana leaving the Ritz that had been released by Mohamed Al-Fayed's press office that afternoon.

'She's wearing white trousers and a black jacket, pushing her way out of the door towards the car, completely unsuspecting. She looks a bit agitated, a bit tired after a long day. It's emotional to watch, knowing what was going to happen next . . . And interestingly, at one point I can see the glint of a silvery bracelet on her wrist. It looks as though the heart I found could have fallen off it.'

'Really?' It felt eerie to know they had something belonging to the Princess in their possession. 'Why do you think Al-Fayed released the video?'

'The main reason is because it shows Henri Paul walking around looking perfectly sober. They are claiming he wasn't drunk at all, and that someone tampered with his blood sample. There's a huge conspiracy theory growing.'

Rachel chuckled. 'I bet there is: all those people who think Kennedy was assassinated by the Mafia and Marilyn was killed by the Kennedys and Elvis is still alive.'

Alex didn't laugh. 'Actually, there are quite a few anomalies. I don't know why it took them so long to get her to a hospital. I spoke to an A and E doctor who told me that because they missed the golden hour straight after the accident, it would have been impossible to save her. When they opened her up, the surgeon even massaged her heart in his hands but it simply wouldn't start again.' His voice sounded choked, but he controlled himself and continued. 'In the UK, the strategy would have been to pull her out of the wreck pronto and get her straight to the nearest hospital.'

Rachel was startled by the image: the heart of the so-called Queen of Hearts being squeezed in a surgeon's hand. 'It's a shame they didn't do it that way, but you can't believe the French ambulance service was part of a conspiracy. That's loony talk, sweetie.' She twirled a finger by her temple.

They stopped to read the menu outside a Chinese restaurant but Rachel decided against it: too many gloopy sauces.

'They think there could have been a motorbike or another car involved in the collision, but it didn't stop at the scene,' he continued.

Rachel hadn't heard that. 'It's possible, I suppose. Maybe one of the photographers crashed into them then legged it. It would be a natural reaction.'

'Or it could have been set up by one of the secret services if they wanted Diana dead.'

Rachel frowned. 'And what motive would they have?' She checked the menu at a Lebanese restaurant: hummus, falafel, shish taouk. 'Let's try this, shall we?' It had the benefit of being cheap, and she had a constant nagging worry about money at the back of her mind.

Alex waited until they were seated in the glass-fronted conservatory-style eatery before answering. 'Diana allegedly hinted to journalists about a wooden box of secrets she was keeping as an insurance policy. If the royal family treated her too badly, she could threaten to release it.'

'But that would make them wary of killing her, wouldn't it? Presumably she had left instructions for its release if anything happened to her.'

Rachel skimmed the menu while Alex ordered a beer for himself and a vodka and tonic for her.

'Some sources are saying she was killed because she was planning to marry a Muslim and Princes Harry and William could have had Muslim half-siblings.'

'That doesn't make sense either,' Rachel murmured. 'Wasn't her last boyfriend Muslim too? That doctor chap . . .'

'Hasnat Khan. True . . .' He cleared his throat. 'Anyway, something doesn't add up about the story and I want to look into it. It means I'll have to spend a lot of time in Paris over the next couple of months.'

Rachel swallowed. She could have used his moral support while she fought to save her business, but he was bursting with enthusiasm for his new project and she didn't want to make him feel guilty for neglecting her.

'Where are you going to film the funeral from?' she asked.

'My cameraman has a spot opposite the Abbey. He's been camping there since early morning. And I've got another cameraman and a sound guy walking round catching crowd reactions. They'll be filming as the princes walk behind Diana's coffin before the ceremony, with Prince Charles, Prince Philip and Charles Spencer.' Suddenly his eyes filled with tears.

Rachel was puzzled. 'Are you OK?'

He dabbed his eyes with a napkin and struggled to stop himself from crying. 'Don't you find it tragic?' he asked. 'Those poor boys.'

There was a strange moment when Rachel peered at him, expecting him to grin and say, 'Ha! Fooled you!' But he didn't. He was serious. Of course, thinking about what the boys were going through must be bringing back the shock of his own mother's death when he was their age.

She leaned over the table, cupped his face between her hands and whispered, 'I do love you.'

It still seemed incredible that this man was soon to be her husband. Her business might be in danger, but she couldn't believe how extraordinarily lucky she was in love.

Chapter 13

Brighton, 6 September 1997

RACHEL OPENED HER SHOP ON THE DAY OF DIANA'S funeral, although the sun-drenched Brighton streets were near-empty and it seemed everyone was staying at home to watch television.

Amongst the items she had found in her charity-shop trawl the previous day was a bias-cut silver and gold lamé evening gown with a handkerchief hem and two panels that knotted just below the hip line. There was no label, but it looked similar to a 1926 gown by the great French designer Madeleine Vionnet that was pictured in one of her fashion history books. Some of the seams were frayed and the ornamental knot had come loose, but Rachel had a reel of silver thread and she sat down to repair it, using her old Singer sewing machine controlled by a foot pedal.

As she worked, her mind was on Diana. The thought that had haunted her in the week since the crash was whether Diana had had any idea she was dying while she was trapped in the car. She hoped not. The papers said she had been due to see her sons the following day after two weeks' separation. Maybe she was thinking about them, hoping her injuries would not prevent her getting home. But she must have felt very alone, especially if she realised her lover was dead beside her.

Just before eleven, the door opened and Nicola popped her head in, her expression nervous. She was wearing navy jogging bottoms and a grey T-shirt, her dark hair wet and straggly from the shower.

'You've opened up, I see?' She glanced around at the half-empty clothes rails and sparsely filled shelves. 'Rachel, I can't forgive myself for what I did. I'm so sorry. Have you heard from the insurers yet?'

'Not yet. But don't beat yourself up about it. We all make mistakes.'

She didn't feel cross with Nicola. It was her own fault for leaving the shop in someone else's care. Nicola was warm, creative, sensitive, a good friend, but she was prone to flakiness. Details escaped her notice, and she was perpetually running late for something or other.

'Is there anything I can do to help? I wish you would let me make amends.'

Rachel glanced around. 'I ordered new glass panels for the display cases and they were delivered yesterday. Do you want to try and slot them in?'

Nicola bounced into the shop, pleased to be given a task. 'Are you not watching Diana's funeral?' she asked, as she crouched on the floor to pull the first pane of glass from its cardboard covering. 'You missed Wills and Harry walking behind the coffin. It was really moving.'

Rachel thought of the tiny portable television set she kept in a cupboard to watch on slow days. Had the thief taken it? She got up to look, and there it was, nestled on a low shelf. She placed it on the counter, plugged it in and switched it on with mixed feelings. The funeral was bound to be a media circus, but she supposed it was history in the making.

'Looks as though they're just arriving at the Abbey,' Nicola remarked, and she called out names as the cameras homed in on celebrities: 'There's Tom Cruise and Nicole Kidman . . . And Tom Hanks with Rita. Diana would be pleased.'

Rachel smiled and carried on with her sewing, wondering if Alex was filming the Hollywood contingent.

The ceremony began and they listened in silence to Diana's brother's speech, in which he called her the most hunted woman of the modern age. Rachel got goose bumps thinking of those loathsome photographers clamouring around the Princess's dying body. It seemed fitting that he had commented on the paparazzi. As the camera panned round the Abbey, she kept an eye out for Susie Hargreaves, but couldn't see her.

'You should stock up on Diana clothes in the shop,' Nicola suggested. 'They would go like hot cakes. Think shoulder pads, tiaras . . . Di liked a good tiara.'

Rachel made a face. 'No chance. I draw the line at the 1950s. I have an uneasy relationship with acrylic.'

Too late she realised that Nicola's jogging bottoms were acrylic, but it seemed no offence was taken.

From time to time the television showed the scene in the streets outside the Abbey, and Nicola suddenly shrieked, 'Look! There's Alex!'

Rachel glanced up from her sewing to see him standing behind a cameraman, giving directions. In the crowd around them, several people were sobbing openly: men and women of all ages, faces red and distorted with grief, leaning on each other for support. The few children present looked baffled by the outpouring of emotion, and Rachel felt the same way. They hadn't known Diana. What was it really about?

'I hear Alex is making a documentary about the crash,' Nicola said. 'He thinks there was something suspicious about it. Do you agree?'

Rachel didn't want to be disloyal so kept her response neutral. 'It seems to me that if you were going to bump someone off, there are easier ways. But I'll see what he digs up. You never know.'

'I hope it didn't spoil your romantic weekend when he suddenly slipped into producer mode. I know what he can be like.'

Rachel put down her sewing and, with a grin, held out her left hand to show Nicola the ring. *Au contraire* . . . He asked me to marry him. I'm sorry we didn't tell you before, but we were waiting till our news wasn't overshadowed by Diana.'

For a fleeting moment, an unguarded expression flickered across Nicola's face: surprise, possibly alarm, maybe even horror. It was very quick, and afterwards Rachel wondered if she had imagined it.

'But that's wonderful!' Nicola exclaimed, her mouth curving into a broad smile. She jumped up and rushed over to hug Rachel, almost knocking a cup of tea onto the lamé dress. 'How on earth could you keep a secret like that all week?'

'How could you not notice my ring last Monday? I kept waiting for you to ask about it – but I guess we had other things on our minds.'

Nicola grabbed her hand for a closer look. 'You know me – observational powers of a mole. It's gorgeous. I'm so happy for you.' She touched the twin diamonds with a fingertip. 'Truly I am.'

Chapter 14

New York City, September 1919

MARRIED LIFE WITH JACQUES WAS GLORIOUS. MARY loved the way he touched her, making her skin tingle, the way he made love so gently and ardently while whispering in his romantic French accent how beautiful she was and how much he adored her.

She liked arranging their apartment, which overlooked Washington Square in Lower Manhattan, and planning meals to please Jacques when he got home from his new job as an insurance broker. She bought his favourite red wine to serve with dinner, although she didn't much care for it herself, and she planned entertainments for them: poker evenings, or visits to tiny jazz clubs in the Village, just walking distance from home, where live bands played so close to the audience you could see the beads of sweat on their foreheads and hear every breath they inhaled. They mixed with other young married couples, either neighbours or Jacques' business colleagues, dining at each other's apartments, drinking and chatting late into the night. Occasionally they visited the Upper East Side home of Renée du Pont and her businessman husband John Donaldson, but they were hugely wealthy and Mary felt embarrassed about issuing return invitations to her much humbler address.

Her happiness was complete when, a year after their wedding, she discovered she was expecting a child. She had missed two monthly bleeds before she called on a doctor, who confirmed the news. Jacques was beside himself with joy, and every day when he returned from the office he brought some small gift: flowers or bonbons for her, a rag doll for the little one.

'I see you have decided the sex of our first child already.' She smiled. 'Have you consulted a fortune-teller?'

'I can sense she is a girl, and that she will grow up to have your extraordinary beauty,' he said, a hand cupping the barely-there curve of her belly.

But one day, as she sat writing a letter to her mother, she felt a twisting of her insides so agonising she screamed out loud. The maid came running and Mary gasped for her to call a doctor and to telephone Jacques. By the time they arrived she was lying on the sofa, blood-soaked towels between her legs, racked with sobs.

'I'm so sorry,' she told Jacques. The disappointment etched on his face made her feel a failure as a wife. She hadn't been able to keep his baby safe.

'It's all right, *mon amour*.' He clutched her hand, squeezing her fingers hard.

The doctor asked Jacques to leave the room while he conducted an intimate examination. He palpated Mary's belly, checked the matter that had been expelled, took her pulse and temperature, then asked her permission to examine her private parts. She coloured deeply but gave her consent.

'You have a little sore patch here,' he said, touching it. 'And another. Have you been feeling tired? Any joint pains, or skin rashes?'

'I thought those were symptoms of pregnancy,' she replied.

The doctor scraped a little material into a test tube and

promised to call on her again just as soon as the results of his tests came back.

It was a week later when he returned, and at first he seemed embarrassed to tell her and Jacques the outcome. 'I'm afraid to say you have syphilis,' he mumbled. 'A disease that is transmitted through sexual relations.'

'That's not possible,' Mary cried, her face burning with shame. 'I have only ever been with my husband.'

Jacques looked pale and shocked. 'I had it several years ago but was assured it had been cured.'

'Which treatment did you use?' the doctor asked.

'I applied mercury every day for several weeks and it burned the sores away. How can the disease still be there?' He seemed close to tears.

Mary stared at him, wondering how he had caught syphilis. She had not known there were others before her. Why had he not told her?

'Mercury is the old-fashioned approach. We have a new treatment now, a drug called Salvarsan. I will give you both daily injections for a month. If you refrain from marital relations during that time, you will both be cured. Give yourself a few months to recover,' he counselled Mary, 'and then there is no reason why you should not fall pregnant again.'

Jacques was crying silently, trying to wipe his tears without her noticing.

Mary had to ask. 'Is it because of the syphilis that I lost my baby?'

The doctor bowed his head. 'I'm afraid so, yes.'

Jacques gave a loud sob, leapt up and ran from the room.

Later that evening, he cried on her shoulder as he told her about the girl who had infected him during the first months of the war, when he was lonely and had sought comfort. He had not realised that she had offered the same comfort to many other soldiers, and had been devastated when the army medic diagnosed the disease.

'It's not your fault,' Mary soothed, stroking his head. He smelled of wine and she guessed he had drunk a few glasses to take the edge off his anguish. 'At least there is a sure way to cure it.'

That should have been the end of it, but Mary found it hard not to dwell on the girl Jacques had taken to his bed. How had *she* caught syphilis? Had there been any other girlfriends apart from her? He refused to answer further questions, saying it had all happened long before he met Mary and there was no point in dragging up the past because it would only hurt her more, but his reticence led her to imagine the worst. It also made her wary of resuming marital relations, in case the infection recurred, but eventually her burning desire for a child overcame her deep humiliation.

She fell pregnant again just over a year after they finished the course of Salvarsan, but almost as soon as the diagnosis was confirmed, she miscarried.

'It was too soon,' the doctor advised. 'Your body wasn't ready. Give it time.'

In May 1921, while Mary was still in mourning for the second child she had lost, a letter arrived from Wallis: *Dearest Mary, I wonder if I might visit you and Jackie for a few days later this month? I must talk to you on a matter of vital importance.*

She was surprised, as they had drifted apart since Wallis had been living on the West Coast. They still corresponded, but much less frequently. Weeks would go by with no news, and when a letter did arrive from San Diego, it was full of descriptions of glamorous parties Wallis had attended in the fashionable Hotel de Coronado and movie stars she had met, including John Barrymore ('the most hilarious drunk') and Charlie Chaplin ('a peculiar little man').

Mary wasn't sure what to reply. She didn't feel like company, would find it hard to put on a gregarious mask and pretend to be the person she used to be as a teenager when she and Wallis were close. But at the same time, she couldn't bear to let her friend down, so she replied asking when Wallis would like to arrive.

~

A maid showed Wallis straight into the drawing room and Mary leapt to her feet to embrace her. On first glance, she could tell something was terribly wrong. Wallis had always been skinny, but now she was skeletally thin, with dark shadows under her eyes, and she looked a good five years older than her age of twenty-five.

She threw herself onto a chair and blurted out, 'I'm leaving Win,' before bursting into a torrent of weeping, her face buried in her hands.

Mary hadn't seen her cry like that since Mr Rasin died. She knelt by her feet, and took Wallis's hands in her own. 'Oh you poor dear. Are things really so bad?'

'They're worse than bad,' Wallis sobbed. 'I have to leave him but no one will support me. Uncle Sol says he won't let me bring disgrace on the family. Mother says that being a successful wife is an "exercise in understanding", and that I must try harder. But it's like serving a life sentence in jail. I won't do it. I can't!' She cried even louder, and Mary took a handkerchief from her pocket and dabbed at the tears.

'There, there,' she soothed. 'We will think of a solution. Let me call for refreshments.'

Wallis managed to calm herself in the presence of the maid. Once she had left the room, Mary asked: 'Now tell me what is so wrong with your marriage. Is Win unhappy too?'

'He's a drunk,' Wallis said bitterly. 'A violent, brutish drunk who doesn't love me. I don't think he ever did.'

'Of *course* he loves you. It's clear to everyone.' Mary wasn't being entirely truthful; she had rarely seen Win behave in a loving manner towards Wallis. 'And hasn't he stopped drinking now that we have Prohibition?' The 18th Amendment, passed the previous year, had banned the manufacture and sale of alcohol throughout the United States.

'Of course not! Alcohol is more popular than ever now that it's hard to buy. Isn't it the same in New York?'

Mary admitted that they always kept some wine and bourbon in the house; she wasn't sure where Jacques bought it and thought it better not to know.

'It's not just the drinking,' Wallis continued. 'It's his completely unreasonable behaviour. Several times now he has locked me in the bathroom and left me there all day while he went out. Can you imagine? One time he even hog-tied me to the bed. You don't do that to someone you love, do you?'

Mary was horrified but not entirely surprised. She remembered the smashed glass in Pensacola, the cruel words, the moodiness. 'Why does he tie you up?'

Wallis turned away. 'It's his pathetic jealousy. To his mind, every man I speak to is a secret paramour. If I dare to dance with another man at a party, all hell breaks loose. Win calls me names you wouldn't believe when he's fried: tells me I'm a whore and that I have a face like a horse. Oh God, Mary, it's unbearable.' Her lip was trembling, and she was clearly on the verge of another crying jag.

'Does he hit you?' Mary whispered.

'A slap now and again. I can put up with that; it's the way he talks to me that is the worst kind of cruelty.' She shook her head. 'I have to divorce him while I'm still young enough to get another husband. I don't want to leave it too late.'

'Divorce is a big step, though.' Mary had heard of couples divorcing but there were no divorcees in her social circle.

Adultery was the only grounds on which a divorce would be granted in New York State, and it always caused a huge scandal. 'What would you live on?'

Wallis looked worried. 'Win must surely pay me some alimony; don't you think? And I suppose I could get a job . . .' she continued doubtfully.

Mary knew Wallis had never wanted to work; she would consider it beneath her to be tied to an office or a shop job. No, she would want to find another husband as soon as she possibly could. And no doubt she would succeed.

~

Wallis changed her clothes before Jacques arrived home from the office and greeted him in a black organdie dress trimmed with white lace.

'You look *très élégant*,' he told her admiringly.

'Black is *the* spring colour in France this year,' she told him. 'If a frock isn't all black, then it's black and white.'

'Oh dear,' Mary remarked cheerily, looking down. 'I'm completely out of date with my cerise gown from last fall. You'll have to buy me a new one, dear.'

Jacques embraced her. 'Anything you want, *mon amour*.'

Over dinner, Wallis monopolised the conversation to ask Jacques' advice on her situation. 'Perhaps you can recommend insurance products to suit impoverished single women,' she suggested. 'Once I am on my own, I will rely on my gentleman friends.'

'You won't be single for five minutes when word gets out,' he replied gallantly. 'In fact, I'm sure I spotted a line round the block. Perhaps we can invite them in for interviews later.'

'Oh yes!' Mary giggled. 'Can we choose your next husband for you? Two heads are better than one.'

'Of course,' Wallis agreed. 'But I want someone just like Jackie: every bit as handsome, with his wit and perspicacity and that divine French accent. Do you by any chance have a twin?' She placed a hand on his arm and Mary felt a fleeting twinge of irritation.

'You should visit Paris,' Jacques suggested, shifting his arm to pick up his glass. 'You won't be able to move for Frenchmen falling at your feet.'

'Doesn't that sound fun?' Wallis twinkled. 'I'll book my ticket next week.'

As they got ready for bed that night, Mary asked Jacques what he thought of her friend. They had only met fleetingly at the wedding so it was the first time he'd had a chance to make lengthy conversation with her.

Jacques paused. 'You've spoken so highly of her in the past that I was curious to compare the real Wallis with the legend. And you were right in most respects: she is clever and entertaining and gay.' He put his arm round her. 'But I was disappointed to see that she is not very loyal to you. I would be wary of her.' He kissed the tip of her nose.

'Do you mean because she flirted with you? Wallie can no more keep from flirting than she can from breathing.'

'No, because she will be your friend only for as long as you are useful to her.'

Mary didn't reply, but the words stuck in her mind long afterwards.

～

Over the course of the week, Wallis and Mary went shopping together and lunched in some of the city's top restaurants: Delmonico's, Sherry's and Henri Mouquin's. They had tea with Mary's lady friends and illicit cocktails with Jacques' business partner and his wife, and all the time they talked endlessly about Wallis's problem.

'Is it completely hopeless with Win?' Mary persisted. 'Are you sure it cannot work if he promises to mend his ways?'

'I know. I should try again. That's what everyone says.' Wallis stared at her lap. 'You're right, of course.'

It felt strange being the wiser of the two; it was a reversal of roles for them. Mary was pleased that Wallis had turned to her in her hour of need, and glad to be able to help. She had a deep love for her childhood friend that had taken root in their teenage years. Secretly she hoped that if Wallis did divorce, she would settle in New York and they could be close again: like sisters but better, because they had chosen each another.

Before she left New York, Wallis said she had decided she would give Win one last chance. But two weeks later, a letter arrived saying that she had moved into her mother's apartment in Baltimore. She simply couldn't bear to spend another night under the same roof as 'that man'.

Mary told her mother, who told her sisters, and all were horrified.

You must cut your ties with Wallis, her mother wrote. *She can blacken her own name if she likes, but I will not have any stain on you because of your association. Her family must be livid.*

Ignoring the instruction, Mary sent a long and sympathetic letter to Wallis, saying that any help she and Jacques could offer was hers, and that their door was always open. She was worried about her friend. Divorced women were generally excluded from polite society, which would make it difficult to find another husband of suitable rank. Wallis might find herself alone and struggling to make ends meet if Uncle Sol refused to support her, and Mary shuddered to think where a woman in *that* position might end up.

Chapter 15

New York, January 1924

MARY HAD HOPED SHE WOULD SEE MORE OF Wallis after the separation from Win, but it did not work out that way. At first Wallis stayed in Baltimore with her mother, then she moved to Georgetown to live with a friend, an admiral's daughter who was supremely well connected. Contrary to Mary's fears, people did not seem to have any misgivings about entertaining a woman who had left her husband: Wallis wrote of receptions and parties and tennis tournaments where she met politicians, diplomats and high-ranking naval officers. There was never anything personal in the letters; she gave no hint as to her state of mind, but Mary assumed she was on the prowl for husband number two.

Buckie wrote that Wallis was rumoured to be having an affair with an Argentinian diplomat called Felipe Espil; according to her, 'simply everyone' was talking about it. Espil had broken the hearts of many society girls and Buckie appeared to take grim satisfaction in predicting that the same thing would happen to Wallis.

Mary found that hard to believe, as in all the time they had known each other, it was always Wallis who had been the heartbreaker. She waited for her friend to mention Señor Espil, but the name never came up, and Mary felt reticent about raising the subject. Perhaps Wallis was unaware of the gossip; perhaps the rumour was pure invention. The next she heard was that Wallis had gone to Paris with her cousin Corinne in January 1924, and later that year, for reasons Mary couldn't fathom, she decided to sail out to Hong Kong, where Win had been stationed, in order to give her marriage one last try.

By that time, Mary had taken a job in a small boutique near Fifth Avenue, where they sold the latest Parisian fashions as soon as they could be shipped over. She enjoyed the sociable aspects of the work and found she had a good eye for helping society matrons to choose outfits that suited them. In the evenings, she and Jacques went to restaurants or to shows, they entertained or visited other couples, and often they made up a four for bridge.

One evening Jacques invited a business colleague, Ernest Simpson, and his wife Dorothea for dinner. As the introductions were made, Mary thought to herself how rare it was to find a couple where the husband was better-looking than the wife; usually it was the other way around. Ernest was extremely attractive, while Dorothea was plump, dowdy, and looked much older than him.

'Are you English, Mr Simpson?' she asked on hearing his accent.

'Good question,' he replied with a friendly smile. 'My father is English, my mother American; I was born and raised in New York City and went to Harvard University, but during the war I took British citizenship in order to fight for them. And now I am married to an American woman. So what do you think that makes me?'

'A half-breed,' Mary replied, returning his smile. 'But you dress like an Englishman, and your accent sounds British to my ear.'

He was wearing an impeccably pressed pinstripe suit and waistcoat, with a hint of handkerchief showing above his breast pocket in the exact dark blue shade as his tie.

'Yet the English think I sound American, so I suppose I am neither one nor the other.'

'Or both,' Jacques contributed. 'Now can I offer you a *real* drink?' He produced a bottle of bourbon and the men had a glass each while discussing its relative merits compared to Scotch whisky, which Ernest preferred.

'I normally drink wine,' Jacques said, 'like a good Frenchman, but it is difficult to find these days. The bootleggers seldom stock it.'

While the men talked about the difficulties of buying alcohol, Dorothea turned to Mary and asked, 'Do you have children?'

'Not yet,' she blushed, 'but we would like to.'

'I have girls. My daughter Audrey is two, and I also have a ten-year-old, Cynthia, from my *disaster* of a first marriage.' She rolled her eyes.

Mary was surprised that she would mention on first meeting that she was a divorcee, but she soon learned that Dorothea possessed a refreshing candidness.

Over dinner, Ernest and Mary got into conversation about books, and she was pleased to hear he was a fan of Edith Wharton.

'I thought her novels were of interest only to women, with their themes of courtship and marriage.'

'On the contrary. I enjoy her descriptions of the nuances of New York society, and think her a talented wordsmith. She can sum up a character in one brief phrase so that you feel you know not just their appearance but their soul.'

They compared notes and when Mary heard he had not read an early one, *Ethan Frome*, she offered to lend it to him.

'Do you enjoy reading, Dorothea?' she asked.

'Me? No. I'm a dumb Dora. I don't have the patience for it. I'm always busy with the children or running the house, but I'm happy that it gives Ernest such pleasure.'

After they had waved their guests off, Mary linked her arm through Jackie's. 'I like them,' she said. 'Let's invite them again.'

~

In the early spring of 1925, when the snow had only recently melted, Mary realised she was pregnant again, four years after her last pregnancy. Her breasts were full and tender, and she had a slight nausea that persisted throughout the day. As soon as her doctor confirmed the diagnosis, she left her job in the shop and gave up socialising, spending her days reading on the sofa or resting in bed. She spoke to the little one growing inside her, and Jacques did the same, kneeling down to whisper endearments to her belly.

'I'm sure it's a boy,' he predicted. 'My firstborn son and heir.'

Mary felt instinctively it was a girl but did not like to argue. She dithered over names – Evelyn, Gloria, Louise – and decided she would let Jacques choose if it was a boy.

At first she resisted telling anyone, superstitious in case it should go the same way as her earlier pregnancies, but when she was around two and a half months gone, she wrote to Buckie, and her elder sister immediately came to visit, full of advice and caution.

'You must take it easy. Twenty-nine is very old to carry your first child. Your body is not so resilient as when you were younger.'

'If I took it any more easy, I would be asleep the entire time,' Mary joked.

She was deliriously happy, and with Buckie's help began to plan the decoration of a nursery and discuss the hiring of a nanny.

And then she woke in the middle of the night with fierce cramps gripping her stomach and warm stickiness between her legs, and knew straight away what it was. Jacques ran to fetch Buckie, groggy in her nightgown, and then to telephone the doctor.

'Perhaps the baby can be saved,' Mary begged her sister, clutching her arm. 'Perhaps she is all right.'

'That bloody man and his syphilis,' Buckie muttered under her breath as she mopped up the copious blood with fresh towels. 'We Kirks have never had a problem carrying babies.'

Mary wished she had never mentioned the syphilis. 'Tell the doctor I *need* this baby. He *must* save her.'

But the blood kept coming, viscous and dark, with a metallic smell, and she knew it was the end. She stayed in bed for over a week, refusing food, turning her face to the wall, crying bitter tears that left her chest aching. Jacques cried too, and clutched her tight, seeking comfort she was unable to give.

The doctor said it might be nothing to do with the syphilis, but in her heart Mary couldn't help blaming Jacques, although she never said as much. Buckie had no doubt who *she* blamed, and went home to Baltimore grim-faced to share the news with the family.

All through the summer, Mary did not leave the house. She couldn't bear to socialise, did not have the energy to drive to the beach for fresh air, as Jacques suggested. She knew he was sad too, as he poured himself a glass of red wine when he got home from work every day, and drank several more over the course of the evening. She often caught him with fresh tears in his eyes and she felt for him – it was his loss too – but was sunk too deep in her own grief to be able to help.

Friends sent invitations but she refused them all, citing ill health. Some delivered cut flowers, others sent their servants round with healthful broths or light custards, but still she could not face company. And then one Saturday afternoon, when Jacques had gone for a solitary walk, the bell rang and her maid announced that it was a Mr Ernest Simpson and he was most insistent upon seeing her.

'Bring him in,' Mary agreed, and blotted the letter she was writing.

'You're so pale,' Ernest exclaimed as soon as he saw her. 'I'm sorry you have been poorly but I simply couldn't let any more time go by without calling.'

'It was kind of you,' she said. 'Let me ring for tea.'

'I've brought you a book that's just been published.' He handed her a brown paper package. 'I'm pretty sure you'll like it.'

Mary untied the string, opened the paper and read the title: '*The Great Gatsby*. It sounds unusual. I haven't read anything by Mr Fitzgerald, but I've heard of him, of course.'

'It's had mixed reviews but I find it a literary gem, and I would appreciate your opinion. We usually see eye to eye.'

Ernest pulled a chair close to where she was sitting and they talked of books for a while. She asked after Dorothea and the girls, then there was a lull in the conversation. Ernest studied her face, trying to gauge her mood, and Mary broke the silence.

'I expect you are wondering about my illness but you are too polite to ask. Well, I feel drawn to tell you the truth, but I ask you pray be discreet about it . . .'

'Of course.' He shifted in his seat.

'I lost a baby in May. It was the third time I have fallen pregnant and then lost the baby quite soon after, and I am in mourning for the child it seems I am destined never to have. That is why I cannot face society. It's something I must come to terms with in my own time.'

He looked so unutterably sad that Mary was touched.

'I am sorry to hear it,' he said. 'You would be a wonderful mother. Perhaps you still can be, as you are young enough.'

'It's kind of you to say so, but I'll be thirty next year and I suspect time has run out. Not everyone can be as blessed as you and Dorothea. I will find some other focus for my life.' It felt good to put this into words. For the first time she felt a sense that life might be valuable without children.

'Perhaps you will be a writer,' Ernest suggested. 'A poet.'

She laughed, an unfamiliar sensation. 'Goodness, I doubt that. At any rate, thank you for not telling me that it was God's will, as my mother keeps insisting. I'm not very impressed with God, if that's the case.'

He looked up at the ceiling, then back at her. 'Nope. You have not been smitten with a thunderbolt from the heavens. That's a relief.'

They chatted for over an hour and Mary had a curious sensation of stepping outside herself and observing that the heavy cloak of grief she had been smothered beneath all summer had lifted. She saw a woman who was interested in life again and she knew that something had shifted. At last she was ready to re-enter the world, as the first leaves cartwheeling to the ground presaged the arrival of autumn.

~

Letters from Wallis had been few and far between while she was in the Far East, but in December 1925 one arrived from close to home.

I'm back and am living in Warrenton, Virginia after receiving a tip-off that it's just about the cheapest place to get a divorce. I have to be resident here for a year and it will cost three hundred dollars, but what a bargain at the price!

There are two or three agreeable people in Warrenton but I fear I shall tire of them before long and I hope you and Jackie will not mind if I land on your doorstep, luggage flying, begging you to revive me.

Mary smiled. Perhaps a touch of 'Wallisification' was just what the doctor ordered.

Chapter 16

Brighton, 7 September 1997

ALEX RETURNED TO BRIGHTON THE NIGHT OF THE funeral and he and Rachel spent the next morning in bed, reading the Sunday papers. She had missed him during the week; it had been a stressful time and she would have liked to talk it through with him.

'How's the shop?' he asked that morning, kissing her shoulder. 'Are you getting back to normal?'

'I opened yesterday but only took a couple of hundred quid because I'm still very short of stock.' She toyed with telling him about the tight band of fear around her chest, the panic that she was going to lose all she had worked for, but she was too proud.

'Is there anything I can do? Shall I get my friends to raid their grandmas' closets for you?'

He was trying to help, but Rachel didn't like the idea of all their friends knowing she was in trouble. 'Thanks, but I would just end up with a load of junk to sort through.'

'Well, remember my offer,' he said, opening the *Sunday Times*, which had a whole section devoted to Diana. 'And just ask if you need money to tide you over.'

Rachel reached for the *Observer*.

All the papers had endless photographs of Diana's funeral procession, the eminent guests, and the car that took her coffin north for burial at the family seat, using its wipers to clear the windscreen of flowers thrown by the public. Most of the broadsheets had focus pieces on the crash and Rachel read them, curious to hear the mainstream media view.

'Do you think it's true that Diana and Dodi were engaged?' she asked Alex. 'It's claiming here that he asked her to marry him the night they died – just when you asked me. Isn't that a coincidence?'

'It does seem odd, especially when they had only been an item for six weeks or so.'

Rachel read on. 'Dodi didn't plan ahead as well as you. It says here he only went to collect the ring at six that evening from a jeweller's shop near the Ritz. You were much more organised.'

'I had to be.' He kissed her. 'Do you have any idea how long I spent looking for a ring that might be acceptable to you? Months of anguish . . .'

'Because I wouldn't have married you if it was the wrong ring, would I? Idiot.' She pinched his stubbly chin affectionately. 'It says she wasn't wearing the ring when she died. Maybe he was planning to ask her later.'

'Maybe she didn't like the ring. Or maybe it didn't fit.'

Rachel wrinkled her brow. In the last pictures of Diana emerging from the Ritz, she looked serious and preoccupied, not like a woman who had just agreed to marry the man she loved. After she and Alex got engaged that same evening, she had been unable to stop grinning. They had giggled like kids, bursting with happiness.

The article she was reading continued by saying that on arrival in Paris earlier in the day, Diana and Dodi had gone straight from the airport to visit the Villa Windsor in Bois de

Boulogne, where the Duke and Duchess of Windsor – formerly Edward VIII and Wallis Simpson – used to live. It was now being rented from the French state by Mohamed Al-Fayed.

'Says here that Diana and Dodi were considering using the Villa Windsor as one of their homes,' she told Alex. 'That would have been rather fitting, don't you think? Both Diana and Wallis were thorns in the flesh of the British monarchy. I wonder if they ever met?'

'They'd have had a lot to talk about,' Alex mused. 'Diana wanted to bring down a future king – she allegedly told Charles during the divorce that she would "destroy" him – and Wallis actually caused Edward VIII to abdicate. Besides, like you, they were both fashionistas.'

'I *love* Wallis's style,' Rachel drooled. 'She was top of the best-dressed list for about ten years in a row after World War Two. Having pots of money helped, of course, but her outfits were elegant and imaginative.'

'When Diana died she was wearing Versace shoes, an Armani jacket and a black crocodile-skin Ralph Lauren belt,' Alex recited. 'This is the kind of information I now have at my fingertips.'

'Impressive,' Rachel chuckled. He had no interest at all in fashion. 'Did I tell you I spoke to a friend of Diana's this week?'

'You did?' Instantly Alex was all ears. 'Who was it?'

'Someone I've bought stock from. She couldn't stop crying on the phone and I got the impression that she and Diana were quite close.' She described the conversation to Alex.

'Do you think you could introduce me?' he asked. 'I need a friend of Di's in my documentary and I hear none of the London set are talking.'

Rachel hated the idea. Susie was primarily a business contact and it would be unprofessional of her to use the connection. 'I'd rather not,' she began. 'She's distraught. It wouldn't feel right.'

'You would really be helping me,' he said, ignoring her objections. 'It's proving difficult to get people to talk on camera.'

He picked up the coffeepot to pour himself a refill but it was empty. 'My turn,' he said and got out of bed to head for the kitchen. Rachel heard the sound of the kettle, then the fridge door opening and closing.

When Alex came back he was grinning, his eyes full of mischief. He put the coffeepot on the bedside table, then suddenly swept the newspapers to the floor and straddled her, pushing her back on the pillows. Rachel smiled lazily as he bent to kiss her, while stroking her nipples with his thumbs.

'What a good idea,' she murmured.

He pinned her arms above her head with one hand and pushed her legs apart. She lifted her hips to meet him, breathing hard, entirely lost in the moment.

~

The phone rang just after Rachel got out of the shower, and she was delighted to hear the voice of her old friend Richard Graham, who specialised in running international auctions.

'I've just heard about your break-in,' he said. 'You poor thing. It's horrible to think of someone trashing your beautiful collection.'

'I'm feeling pretty sick about it,' she admitted.

'I heard you're looking for new stock and wanted to let you know I'm organising a sale in New York on Wednesday that it would be really worth your while coming over for,' he told her. 'Have you heard of the Van der Heydens? Diamond merchants from Amsterdam, crème de la crème of New York society in the 1920s. You should come and have a look.'

'Is it reasonably priced?' Rachel asked. 'Worth the cost of the air fare? I'd love to see you but I've got to watch the pennies.'

He listed some of the items for sale: sequinned flapper dresses, loose chiffon printed tunics, fur-trimmed jackets and embroidered silk capes. The exchange rate meant they would be relatively cheap for her.

'Tell you what,' he suggested. 'If you come on Tuesday, I'll give you a personal preview.'

Rachel was tempted. 'What about import duty? Won't that make it prohibitive?'

Richard chuckled. 'We have ways and means of minimising it. And you're welcome to stay with me. I've got a place in the Village, near Washington Square.'

When she came off the phone, Alex called, 'What was that about, darling?'

She explained, but when she said she was planning to fly to New York on Tuesday, he frowned. 'It's the TV industry awards ceremony on Tuesday, remember? You're coming to the dinner with me. I've got your ticket.'

'Oh, rats!' Rachel had clean forgotten. 'Can't you go without me? This sale sounds too good to miss.'

Alex pleaded. 'There will be other sales; you're always going to sales. The awards ceremony is only once a year.'

'But you're much better than me at all the social chit-chat. I just stand there with a smile pasted on my face. Please, darling. This trip is important to me.'

'It's just that I love to show you off. I'm proud to have you by my side.' His face was beseeching.

'I promise I'll come with you next time.'

Alex went to shower without another word but Rachel could sense that the intimate, loving atmosphere of their morning had dissipated. Should she back down? But she didn't want to; the thought of the sale was far too tantalising.

Chapter 17

Brighton, 7 September 1997

HEN RACHEL HAD TOLD HER MUM ON THE PHONE that she and Alex had been in the Alma Tunnel just after the crash, she was eager for details, keen to hear some small fact no one else knew. Rachel had noticed this reaction all week: people felt possessive about the story, competing over who knew most about the paparazzi who'd been arrested, the airbags and seat belts in the car, the exact sequence of events. After describing what she had seen, it didn't feel like the right moment to announce her engagement, then the shop break-in preoccupied her. But once Nicola knew, word would spread quickly, so on Sunday afternoon she rang to tell her mum, who reacted by inviting both families for an impromptu celebration.

Rachel's parents lived in Hove and she and Alex walked there along the promenade. Neither mentioned the New York trip, but it was there, a source of tension between them. The sea was metallic grey and choppy, with intermittent sunbursts warming the dilapidated wooden pavilions of the old West Pier. Seagulls still swooped around, although it was structurally unsound and there were no tourists left to feed them, no stray chips dropped from newspaper cones. The architecture spoke of genteel times when Victorian ladies strolled beneath parasols, linking arms with gentlemen in top hats and waistcoats. Rachel loved the sense of history in Brighton, the feeling that you had stepped through a portal into the nineteenth century.

Her parents' front room was already crowded when they arrived and, looking around, Rachel mused that her family and Alex's could not have been more different. Her parents, along with her brother, sister and their partners, were glugging Veuve Clicquot and immediately began teasing Alex and Rachel.

'You can't possibly be engaged,' her dad joked, 'because Alex hasn't come to ask my permission.'

'Permission?' Alex retorted. 'I was hoping to speak to you about the level of the dowry.'

Rachel's sister asked: 'Is there going to be a pre-nup, Rachel? If you break up, you can't risk him getting your Chanel dress.'

'He's tried it,' Rachel replied. 'It's far too tight.'

There weren't enough chairs, so the younger generation sprawled on the cream and green-flecked shagpile carpet – how I loathe that carpet! Rachel thought every time she visited – with a huge platter of smoked salmon on brown bread resting on the glass coffee table between them.

Alex's dad and stepmum Wendy sat side by side on the sofa, thighs parallel and postures very straight. Both had dark hair streaked with grey, both wore drab, shapeless garments. Neither of them was drinking and more than once Rachel caught them surreptitiously checking their watches, as if deciding how early they could slip off.

They were a funny pair, who gave little away. Although she had met them dozens of times, Rachel still couldn't imagine what they talked about when they were alone. They conversed in generalities and never divulged anything personal.

Rachel felt sorry for Alex that he had grown up without the easy camaraderie she took for granted in her own family. It was astonishing that he had such highly developed social skills as an adult, given the coldness of his background.

'You have to work harder at friendships when you don't have siblings,' he explained once. 'I thought I had to study people and learn how to make them like me.'

It had worked, because he had a vast universe of friends that kept expanding outwards. Everywhere they went Alex made new contacts, and he had the energy to follow them up and invite newcomers to gatherings, drawing them easily into his network. It was a skill that had proved useful in his TV career. He liked people, enjoyed learning about them. Rachel's circle was much smaller, more exclusive.

'When are you thinking of having the wedding?' Rachel's mum asked them.

Alex and Rachel looked at each other, and he answered. 'We haven't discussed it yet. I don't know about you, darling' – he slung an arm round her – 'but I've always fancied a Christmas wedding: snow on the ground, twinkling lights, you swathed in furs arriving on a sled like the Snow Queen . . .'

'What, *this* Christmas?' Rachel was horrified. She had far too much on her plate with her struggle to keep the shop afloat.

'There's no point in a long engagement, is there?' her mum said. 'You're both old enough to know your own minds.'

'I can't possibly organise anything over the next three months,' Rachel said. 'And Alex, I thought you were going to be spending most of your time in Paris?'

'I'll arrange it!' Her mum clapped her hands in glee. 'Just tell me what you want. I'm not sure I can guarantee snow, mind.' She had too much free time since retiring earlier in the year and seemed excited at the thought of a new project.

Rachel opened her mouth to say she thought this was too precipitous, but Alex spoke first. 'That would be wonderful. What do you think, darling?'

'I can't afford much just now,' she said. 'If we leave it till next year, I should be in a stronger position . . .'

'Your father and I will pay,' her mum butted in. 'Father of the bride always pays for his daughter's wedding.'

'And we'll help,' Wendy volunteered.

Rachel felt her arm being twisted. If only she and Alex had discussed it on their own first. She had a vision in her head of exactly how she wanted her wedding to be and wasn't sure her mum would be able to achieve it, but it seemed churlish to say so. 'It's very kind of you all. Let us think about it,' she conceded.

When wedding talk had been exhausted, conversation turned to Diana, and Rachel's mum asked Alex if he believed that Henri Paul, the driver, had caused the crash.

'It remains to be seen,' he replied. 'There are some strange stories coming from the first witnesses. One claims to have seen a motorbike swerving in front of the Mercedes and flashing a bright light at the driver a split second before the crash.'

'Do you mean a camera flash?' her mum asked, eyes widening.

'The witness thinks it was much brighter than that. And what's interesting is that British secret services once had a plan to assassinate Yugoslav president Slobodan Milosevic by shining a powerful light into his driver's eyes at a dangerous spot on the road.' Alex spoke passionately and everyone stopped to listen. 'Anyway, I'm not saying secret services were involved, but the more I dig into the Princess's death, the more peculiarities I find – and I've only just started. I genuinely think there's at least a possibility she was murdered.'

'Nonsense!' his father snapped. 'You've been reading too many spy thrillers. I read that they ran three separate blood tests on the driver and all of them showed him to have excessive alcohol in his blood. Case closed.'

'Yes, Dad, but several witnesses saw the motorbike overtake the Mercedes inside the tunnel yet no one has come forward to say who it was. There also appears to have been a car just in front of the Mercedes that forced Diana and Dodi's driver to swerve into the left lane as he entered the tunnel. There's a story about it in the *Journal du Dimanche* today.'

His father snorted. 'Oh well, if it's in the press, it must be true.' He glanced at Wendy, but she focused on the smoked salmon she was eating.

Suddenly the atmosphere was charged. Rachel had heard Alex and his dad argue before and knew both were too pig-headed to back down. In an effort to deflect them, she picked up a bottle of champagne and asked, 'Anyone for a top-up?'

'Yes, me!' Her sister thrust out her glass, and took the bottle to fill up the others on her side of the room.

'It's strange no one saw Henri Paul drinking,' Alex continued, his tone clipped, and Rachel could tell he was annoyed. 'In the footage from the Ritz he is completely steady on his feet. And the two bodyguards would never have let him drive the Princess if they had smelled so much as a hint of alcohol on him. But *you* think you know better . . .'

Rachel's mum broke in to try and defuse the argument. 'It's such a tragedy, we are all having trouble comprehending it. I'm sure it's even harder for Alex and Rachel, since they were there. Still, at least we have a joyous occasion to look forward to.'

Alex's father hadn't finished having his say, though. 'I think you're making a mistake rushing to find conspiracies in a simple drink-drive accident. You'll only make a fool of yourself and damage your reputation.'

'I'm the one with an open mind here!' Alex growled. 'I'm going to explore all the possibilities, sift the evidence and see what I find. You're the one who—'

'Alex,' Rachel cautioned, putting a hand on his thigh.

He caught her eye and managed to control his temper. Taking a breath, he looked round the assembled company and raised his glass. 'Sorry about that. And thank you for welcoming me into the Wainwright family. Let's have a toast: to happy families!'

His father and Wendy raised their glasses of fruit juice, ignoring the irony in Alex's tone. Shortly afterwards they announced they would have to be on their way.

'Early start in the morning,' Wendy apologised. 'Thank you for including us tonight. And Rachel, let me know how I can help with the wedding.'

~

As they walked home later that evening, slightly tipsy, Rachel was mulling over the argument. Alex usually avoided arguing with his father, whose views were dyed-in-the-wool establishment; there was no point in confronting him. Was he still upset about her going to New York? Had that put him in a belligerent mood?

She felt sorry that his dad did not seem more pleased about their engagement. Wendy had said all the right things and her heart was in the right place, but she and Alex weren't close. He was fond of her, enjoyed teasing her about her coasters and carefully swagged curtains, but they had little in common.

'Do you think your dad likes me?' Rachel asked, linking her arm through his. 'He's never given the slightest hint one way or another. I reckon he's indifferent.'

'I don't think he likes women full stop,' Alex replied. 'Not even Wendy; he tolerates her rather than liking her.'

'You shouldn't let him get to you.' She squeezed his arm and quoted in a nursery voice something her mum used to say to her and her siblings: 'Grizzly bears don't get the honey.'

In a sudden movement, Alex whirled her around and bent her backwards over his arm in a tango move. 'Christ, you can be infuriating sometimes,' he muttered before kissing her long and hard.

Chapter 18

New York, spring 1926

WALLIS ARRIVED AT NUMBER 9 WASHINGTON SQUARE looking pale beneath her rouge and face powder. She winced as she slipped off her coat and handed it to the maid, and walked slowly into the drawing room, seeming frail.

Mary was alarmed. 'What's up? Have you been overdoing the parties?'

Wallis lowered herself into a chair. 'It's such a bore. I had to have emergency abdominal surgery in Seattle, as soon as I got off the boat from China, and things haven't been right since. I plan to consult a specialist while I am in New York. But let's not talk of that.' She waved a dismissive hand. 'How is Jackie? And how are you, my dear, *dear* Mary?'

Mary lied, saying that everything was fine and dandy. She didn't feel like talking about her miscarriages, not yet anyway. Jacques' business was going well, and they often went to the theatre, or to jazz clubs such as the legendary Cotton Club or the recently opened Savoy dance hall in Harlem. 'Perhaps we should go dancing,' she suggested. 'It's very gay.'

'I don't think I am able to dance just yet,' Wallis said, laying a protective arm across her belly, 'but I yearn for some decent conversation. I swear, my companions in Warrenton tell the same stories every week, expecting me to laugh raucously each time. I need someone smart and funny, someone to make me *think* again, and that's why I have come to throw myself on your sweet mercy.'

'I will be as entertaining as is in my power. But first I want to ask about you. How was China? And is there a lucky man waiting to walk you down the aisle once the divorce goes through?'

Wallis shook her head. 'Nix. No one. I am thirty years old and entirely alone in the world. China was an interesting experience, but the Americans and Europeans there all have Win's problem with their elbows.' She mimed bending the forearm to pour alcohol down the throat from an imaginary glass.

'You must be holding out on me,' Mary teased. 'You're the world's greatest romantic. Surely you would not have stayed away so long if you were not in love?'

Wallis smiled, with a faraway look in her eyes. 'I was in love before I went. He let me down very badly. But I have found that the ideal cure for heartache is to put an ocean between yourself and the cause of the affliction.'

Mary guessed she was talking about the Argentinian diplomat Felipe Espil. She had heard on the grapevine that he had refused to marry Wallis, and instead took up with a younger woman from a wealthy, aristocratic family. It must have been the first time Wallis had failed to win the object of her affections, and it was bound to rankle.

'I'm sorry,' Mary said. 'But I'm glad you found the cure. Perhaps you should register it at the Patent Office.'

Wallis laughed. 'That's not a bad idea. I need to find *some* way to make my fortune.'

They soon slipped into an easy friendship, similar to the one of old, but more guarded. They were no longer teenagers, but thirty-year-olds with emotional scars they did not wish to probe. It was fun trying on each other's clothes, gossiping about the marriages of former acquaintances, shopping in Fifth Avenue, getting their hair done, and lunching at upscale restaurants, where Wallis toyed with a fillet of fish or a lamb chop but seldom ate much. If they dined at home, she flirted with Jacques but Mary no longer felt annoyed by it. It was a game, and Jacques was perfectly capable of returning her compliments without leaving any doubt about his devotion to Mary.

They both enjoyed hearing her stories about the Far East, and one evening, Wallis told them about the sing-song houses, where young girls were trained in the art of love. 'Win and I visited an establishment in Shanghai,' she told them. 'We were led into a sumptuous room with mahogany furniture and gold lattice decorations, where we sat as the girls were led in. They wore very simple silk frocks in either blue or red, and you could clearly see they wore nothing underneath.'

Jacques and Mary were agog. 'Did they speak any English? Did you talk to them?' she asked.

'They all learn a bit of English so they can entertain English guests, but one was more fluent than the others and Win quizzed her about the special techniques in which they are trained.' Her eyes glittered; she was clearly enjoying the effect she was having on her audience. 'She told us of a tantalising style of massage called fang-chung, of the erotic dances they learn, and of a special muscle technique called the Singapore Grip.'

'I've heard of that,' Jacques interrupted, leaving Mary to wonder what it was and where he might have come across it. She still brooded about the women he had known before they met, but he hated to talk of the war years and changed the subject abruptly if she ever brought them up.

Wallis continued: 'The girls parade in front of invited guests, then they retire to private rooms on the upper floor with the customer who has chosen them for the evening.'

'My goodness, how fascinating!' Mary exclaimed. 'What kind of girls do you think they are? I suppose they come from very poor families.'

'Not necessarily,' Wallis said. 'Some well-to-do families send their daughters there to learn ways of pleasing their future husbands. All the girls are very beautiful, with shy expressions, like so.' She mimicked a girl with head bowed, looking up sideways through her lashes.

Mary wondered if Wallis had learned seduction techniques herself but did not like to ask. 'I would love to come to a sing-song house with you, Wallie. What adventures you've had!'

In company, Wallis sparkled as only she could, but when they were alone, Mary noticed that she was tired and guessed she was not sleeping well. She winced in pain sometimes, and most of all Mary could sense loneliness deep as an ocean. Her old feeling of protectiveness returned as strong as ever: poor Wallis with a broken heart, a failed marriage and no family money to fall back on, because Uncle Sol still firmly refused to support her. She had a small allowance from Win, but her position was horribly vulnerable.

'You must come here whenever you like,' Mary told her. 'Treat Washington Square as your second home.'

◠

Over the summer and fall, Wallis took her at her word and visited every few weeks. She spent Thanksgiving with them, and Mary thought it only fair that she invite her for Christmas as well. No one should be alone at such a time, and Jacques never seemed to mind Wallis's presence. Mary suspected he was relieved that Wallis kept her entertained, taking the pressure off him so he could spend time with some French and Italian friends he had made in the neighbourhood.

On the evening of Christmas Day, the three of them, along with various family members and friends, were drinking cocktails when the maid came into the room to announce a visitor: 'Mr Simpson to see you.'

Mary rose with pleasure to greet him. 'I'm so glad you could join us. Is Dorothea not with you?'

'Sadly she is unwell, so I have left her at home with the girls. I had to come and bring you this gift, Jackie.' He handed over a bottle of Scotch whisky.

Jacques hooted with laughter. 'Bourbon versus Scotch. We must have a head-to-head contest some evening.'

'If ladies are permitted, I should very much like to join you,' Wallis butted in. 'Do we drink shots of each, turn about, until we fall off our chairs?'

Jacques introduced her to Ernest and he gave a slight bow.

'We shall have to agree the rules of engagement,' he smiled, 'but you would be welcome.'

'What is your line of work, Mr Simpson, when you are not tempting folk to imbibe the demon drink?' Wallis fixed him with her most scintillating gaze, and he sat in the chair next to her to tell her he worked in shipping.

'Do you have a job I could apply for in your shipping office?' she continued. 'I'm a poor single woman in need of money and qualified for precisely nothing. I can't type, can't sew, can't wait table, and I'm not terribly good with numbers. But I need to earn around seventy-five thousand dollars a year. Might you have a position for me?'

They all laughed. 'I shall certainly ask around,' Ernest promised.

'What a wonderful suit!' she exclaimed, stroking his lapel. He was wearing a double-breasted pin-striped suit with a waistcoat underneath. 'Do I detect English tailoring?'

'Savile Row,' he replied. 'The same tailor my father uses and his father before him.'

'I love your British traditions: all the pomp and ceremony, the rules and standards. It's terribly civilised.'

'I agree,' Ernest said. 'I'm very proud of my English half.'

As he explained to Wallis about his fluctuating nationality, Mary watched them with narrowed eyes. Wallis was unleashing her charm, making him feel as though he was the most interesting person in the room and she simply had to hear every word he uttered. She leaned closer, her face artfully tilted. Just like the sing-song girls, Mary thought. She didn't like it; Ernest was *her* friend and she didn't want to share.

After an hour, Ernest stood up, announcing that he must return to his invalid wife. Mary reached beneath the Christmas tree, where she had wrapped a novel entitled *The Sun Also Rises*, by the journalist Ernest Hemingway, to give him as a Christmas gift. They met in the hall as he was putting on his coat, and she handed over the parcel.

'I do hope you like it,' she said, feeling shy all of a sudden. 'I was most impressed by the honest style of writing.'

He spoke warmly. 'If you enjoyed it, I know I shall too. We have never yet disagreed over a book, have we? Thank you. I shall treasure it.'

~

Eight days later, just after the New Year, Wallis announced that she was going out.

'Are you seeing one of your friends from Europe or from China?' Mary asked.

'No. In fact, your Mr Simpson has invited me to luncheon. I think he may have been trying to find work for me.'

Mary was shocked. 'He's a married man, Wallie. You can't have luncheon together without a chaperone. Word travels around Manhattan faster than you might think, and you'll get a reputation.'

Wallis gave her a pitying look. 'Oh Mary, it's 1927, for goodness' sake. Men and women can have friendships without anything more being read into it. I like your Mr Simpson and I didn't think you would mind if I saw him again.' Her eyes narrowed. 'You seem to be cosy with him yourself. I saw you giving him a package on Christmas evening.'

Mary blushed. 'We both like reading, and we often exchange books.'

Wallis smiled. 'That's all right then. Now, shall I wear the blue frock or the amber?'

Wallis was gone for over three hours and Mary paced the house in a sour mood. She did not mind sharing her home, her wardrobe or her female friends with her, but this was too much. It was true that she was very fond of Ernest herself, but the difference between her and Wallis was that *she* could be trusted.

Chapter 19

*M*ARY WAS SURPRISED WHEN DOROTHEA SIMPSON telephoned asking if she might call on her. They had never seen each other alone before, although their relationship was always cordial when the two couples got together.

'I'd be delighted,' she replied.

Dorothea was shown into the drawing room, greetings were exchanged, tea was served, and as soon as the maid had left the room, she got to the purpose behind her visit.

'I'm sorry to bring my troubles to your door,' she began, 'but could you please do something to rein in your predatory friend?'

Mary paled. What had Wallis done now?

Dorothea continued: 'I came home from a shopping trip yesterday afternoon to find Wallis in *my* house with *my* husband wearing one of *my* blouses.' Mary gasped, quickly covering her mouth with her hand. 'She claimed a cup of coffee had got spilt on her blouse and Ernest insisted on lending her a fresh one.'

'Wallis doesn't drink coffee . . .' Mary said slowly, trying to work out what must have happened.

Dorothea's tone was almost hysterical. 'Do you have any idea how much time she is spending with my husband? If I telephone his office in the afternoon, he is never there. In his pockets I find tickets to lectures, art galleries and concerts, and he is certainly not attending them with me. There are receipts for luncheons and – you won't believe this – I found a ticket from the Savoy dance hall dated for an evening three weeks ago when I was in hospital.'

Mary remembered telling Wallis about the dance hall and felt furious with her. What was she playing at?

'I'm sure it is all perfectly innocent,' she said, trying to remain calm. 'Wallis enjoys male company but she would never dream of fooling around with a married man.'

Dorothea's tone was scathing. 'She might be able to pull the wool over your eyes, but not mine. I am sure that they *are* "fooling around", as you put it.'

Mary blushed scarlet. She could feel the heat in her cheeks and temples, right up to the roots of her hair. She didn't want to believe it – couldn't bear to.

Before she could reply, Dorothea continued: 'Your friend has a reputation for pursuing married men. Stories filtered back from China about an Italian count by the name of Galeazzo Ciano. And there was talk that she was over-friendly with Herman Rogers while staying with him and his wife . . .'

Mary held up her hand. 'Stop! Please . . . I am surprised you listen to tittle-tattle. I know Wallis better than anyone, and while she is naturally flirtatious, she would never cause any harm.'

'She has already caused harm. Had my health been better, I would have confronted her myself, but I do not have the strength. So I am asking you to tell her from me: Ernest might toy with her for a while, but he will never divorce me. He loves his girls too much.'

'Of course he wouldn't . . .' Mary breathed.

'And if she doesn't back off, I will blacken her name in New York society. I'll make sure the news reaches her family in

Baltimore and will personally tell the judge who presides over her divorce case. Don't doubt that I am capable of this.' Dorothea was shaking with anger. Her tea sat untouched on the table beside her.

'I feel responsible for introducing them,' Mary apologised. 'I'm sure it's not what you think, but I will have a word with Wallis. I know she will be horrified to hear that her actions have hurt you.'

Dorothea shook her head, in a way that implied she thought Mary impossibly naïve.

~

On this visit, Wallis was staying in the Upper East Side with Mona Van der Heyden, a new friend, so Mary telephoned and asked if she might call round for a word. She found Wallis fixing her hair, preparing to dine out.

'Who are you dining with?' Mary asked, perching on the edge of the bed. 'Anyone I know?'

'I'm introducing Mona to Gerald and Sara Murphy, a couple I met in China. They live on the French Riviera but are here for a few weeks, and I can't *wait* to see them.' She smiled at Mary in the mirror, drawing her comb firmly across her scalp to straighten the centre parting she always wore these days.

'Are they connected in New York society?' Mary asked.

'I believe so. Her mother's family are Shermans, direct descendants of the Civil War general.'

'Very impressive. And the Van der Heydens have a wonderfully grand house. You are clearly becoming well established in the city.'

Wallis wrinkled her nose. 'I wouldn't say so. Lots of *Social Register* types won't invite me because of the divorce.'

Mary saw her opening. 'I came to warn you that Dorothea Simpson thinks you are having an affair with her husband and is threatening to spread the rumour around New York society. I thought I should tell you because gossip travels like wildfire. She is also threatening to inform the divorce court in Warrenton, and to get word to your mother . . .'

She tailed off, surprised by the lack of reaction. Wallis continued fixing her hair without her expression changing one iota.

'Ernest tells me their marriage has been dead as a stuffed dodo for over a year. They have nothing in common; she never wants to go out or do anything except lie on a sofa.'

'Dorothea has poor health. I'm not surprised she doesn't want to go out. But surely it's not true, is it?' Mary had a knot in her stomach: please let it not be true.

'I've been seeing him, yes. And he's in love with me.'

The words slipped out, shattering Mary's illusions. Her mouth fell open.

'Oh don't look like that. It's not my fault he's in love with me. It wouldn't have happened if his wife hadn't neglected him so.' She put the final pin in her hair, then reached for a lipstick in a gold push-up case.

'What about the children, Wallis? His girls, Audrey and Cynthia. He can't leave them.'

'I'm not asking him to.' She smeared red lipstick onto her top lip first, then the bottom, and pressed them together, peering in the mirror to check for smudges. 'That's his choice, not mine.'

Mary's chest was tight with horror. 'Do you love him?'

'No.' Wallis cocked her head to one side. 'But I like him. Perhaps I could love him in time.' She swivelled to face Mary. 'You don't mind, do you? You, me, Ernest and Jackie all get along so well. We could double-date. It would be fun.'

'Aren't you worried about the gossips ruining your chances of getting a divorce?'

Wallis shrugged. 'What are they going to say? That Ernest and I are close friends? That's true. Anything more, I will deny.'

Are you going to bed with him? Mary wanted to ask. It was on the tip of her tongue, but something stopped her. Would Wallis lie to her? Did she want to know the truth?

Wallis came over and put an arm around her. 'Your conversation with Mrs Simpson must have been very awkward. I'm sorry for that. But I have done nothing wrong.' She kissed Mary on the cheek, then wiped away the lipstick mark with the edge of her finger. 'You worry too much.'

She glanced at the clock and announced she was late, then grabbed her evening cloak and bag from a chair.

'Please will you stop seeing him?' Mary begged, standing to follow her down the stairs. 'For me?'

Wallis laughed affectionately. 'Goodness, you have become a prude, darling. Come now, I must dash.'

~

The knowledge of Wallis and Ernest's liaison burned inside Mary like poison. She did not tell Jacques of her discovery because he had rather a French attitude to affairs and she suspected he would make a joke of it. To her, it felt like a betrayal on both their parts. She had believed Ernest to be the perfect gentleman with impeccable moral standards, but it seemed she was wrong; she knew Wallis was a flirt but had not thought her a husband stealer. She was disappointed in both of them and could not face seeing them for the time being.

Some weeks later, however, she arrived at a cocktail party and spotted Ernest standing on the other side of the room by some floor-length drapes. She felt a wave of anger and resolved to have a word. Without planning her next move, she grabbed a cocktail, swallowed a gulp for courage, then made her way across.

'It's such a long time since we've seen you, Ernest. I hear you've been very busy of late.' She smiled, but there was an edge to her voice.

'Indeed. I don't know where the time goes. You're looking ravishing, if I may say so.' He smiled broadly and bowed his head.

She took another slug of her cocktail. 'It's good of you to spend so much time with poor Wallie while she is going through her divorce. I know she appreciates it.'

He cleared his throat, refused to meet her eye. 'It's a difficult period for her.'

'I've known Wallis since we were at school together and it's remarkable how little she has changed. Back then she used to collect beaus the way other people collect stamps, just for the hell of it.'

Ernest's face froze and he glanced around, hoping for rescue, but Mary was in full flow and not about to stop.

'Men always fall in love with her. She's got that mysterious something: sex appeal, I suppose you'd call it. But as soon as she senses she has captivated any man, she gets bored. I've seen it happen time and again. She doesn't mean to hurt them, of course, but she has left a trail of broken, bloodied hearts all the way from here to China. It's quite a talent.' She smiled at him. 'I wonder if I could ask you to fetch me another gin and lime? This one seems to have evaporated.'

He grabbed her glass and disappeared like a shot. When he returned with her replenished glass, he brought their hostess with him so she did not have a chance to continue on her theme. No matter; she'd said enough. She felt terribly disloyal to Wallis, but told herself she was only thinking of Ernest and Dorothea's children. She was doing them a service.

~

A few days later, Wallis telephoned, clearly annoyed. For a moment Mary worried that Ernest might have repeated what she had said, but it wasn't that.

'Ernest has told me he will never divorce his wife,' she complained. 'What a flat tyre he turned out to be.'

'It's all for the best,' Mary soothed.

'Best for whom? Dorothea has no brains, a face and figure like a bison, and they don't have any interests in common. I simply don't know what is going through his mind.'

'He's not your type anyway,' Mary told her. 'Far too boring and bookish.'

Wallis snorted. 'Anyhow, Aunt Bessie has invited me to Europe for the summer and I'm going to accept. We'll be staying on the French Riviera, so Gerald and Sara Murphy can introduce me to the "it" crowd.'

'Darling, you'll have a gay time. I wish I could come too. If only I didn't have to look after Jacques . . . Poor dear would be lost without me!'

When she hung up the telephone, Mary remained sitting in the hall chair for several minutes, pleased with herself. Wallis would surely find a new admirer amongst the glamorous set in the South of France, and the threat to Ernest and Dorothea's marriage would have passed. She had been right to meddle. She just hoped Wallis never found out.

Chapter 20

Brighton, 9 September 1997

ACHEL'S LOCAL TRAVEL AGENT HAD MANAGED TO
secure a cheap return to New York, flying out on the
Tuesday morning and back on Wednesday night's red-eye. Alex
didn't comment when she told him and she felt guilty for
letting him down, but once she was on the train to Heathrow,
excitement took hold. It was years since her last visit to New
York, and several months since she had seen Richard, but most
of all she was thrilled at the prospect of inspecting the contents
of the Van der Heyden wardrobes. She knew Richard wouldn't
have invited her if the sale wasn't going to be well worth it.

Rachel picked up some magazines to read on her flight to
JFK, even though she'd had an early start and was hoping to
snooze part of the way. She got a window seat and gazed out
at the River Thames snaking its way into the city, growing less
distinct by the second as they climbed through cloudless sky
marked only by criss-crossing jet trails. It seemed no time before
they were crossing the Irish Sea, skimming the rocky coast of
Ireland then heading west across the petrol-blue Atlantic,
featureless apart from sun blinking on white-crested choppiness.

The previous day she'd had word from the insurers that, as
she had feared, they were not going to pay up. She had

immediately made an appointment with her bank manager and agreed a short-term extension of her overdraft facility, but she was pinning her hopes on the Van der Heyden sale to replenish her depleted stock. Until she could start making money again, her finances would deteriorate by the day, so a lot was resting on this trip.

A stewardess handed her a breakfast tray: cheese and ham croissant, yoghurt, fruit salad. She ate the fruit and drank a cup of coffee before closing her eyes to try and sleep, but her mind was buzzing. She had shut her half-empty shop for the two days she would be away. Nicola could have looked after it – she was bound to be fastidious about security from now on – but something stopped Rachel from asking. It wasn't that she hadn't forgiven her, but she didn't quite trust her in the same way. Besides, midweek takings when stock was low would barely cover her wages.

She took out her Filofax and began to scribble a list of what she wanted at the wedding: registry office then a reception at the Bonne Auberge, their favourite French bistro; a bouquet with lilies of the valley; arty black-and-white photography. She would find her own dress: maybe a 1930s long-sleeved satin gown in ivory or cream.

Turning the page, she came upon a cartoon by Alex. It showed a shaggy dog holding out his heart towards an elegant Siamese cat, and the caption read: *What's a classy dame like you doing with an old dog like me? Can't get over my luck.* She laughed, wondering when he had drawn it. He seemed to be apologising for being in a bad mood about her trip. His animal characters often expressed sentiments he found hard to say out loud. The first time he said 'I love you' to her had been in a speech bubble.

She picked up a magazine whose headline proclaimed an article on Diana's 'troubled' love life. There had been James Hewitt, the one Diana said in her *Panorama* interview had let her down badly; then James Gilbey, famous for calling her Squidgy in a phone call leaked to the media. Rachel thought of the platinum heart with the initial J and the number XVII, still zipped in her purse. Could one of those Jameses have given it to her? If so, what did the XVII stand for?

The article claimed that there had been a number of married men amongst Diana's dalliances in the early nineties. It must have been difficult for the Princess to find lovers, Rachel mused. She was rich and beautiful, but most normal men would run a mile from the media interest she attracted. Alone and vulnerable as she negotiated her divorce from the heir to the throne, perhaps a married man had seemed a good idea. Discretion would be in his interests too, and if he was a slightly older father figure, perhaps she hoped he could offer wisdom and the security she craved.

Diana had ricocheted from one unsuitable liaison to the next in her late twenties and early thirties – just as Rachel herself had. She ticked off her own list of failed love affairs. One man who was separated from his wife but tellingly not divorced, and who jumped whenever his ex snapped her fingers. Another who lived in Rome; he had been an exciting lover for a few expensive months before she realised the relationship had nowhere to go because neither was willing to relocate. And then the man she'd been dating just before she met Alex, who had been serially unfaithful to her. She had broken up with him as soon as she found out but had been wounded by the experience. Her ego was bruised, if not her heart, and when Nicola invited her to her birthday party soon afterwards, Rachel decided to wear her Chanel 'little black dress' accessorised with six long strings of pearls. The right outfit could always boost her confidence.

She had made a large birthday cake and was carrying it awkwardly in front of her, with a bottle of wine and a gift swinging in an overstuffed shoulder bag, when one of her stiletto heels got caught in a drain cover down the road from Nicola's flat. She tugged at her foot but it came out of the shoe, which remained firmly stuck in the drain. Stockinged foot resting on the pavement, she was glancing around, looking for somewhere to put the cake down, when a man appeared by her side.

'Allow me,' he said. He crouched and wiggled the shoe to dislodge it then, still on bended knee, held it out for her to insert her foot.

'Like Prince Charming,' she giggled.

'And the shoe fits!' he announced triumphantly.

He stood up and she saw that he was a tall, slim man with sandy hair and a winning smile. He wasn't conventionally handsome but he had an interesting face, one you wanted to look at.

'Are you by any chance going to Nicola's?' he asked. It wasn't a huge feat of deduction since her name was iced on top of the cake.

'Impressive detective work,' she smiled.

He nodded his head towards the cake. 'Maybe you should let me carry that the rest of the way, in case of any more footwear malfunctions.'

'OK,' she agreed. 'So long as you don't claim the credit for baking it.'

He laughed out loud. 'Nicola would never believe that. Trust me.'

Once inside the party, Alex fetched her a glass of wine, getting a beer for himself. He clearly knew most of the guests; several groups called greetings and beckoned him to join them, but he hovered by Rachel's side, clearly keen to chat to her.

'You look as though you work in fashion,' he guessed. 'Am I right?'

She told him about Forgotten Dreams and he told her about his TV production company, based in a tiny office in north London. He had been living near there until recently but when rents grew astronomical he headed south to the seaside town where he'd attended art college and where a lot of his friends still lived – including Nicola.

People who wandered over to talk to Alex soon took the hint that he did not want to interrupt his conversation with Rachel. They sat in a corner together and somehow segued into reminiscing about their favourite childhood TV programmes: *The Man from U.N.C.L.E.*, *Doctor Who* and *Star Trek* were his choices, while she said she liked *Bewitched* and demonstrated the side-to-side nose twitch that Samantha used to cast spells.

'It's worked,' Alex said, gazing into her eyes, his voice a little husky.

'It should do,' she replied. 'You have no idea how many hours I spent practising in the mirror.'

He touched her hand, just a feather touch. 'When will I see you again?' he asked. 'Dinner tomorrow night?'

'Yes,' she said straight away, feeling a tug of lust in her belly.

The relationship progressed quickly: he had been staying in a friend's spare room while looking for a place of his own but somehow there seemed no point when he and Rachel wanted to spend every night together. She gave him a door key, despite feeling nervous that she was jumping in too deep, too quickly. Since then he had never given her any cause to doubt him: he was consistently romantic and attentive – and, most important of all, they had fun.

Rachel worried sometimes that it had been too easy. They seldom argued, and if they did, it was quickly over. Maybe this was what other people felt when they fell in love; maybe she had been doing things the hard way before. She had no misgivings about marrying Alex and having his children, then spending the rest of her life with him.

The stuffy air of the aeroplane cabin and the diamond light piercing the window made her drowsy and she closed her eyes. Her thoughts drifted back to the woman who was alleged to have got engaged in Paris the same night as her. Would Dodi have been the right man for Diana? Would she have had children with him?

Rachel dozed for a while but was wakened by the rattling trolley of the stewardess bringing drinks. She accepted a cup of tea and took a sip then picked up another magazine. This one had an article about the final twenty-four hours of Diana's life, starting as she swam with Dodi in the sea off Sardinia and ending in the mortuary of a Paris hospital.

Paparazzi had captured most of the time Diana had spent in Paris. There she was shading her eyes from the sun as she arrived at Le Bourget airport on the afternoon of 30 August, dressed in an oatmeal trouser suit with a black top and dark sunglasses. They didn't have an image of her at Villa Windsor but showed the house instead, and added the detail that Diana and Dodi had been meeting an Italian interior designer who was going to remodel it for them. Next they pictured her arriving at the Ritz, where she had her hair done; you could see the difference in the before and after pictures, as she went from tousled to coiffed. The following image showed Diana dressed for dinner that evening in slim white trousers, black jacket and black top, and the article explained their change of plans: the paparazzi were staking out the restaurant where Dodi had wanted them to eat, so they dined at the Ritz instead.

Suddenly Rachel noticed something else. When Diana arrived at the Ritz to have her hair done, the silver-coloured bracelet Alex had mentioned was on her right wrist. It looked as though a charm was dangling from it. She stretched down to her handbag, tucked under the seat in front, pulled out her purse and retrieved the platinum heart from its zipped pocket. It looked the same shape and size as the one shown in the magazine. She polished it on her sleeve, turned it over in her hand, feeling the weight, running her finger over the engravings. Definitely platinum, she thought; it was much shinier than silver.

She looked to see if there was a clearer shot of the bracelet in any of the other pictures. In the shot taken at Le Bourget, Diana's wrist was clearly visible and she was not wearing a bracelet, just a gold watch on her left wrist. But she *was* wearing it when she arrived at the Ritz that afternoon. When had she put it on? She had not been back to Dodi's flat, and hadn't changed her clothes in the intervening period.

In the evening shots she wore gold earrings, and there was that bracelet again, still on her right wrist, alongside a pearl bracelet now. There was a gold ring on her right hand but nothing on her engagement finger. Strange to wear gold, pearl and platinum jewellery together; she clearly hadn't given it much thought.

Suddenly Rachel realised that all the photographs in which Diana was wearing the silvery bracelet were taken after the Villa Windsor visit. Perhaps she had been given it while they were there. Maybe it was a gift from Dodi and the engravings marked a significant date in their relationship. Rachel felt like a detective, and wondered if anyone else would notice this detail, or if she was the only one.

Chapter 21

New York, 9 September 1997

RICHARD LIVED IN THE LOFT OF A BUILDING ON Bleecker Street, above a nightclub called The Bitter End. Rachel was stunned by the vast open-plan space, topped by a glass skylight roof. There was a sitting area in one corner, a double bed in another, a dining table and kitchen at the far end, a camp bed with a folding screen around it, which she assumed was for her, and acres of wooden floorboards in between.

'This place would be great for skateboarding,' she commented. 'Is that why you bought it?'

'I'm only renting,' he said, 'but isn't it cool? I love this area.'

'You look well.' She smiled, taking in his Black Watch tartan trousers, which he'd teamed with a black T-shirt. He was tanned, his fair hair sun-bleached, and he had a trendy new pair of bright-blue-rimmed glasses. 'It's wonderful to see you.'

'You too.' He kissed her on both cheeks. 'It's been far too long.'

Richard made a pot of coffee while she freshened up in the tiny old-fashioned bathroom, where the plumbing looked as old as the century and the cistern gurgled as it refilled.

'So what's new?' he asked when she emerged. 'Tell all.'

She had already mentioned on the phone that she was engaged, but now she showed him her ring and he made admiring noises.

'Gorgeous.'

'Alex chose it himself,' she said proudly, sitting down at the table.

'He's good at jewellery. I remember when you two had only been dating a couple of months he bought you those pearl earrings surrounded by tiny chips of diamanté. It was impressive that he noticed you wore clip-ons not pierced earrings, and he managed to choose a style that would suit you.'

'He's got an eye for it,' Rachel admitted, 'but I've trained him to keep receipts.'

'I'm really happy for you both. Now, where's my invitation?'

She laughed. 'Mum's organising the wedding, but don't worry – you're on the list.'

'Tell me about the proposal. Did he get down on bended knee?'

'Not quite.' She shook her head. 'We were in Paris for the weekend and it was all perfect – until later that night our cab screeched to a halt in the Alma Tunnel right behind Diana's wrecked Mercedes, which put a dampener on things.'

'Oh my God!' He patted her hand across the table, concern in his eyes. 'That must have been traumatic.'

'It was horrible, with all the photographers milling around, snapping away . . .' She paused. 'I've been dreaming about it ever since; just general anxiety dreams in which I feel I should be doing something to help but don't know what.'

As she spoke, an image came to her from a few nights earlier. 'In one dream, I was pulling on Diana's hand, trying to drag her out of the wreck, but her fingers kept slipping from my grip.'

Richard stirred his coffee. 'I helped some survivors out of a fatal car wreck once and it haunted me for years. Don't underestimate how much it affects you.'

He was the first person Rachel had told about it who hadn't wanted all the gory details, and she appreciated that. 'Anyway, Diana's funeral is over and life in the UK is returning more or less to normal – apart from me having a half-empty shop. Tell me about this sale you're organising.'

He rubbed his hands and grinned. 'The Van der Heydens were one of *the* New York society families, up there with the Rockefellers, the Vanderbilts and the du Ponts. It was the Jazz Age, when Louis Armstrong and Jelly Roll Morton were playing dance music and the more daring white people slipped out to speakeasies to drink cocktails, or to the Cotton Club or the Savoy dance hall in Harlem. And their dresses . . .' He kissed his fingertips. 'Have I got a treat in store for you!'

~

They walked down shady, tree-lined Bleecker Street, with cafés spilling onto the sidewalks and metal fire escapes making the building frontages look like a giant game of snakes and ladders. After turning down a cross-street, they walked a couple of blocks north and skirted across the corner of Washington Square. Chess players were huddled around little tables, deep in concentration, and everywhere there were street performers: musicians, jugglers, mime artists and break-dancers. They looked incongruous amidst the historic buildings that ringed the park and the memorial arch at the north side but had clearly made this their home territory.

Richard had keys to a warehouse down a side street and he unlocked the door and led her into a hangar where rows of clothing hung under plastic sheets, with code numbers on each rail.

'Let me get you the listing,' he said, and disappeared into an office.

Rachel inhaled the musty, dusty scent, excited by the prospect of looking through this collection. Richard's description sounded alluring.

'Some of them are in lots, some for individual sale,' he said. 'You'll see guide prices in the margin. Do you want to browse on your own for a while? I've got some admin to do.'

'I can't wait,' she breathed.

She lifted the plastic from the first row to find some extraordinary dresses by well-known designers of the 1920s: a cerise satin gown by Piguet, draped in chiffon scarves decorated with silver leaves, and with matching harem pants to wear underneath; a Vionnet black crêpe gown with a black lace bodice; a coral velvet gown by Worth with pearl strands strung from the bodice over the arms, like fairy wings; a Chanel dancing frock in flouncy black and pink chiffon. She doubted she would be able to afford any of them, but made notes beside the ones she liked, estimating the price she could charge in her shop, then calculating how much she could afford to pay in dollars, allowing for the auctioneer's fee, the exchange rate, plus shipping and import duties.

She had brought a calculator and went along each row doing the same sums, working out which garments might fall within her budget. Coats, skirt suits, hats and shoes, costume jewellery, even some early swimsuits and matching beach robes were in the collection. It was phenomenal.

When Richard emerged an hour later, he laughed at the sight of her price list, covered in pencil jottings. 'Why not take it all?' he suggested.

'I'd love to. This is paradise on earth for me. I wish I could be reincarnated as a Van der Heyden and have this as my personal wardrobe.'

'There's one thing you won't have seen yet,' he said. 'The *pièce de résistance*.'

Intrigued, she followed him to a separate rail where a full-length zip-up bag was hanging. He unzipped it and lifted out a dress that made her gasp: it was ivory crêpe georgette decorated with crystal beads, with a tight sash round the hips and a back that scooped to waist level.

'It's a 1928 Molyneux original that was worn by the actress Gertrude Lawrence. Isn't it divine?' He turned it around so she could see both sides.

Hundreds of tiny crystals had been painstakingly hand-sewn all over the silky fabric. Rachel took the dress and held it in front of her. Instinctively she knew it would fit.

'Why did you show me this?' she sighed. 'It's the ultimate wedding dress but I know without looking at your price list that I could never afford it.'

'Give it a try,' he urged. 'You can change behind that curtain.'

She couldn't resist. When she slipped the dress over her head, the weight of the fabric made it hang perfectly.

'It looks as if it was made specially for you in Molyneux's atelier,' Richard said as he directed her to a full-length mirror.

She admired the snug fit around the hips, the cut of the neckline resting below her collarbones, and the deep swoop at the back, displaying her shoulder blades and spine.

'That was cruel,' she said, turning away with a wan smile. 'You've spoiled me for any other dress.' Whatever else she tried on now, it would never live up to this.

'Sorry.' He grinned. 'I'd better buy you a cocktail to apologise.'

They went to a speakeasy bar on Bleecker Street, a cramped one-room place with brick walls that was entered along a passageway and up a back staircase. Richard ordered her a sidecar, a Prohibition-era cocktail made with Cointreau, cognac and lemon juice, and she sipped it appreciatively. First of all they discussed the lots she was planning to bid for, and Richard offered to reduce her shipping costs by including her purchases in a shipment he was sending to London. Next they chatted about mutual friends, and finally the conversation returned to Diana, and the media obsession with her on both sides of the Atlantic.

'I liked her,' he said. 'She had a lot of charm, but who would have thought she would be deified in death? You don't dare criticise because people get very heated.'

'Alex thinks the crash might have been caused deliberately by some secret-service operation,' she told him. 'He's making a programme about it.'

'I've heard the rumours.' Richard looked thoughtful. 'I suppose it's possible. Wouldn't that be awful?'

They ate dim sum in a Chinese restaurant across the street from his loft apartment, and Rachel was so exhausted by the time they got back that she fell onto the camp bed and was asleep within seconds.

~

At the auction next morning, Rachel was uncharacteristically nervous. She had decided to bid on twenty-four separate lots and had a budget of up to ten thousand dollars to spend from the overdraft her bank manager had arranged. Richard gave her a paddle to raise when she wanted to bid. She had never mastered the tiny twitches and raised pinkies some folk used to attract the auctioneer's attention.

It started well when she bought an extensive lot of costume jewellery, including several strings of black, pink and cream pearls, for a hundred dollars. She was amazed to get the Chanel dance dress and the black Vionnet for their guide prices, and she picked up several lots of daywear, coats and jackets. All in all, she won fourteen of the lots she had decided to bid on, for prices that were well below her self-imposed limits.

The Molyneux dress was up last and she decided to wait and watch, even though bidding started at eight hundred dollars, ruling her out straight away. Someone at the back of the room – bidder number 54 – secured it for $2,500 and she sighed. She had to scrub the memory of it from her brain before she started hunting for her own wedding dress.

She signed all the necessary forms and arranged a money transfer, and Richard assured her the goods would be delivered to her shop in mid November, in plenty of time for the Christmas trade.

'You'll find a little something extra in there,' he said. 'But it's just a loan. You can give it back in the New Year.'

'What on earth are you talking about?'

He showed her his bidding paddle with the number 54 on it. 'I won the Molyneux and you *shall* wear it to your wedding. Now you *really* have to invite me.'

She flung her arms round him, almost bursting into tears. 'That is the best wedding present you could ever have given me. I can't tell you how much it means.'

On the subway to the airport, Rachel couldn't stop smiling as she imagined herself in the Molyneux on her wedding day. The trip had been a great success all round and she couldn't wait for her purchases to arrive in Brighton. She took out her Filofax and began sketching ideas for a spectacular Van der Heyden shop window display to let the locals know about her glamorous new acquisitions.

Chapter 22

New York, July 1927

*I*T WAS A MUGGY EVENING WITHOUT A BREATH OF breeze. Mary wore a loose white cotton dress with apricot embroidery and sat fanning herself by the open window. Ernest had telephoned earlier to say he would drop by and she waved when she saw him turn the corner. Despite the oppressive heat, he was wearing a suit and tie with a bowler hat on his head, and she giggled at the quintessential Englishness.

'Aren't you positively baking?' she called as he climbed the front steps, tipping his hat at her.

'Like a hog roast,' he grinned as the maid opened the door for him.

'Ernest, good man, what's your tipple?' Jacques greeted him. 'Mary's having a mint julep and I'm on the *vin rouge*.' His words were slurred and Mary could tell he was drunk already, although it was only just after six. She sighed.

'Mint julep sounds delicious.' Ernest laid down his hat and asked Mary's permission to remove his jacket, then rolled up his shirt sleeves, taking a chair close to hers.

She asked after Dorothea, and he said that unfortunately her health continued to be poor, then added: 'On that front, I have some news for you.'

Mary scrutinised him; he seemed uncharacteristically sombre and was avoiding her eye. 'Don't keep us in suspense,' she prodded, as Jacques handed him the drink.

He took a sip. 'I think you know that I have always felt torn between my British and American sides. My father has recently been in touch to ask if I will go back to London to run the office there, so he can begin to step down from the business. My sister Maud is also based in London and keen for me to be nearby. So I have said I will sail within the next few weeks, just as soon as arrangements can be made.'

'You can't go!' Jacques exclaimed. 'Where will we find someone else for our bridge tournaments? Seriously, *mon ami*, we'll miss you terribly.'

Mary had a lump in her throat. She missed him already. 'How does Dorothea feel about the move?' she asked.

He gave a little cough. 'In fact, Dorothea and I have . . . I'm afraid we've decided to divorce.'

There was a shocked silence. Mary's mind was whirling. Wallis was in France, on the same side of the Atlantic as London. 'You're not going because of . . .' she started, then stopped, remembering that she had never told Jacques of the affair.

'Our marriage has been unhappy for some time, and recent strains have proved insurmountable. It's best for all concerned.' He stared at his lap as he spoke, clearly embarrassed.

'Wallis is in Europe just now. Perhaps you'll bump into her,' Mary said tartly.

At the mere mention of the name, she saw his eyes go sappy and it enraged her. The first thought in her head was: *What about me?* Ernest had been her confidant since the day she had told him about her miscarriages, and until the Wallis debacle she had felt she could talk to him about anything. They had their shared love of books, and he was a good influence on Jacques, restraining his drinking by example. He was her safety net, her shoulder to lean on, and he couldn't go to London. She wouldn't allow it.

Then another thought came into her head, one she had never put into words before: *If he is leaving his wife, it should be for me.*

It surprised her as soon as she formed the thought because it was patently obvious. In her fantasy life, Ernest was her ideal husband, someone who was both friend and lover. He would ask her opinion in a way that Jacques never did; there would be no subjects she was not allowed to raise, no restless nights spent listening to his drunken snoring. She had sometimes imagined his face when she and Jacques made love, always with a twinge of guilt afterwards. But it had never seemed possible that they could be together because he was with Dorothea – and now Wallis had turned his head and he was chasing off to Europe on her trail. Of course, she would treat him with contempt, as she did all her admirers. She would take his heart in her hands, drop it on the floor and grind it beneath her heel.

'I always thought you were more of a gentleman than that,' she said sharply. 'I guess I was wrong.'

'Mary!' Jacques rebuked. 'It's none of our business what goes on in Ernest's marriage.'

'I'm just surprised that he should be so easily taken in,' she continued, aware that Jacques would have no idea what she was talking about. 'You men can be so gullible.'

'Hey, what have I done?' Jacques exclaimed, while Ernest looked as though he wished he were anywhere but there.

'I'm disappointed in you. You have plummeted in my estimation,' she told Ernest, and he mumbled a few indistinct words that sounded like an apology.

'Is someone going to tell me what's going on?' Jacques asked.

Mary stood up. 'I'll let Ernest tell you. I have a headache and am going to retire. Goodbye, Mr Simpson.'

He rose to his feet but she did not stop to give him her hand as she fled the room. She was so angry she felt she might cry. Why did Wallis always get what she wanted? It simply wasn't fair.

The week after Ernest sailed, Mary received a letter from Wallis on the Côte d'Azur. She and Aunt Bessie had befriended a young Philadelphia lawyer who at first had seemed sedate but turned out to be the most exceptional dancer. When he got on the dance floor, others drew back to admire his Charleston and his Black Bottom. She also mentioned a very amusing Irishman, who entertained them at dinner. It was clear she was not pining for Ernest. Mary ripped the letter into tiny pieces and dropped it in an ashtray.

~

On 25 October, the front page of the *New York Times* ran the story that Wallis's Uncle Sol had died. Mary read his obituary with curiosity. She had known he was director of a railroad company but not that he was responsible for the extension of the Seaboard Air Line Railroad to southern Florida. She had ridden on that very line when she visited Wallis in Pensacola. Various worthy businessmen wrote of his great contribution to the country's transport infrastructure and of his fortune, estimated to be around five million dollars. Of course, it meant that Wallis would be coming home from France. She must have high hopes of an inheritance, since Sol had never married and had no children of his own.

By the time Wallis returned, Uncle Sol was already lying in the family vault and his will had been read to family members. Wallis was met at the station by her mother Alice, who explained the terms, and she was soon on the telephone to share them with Mary.

'Can you believe it? He's left the bulk of his fortune to a home for impoverished ladies of gentle birth. I will receive a minuscule trust fund – and even that will cease in the event of my remarriage.'

'Why would he do that?' Mary sympathised. 'Why not look after his own flesh and blood?'

Wallis sighed. 'Because he never forgave me for leaving Win, against his express orders. Looking on the bright side, at least I don't have to sit through another of his tedious moral lectures. He had no respect for me, or for any women. In his book we were frail creatures without principles or common sense.'

Mary's recollection was that Wallis only ever visited Uncle Sol to wheedle and cajole money for one thing or another: a new dress, a trip to Europe, a divorce. Perhaps he got fed up with it.

'I'll appeal, of course,' Wallis finished. 'He's not getting away with it.'

'Are you coming back to live in America now?' Mary asked.

'Not for long. I'm going to Warrenton to finalise my divorce in early December, then I wondered if I might impose on your hospitality over Christmas? I sail for Europe early in the New Year.'

Mary paused. Wallis clearly had no idea how cross she was with her. It would have been easy to make some excuse, to say that Jacques' family were staying, but she couldn't resist the allure of her old friend. She heard herself saying the words: 'Yes, of course you can stay.'

For the first day or so of the visit, Mary did not ask Wallis about Ernest. She couldn't bear to torture herself. But before long her curiosity got the better of her.

'Did you know that Ernest is in London and is divorcing Dorothea?' she asked, watching for the reaction.

'He's such a dear,' Wallis replied, tipping her head to one side with a distant smile. 'He keeps asking me to marry him and I really can't make up my mind. I'm very fond of him, and he is *kind*, which would be a marked contrast to the last husband. But I'm not sure he is *temperamentally* my type.'

'I'm not sure that anyone is,' Mary replied, unable to keep the acid from her tone.

Chapter 23

New York, August 1928

MARY WAS HEARTSICK BUT NOT SURPRISED WHEN Wallis wrote to say that she and Ernest had married. The ceremony took place on 21 July in a grim London registry office that Wallis described as *more appropriate for a trial than the culmination of a romance.* She wrote of their honeymoon driving through France and Spain, in which Ernest took the role of tour guide, with his impeccable French and his detailed knowledge of the architecture and customs: *like a* Baedeker, *a* Guide Michelin *and an encyclopaedia all wrapped up in a retiring and modest manner.*

Reading between the lines, Mary could tell that Wallis was already bored. She had sought security, but the constraints of a safe marriage were for her like a straitjacket. *Ernest's sister Maud is trying to launch me in London society but I find the English are easily shocked by my conversation; their women do not follow politics and current affairs and seem to feel it is not a woman's place. As you can imagine, I disagree strongly.*

She wrote that she had little to occupy her from nine, when Ernest left for work, until his return at six, and complained that he would rather spend the evenings reading books than attending parties. At weekends he wanted to drive around the countryside looking for dreary old churches or castles. The weather was gloomy and grey, the people largely unfriendly, and Wallis sounded restless.

Good! Mary thought. It serves you right.

She wrote to both, congratulating them on their marriage and wishing them every happiness, in a letter that was a study in diplomacy.

Her own life in Manhattan was increasingly lonely, and she had to admit that despite being cross with the two of them, she missed them dearly. She pined for her wide-ranging conversations with Ernest and the comfort of his friendship. She yearned for the zing of Wallis's visits, when she swept into Washington Square in a whirlwind of gossip and humour. They had been her two best friends, and she resented them doing anything without her. It was like being back at school when Mary felt jealous if she saw Wallis strolling in the grounds with another girl. Back then, she would invariably be invited to join in, but now Wallis and Ernest had struck out on their own and left her behind. It wasn't fair.

Although she still loved Jacques, he was no longer the dashing, romantic pilot she had married. He brooded for hours on end, but would never tell her what troubled him, and their marriage was increasingly strained by his drinking. Several evenings a week he went out to guzzle red wine with his French and Italian friends, and came home in the early hours reeking of booze and garlic. He had stopped talking to her about anything of importance and never brought her gifts or paid her compliments. It was as if she was his housekeeper rather than his wife. Mary grew to prefer the evenings he went out, when she could entertain her female friends or sit reading on her own. Wine made him belligerent and they had stupid rows over trivial matters, while the true source of their unhappiness was unexplored.

In April 1929, Mary turned thirty-three and her grief at remaining childless intensified. If only she could have a baby, she believed it would give her life focus and make everything else tolerable. Her sister Anne had two children, Buckie had one, and Mary adored them, always happy to read stories as they sat on her lap or answer their innocent questions. She had no remaining sexual desire for Jacques but forced herself to go through the motions, then she counted the days of her cycle on a calendar and cried every month when her bleed began yet again. Margaret Sanger opened a birth control clinic to help women prevent pregnancy and Mary felt like turning up at her office and begging advice on how to promote it.

~

In June, Wallis wrote with the sad news that her mother Alice had developed a cancerous tumour behind her eye that had caused her to lose her sight on that side. Mary grimaced; it sounded horrid. The letter continued that Wallis and Ernest had made a whistle-stop trip to visit her in Washington, the first time he and Alice had met.

I was much amused to hear the advice she gave him, Wallis wrote. *She said that, as with explosives, he must handle me with care. He replied that he was well aware of my explosive possibilities and felt sure he was equal to the task.*

Ernest had to return to London on urgent business and Wallis was left in a quandary, torn between her desire to be with her mother and her duty to her husband. Although the cancer was incurable, doctors hoped Alice might live another two or three years. The upshot was that Wallis stayed an extra two weeks before following Ernest. Her letter finished by saying that she planned on visiting her mother regularly and promised they would meet on her next trip.

Mary's first reaction was to feel wounded that they had come to America without visiting her. Was Ernest still cross with her for opposing his relationship with Wallis? She had hoped that was water under the bridge. But she also sympathised with Wallis's dilemma; it must have torn her apart to leave with that diagnosis hanging over her mother.

In October, Mary received a cable: *MOTHER CONDITION WORSE STOP SAILING ALONE ON MAURETANIA STOP DUE 29TH STOP CAN YOU MEET ME? STOP WALLIS.*

Wallis had obviously told her Aunt Bessie that Mary was going to meet her, because on the 28th she received a phone call: Aunt Bessie said that Alice had slipped into a coma and death could not be far away. She asked Mary to tell Wallis when she came ashore so she would be prepared for the sight that met her in Washington.

With heavy heart, Mary made her way to the pier on the East River and waved as she saw Wallis hurrying down the gangway, a porter wheeling her luggage. She was anxious and drawn as she reached Mary and embraced her quickly.

'Is there any news?' she asked.

Mary took her hand. 'She's still here, but she's no longer conscious. I'm so sorry, Wallie.'

Wallis gave a scream and her eyes filled with tears. 'I must get to her.'

Mary had a taxicab waiting and asked the porter to load Wallis's luggage onto the roof as they climbed into the back seat. 'Pennsylvania Station, please,' she told the driver.

As soon as the door closed, Wallis began to sob. Mary gave her a handkerchief and rubbed her shoulder, feeling desperately sad for her.

'What shall I do, Mary? I don't know what to do.'

Mary spoke in a gentle voice, her heart full of compassion. 'She will still be able to hear you. I have heard many stories in which people have revived from comas and remembered what was said to them. Go to her bedside, take her hand and tell her how much you love her. Tell her what a wonderful mother she has been. Tell her everything so that at the end you will know that nothing has been left unsaid. I promise she will hear.'

Tears were streaming down Wallis's face and falling unchecked, while she crushed the handkerchief in her fist. 'I don't know how I shall live without her. I've had so little stability in my life, but I could always rely on her being there if I needed her.'

Mary put an arm around her. 'You have Ernest, and you have me. You will always have me.'

Wallis turned and gripped her hand fiercely. 'Come to Washington, Mary. I can't face this on my own.'

Mary paused. 'It's a time for family. You will have Aunt Bessie, after all.'

'But you are my sister. Remember? Sisters who chose each other. Please come, Mary. I need you.'

'Then of course I will. I will put you on the first train, then go home and pack, and join you shortly.'

When Mary arrived in Washington, she found Wallis, her mother's new husband and her Aunt Bessie keeping a round-the-clock vigil by Alice's bed. She made herself useful in briefing the cook to prepare light meals and hot drinks for them and urging them to eat or drink. When they fell asleep by Alice's bedside, she covered them with quilts. All the while the invalid's chest rose and fell, her face grey in colour and her eyes firmly closed. Sometimes she stirred and her lips moved as though in response to some remark, but she soon settled into deep sleep again, her withered hands motionless on the bedcover.

'Does she know I am here?' Wallis despaired. 'She gives no sign.'

'Of course she knows,' Mary assured her.

The end came early in the morning of 2 November. It was hard to tell at first because Alice's breathing had become so faint, but Aunt Bessie held a mirror to her mouth and nose and there was no misting.

'Mother!' Wallis shook her shoulders, trying to force her to breathe again. 'Mother!' she screamed, growing hysterical.

'Come along, Wallie.' Mary put an arm around her. 'You need to rest. Everything will seem manageable if you have some sleep.'

'How can I sleep?' Wallis wailed. 'I've lost the person who loved me most in the world.'

Her legs almost gave way beneath her as Mary led her out of the room, and she leant heavily on her arm.

'Lots of people love you,' Mary whispered. 'More than I could ever count.'

Wallis shook her head. 'Not love. I entertain and amuse people but they don't love me, not the way they love you. You've always been the lovable one of the two of us.'

'That's silly,' Mary chided her.

'Ernest doesn't even love me; at least not in the all-consuming way Jackie loves you.'

'Of course he does,' Mary soothed, leading her into her own bedroom. 'And my marriage is not as perfect as you might imagine.'

'Really? What's the problem?' Wallis sat on top of the bedcover and swung her feet up, lying back on the pillows, her eyes red and swollen. Mary unfastened her shoes and pulled them off.

'Oh . . .' She felt disloyal to talk of it, but decided that perhaps it might distract Wallis from her grief. 'The usual thing: he drinks too much. It seems to me that Prohibition has had the opposite to its desired effect, making alcohol more alluring than ever.'

'Does he hit you?' Wallis was wide-eyed.

'No, never. Nothing like that. But it's rather lonely trying to converse with a drunk, as I'm sure you remember from your first marriage.'

'Have you threatened to leave him if he doesn't stop?'

'No. I still love him.' Mary didn't like to admit that thoughts of divorce had sometimes drifted to mind, but she always pushed them away. She couldn't bear to be a divorcee in a city where that status reduced women to second- or third-class citizens. She remembered how people had gossiped about Wallis behind her back and stopped inviting her to society events.

'Come back to London with me after the funeral,' Wallis pleaded. 'I need a friend there and it will give Jacques time to buck up his ideas. Either that or we'll find you a new English husband. *Please* come.'

Mary put her arms round her and hugged her tight. She realised she had got over the hurt she felt about Wallis marrying Ernest and she longed to see him – to spend time with them both. And she felt enormously protective of poor, orphaned Wallis, who needed her more than ever.

'I'd love to,' she agreed. A change of scene, a holiday with two close friends in a country that had long fascinated her: she couldn't think of anything she would enjoy more.

Chapter 24

Brighton, 11 September 1997

ACHEL GOT BACK TO BRIGHTON AT LUNCHTIME on Thursday, her neck stiff from sleeping hunched awkwardly on the overnight flight. Her flat looked tiny and cluttered compared to Richard's loft, but she preferred her decor: the gilt-framed turquoise-velvet chairs and sofa, the chaise longue at the foot of her canopied bed, the chandelier and the groupings of sepia photographs in mother-of-pearl frames. She felt energised by the trip: at least now she could tell her regular customers there was new stock on the way. Maybe this would mark a change in her fortunes. Good old Richard: they didn't see each other often because of the amount of travelling he did, but he had proved a true friend in her time of need.

The answer machine was blinking so she played the messages: her mum's cheerful voice told her that the registry office was booked for 5 p.m. on 18 December, a Thursday; it was the only time they had available in December, she said. The next message was from Nicola, who sounded upset that the shop was shut and hoped it wasn't closing down because of her. And then there was a call from Alex in Paris and she could hear from his tone that he was stressed so she called him on his mobile, wondering if he was still cross with her.

'I'm back,' she said. 'How did your awards ceremony go?'

'Brilliant!' he exclaimed. 'I won an award for "rising star". Ironic that I'm only "rising" now when I've had my company for eight years, but it's good to feel appreciated.'

Rachel gasped. 'Alex, that's wonderful news. I'm so proud of you. But I feel awful I wasn't there to see you collect the award.'

'I thanked you in my speech anyway. You weren't forgotten.'

'Now I feel even worse. You'll have to tell me how I can make it up to you.'

He continued, his tone becoming subdued: 'But meanwhile, the Diana programme is turning into a fiasco. Remember I told you about the witness who saw the motorbike pillion passenger flashing a light in Henri Paul's eyes? Well, it seems his wife, who was sitting beside him, has a completely different story. Every lead I uncover turns to dust when I look more closely . . .'

'That's frustrating.' She wished she was there to give him a hug; she felt guilty about missing his awards ceremony, guilty about her lack of enthusiasm for his Diana documentary. 'Can't you present the contradictions and leave the viewer to draw their own conclusions?'

He sighed. 'It would be nice if at least some of the witness stories were corroborated. Beats me how twenty people can watch the same event and all give a different account of it.'

'You sound knackered,' she soothed.

'That's an understatement.' He laughed half-heartedly. 'How about you? How was New York?'

'Good. I picked up some wonderful pieces. Mum's booked the registry office for the eighteenth of December, by the way, so stick that in your diary.'

There was a pause and she heard the tapping of his fingernail as he checked his Psion organiser. 'Yeah, that's fine for me. I'll take the day off.'

'Just a day?' she laughed. 'Actually, I can't afford to take any more than that right before Christmas. We can honeymoon in the spring.'

'Got to go,' he said, and she heard another voice in the background. 'See you tomorrow night.'

Alex never stayed on the phone long when he called from overseas because the charges on his mobile were prohibitive, even for receiving calls.

Rachel called her mum next and ran through her list of requests for the wedding. It felt awkward since she was not paying, and she tried to think of ways of cutting costs. 'One of Alex's production team can make the video,' she suggested. 'And I'll ask Wendy to make the cake. She said she wanted to help.'

'I'll call this morning and see if I can book the Bonne Auberge,' her mum said. 'Fingers crossed.'

Next Rachel sat down to open some post that had arrived. There was a notification about an increase in business rates for the shop, a credit card bill and a letter from the bank confirming her revised overdraft facility. Her stomach clenched. The business was still in a deep black hole. Once she had paid the rent, the VAT and the costs of the New York trip, she would have spent up to the new overdraft limit and there would be nothing left in either her personal or her business account. Meanwhile she would not be able to start selling her Van der Heyden stock until mid November. Something else was needed to get her through the next eight weeks, and at that precise moment she couldn't think what.

～

After changing and grabbing an apple, Rachel headed to Forgotten Dreams. As she walked past the modern shops of

Churchill Square, she saw 'Sale' signs in several windows and that gave her an idea: she had never held a sale at the shop before, but perhaps she could have a limited one, just offering twenty per cent off the old stock. She stopped at a print shop and asked them to make her a banner.

On entering Forgotten Dreams, she paused and surveyed her empire. It was heartbreaking to think of all she had lost. The interior no longer had that cluttered 'flapper's boudoir' look, and the shop window still looked sparse, even with her own dresses and jewellery. A note had been pushed under the door: a local craftsman whom she had asked to repair the art deco lamp said it was ready for collection. That was good news at least.

The holdall of charity-shop goods she'd bought in London was at the back of the shop. The clothes were being dry-cleaned, but she had also picked up a range of accessories and trinkets and Rachel brought them to the counter to sort through. A 1920s black-sequinned evening bag was shedding its sequins, so she threaded a needle and began reattaching them.

Nicola's head popped round the door. 'Thank goodness you're open. I was beginning to think . . .' She didn't finish the sentence.

'I've been away. How are you?'

'I still feel awful about the robbery and wish there was something I could do. Can I help you today? No charge, just so we can spend time together?'

'There's an offer I can't refuse,' Rachel said with a smile. She reached into the holdall. 'Fancy polishing these silver photo frames? There's some liquid polish in the cupboard.'

Nicola pulled up a chair and before long the shop had the sweet chemical scent of a well-kept stately home. Rachel told her about the New York trip, then mentioned the date of the wedding.

'Are you bringing Tony?' she asked. He was Nicola's latest. 'I've got you down on the list as a plus-one.'

Nicola lowered her head. 'What a creep Tony turned out to be. The band are going on tour for a couple of months and he said I'm not allowed to contact him. What happens on tour stays on tour.'

'Oh no, I'm sorry.' Rachel wasn't surprised. Whenever they'd met, Tony had given her lecherous looks and too-intimate hugs of greeting, and had clearly not seen Nicola as any more than a pit stop.

'I need to stop picking musicians. I've always been a sucker for a man who sings to me in bed.'

Nicola was a year older than Rachel, but her love life was a series of disastrous flings with musicians she met in pubs and clubs round Brighton, none of whom had any intention of settling down.

'Why not get an Eric Clapton CD,' Rachel suggested, 'and date grown-ups instead of perennial teenagers?'

'Good idea,' Nicola agreed. 'Alex says I need to retune my antennae because I have an unerring knack for picking the bastard in the room.'

'Did he suggest how you should do that? Aversion therapy? Maybe listening to your friends for a change?' She rubbed Nicola's shoulder in sympathy.

Nicola concentrated on her polishing, rubbing so hard Rachel worried she might wear away the silver. 'I hear you and Alex aren't going to manage a honeymoon until spring. He says he'll have to work through Christmas Day now the programme is airing in January.'

Rachel frowned. 'Is it January? I didn't know that.'

'He mentioned it when he rang the other day, and I thought that would make timing tight for a Christmas wedding because he'll be in the middle of editing.'

'I wonder why he didn't mention January to me?' Rachel mused. 'Maybe he did and I wasn't listening properly.'

'Must have been while you were away. He got a call from the channel a couple of days ago.'

The bell rang as a customer came in looking for a necklace to match a gown she had bought a few weeks earlier. Rachel only had a few necklaces in stock – her own ones, brought from home. She helped the customer to try them on, fastening the catches as she lifted her long hair out of the way, but none were quite right. There had been dozens of necklaces before the break-in, and Rachel could picture one that would have been perfect.

All afternoon she watched browsers, noticed what they picked up and willed them to buy, but she only sold one angora cardigan. It felt as if her luck had changed, like the wind blowing from the north instead of the south. The thought crossed her mind that it might be something to do with that broken mirror, and she murmured, 'Idiot!'

'What was that?' Nicola looked up.

'Oh, nothing. I stabbed my finger with a needle.' She couldn't tell Nicola how stressed she was about the shop because it was clear she was already consumed with guilt. She couldn't tell Alex because he had his own stress. It was something she would deal with on her own.

As she cashed up and prepared to close for the night, her thoughts returned to the earlier conversation with Nicola and she realised that Alex must have rung her from Paris. Why would he do that when he was careful about his phone bill?

She was about to ask Nicola but stopped herself. Their friendship was their business. And she had always believed that men who had female friends were more trustworthy than those who didn't.

Chapter 25

Brighton, 4 October 1997

RACHEL STARTED A SALE IN THE SHOP AND advertised it in the local paper, but it was that post-summer lull when the weather was still mild so no one was buying winter clothes yet, but they weren't thinking of topping up their summer wardrobes either. Trade was slow, even with the discounts, and every afternoon when she closed the door after taking only a fraction of what she would have turned over before the break-in, she felt the iron band tighten around her chest. She had no idea how she was going to pay the rent at the end of October.

One day her hopes were raised when an intern arrived from Gazelle Films with a list of 1920s dresses they needed for a period drama. The girl looked like a college leaver, wearing a Radiohead T-shirt and ripped jeans, with a long strand of maroon hair hanging over one eye. Rachel scanned her list with mounting excitement.

'I've got everything you need arriving from New York in November,' she promised. 'Dresses, shoes, velvet evening coats, jewellery. It's on its way as we speak.'

The girl wrinkled her nose. 'Do you have any photos? I'm supposed to take photos so the art director can choose.'

Rachel kicked herself. If only she'd photographed her purchases; there hadn't been time. 'No, but tell your art director it's from the Van der Heyden estate sale in New York. It would be perfect for your drama. These are originals that haven't been seen on TV before.'

She scribbled a note on the back of her business card and handed it over, feeling anxious as the girl stuffed it casually into an untidy satchel.

'Shall I give the art director a ring myself?' Rachel offered. 'I can email a list of what I've got if that would help.'

'I think they want to see pictures so they can co-ordinate. They don't want every character wearing the same colour, you know?'

Rachel swallowed her irritation. She had worked for a film company back in the eighties and knew exactly how it worked. She decided she would ring and try to get through to the art director after the weekend.

It was a Saturday and she was hoping to spend time with Alex later. They'd barely seen each other over the last month, as he got back late on Friday nights and spent his Saturdays and Sundays poring over scripts, doing research on the home computer or talking endlessly on the telephone. That evening she planned to cook dinner for a change, to open a bottle of wine and have a proper conversation with him, then later, with any luck, some sex. There hadn't been nearly enough lately; they were both working long hours so when they did manage to spend an evening together the mood was more fatigued than flirtatious.

∼

As she walked into the flat, she could hear Alex on the phone and he sounded irritable. 'It's not good enough,' he snapped. 'Do I have to do everything myself?'

She kicked off her high heels and went through to the kitchen to open a beer for him. As she placed it on the coffee table, he acknowledged it with a quick smile and carried on talking. 'It's got to be ready by Wednesday at the latest.'

She poured herself a vodka and tonic in her special glass with hand-painted edelweiss on the sides. It had been in the shop but there was only one, and most people liked their glasses to be a set, so she'd brought it home.

Next, she began chopping the ingredients for her sausage casserole, a cheat's version of French cassoulet. It was one of Alex's favourites. There were piles of neatly diced celery, carrot and onions in front of her and the sausages were browning in the pan when he came through, swigging his beer.

'Your mum just emailed that the Bonne Auberge can only take sixty guests. That's not going to work, honey. I've got dozens of people who will take it as a personal slight if they're not invited.'

She frowned. 'Alex, we discussed using the Bonne Auberge and you agreed. How many did you think it would take?'

'I thought they would squeeze in at least a hundred . . .'

'Only if they removed the tables and we ate off our laps.'

He sat down and started nibbling a piece of carrot. 'Maybe we can find another restaurant that will do a buffet. I've been to loads of buffet weddings.'

Rachel felt annoyed. 'It's too late to say this now. The booking is made. Besides, I don't think we can ask my parents to stump up for more than sixty dinners.'

Alex was intransigent. 'We can pay the difference ourselves. How much is it?'

'Twenty-five quid a head for the set meal. And speak for yourself: I don't have any spare cash right now.' She tipped the onions into the pan and stirred them in the sizzling sausage fat.

'That's extortion. Did your mum not try to bargain with them? I hope they've given us reasonable prices for the booze.'

Rachel chopped some chicken thighs and tossed the pieces into her pan. 'Alex, stop bringing your TV producer head to this. It's not your gig. We asked Mum to organise the wedding and you can't waltz in later and criticise what she's done, especially not when she is paying.'

'You keep banging on about who's paying. I wish they *weren't* bloody paying so we could have the wedding we actually want.'

Rachel tossed her knife into the sink with a clatter. 'Could you try to be a little less ungrateful? You were the one who pushed for a Christmas wedding and you've got everyone bending over backwards to arrange it for you. My dad's hired a car to take us to the registry office, Mum's booked the photographer and the flowers, Wendy's making the cake . . .'

'Oh Christ, why did you ask Wendy? She'll come up with something tacky. I bet it will have grinning shop-bought bride and groom figures on top.' He finished his beer and brushed past her on his way to the fridge for another. Her vodka and tonic was finished but it didn't occur to him to ask if she wanted a refill.

'If you don't want Wendy to do it, tell her and find another cake.' Rachel's voice rose. 'I've had it to the back teeth with you sniping at everyone while contributing nothing but criticism.'

'I'm marrying you – isn't that enough?' He looked at her quickly, as if realising he might have gone too far.

Rachel blanched. 'I'm sorry. I didn't realise you were doing me a huge favour. *You* were the one who wanted to get married.'

'Come on, that's not what I meant.' He sighed ostentatiously, with just a hint of implication that she might be overreacting, as he reached out to give her back a friendly rub.

Rachel didn't reply but crashed a casserole dish onto the hob and began pouring in the contents of the frying pan, followed by chopped tomatoes, red wine, a bay leaf and a sprinkling of thyme. The flageolet beans would be added later.

Alex got up. 'I've got a phone call to make,' he said, and left her stirring the casserole with gritted teeth.

Over dinner that evening, Alex talked about the problems he was having with filming, seeming oblivious to the fact that she was still cross with him.

'We know there was a minor collision with a white car when the Mercedes entered the tunnel, because there are white paint scratches on the wing that weren't there before, and they found shards of glass from a side light on the road, but no one has come forward to own up. And get this: *none* of the CCTV cameras in the tunnel or on the route they took from the Ritz have captured anything. The police are saying they were all inoperative.'

'You're lucky. That means they don't have any footage of you making off with Diana's platinum heart.'

He frowned. 'You're missing the point. I could believe it about one or two cameras, but *all* of them? That's definitely fishy.'

The two vodka and tonics she'd drunk were not helping Rachel's mood. She separated her dinner into little mounds with a fork – sausages, chicken, beans, veg – feeling argumentative. 'It could be coincidence. Not all the cameras in London are switched on all the time, and we're supposed to be the surveillance capital of the world.'

'Too much of a coincidence, if you ask me. I was hoping for a chunk of CCTV footage to show in the programme, but I guess, in the best traditions of broadcasting, we'll have to fake it with our own camera and a hired Mercedes.'

'With a Diana lookalike in the back seat, no doubt?'

He ignored her. 'I've got to do something. I've got interviews with three of the paparazzi, and the doctor and his friend who were in the tunnel, but at the moment I don't have any footage that wasn't in the BBC *Panorama* programme screened two weeks after the crash. What's more, I hear there is another crew working on a crash documentary. I don't suppose you could talk to Susie Hargreaves this week about me interviewing her?'

'Alex, you're kidding.' She put down her fork. 'I didn't think you were serious about that. You can't expect me to call a business contact and ask her to appear in your programme. It's too much of a blurring of boundaries.'

He slammed down his cutlery. 'You promised.'

'I didn't promise . . .'

'You did, and I was counting on it.' He glared at her. 'It would be nice if you could act like you care about my work instead of criticising everything I tell you.'

'Yes, ditto,' Rachel reiterated, her temper rising. 'You never ask me anything about the shop. I'm struggling to survive after Nicola's idiocy wiped out my stock, and all I get from you is grief because a few of your friends can't come to our wedding.'

Alex shook his head in annoyance. 'It's not just a few friends. There are important industry contacts, commissioning editors and the like. It's a great opportunity to schmooze . . .'

'Oh, so our wedding is just another business opportunity? Well, I hope you enjoy yourself, because the way things are going, it's unlikely I'll turn up.'

Rachel shoved her chair back and swept out of the room, leaving her dinner virtually untouched. It was a one-bedroom flat, albeit a sizeable one, and the bathroom was the only place to find privacy. She locked the door and sat on the edge of the bath, her emotions engulfing her. Was she being unreasonable? She'd hoped for a peaceful, intimate evening and that row had erupted from nowhere. What was happening to them?

They never used to argue before they got engaged. If there was ever a tetchy moment, they'd be laughing about it minutes later.

She tried to think of a way to calm the situation but was overcome by a wave of tiredness and decided they could talk in the morning. She wiped off her make-up, brushed her teeth and went down the hall to bed without glancing into the sitting room, where she could hear Alex was watching television.

He came in later and she felt the mattress rock. She pretended to be asleep but knew he could tell she wasn't.

'I'm sorry I snapped,' he whispered. 'I'm so bloody wound up at the moment.'

She moved slightly, just enough so he knew she was listening.

'Can we make up?' he asked, snuggling in behind her.

She didn't reply, but she didn't pull away when he wrapped his arms around her and kissed the back of her neck before drifting off to sleep.

~

Next morning, the television news announced that Trevor Rees-Jones, the bodyguard in the Paris crash, had been released from hospital and flown home to recuperate in England. While spreading marmalade on a slice of toast, Alex dialled the number of one of his researchers, asked where Rees-Jones was staying, and jotted down an address. Rachel was in the next room but she overheard them talking about how an approach might be made to see if he would give them an interview.

'Is he well enough to talk?' she asked, entering the kitchen as Alex's call ended. 'I thought he was badly injured.'

He nodded, making a note in the book that was never far from his side. 'Yeah, he had reconstructive surgery on his face. Sounds ghastly.'

'Do you think he remembers what happened?'

Alex looked grim. 'Even if he does, I bet he won't say. If secret services were prepared to kill Diana, they wouldn't hesitate to bump him off too.'

Rachel frowned. 'You seem to have made up your mind it was a conspiracy. In that case, aren't you worried the spooks might come after you too? They won't want you broadcasting any of this.'

'What's your point exactly?' He looked at her coldly.

She felt an underlying irritability from the fight of the previous evening. 'To be honest, I think you should leave the poor bodyguard alone. He must be horribly traumatised. I feel sorry for him.'

Alex spoke between mouthfuls. 'If I don't contact him, the other crew working on the crash story will. He'll talk to them, they'll get the scoop, and in comparison my programme will just be a succession of night-time shots of traffic driving into the Alma Tunnel with a voiceover. Is that what you want?' His tone was scathing and she could feel another fight brewing.

'I can see it's a tricky judgement call.' She busied herself cleaning the sink.

Alex sounded annoyed. She had obviously hit a nerve. 'I'm doing my best to find a balance and come up with something more interesting than a mash-up of cuttings. It is possible to ask searching questions of the protagonists without being exploitative. It's what we call journalism.' He checked his watch and stood up, taking his toast with him. 'I'm heading up to London.'

Rachel went over to kiss him and they had a brief hug before he went into the sitting room, clenching the toast between his teeth as he gathered his bags.

After he'd left, she found a cartoon in her make-up bag of two angry raccoons wearing boxing gloves and the message *Let's be friends again*. He must have drawn it after she went to bed. She sighed. There was nothing she wanted more.

Chapter 26

London, 29 May 1931

WHEN MARY'S SHIP DOCKED AT SOUTHAMPTON, SHE was standing on deck with some friends she had made during the crossing, watching as tugs manoeuvred the huge liner into an unfeasibly narrow space. They all cheered at the skill of the feat. When she returned to her cabin, she found a radiogram from Wallis, left by a steward: *SORRY CAN'T MEET YOU SOUTHAMPTON STOP CATCH 11 A.M. TRAIN TO WATERLOO STOP WILL BE STANDING ON PLATFORM WAVING STARS AND STRIPES.*

Mary felt a momentary twinge of panic. She had never been to England before. Where would she catch the train? Jacques had always made the arrangements when they travelled, but now, after much soul-searching, she had decided on a separation. His drinking had gone from bad to worse and communication between them had dwindled to nought, as he went out with his friends every night and staggered home in the early hours. She had crossed the Atlantic on her own to clear her head while she contemplated the unthinkable: a divorce, followed by life as a single woman.

She looked out of the cabin door and a passing steward promised to organise a taxi to the station for her. It all worked seamlessly, with a porter buying her ticket, wheeling her trunk on his trolley and loading it onto the train. She handed him a shilling as a tip, which he seemed pleased with.

The English countryside was resplendent, the greens so vivid they made her eyes ache. It was thrilling to be there, alone, starting a new adventure. She hadn't slept well on the ship, with a bout of seasickness and a mattress that was too firm for comfort, so she nodded off for a while, lulled by the rhythmic chuntering, and only wakened when the locomotive braked as it pulled into its destination.

Waterloo station was a vast iron and glass pavilion, and glancing out, she feared getting lost in the milling crowds, but as soon as she alighted, there was Wallis, wearing a sharp blue suit and a jaunty cloche hat.

'Mary! You made it!' She hugged her. 'It's *so* good to see you. I have a taxicab waiting. We're off to lunch with Consuelo and Benny Thaw. She's one of the Vanderbilt sisters; he's first secretary at the Embassy.'

Mary felt dizzy. 'Couldn't I go back to yours to change first? I look rather dishevelled.'

Wallis eyed her up and down, smoothed her lapel. 'You're fine, dear. They're expecting us any moment. I'll get the driver to take your trunk home.'

She hurried Mary out of the station to a black Austin taxicab with a luggage rack on the roof. As Mary handed the porter a shilling tip, Wallis hissed, 'That's too much,' but it was too late to retract.

Mary looked around in wonder as the taxi nudged its way into the London traffic. All the buildings were centuries older than those in New York, with fancy stonework and impressively tall windows. As they drove over a bridge and past the Palace of Westminster, she was awestruck by the intricacy of the sand-coloured stone carvings; her mouth actually fell open. She turned to Wallis to comment, but her friend seemed immune to their splendour.

'We saw the Prince of Wales *again* last week,' Wallis confided, clutching Mary's gloved hand. 'That's three times now. He's *quite* the character.'

Wallis had written with great excitement about her first meeting with the Prince the previous January, at a house party given by her friend Thelma Furness. She said she had been surprised by how natural and informal he was in person. Mary was glad that Wallis appeared to have found an entrée into London society in the two years since they last met. She had been worried the English might be too stuffy to appreciate her sharp sense of humour, but it appeared not.

'You said your friend Thelma is the Prince's mistress. Doesn't her husband mind?'

Wallis laughed. 'I'm sure he would mind if she was hopping into bed with the butler, but since her lover is heir to the throne, there's a certain cachet. Perhaps you'll meet him during your visit. Remember back at school you used to have a crush on him? Well, he's still unmarried, so you never know your luck.'

'He may be single, but I'm not,' Mary said gloomily, then turned to gaze out of the window.

~

Mary's brains felt scrambled that first afternoon in London. She was still on American time so it felt like first thing in the morning when wine was served with lunch at the Thaws'. They played bridge all afternoon then went directly to the home of another friend, Ethel Lewis, for what Wallis called a 'KT'. There was an extraordinary array of liquor on display in a miniature bar in Ethel's drawing room, and a butler made their cocktails of choice in a shaker before pouring them into martini glasses. Mary chose a Tom Collins because she'd heard of it but had never tried one; she found it to be a refreshing concoction of gin, lemon and club soda.

By the time they returned to Wallis's home in Bryanston Court, Mary was almost sleepwalking, and that helped her to get over the awkwardness of seeing Ernest for the first time since his marriage to Wallis. He was waiting for them in the drawing room, dressed for dinner in white tie, and looking very suave. He took Mary's hand and bowed.

'I'm delighted to welcome you to our London abode. It's been far too long since we've seen each other.'

'Thank you for the invitation. I've already seen a lot of the city in one afternoon.' She smiled. 'It's been a whirlwind introduction.'

While Wallis was out of the room, changing her shoes, Ernest said: 'I'm terribly sorry to hear about your marital problems. If you and Jackie can't work it out, there's no hope for any of us.'

'Thank you,' she said, pursing her lips. She didn't want to talk about Jacques, not yet. She was on vacation and planned to enjoy it to the full – once she had caught up on sleep.

'You look exhausted, my dear. The journey must have taken it out of you.' His concern was touching.

Coming back into the room, Wallis overheard. 'Why don't we change into tea gowns for an informal dinner? Then you can fall straight into bed afterwards.'

'Won't it look incongruous, with Ernest in white tie and us in tea gowns?'

'Nonsense. We don't stand on ceremony,' Ernest assured her.

The maid had already unpacked Mary's clothes and she found her tea gown and changed. She ate dinner quickly, while Wallis toyed with her food and relayed to Ernest some gossip she had heard that afternoon.

As soon as the dessert dishes had been cleared, Mary made her excuses. She blinked when she contemplated the bed in the guest room: a circular white satin one with rose-pink sheets. But the mattress was comfortable and she was asleep as soon as she closed her eyes.

~

Next morning, Wallis came to sit on Mary's bed as she sipped a cup of tea brought by the maid.

'It's wonderful to have you here. It feels just like the old days when I stayed over at your folks' house and we chatted in our pyjamas about boys and decided what we were looking for in our ideal husbands.'

'Did you find all the qualities you wanted in husband number two?' Mary asked.

'Isn't he a dear?' Wallis smiled. 'Such an English eccentric. I do love his funny ways. You'll see him in the evenings and at weekends, but I have a hectic schedule lined up for our days: lunch at the Ritz today, then KTs are at ours tonight. I do like hosting cocktail hour.'

She got up and opened the wardrobe door to look through the clothes Mary had brought. 'Do you only have three evening gowns? We'll have to get you more.'

'I was hoping not to spend too much, Wallie.' Jacques had taken a job in real estate after his insurance business went bust in the Wall Street Crash, but people weren't buying many new properties in the uncertain times. 'I'm on a shoestring.'

Wallis was looking critically at her suits. 'They wear a different silhouette here: slim on the hips with a long slender jacket.'

Mary, whose hips were decidedly not slim, asked, 'Does it really matter? All your friends know I'm a hick from hicksville.'

'Of course not. I'll swallow my pride and appear in public with you all the same,' Wallis teased. 'Actually, I'm jealous that you don't have the slightest hint of a wrinkle and not a single grey hair. You are positively blooming. We'll be fighting off the men when they hear you are free.'

'Why bother fighting?' Mary retorted blithely.

Suddenly Wallis flung herself on the bed and pulled Mary in for a tight hug. 'I can't describe how glad I am that you're here.'

'Why? Is something wrong?'

'No,' Wallis assured her. 'Not that. It's just that you ground me. Now Mother's gone, I think you are the only person in the world who knows who I really am.'

'I'm sure Ernest has a pretty good idea.' Mary stroked Wallis's hair, feeling a rush of love for her. 'Now I had better get dressed before the morning is over – I want to treasure every day that I'm here.'

In the Ritz that lunchtime, Mary glanced around and real- ised that Wallis was right: the length and shape of her suit were old-fashioned. It was warm outdoors but several women wore furs in a loop round their necks, with the poor creatures' heads slipped through openings in their tails. Most wore hats as well, and did not take them off indoors. She imagined they must be stifling.

Wallis had always dressed well; even when she was reliant on stingy Uncle Sol for cash she had a knack for putting elegant outfits together. Now, with Ernest's salary to spend, she had discovered a style that truly suited her: slinky tea dresses that accentuated her slim figure, and tailored skirt suits with wasp waists, accessorised with a striking brooch. Her hair was more severely styled than ever: she wore the same centre parting but pulled each strand tightly into a bun. It had the effect of focusing all your attention on her strong-boned face with those incredible sapphire eyes. Truly she had never looked better. She wasn't conventionally beautiful, Mary thought, watching her, but by God she was striking. And so alive!

Chapter 27

London, June 1931

MARY LOVED THE SOCIAL WHIRL IN LONDON AND according to Wallis was soon 'a hit' with her friends. There was a cocktail party every evening at six, more often than not in the spacious drawing room at Bryanston Court, where Wallis herself mixed the KTs and served tiny sausages and little biscuits with caviar. There were a lot of Americans in their set: Wallis's cousin Corinne and her husband George, who worked at the US Embassy; the three glamorous Vanderbilt girls, Thelma, Consuelo and Gloria; and the US air attaché Mike Scanlon and his wife Gladys. There were also some British friends of Ernest's sister Maud, but they tended to be older and more staid.

One evening Wallis threw a dinner party for the American set, where she served Southern recipes from her and Mary's youth: Maryland fried chicken and biscuits, pork cake, shrimp and corn pie. Conversation was about whether Judge Wilkerson would manage to pin tax evasion charges on Al Capone.

'They have to find some way of getting him behind bars,' Corinne insisted. 'Did you see those photographs of the St Valentine's Day massacre? We can't live in a country where his gang can mow down seven men in broad daylight.'

'The Eighteenth Amendment is responsible for the creation of gangsters like him,' Mike Scanlon argued. 'As soon as governments ban a popular substance like alcohol, they invite criminals to step in and even give them a veneer of respectability.'

'It made criminals of us all,' Wallis declared. 'We each crossed a line when we took our first sip of illegal hooch, and who knows where it will end? Perhaps we will progress to more serious crimes – like exceeding the speed limit.'

'As they say here in Britain, the law is an ass,' Ernest commented. Two of the women gasped and he quickly corrected himself: 'An ass as in a type of donkey, that is.'

Mary admired Wallis's skill as she ensured everyone was engaged in conversation, asking questions about areas she knew they could discuss, and never permitting a lull. They moved on to talk of the Empire State Building, which had just opened in New York – 'It's breathtaking,' Mary was able to report, 'but I'm sure there are many collisions on the sidewalk as passers-by crane upwards at its soaring heights' – and of hailstones the size of golf balls that had recently fallen in New Jersey, breaking hothouse windows and causing many sore heads.

'No one wants to leave Wallis's parties,' Mike Scanlon whispered to Mary, 'because they have so much pep in them.'

Ernest took a back seat, happy to let his wife be the centre of attention, and Mary gravitated towards him after the meal. In no time at all their old friendship had been re-established, as if she had never quarrelled with him back in New York. She enjoyed asking what books he had read recently, and questioning him on architectural sights she had spotted while gadding around in a taxicab with Wallis. It was clear he had never told Wallis what Mary had said about her, and she appreciated his discretion.

On the rare occasions when it was just the three of them at home for an evening, Mary watched Wallis and Ernest together. She loved them both dearly and wanted them to be happy, but she could sense Wallis was not in love. She liked Ernest – everyone did – but she wasn't giddy the way she had been when she met Win; her eyes didn't light up the way they had when she spoke of Felipe Espil. Did Ernest love her, or was he just swept away by her? She was great fun to be around, but Mary wasn't convinced they had enough in common. Could Ernest see the vulnerability beneath the carapace, the part Mary thought made Wallis human and lovable?

~

On the morning of 1 June, Wallis came rushing into Mary's bedroom with news. 'The Prince of Wales is going to be at Consuelo and Benny's later, so you'll get a chance to meet him. Won't you wear the green silk? It's your most fetching gown. I'll lend you my emerald necklace. And let's get our hair done this afternoon.'

Mary laughed. 'Anyone would think you were trying to match me with the poor man.'

'Don't you want to make a good impression? He is your childhood pin-up after all.' Wallis seemed more effervescent than usual.

'Fine, but before we go you'll have to remind me how to curtsey and what to call him . . .'

The day was spent in a flurry of hair, nails, make-up and careful accessorising before they took a taxicab to Consuelo's at six. Every guest was formally announced by a butler as they entered the room, a system Mary rather liked because it helped her to remember the names. It was half past six and she had almost finished her first drink when the butler announced: 'His Royal Highness, the Prince of Wales, and Mrs Thelma Furness.'

Mary looked over and was startled to see how short the prince was: probably only five foot six or seven. He was wearing a loud houndstooth-check suit and had prominent bags under his eyes, nothing like the handsome blonde youth whose picture she used to kiss in magazines. Of course, he was thirty-seven years old and not a youth any more. Thelma was an exotic raven-haired beauty with a pretty laugh.

The Prince chatted first to a group near the door, but moved from one circle to the next every few minutes, making his way slowly around the room, cigarette in one hand and drink in the other. Mary smiled as she saw Wallis manoeuvre into position so that he would have to talk to her next. He greeted her warmly, seeming pleased to see her, and Wallis was clearly at her most animated, but Mary was not close enough to hear what they were discussing.

At one stage they both turned to look at her and Wallis beckoned. Mary approached, feeling a flutter of nerves, and dropped a curtsey of sorts.

'It's an honour to meet you, Your Royal Highness,' she said, then she looked into his face and saw a turned-up nose and the saddest blue eyes she ever had encountered. It was a shock; not what she had expected at all. What did he have to be sad about?

For a moment they examined each other, then he said, 'I hope you will enjoy your stay in London, Mrs Raffray. We do like welcoming American visitors.'

'I'm already entranced by the history in every street; you have so much architecture,' Mary gushed.

'A wonderful setting to show off the beauty of you American women.' The Prince smiled, looking at Wallis.

She replied in her best flirtatious style: 'Why, sir, you are just a heartbreak to any woman because you flatter her but you can never marry her.'

He laughed at that, throwing his head back. 'Mischievous as ever, Mrs Simpson. Keep up the good work.'

Mary was shocked. After the Prince had moved on to talk to the next group, she whispered in Wallis's ear: 'Bessiewallis Warfield Simpson, I do hope you are not trying to seduce that poor man.'

'Good Lord, no!' Wallis whispered back, wrinkling her nose.

Chapter 28

Brighton, 5 October 1997

RACHEL DECIDED TO CALL HER MUM AND ASK IF there was any chance of increasing the number of guests at the wedding if Alex were to pay. Her mum suggested that instead of finding a bigger restaurant, they have a party afterwards for all the guests they couldn't fit on the eighteenth.

'That's a good idea,' Rachel mused, 'but I don't want you and Dad having any more expense. I suppose we could hold it here at the flat.' She hated the thought – it had taken days to tidy up after their New Year's Eve party – but that would be the cheapest option.

'I'm happy to buy a case of champagne and help you prepare some food.'

'Mum, you're doing enough as it is. It's Alex's turn to contribute something to this wedding.' Her tone must have revealed her mood, because her mother picked up on it straight away.

'What's he done?'

It felt disloyal to talk about the previous day's argument, but she couldn't help herself. Her mum listened, and when Rachel had finished her rant, she was reassuring. 'It's only natural to argue during an engagement. Every couple does. You're looking for faults in the other person, and worrying about whether you can put up with them for the rest of your life. No one's perfect. We all have annoying habits – even you!'

Rachel swallowed. It was true. She wondered how Alex put up with her pickiness over clothes and decor. He was usually laid-back in those areas and let her make the decisions.

Her mum continued. 'You need to stop criticising the documentary. Remember, it's his career on the line. Next time he says something you consider tasteless, just button your lip.'

Rachel knew this was good advice.

'And let him bring whoever he wants to the party. Why can't it be a chance for him to invite his colleagues?'

Rachel didn't like the idea of their wedding being turned into a networking event, but she supposed the main thing was that he turned up, they both said their vows and became man and wife. All the rest was window-dressing.

When Alex called that evening, he was frustrated that a manager at the Villa Windsor had refused to give them an interview about Diana and Dodi's visit there on 30 August. He wouldn't confirm anything about it, either on or off the record.

'I've worked out that they could only have been there for around half an hour, so I'm guessing Diana took one look and said she didn't like the house and didn't want to live there,' he said.

'I read they were meeting an Italian interior designer,' Rachel mentioned.

'Yeah, I heard that too, but I don't think it's true. They would have been there much longer with a designer. Something else was going on and I'm determined to get to the bottom of it.'

'I wondered if it might be something to do with the bracelet with the heart on it,' she suggested. 'Diana was wearing it after their visit but not before.'

Alex was silent for a moment. 'How do you know?'

Rachel explained.

'Genius,' he said. 'Top marks for observation. I'll look into that.'

Pleased that he was in a better mood, Rachel tentatively suggested that they have a party at the flat, perhaps on the Saturday after the wedding, for those who couldn't be at the dinner.

'Don't you think that's a bit like having A-list and B-list guests?' Alex retorted.

'I don't think so. The eighteenth is about family and close personal friends, but the twentieth is the drinking and dancing bit that everyone likes best.'

'OK, I'll make up a list. But if you could drop some of your interminable aunts and cousins, that would help.'

When Rachel came off the phone, she stared at it for a few moments. There had been no questions about how she had spent her day, no mention of the argument, no words of affection. It was hard to feel close to him when the only topic filling his head was Princess Diana's death. Soon after they got together Alex had warned her that his previous relationships had tended to fail because of his obsessive attitude towards work but she had never known it to be like this.

Rachel was a self-sufficient type, and Alex seemed to appreciate that side of her. On holiday in Vietnam, when there was a mouse in their room, she was the one who trapped it in a wastebasket and got rid of it while he stood on the bed nervously giving directions; she was the one who did the DIY at home, and her knowledge of car mechanics far outstripped his. She had turned down his offer of money after the break-in and perhaps that made him feel she didn't need any support – but she did. It was partly her own fault; she hadn't told him about the huge financial pressure she was under. She had expected him to guess – and it seemed he hadn't.

When Rachel woke next morning, the weather had turned grey and overcast, with squally rain battering the windows and the cold forcing her to turn on the central heating for the first time that autumn. As she walked to the shop, her umbrella kept blowing inside out and the spokes bent backwards so that it was limp and bedraggled by the time she reached the North Laines. This was clearly the end of summer.

The shop was deathly quiet all morning, the door only opening when the postman dropped off some bills. Rachel sat poring over the accounts, trying to devise cost savings, and filled out an application for an extra credit card. She called the art director at Gazelle Films, the company that was looking for 1920s items, but was told abruptly that they couldn't consider any of her costumes without photographs and that their decisions would already be made by November. That was yet another blow. During the afternoon a couple of regular customers came in and browsed for five minutes, but she knew they wouldn't buy because she had nothing they hadn't seen before.

'I'll have new stock soon!' she called as they were leaving. Not soon enough, though. There was an auction in Reading the following week, and she could do another charity-shop trawl, but both would entail closing the shop since she couldn't afford to pay Nicola to be there.

Suddenly she thought of Susie Hargreaves. It had been over a month since Diana died. Would she be ready to make a date to clear out more clothes?

'I'm sorry I haven't been in touch,' Susie apologised. 'It's been a difficult time.'

'Of course. I understand.'

'I keep going to the phone absent-mindedly, thinking, "I must call Duch," then remembering I can't any more. Her death hasn't sunk in yet.'

'How was the funeral?' Rachel asked.

'I wept like a baby, but fortunately I was sitting behind some large military type who got between me and the cameras. His wife kept turning round and tutting at the noise I was making.' She gave a little laugh that had no mirth in it.

'I watched a bit on TV and it seemed a strange mixture of royal funeral and show-biz tribute. The scenes outside were extraordinary.'

'Diana was an extraordinary woman,' Susie said. 'But I suppose you're ringing about setting a date to come over and clear some cupboards?'

'I could use more stock, so it would really help me.'

'And I could use some cash. Let me find my diary.' She put the phone down and there was silence, punctuated by the sound of footsteps crossing a wooden floor.

Rachel tried to decide whether to mention Alex's documentary. At least it would prove to him that she was supportive of his career, even if Susie dismissed the idea out of hand.

When Susie picked up the phone again, Rachel ventured: 'I don't know if I mentioned that my partner, Alex, is a documentary maker? He's making a programme about Diana and I wondered if you would consider speaking to him.' There was silence on the line. 'Of course I'll completely understand if you don't want to. Sorry, just thought I'd mention it.'

When Susie spoke, her tone was cool. 'Have him fax through some information about his programme and I'll consider it.' She gave the fax number and Rachel jotted it down on the corner of a page in her accounts book.

'Thanks, Susie. And when do you want me to come to the house?'

'I'll get back to you,' she said, and hung up without saying goodbye.

Chapter 29

Brighton, 16 October 1997

ALEX WAS DELIGHTED THAT RACHEL HAD ASKED Susie about appearing in his documentary, but she was furious with herself, and deep down she felt cross with him for putting her in that position. It had been crass to mention it, and when days went by without any word, it looked as though it might have cost her a much-needed client.

Rachel began spending her mornings touring charity shops and antique markets in the wealthier districts of the south-east and only opening Forgotten Dreams at lunchtime. Each week she found a few saleable items, but trade remained slow and her fears mounted that she wouldn't be able to pay the rent at the end of October. Her only hope now was getting approval for the new credit card and withdrawing cash from it.

She still dreamed about Diana some nights and woke with a mixture of anxiety and guilt that coloured her mood for the day. She often thought about the Princess's sons and wondered how they were coping with the unthinkable loss. One was fifteen, the other twelve, she had read: old enough to comprehend the tragedy but too young to have any kind of adult perspective on it. Alex had been twelve when his mother died suddenly of a stroke. He had found her lying on the floor when he got home from school and had rung for an ambulance, but they couldn't save her.

When Rachel asked him about that period, early in their relationship, he told her he had a week off school before the funeral but was glad to return straight afterwards because it was ghastly being stuck in the house with his grieving dad. There were reminders everywhere of the loss: the empty chair at breakfast, her cosmetics in the bathroom, her coat in the hall. His father carried on, not dealing with practicalities for months on end.

At school, the teachers were unusually kind and Alex took advantage. He didn't get pulled up for skipping lessons, so he took to hiding in the bike shed having a fag with some older boys instead of doing double maths. When he tipped his lunch over a lad who was annoying him, they said it must have been an accident and there was no punishment.

'The sudden lack of boundaries was scary,' he said. 'As if I could do anything and no one would stop me. I felt as if I was floating and rootless, that nothing mattered any more. I wasn't suicidal but I remember thinking it wouldn't matter if I died too. Death can come to any of us at any time, so why worry about it? Does that make sense?'

She hugged him, her heart aching for the lost little boy he had been. 'What got you through it?'

He gazed out of the window before answering. 'I just shut Mum out of my head. It sounds cruel, but it was my way of coping. Then Wendy came on the scene, doing all the things that mums do – laundry, giving me lunch money – and I thought, "That's all right then." It wasn't until I was in my twenties that I allowed myself to think about my real mum again. By then the memories were distant and felt more manageable.'

Rachel wondered if Diana's boys were going through something similar. And she wondered if Alex's current volatility was because the parallels reminded him of that period in his own life. If so, he probably wasn't even aware of it.

She suddenly realised she had never seen a photo of Alex's mum, had no idea what she looked like. A thought popped into her head. She was driving out to Arundel one evening later that week to discuss the cake with Wendy. She could ask to see a photo of his mum then. Maybe if there was a particularly nice one she could blow it up and frame it as a wedding present from her.

~

'We don't have any prints,' Wendy told her as they sat at the kitchen table over mugs of Nescafé. A few undissolved granules floated on top of Rachel's coffee. 'Alex's dad had a camera that produced slides, so we've got a boxful of them and a little slide viewer. You're welcome to borrow them if you like. I think it's a lovely idea to give him a framed photo.'

She fetched the cardboard box, along with an old-fashioned grey plastic viewer. You slotted a slide in at the side and viewed it on the screen. There was little Alex posing in navy swimming trunks with a medal he had clearly just won, his ribs sticking out and his grin displaying a missing front tooth; by a riverbank proudly holding a tiny fish while wearing some wide flared jeans and a dodgy patterned shirt; hanging on grimly as he rode a donkey at an English seaside resort. The colours had an old-fashioned magenta tint.

'Isn't he cute?' Rachel laughed. 'He looks so happy. And cheeky.'

None of the slides had captions and lots showed people and scenes that neither she nor Wendy could identify.

'That's his mum,' Wendy said when they came to a shot of a blonde woman in a high-waisted 1960s bikini wearing huge

Jackie Kennedy sunglasses. She was holding up her palm in a 'Don't photograph me' gesture but laughing at the same time.

'She looks very chic,' Rachel commented.

'Yes, I believe she was,' Wendy agreed, obviously without any sense of insecurity about her own lack of interest in clothes. 'Feel free to borrow all the slides and have a look through. Now, shall I show you my idea for the cake?'

She shyly produced a picture she had found in a bridal magazine of a 1930s-style wedding cake. It was in three tiers, with festoons of pearls made of white icing around the sides and a spray of real orchids on top.

'I picked this one because I know the thirties is your favourite era, but if you don't like it, we can look for another.'

Rachel was stunned. She leaned across, grabbed Wendy and kissed her on the cheek. 'You genius! I am the fussiest person in the world, but this is perfect. It's simple and classic. I love it.'

Wendy grinned, clearly delighted. 'Oh good. I had an inkling you would.'

~

When he arrived home from Paris that Friday evening, Alex was whistling, his mood transformed. He produced a parcel wrapped in tissue paper from his case and kissed Rachel on the lips before handing it over. 'I saw this and thought you might like it. If not, you can sell it in the shop.'

She opened the paper to find a forest-green velvet turban with a paste brooch of pale green and amber stones on the front.

'It's gorgeous,' she remarked, looking inside for a label. 'Lanvin – *wow*!' She rushed to the hall mirror to try it on, tucking her short hair underneath except for a few tufts at the forehead. 'What a wonderful present. Thank you, darling.' She modelled it for him, then threw her arms round him. 'What did I do to deserve this?'

'Glad you like it. You've given me a present too, as it turns out. Susie Hargreaves has agreed to talk and we're going to film her next Tuesday. She suggested you might like to come. Said you could pick up more clothes.'

'I was sure she would refuse.' Rachel was delighted to hear that Susie was still prepared to do business with her, but alarmed by the prospect of the interview.

Alex flicked on the television, as he invariably did when he got home these days. 'I used the old charm . . . and money seemed to be a factor. She drove a hard bargain.'

'But she's so protective of Diana!'

Alex turned to her, frowning. 'And you think I'm going to trash her. Is that it?'

'No, of course not . . .'

He was defensive now. 'If I were Diana's friend and I suspected she'd been murdered, I'd be happy to help anyone investigating her death. The French police seem to have decided on day one that it was a drink-drive accident and are not exploring any other possibilities.'

Rachel went to the fridge to get him a beer, flipping the top off the bottle, then poured herself a vodka and tonic in her edelweiss glass. When she returned, she asked: 'Does Susie think Diana was murdered?'

'Thanks.' Alex took a sip of the beer. 'I haven't asked. She thinks we're going to talk about Diana's charity work – they were on some committee together. I'll warm her up gently and ask about the crash later.'

'So basically you've tricked her into agreeing?' Rachel was alarmed. She pulled the turban from her head and laid it on the table. There was a price tag on the back: 180 francs. Not bad if it was a Lanvin original, she noted; far too much for a replica.

'She didn't place any areas out of bounds. She knows what the media are interested in – and she needs the money.'

He turned up the sound as the news headlines were read out: the Queen and the Duke of Edinburgh were planning celebrations for their fiftieth wedding anniversary the following month. It seemed awfully soon after Diana's death for the royal family to be celebrating anything. Rachel wondered if she and Alex would ever get to their fiftieth anniversary: if they did, she'd be eighty-eight and he'd be eighty-nine. What kind of old people would they be? Crotchety ones, if the current atmosphere was anything to go by.

Chapter 30

London, 13 June 1931

ARY WAS KEEN TO SEARCH FOR THE TOMB OF A Kirk ancestor in Westminster Abbey, so one Saturday afternoon, while Wallis was at a dress fitting, Ernest took her there in his yellow Lagonda motor car. As they entered through the Great West Door, she got goose bumps all over and felt for a second as if she couldn't breathe.

'I had no idea it was so big . . . so magnificent,' she exclaimed, then immediately felt embarrassed. Of course it would be: all the British kings and queens had been crowned there since 1066, and many were entombed there.

Ernest was amused. 'We know how to do pomp and ceremonial in England; it's our speciality.'

As he led her around, he pointed out the cobweb-like fan vaulting in the Henry VII Chapel, the French-style tracery on the rose windows and the tall, slender proportions of the building. They stopped at Poets' Corner, examining the memorials to writers from Chaucer and Dryden through to Dickens and Mary's compatriot Henry James. They wandered for hours, not managing to find her ancestor but enjoying every moment.

Since Mary had shown such interest in the history of the monarchy, on 6 June Ernest arranged for the three of them to watch the Trooping of the Colour from private windows at the Admiralty, which offered a perfect view. First there was the procession of King George V and Queen Mary in state coaches, then Mary was enthralled as they inspected the troops in their dress uniforms glittering with gold.

'All this could be yours, Mary,' Wallis teased. 'Just think . . .' She turned to Ernest. 'Mary was crazy about the Prince of Wales when we were at school.'

'Mary is still a married woman, dear. I don't think it's our place to be matchmaking for her,' Ernest rebuked.

Mary had told Ernest about the problems in her marriage when they were on their own one evening. She liked the fact that he had not offered advice, had merely listened and sympathised. Wallis, on the other hand, was adamant that she should get divorced and find a new husband as soon as possible: preferably one hand-picked by her.

～

June flew by in a flurry of engagements and visits and Mary barely had time to think about Jacques. Wallis asked her to help pick some new furniture for Bryanston Court and they spent hours wandering round Heal's department store on Tottenham Court Road, sitting on four-poster beds to test their comfort and looking at the new Bauhaus chair designs of Mies van der Rohe made in chrome and leather.

'Very stylish,' Mary said, trying one, 'but not entirely comfortable. I like more padding.'

'Look at this.' Wallis waved her over to an old-fashioned dressing table in rococo style. 'I've seen these before,' she said. 'Watch.'

She slipped her gloved hand along the coving on the left underside of the dresser top until she triggered a hidden mechanism and a drawer sprang out. It was about six inches long by four wide and two deep, but when Mary pressed it back in there was no sign of it. You'd never have guessed it was there.

'How clever!' she remarked. 'But whatever would one keep in it?'

'Secrets, of course,' Wallis said. 'Everyone has secrets. Even you, Mary.'

Mary laughed, but the word did not have positive connotations for her. She thought of the syphilis Jacques had given her, and the wartime memories he would never talk about. Secrets were seldom good in her experience.

Wallis and Ernest made her feel so welcome that she began to consider whether she might move to London after the divorce and lease an apartment close to Bryanston Court. She got on equally well with both of them, sharing Ernest's intellectual interests and Wallis's love of sparkling conversation. Would they feel she was encroaching on their territory? She was sure they wouldn't.

And then one evening, as she left the guest room to join them for dinner, she heard them through the open door of the drawing room.

'Could you bring me a drink, darling?' Wallis asked, then there was the clink of a glass and the murmur of Ernest's voice before Wallis continued: 'Where's the house pest?'

Mary stopped dead in the hallway.

'Stop that!' Ernest snapped in a whisper. 'She might hear you.'

There was a sotto voce discussion. Mary felt herself flush scarlet. She turned and tiptoed to the bathroom, locking the door behind her, then perched on the edge of the bath, blood pounding in her ears.

Could Wallis have meant someone else? No. It had to be her. She was the house pest. She'd had absolutely no indication that she was outstaying her welcome. Did Ernest feel the same way? It was a horrible thought. She was so hurt, she felt like packing her trunk and leaving that very evening, but then they would know she had overheard. Instead, she decided to plead homesickness and bring forward the date of her return sailing.

She splashed some cool water on her cheeks, refreshed her lipstick, then took a deep breath before walking through to join her hosts, deliberately coughing so they would hear her approach.

'You can't possibly leave early,' Ernest protested, seeming completely sincere. 'I was planning to take you to Canterbury Cathedral this weekend. And then we are going to Paris next week, and you absolutely must see Paris.'

'Oh yes, do come to Paris, Mary,' Wallis pleaded. 'We can visit the fashion houses and see what's new for fall.'

Mary couldn't bring herself to look either of them in the face. She argued that she felt it was time for her to resolve matters with Jacques, but Wallis replied: 'What's another ten days? Come to Paris and you can change your sailing to leave from Cherbourg when I head down to the Côte d'Azur.' She was joining friends for a holiday in the South of France, while Ernest returned to London to work.

Their arguments were determined and their desire for her to stay seemed genuine, so Mary allowed herself to be persuaded. But in bed that night, when she thought of Wallis's casual words, two tears of humiliation trickled down her cheeks and the hurt nagged like a shard of broken glass in her heart.

~

As if they sensed her emotional withdrawal, both Ernest and Wallis showered Mary with generosity during her last days in London. Nothing was too much trouble, and both stressed how much they had enjoyed her visit and how strongly they hoped she would return soon. Guilty consciences, she thought to herself.

On arrival in Paris, she was pleased she had let herself be persuaded to come as soon as she saw the wide tree-lined boulevards, the iconic Eiffel Tower, and the *bouquinistes* selling antiquarian books on the banks of the Seine, where Ernest was soon lost in a world of his own. Mary had never been to the country of Jacques' birth, and she enjoyed hearing the language spoken all around, and sitting in street cafés with a large bowl of milky coffee and a type of pastry they called a *croissant*.

On their second day there they were invited to the apartment of Gloria Vanderbilt for a very pleasant luncheon. Gloria was the twin of Thelma Furness and had the same darkly exotic looks. Her seven-year-old daughter, also named Gloria, was there, and Mary enjoyed chatting to the girl, asking the names of her dolls and admiring their hand-stitched clothes.

As the three of them left the apartment, they stepped out to cross the street, Mary slightly ahead. Suddenly there was a screech of tyres, a shout, and Mary saw a speeding taxicab heading straight towards her. She had no time to leap out of its path, no time to react, before there was a thump and she was tossed into the air and landed in the gutter.

Isn't it strange I feel no pain? she thought, just before she lost consciousness.

Chapter 31

Paris, 2 July 1931

MARY FELT A SENSE OF MOTION AND OPENED HER eyes a fraction. There was a man she didn't recognise wearing a sort of uniform. That was odd. She was lying in some kind of moving vehicle. She rolled to the left as it turned a corner, and realised someone was holding her hand, clutching it tight. She opened her eyes further.

'Oh Mary, my God, I thought you were dead,' Wallis cried. Tears were rolling unchecked down her cheeks. 'Please don't die.'

Mary tried to speak but found it difficult. 'Won't,' she managed, before closing her eyes again, overcome with exhaustion.

When she next woke, she was in what was clearly a hospital, being lifted from a stretcher onto a crisp white bed. The sheets felt cold and the air smelled of disinfectant and starch. She wanted everyone to leave so she could sleep, but a doctor was ordering that she be X-rayed. He spoke with an American accent and Mary wondered if she had been unconscious for a while and had been shipped back to America.

'Where am I?' she mumbled, and a nurse in a white headdress replied: 'You're at the American Hospital in Neuilly. Your friends thought that was best. We all speak English here.'

Mary nodded. That was good.

After the X-ray, she was taken to a private room, where a doctor shone a light in her eyes, took blood from a vein in her arm, and generally poked and prodded her. She just wanted to sleep, and at some point told them so. She was dimly aware of Wallis and Ernest asking the doctor how she was, and she strained to listen.

'Damage to spine . . . emergency surgery to remove one kidney . . . condition critical . . . wait and see.'

Ernest, ever practical, was asking the questions and it sounded as though Wallis was still crying. Poor Wallie.

Mary slept again, and wakened in the dead stillness of night. There was no sound apart from a low hum of machinery. Outside the window the sky was dark, without so much as a hint of dawn. She turned her head and realised Wallis was still there, sitting in a chair by her bedside.

'Mary, darling,' she whispered. 'You're here. I'm so glad you're awake. Are you in pain?'

Mary shook her head, squeezed Wallis's fingers. 'Thank you for staying with me.'

'Of course I stayed with you!' Wallis exclaimed. 'You're the best friend I ever had and I couldn't bear to lose you. Do you have any idea how much I need you? I don't think you do.' She started crying again. Mary could see in the dim light filtering in from the hallway that her eyes were swollen.

She squeezed Wallis's hand again. 'You're not going to lose me.'

Wallis leant over the bed, sobbing. 'Promise me,' she managed to say, her words smothered in Mary's shoulder.

'I promise,' Mary said, before the veil of exhaustion fell again and she drifted off to sleep.

When she opened her eyes, she could tell it was morning from the shafts of brilliant sunlight slanting into the room.

'Hello, Mary,' said a man's voice, and she was startled to see Ernest sitting in the chair beside her. She felt self-conscious that she was wearing only a hospital gown.

'Where's Wallis?' she murmured, her lips parched and throat dry.

'She's gone to change but she'll be back soon. She's terribly distressed. We all are. I cabled your mother and Jackie, and Jackie wanted to catch the next sailing but I persuaded him to wait until there's more news of your condition. He has cabled his Aunt Minnie to come and look after you. She'll be here later in the day.'

Mary frowned. She had only met Jacques' aunt once before, when she visited New York. She liked her but did not know her well. Still, she supposed Minnie was her closest relative on this side of the Atlantic.

'Can I get you anything?' Ernest asked.

'Water,' she begged, and he poured a glass from a jug by her bed and held it to her lips while she took a sip. Close up, Mary could see brown shadows under his eyes. Was he worried about her? Ernest was always so self-possessed, it was hard to tell what he was thinking.

'You've given us quite a fright, old girl,' he said, trying for a lightness of tone. 'Glad to see you are still with us.'

'You know me,' Mary managed to reply. 'I never like to be the first to leave a good party.'

~

By the time Aunt Minnie arrived, wearing a voluminous umber dress that swept the ground as she walked, Mary had been pronounced out of danger. There was no need for emergency surgery on her kidneys, which appeared to be functioning again, but the doctor warned that it was likely to be a long, gruelling convalescence because of the spinal injury she had incurred. She had stitches to cuts on her arms and legs, a giant bruise on her forehead, and every part of her body ached.

'You go join your friends and enjoy your holiday,' she told Wallis. 'I'll be fine. If I'm still here when you're travelling back to London, drop in and bring me a KT.'

'Yes, you go,' Aunt Minnie urged. 'I'll rent an apartment near the hospital and stay with Mary until she's well enough to sail home.'

'I can't . . . I feel as though the accident was my fault,' Wallis insisted. 'It should have been me.'

Mary smiled. 'What kind of twisted logic is that, Wallie? You should have stepped in front of me and got hit instead? You prize idiot! No, I insist you have your holiday. I'll write and describe my progress in tedious detail.'

Later that afternoon, two nurses held Mary as she swung her legs to the floor to try and stand for the first time. There was a sickening pain on either side of her lower back and pins and needles shot down her legs, worse on the right side. She willed her feet to move one in front of the other but it felt as if the signals from her brain were not getting through. Eventually she managed one step before collapsing back onto the bed.

'One step today, two tomorrow,' Minnie soothed. 'We'll get through this. Never fear.'

Ernest came that evening to say goodbye. He had to return to London for work the following morning. Everyone else had left the room so they managed a few words alone.

'What will you do when you get back to New York?' he asked. 'About your marriage, I mean.'

In the forty-eight hours since her accident there had already been several heartfelt cables from Jacques, saying how much he loved her, that he couldn't lose her, and promising the earth if she would just come back to him.

'I'm going to see if it can be fixed,' she said.

He nodded and cleared his throat, but did not meet her eyes.

Chapter 32

West Sussex, 21 October 1997

ON TUESDAY MORNING, RACHEL AGREED TO DRIVE ALEX to Susie's house near Chichester, while the cameraman and sound man travelled from London with their equipment. Her car was a 1938 Lancia with sleek curves and diagonal grilles on the wings, like the gills on a fish. It was a beautiful vehicle, with a taupe exterior and pale grey leather seats, but something of a money pit that spent a lot of time in the garage for repairs, and this particular morning it was reluctant to start.

'For God's sake, when are you going to trade it in for one that actually works?' Alex huffed, glancing at his watch.

'It's not worth much unless I could afford to put in a new engine. The original number plates were valuable but I sold them to finance the last repairs I had done to the bodywork. Besides, I love my car.'

Patience was the best tactic when it wouldn't start. It was easy to flood the engine with repeated attempts, but after waiting a few minutes she was able to coax the motor to turn over and they set off.

Since the car crash in Paris she always felt a flutter of anxiety about driving, remembering the way Diana and Dodi's Mercedes had crumpled on impact with the tunnel wall, like tissue paper in a fist. She turned on an easy-listening radio station for distraction. Alex was busy scribbling in the notebook he carried while she hummed along to Fleetwood Mac and Simon & Garfunkel.

Suddenly she thought of the first time she took Alex out in the car, a grey January day when on a whim they drove to Whitstable to eat oysters at a restaurant on the beach. He'd ordered an expensive bottle of wine and they sat getting drunk and talking for hours then had to find a room for the night because she was way over the limit. A gale was blowing as they walked the dark streets, wrapped in each other's arms, shrieking with laughter as they were buffeted in the wind, and it came to her in a flash of clarity that she was in love. It was terrifying and exhilarating at the same time. She glanced round at Alex and smiled at the memory.

Susie came out to meet them as they scrunched to a halt in her gravel-covered driveway, and Rachel made the introductions. The crew were already waiting inside.

'Have you been on television before?' Alex asked as they walked into the entrance hall. Susie said no, never, and he seemed surprised. 'You've chosen the perfect outfit: I love the simple neckline of your dress with the lovely red colour complementing your hair. It will look terrific on screen.'

'Thank you.'

It was true: the sienna shade of her dress went well with her highlighted blonde hair, which she wore in a short feathered style, not dissimilar to the cut Diana used to have.

He stopped in the wood-panelled hallway. 'Is this oak? I love the curve of the banister. The house looks like a Sir John Soane design. Am I right?'

'I think it was an imitator rather than the great man himself, and bits have been added over the years. It's rather a mishmash.' Susie glanced around with obvious pride.

'It doesn't look it to me. Now, did you have an idea of where you would like to sit for the interview? Perhaps you wouldn't mind giving me a mini tour?'

Susie was happy to show him around, and Rachel followed, fascinated to see bits of the house she hadn't visited before. The main drawing room had ceiling-height picture windows looking over the sweeping lawn, and a huge fireplace with carved marble pillars on either side; the long dining-room table, which would easily seat twenty, was overlooked by a tapestry featuring a unicorn in a forest; the morning room had a window seat scattered with blue cushions that looked like a comfortable place to curl up with a novel or the morning paper. None of the rooms had a television set, she noticed. All except the kitchen were furnished largely in eighteenth-century style.

They settled on a corner of the drawing room beneath a portrait Susie told them was of her grandmother, a woman in a high-necked brown dress with a cameo brooch at the collar, her hair pulled into a severe bun. 'It was painted by my late grandfather,' Susie told them, and Rachel saw the signature *R. Hargreaves* in one corner and the date '32.

Rachel could tell Susie liked Alex. She seemed relaxed as he talked her through the procedures, laughing at the little jokes that Rachel guessed he used on every interviewee.

'If I ask some questions twice,' Alex explained, 'don't assume it's early-onset dementia. Just answer as though I haven't asked you before and we'll choose the best take.'

His cameraman, Kenny, took light readings, and the sound man, Pete, attached a tiny microphone to the collar of Susie's dress.

'Let me powder your forehead and nose,' Alex said, then patted her face with a giant puff. 'We don't want you too shiny.'

'Shall I leave the room?' Rachel asked, wondering if Susie might feel self-conscious.

'I'll be fine so long as you don't heckle.' Susie smiled.

The camera was switched on and Alex positioned himself out of shot, where he would ask the questions.

'I wonder if you could tell me how you and Princess Diana met?' he began.

'I've known her all my life,' Susie replied in her Home Counties accent. 'Our mothers came out together back in 1953 – at a time when that phrase meant something quite different than it does now.' She chuckled.

'They were debutantes,' Alex prompted.

'Yes, then they remained friends once they were married and had babies. They didn't live close – the Spencers were in Norfolk – but we visited from time to time, or they visited us. Mostly in summer. Duch and I were the same age and we liked playing with dolls. Both of us loved animals, so that was a bond.'

'Duch – is that what you called Diana?'

Rachel was fascinated to see Alex in professional mode, already thinking about how each answer would work in the final programme.

'Everyone called her Duch when she was little. Short for Duchess, I suppose. It suited her.'

'And you maintained that friendship as adults?'

Susie nodded. 'Diana was a tremendously loyal friend. If she heard you were ill, there were always flowers and fruit baskets delivered, and she wrote the most touching notes. Of course, she was terribly busy after she got married, so years went by when we scarcely saw each other, but recently we were both working for the Leprosy Mission.'

'Tell me about your work there,' Alex prompted, and she spoke passionately about the possibility of eradicating the disease one day, while providing support for current sufferers. Rachel guessed he would not be using this section of the interview in his programme, and it made her cross on Susie's behalf.

'The news of her death must have come as a terrible shock,' Alex said. 'Could you tell me how you heard?'

Susie looked down, composing herself for a few moments before she answered. 'I don't watch television or read newspapers so I didn't know until the following morning, when a friend rang to offer condolences. I couldn't believe it at first. I was sure she must be mistaken, but I rang Ken Palace and they confirmed it.'

Her voice was very quiet and the sound man glanced at Alex, but he shook his head slightly. It wasn't a good time for a retake.

'When did you last speak to her?'

Susie was clearly emotional when she answered, her voice wobbling. 'A couple of weeks before she died. She was happy. Said she was having the most wonderful summer.'

'Was that because of Dodi Al-Fayed?'

Susie nodded slowly. 'I think so.'

'Was she in love with him?'

Susie frowned. 'She was clearly enjoying herself. That's all I know.'

'Do you think it's true they were engaged?' Alex's tone invited confidence.

'I have no idea.' Rachel could tell Susie was uncomfortable because she was fidgeting with her sleeve.

Alex asked: 'Do you think she could have been pregnant?'

Her head snapped up and she glowered at him. 'Absolutely not. Do you really think the mother of the heir to the throne would not be scrupulously careful about that? She was far smarter than any of you lot give her credit for . . .' She shook her head. 'Anyway, I don't want to talk about this. Can we move on?'

Alex signalled to Kenny to stop the camera. 'Let's take a break for a moment. You're doing a great job, Susie: you're speaking naturally and managing to ignore the camera. Most people are terribly self-conscious at first, but this is wonderful. I know it must be difficult for you.' He moved his chair closer. 'Would you like a glass of water before we carry on?'

She shook her head. 'There's something I wanted to ask you.' She looked at Alex. 'Rachel told me you were in the tunnel and that you went to the car to translate for Diana. I wonder if you could tell me what you said? How she was?'

'Of course,' Alex agreed. He paused to gather his thoughts, then began. 'She was conscious when I got there. Her eyelashes were flickering as she breathed through an oxygen mask the doctor had placed over her face, and occasionally she opened her eyes slightly. The doctor told her she had been in a car accident and I added: "Don't worry, Your Royal Highness; you're not seriously hurt."'

Susie gave a little squeak and a solitary tear trickled down her cheek. 'Carry on.'

'The doctor reassured her that an ambulance was on the way. I guessed she would be able to tell that the photographers were there and would be worried about the pictures getting out, so I told her the police were rounding them up and taking their film away.'

At that, Susie started crying properly and Rachel hurried over to hand her a tissue. She was surprised Alex hadn't mentioned this to her at the time.

'After that I just kept telling her to stay calm and that she would be fine. I continued reassuring her until the ambulance crew took over.'

Susie blew her nose. 'She would be happy you called her HRH. It was outrageous that she was stripped of the title after her divorce. I'm sorry about the waterworks. I'm still finding it hard to accept.'

'She wasn't in any pain,' Alex said quietly.

That was the final straw. Susie burst into fits of sobbing, covering her face with her hands. Alex put a hand on her shoulder and let her cry.

'Shall I go and make tea for everyone?' Rachel suggested. She couldn't bear to watch Susie's distress from the sidelines, but she knew Alex would not thank her for intervening. It was his show. Susie nodded agreement, dabbing her eyes with the tissue, clearly struggling to control herself.

Rachel left the room, and when she returned five minutes later with a tray, Susie was composed, her make-up had been touched up and the interview was under way again. Pete put a finger to his lips as she tiptoed into the room and placed the tray on a table with a slight rattle of cups.

Alex had reached the controversial area of his questioning. 'Because of her relationship with Dodi, some sources are suggesting that Diana could have been killed by people who did not want her to marry a Muslim. What do you make of that?'

Rachel blinked. How would Susie know?

'She did worry that she might be bumped off, but not because of the religion of her boyfriend. Her divorce got rather heated and she was anxious that what she called "grey men" might try to get rid of her one day – but that was patently ridiculous.'

'She didn't mention that any anti-Muslim sentiments had been expressed to her?'

'Absolutely not.'

Alex consulted his notes, turned a page in his book. 'On arrival in Paris, Diana and Dodi went to the Villa Windsor, the Duchess of Windsor's old house. Do you have any idea why?'

Susie placed a hand over her mouth and seemed on the verge of tears again. Alex continued with his questioning. 'Do you think she and Dodi were considering living there?'

'I don't know why you are asking me about this . . . How would I know?'

Susie stood up suddenly, tugging at the microphone. Pete leapt forward to help her, scared she might break it.

'I didn't mean to upset you.' Alex rose and placed a hand on her arm.

'I'm afraid that's all I can tell you.' Seeming very distressed, she yanked her arm away and rushed from the room.

Rachel ran after her. 'Susie, what is it?'

Alex had followed too. 'Would you like to take a break for half an hour? I only have a few more questions.'

Susie was hurrying up the stairs. When she reached the first floor, she turned back. 'I'm not answering any more. I should never have agreed to this. Please will you leave.'

She disappeared into a bedroom and closed the door hard. Rachel looked at Alex. He was scrolling through his notes, frowning in concentration.

'We'd better stop, guys,' he said to Pete and Kenny. 'That's a wrap.'

~

In the car on the way home, Rachel concentrated on her driving, upset about what had happened. She had closed the shop for the day in the hope of picking up more stock, and was coming back empty-handed all because Alex had upset Susie with his tactless questioning.

He either did not pick up on her mood or chose to ignore it. Most of the way back he was taking calls on his mobile: making decisions, setting up meetings, checking flight times. It appeared he was flying to Paris that evening to interview someone the following morning.

He got cut off mid conversation as he lost signal in a dip in the road, and after calling, 'Hello? Hello?' into the ether for a few moments he gave up.

'You never told me what you said to Diana in the car,' Rachel commented. 'Susie obviously found it very moving.' Could he have invented it? Somehow it sounded too glib.

He seemed puzzled. 'I'm sure I told you that night, in the hotel.'

'I would remember if you had.'

He shrugged. 'It was a surreal night. I'm not sure I remember everything we talked about.'

Rachel was silent and Alex continued: 'I think Susie knows something she's not telling us. Did you get that impression?'

Rachel didn't answer. The whole interview had been excruciating for her. It had felt horribly manipulative, almost as if Alex had been trying to make Susie cry for the cameras. Surely he wouldn't do that? If he would, then he wasn't the man she'd thought he was.

Chapter 33

Brighton, 22 October 1997

ATER, WHEN RACHEL PONDERED THE ABRUPT END of the interview with Susie, something niggled: it seemed as though it was the mention of Villa Windsor that had upset her the most. Alex had asked many more intrusive questions than that. Why had she leapt from her seat and refused to carry on when he asked if Diana and Dodi were thinking of living there? Did she know more about the visit than she was admitting?

On her way to Forgotten Dreams the next morning, Rachel stopped at a bookshop and bought one of the biographies of Diana that were stacked high on the table nearest the door. When she got to her shop, she made a cup of tea then checked the index.

There was just one entry for Hargreaves: a mention that when Diana's mother, Frances Shand Kydd, left her father, Earl Spencer, she had stayed for a while with her old friend Elizabeth Hargreaves at their home near Chichester. In the court case that ensued, Frances lost custody of her children after her own mother, Lady Fermoy, testified against her, calling her 'a bolter'. Women weren't supposed to leave marriages in the 1960s, it seemed, no matter how unhappy.

There was nothing about the Villa Windsor. Rachel closed the book and checked the time: 10 a.m. Not too early to phone. She dialled Susie's number.

'I just wanted to check you were OK,' she began. 'And to say sorry the interview was gruelling.'

'Honestly, don't worry,' Susie replied. 'I'm so emotional at the moment, I burst into tears at the drop of a hat.'

'I hope you weren't upset by Alex's questions . . .' Rachel twirled the cord of the phone in her fingers.

'No, I'm not an idiot. I knew that was what he would be looking for. The story of Diana's charity work is not nearly as attractive to the media as tittle-tattle about her romances. That was always the case when she was alive and it remains true now. Poor Diana. She had terrible luck with men.' There was a pause, as if she was inviting Rachel to ask more.

'Did she often confide in you about her love life?' Rachel held her breath, worried that Susie might find the question intrusive, but she didn't appear to.

'Sometimes, yes. She was stuck in a terrible pattern of picking wrong 'uns, then getting needy and anxious and driving them away. You know her mother left home when she was six? I always think it's harder for those who've lost a parent in child-hood to form healthy relationships in later life.'

That was Alex, Rachel mused. He lost a parent. But he certainly didn't come across as needy or anxious. Out loud, she asked: 'Do you think it might have worked with Dodi?'

'I have no idea if he would have been the one to break the mould, but he seemed nice. I'm just glad she was happy in her final weeks.' Her voice trembled.

Rachel remembered the other reason for her phone call. 'We didn't have a chance to go through any clothes. Do you want to set a date?'

'How about Friday?' Susie suggested.

Rachel couldn't afford to close the shop on a Friday; it was one of her busier days, when women were seeking new outfits for the weekend. She would have to ask Nicola to help for the first time since the break-in. 'Let me check and get back to you,' she said.

'I can't do Friday,' Nicola replied straight away.

'What's up? Have you got a hot date?' Rachel asked. Nicola usually found her next boyfriend soon after the door closed on the last.

'I should be so lucky,' Nicola replied. 'No, I'm going to London for the day. Sorry.'

Rachel rang Susie back. 'I can't get cover for Friday. Is there another time you can manage?'

'Why not come this evening?' Susie suggested. 'You can drive across after the shop closes. I'll even throw in a light supper.'

That was a relief: it meant there was no residual awkwardness over Alex's interview; it sounded as though she still wanted to be friends.

Rachel spent the afternoon cleaning the shop, washing the window inside and out, dusting and polishing shelves, and as she worked her mind strayed back to her recent arguments with Alex. Combined with the stress of trying to save the shop, they were wearing her down. The interview with Susie had revealed a side of him she disliked: he had come across as ruthless, using her for his own purposes rather than treating her as a woman who had recently lost a close friend. It was as if his brain had been infected by this crash conspiracy nonsense and he thought everyone who couldn't see his point of view was stupid.

Had he invented the words he claimed to have said to Diana while she was trapped in the car? That would be unforgivable. Rachel felt as if he was losing sight of the fact that this had been a tragedy in which three human beings had died and one had been seriously injured. He should be more respectful. In her view, he shouldn't be making this programme at all.

~

Later, when Alex called from Paris, she mentioned that she had spoken to Susie, and that she had recovered from her earlier distress.

He snapped back: 'Are you implying that she was distressed because of the nasty questions I tricked her into answering? Why are you always having a go at me these days?'

'That's not fair!' she protested.

'I could really use your support right now, but perhaps that's too much to ask.'

'It was my introduction that got you the interview in the first place.' He wouldn't have heard of Susie without her, because she wasn't one of the Sloane set with whom Diana used to be photographed having lunch in Fulham restaurants; she wasn't mentioned in the biography Rachel had bought.

Alex wasn't finished. 'I keep getting the feeling you're criticising me from your lofty position of moral superiority. It's not your most attractive quality.'

Rachel gasped at the criticism. She opened her mouth to snap that she thought what he was doing was shoddy, but stopped herself just in time. She would talk to him at the weekend rather than having a full-scale argument on the phone.

'I'm flying back on Thursday evening,' Alex told her, 'but I'll stay at Kenny's in London so I can get to the office first thing Friday morning.'

'Nicola's got some secret mission in London on Friday,' Rachel told him. 'Maybe you two could catch the train together.'

'Has she?' he asked, and she could tell from a false note in his voice that he already knew. That was odd.

'Do you have any idea what it's about? She avoided telling me.'

'Haven't a clue!' Alex replied, then made a feeble excuse to get off the phone before she could question him further.

Rachel mulled it over and decided they must be planning a wedding surprise for her. Maybe Nicola was helping him to choose a special present. If that was the case, she wished they would tell her. Even as a child, she had never been keen on surprises.

Chapter 34

Paris, 9 July 1931

MARY WAS RELEASED FROM THE AMERICAN Hospital after a week of treatment, still unable to stagger more than a couple of steps on her own. She moved into the apartment Aunt Minnie had leased, where a nurse came to massage her legs and back every day, then supported her as she tried to relearn how to walk. She still had debilitating pins and needles down her legs, especially the right one, and the summer heat made her feel constantly exhausted and enervated.

One bright spot was getting to know Jacques' aunt. Minnie was an artist, and she often sat in the square opposite their apartment painting the trees, the buildings and the passers-by, using thick brushstrokes and bold colours. She was also a wonderful cook, who made chicken roasted with whole bulbs of garlic and steaks in pepper sauce, buying all the ingredients fresh from the market each day. Mary grew plump with her forced inactivity and had to find a dressmaker to let out her clothes. Ernest sent parcels of books from London, so she was never short of reading material, and letters came regularly from the Côte d'Azur, enquiring anxiously about her progress.

I still feel very shocked by your accident, Wallis wrote, *and the realisation that I came so close to losing you. It's made me wary of going out on the hairpin roads around here with their vertiginous drops to the sea. Instead, I'm spending my summer quietly on the beach by the house and dining at local restaurants.*

'That's not like her at all,' Mary commented to Minnie. 'She's usually only happy in a crowd.'

They often talked about Jacques, and Minnie told her how adorable he had been as a little boy, how he charmed everyone with his happy nature. It made Mary nostalgic for the man she had fallen in love with, the chivalrous pilot who'd brought her French perfume and pale yellow roses, and played her French music on his phonograph.

'Did he ever mention that he was a war hero?' Minnie asked, and Mary was astonished. 'No, I'm sure he didn't,' Minnie answered herself. 'He never speaks of it, but he was awarded a medal for rescuing a fellow pilot from a burning plane. He felt he didn't deserve it because he said any of them would have done the same.'

'I've never seen a medal among his possessions.' Mary was wide-eyed at this new insight into her husband.

'He told me once, near the beginning of the war, that he'd seen some appalling sights; when their fuel tanks exploded, the airmen's faces melted like candle wax and their screams were like those of wild animals rather than human beings. Then he stopped talking about it, but I know that each one of those pilots was braced to die an agonising death whenever they took to the air. And yet after the war, they were expected to return to normal family life and forget all about it.' She shook her head at the ludicrousness of the notion.

'He won't ever speak about the war. I've asked many times,' Mary said.

'I just want to explain to you: I'm sure he is not the only man who used the bottle to try and forget. Have some patience with him.'

By September, when Mary was judged fit to sail home, she was looking forward to seeing Jacques and hopeful that the four months' separation plus the shock of her accident would bring about a real change in their marriage.

She could still only walk with the help of sticks, so Jacques came on board to help her hobble down onto the quay.

'I will never, ever drink again,' he told her in the taxicab back to Washington Square. 'I want us to pretend we are newly-weds starting afresh. And I want us to try for another baby. Can we do that?'

She looked at him and saw a man with a ruddy complexion, thickened waistline, thinning hair and eyes that had lost their zest, but underneath it all he was still her Jacques, her first love. 'Yes, let's try,' she said, and meant it.

Lovemaking had to be cautious because of Mary's back problems. She could lie on one side but not the other, and sometimes sciatica caused a sensation like an electric shock to travel down her leg, making her kick out involuntarily. Jacques learned to massage her the way the nurse had done in Paris, and he was especially tender when touching her scars. He was trying, but Mary didn't feel like a newly-wed; somehow that spark had gone.

If only she could have a baby, she would never leave Jacques because she would not deprive the child of its father. But she was thirty-five years old and it was probably too late. Every time her monthly bleed came, she fell into a depression. She loved him, but if they weren't going to have a child, she wasn't sure she loved him enough to grow old with him. Was that terrible of her? If she left, what would she do with her life? She could not go back to work in the shop because she couldn't stand up for long. And she could not move to London, because no matter how affectionate Wallis was being now, the stinging hurt of being called the 'house pest' had not faded.

~

From Wallis's letters that winter, it was clear that she and Ernest were becoming more of a fixture in the Prince of Wales's social circle. They even entertained him and Thelma at Bryanston Court in January 1932, and Wallis wrote listing the menu for Mary: black bean soup, lobster, fried chicken and a raspberry soufflé. She felt proud of her cook, she wrote; everything had gone exactly as planned. Mary smiled, knowing that Wallis would have run the entire event with military precision, with nothing left to chance.

Soon afterwards, the Prince invited Ernest and Wallis to spend a weekend at his home, Fort Belvedere, near Windsor, and she wrote describing the visit:

> *He wore a kilt, for goodness' sake! I have been in Britain some years but still can't get used to the sight of a man in a skirt. This impression of femininity was compounded when I came downstairs to find him working at some needlepoint, making a cover for his backgammon set. What can one say? He is the Prince of Wales, and can do as he wishes.*

She described the Fort – *like an enchanted castle* – and the two Cairn terriers, Cora and Jaggs, that Wallis had to pretend to like: *You know me, Mary. I find dogs rather unhygienic, but when in Rome . . .* Ernest got along marvellously with their host over a shared love of history: *dates and circumstances were flying back and forth across the table like ping-pong balls.* Mary was glad of that. Ernest needed his intellectual stimulation, and he was proud of his English heritage so was bound to feel honoured by their connection with royalty.

It was a difficult year for Mary and Jacques, with the aftermath of the Wall Street Crash continuing to restrict their financial situation. Mary consulted a specialist about her failure to get pregnant, and was told that he could not rule out the accident in Paris having caused some long-term damage to her innards that would make conception difficult or perhaps impossible. She was devastated by this news. All she asked for was a child, and it seemed her last chance might have been stolen by a distracted taxi driver in a random moment. Anger burned inside her like a hot coal, but she kept the news from Jacques. He seemed preoccupied with his work, as deal after deal fell through. The first time he came home in the evening with the smell of wine on his breath, she did not even comment. She'd been expecting it.

In March 1933, Mary was overjoyed when Wallis came to stay for a few days, on a quick trip to see her Aunt Bessie. She arrived like a tornado, blasting fresh air and energy into the household, and entertaining them with gossip from London.

'We visit the Prince's home most weekends when he is not off "princing",' she told them. 'Thelma seems to appreciate my help in entertaining the crowd. The Prince is trying to tempt me to take up needlework, but I told him, "Where I grew up, the help take care of that."'

Jacques handed Wallis a bourbon with water and poured himself a glass of wine, 'just to keep her company'. Mary noted this but did not comment, and Wallis seemed to forget that Mary had written to her of his promise never to drink again.

'How do you pass weekends at the Fort?' Mary asked.

Wallis sipped her drink, smiling slowly. 'We go for walks, play cards, do the most fiendish jigsaw puzzles, and in the evening there is often dancing. The Prince is a good dancer, light on his feet, with a true sense of rhythm.'

'It sounds as though your admiration for him is growing,' Mary probed. 'I wasn't sure if you liked him before.'

Wallis cocked her head to one side. 'He's a strange man.'

Mary was curious. 'In what way strange?'

'He's most particular: he will only eat certain foods prepared in a certain way, and generally eats very little at all; he's very keen on exercise in the fresh air and windows being kept open even in freezing-cold weather; and his clothes must be just so, with no creases. Should he get the slightest mark on a sleeve, he will rush to change, even if it means holding up dinner for everyone else. I suppose when you are a prince you become accustomed to people pandering to your whims.'

Mary noticed that while Wallis was speaking, the level of drink in Jacques' glass had risen from almost empty to two-thirds full. He was sitting beside the table on which the bottle stood and must have topped it up surreptitiously.

'I shouldn't speak ill of him,' Wallis continued. 'He's a charming host and has been most generous to us. Look at this!' She fished in a pocket of her suit and handed Mary a folded sheet of paper, cream with green letterhead. There was a tiny smile on her lips.

Mary opened it to find a typed radiogram message: *Wishing you a safe crossing and a speedy return to England. Edward P.*

'Is that from the *Prince*? To *you*?' Mary exclaimed. 'I had no idea you were so close.'

'He's such a darling. It arrived just as the ship was about to sail, and all the crew heard of it so I enjoyed the most flattering attention during the crossing. It's good to have friends in high places!'

Mary looked closely at Wallis, trying to fathom what was going on in her head, but her expression was inscrutable and she soon changed the subject to ask Jacques about the Manhattan property market.

Later that evening, Mary crept into Wallis's room in her nightgown, just as Wallis was cleaning her face with cold cream, massaging it upwards along the jawline.

'Don't you find ageing so dispiriting?' Wallis asked, regarding her reflection in the mirror. 'No, perhaps you don't. You still have not a hint of a wrinkle, while I fight a daily battle against the collapse of my entire face.'

Mary laughed. 'Don't be silly. No one would guess you to be a day over thirty.'

'And yet we will both be forty in a few years. Positively ancient!'

'You seem full of high spirits. Are you enjoying your place in the top echelon of English society?' She sat on the bed just behind Wallis, watching her expression in the mirror.

'Money's been a bore. Shipping is in the doldrums and we've had to cut back on entertaining and the purchase of new clothes. I haven't been to the Paris collections for the last two seasons and feel a positive frump!' She used a pad of cotton to pat the cream from her face.

'But you enjoy your time with the Prince. Tell me, do you find him attractive?'

Wallis whirled round. 'Goodness, no. Not in the romantic sense.'

Mary narrowed her eyes, suddenly sure that Wallis *was* after the Prince, but that she had not admitted it to herself. For someone who was insecure about her family background and her financial circumstances, what greater coup could there be than adding him to her list of conquests? She would win his heart if she got the chance, not because she had fallen for him but because it would make her feel better about herself.

Poor Ernest. What would he think of it? Would he stand being cuckolded the way Thelma's husband had? She felt troubled for him.

Wallis gave a beaming smile and threw her arms round Mary, laying her head on her shoulder. 'It's so good to see you. Whenever I visit you, wherever we both are, it always feels like home.'

Chapter 35

New York, November 1933

AFTER WALLIS'S VISIT, THE REMAINDER OF 1933 was hard for Mary. Her father died suddenly, of a heart attack, and her mother, Edith, simply fell apart. She couldn't adjust to life without him, but sat crying all day long, without eating, without dressing properly. As the childless daughter, the responsibility for looking after their mother fell to Mary, even though she was still suffering brutal back pain from her accident that made it hard to sleep at night.

'I can't leave her on her own,' she told Jacques. 'I must stay with her in Baltimore until she has begun to build a new life for herself.'

'Why not bring her here, to Washington Square?' he suggested. 'I can help you to entertain her, and you will not be cut off from your own home and friends.'

Mary thought this a generous offer: what man would relish the prospect of his mother-in-law moving in? Jacques was kind to Edith, sitting down to make conversation with her and always remaining patient with her tears and fretting – something Mary found increasingly trying. But he had begun drinking the best part of a bottle of red wine at dinner, and often he went out to join friends in the Village afterwards.

Mary watched the level of the bottles silently at first, but finally she confronted him. 'You have broken your word to me,' she said. 'I was clear that this was your last chance.'

'It's only wine,' Jacques argued, as if that made everything all right. 'I never drink spirits.'

'It still has the effect of making you unpleasant company,' she told him. 'I love you, Jacques, but I can't live like this. I know you had a terrible time in the war – Minnie told me about it and I sympathise – but I can't bear it.'

'It's got nothing to do with the war . . .'

Mary continued: 'A failed marriage is the last thing I ever wanted, but I can't spend the rest of my life with a drinker. We tried our best, but I think we both know it is over.'

He began to cry. 'Please, Mary. Don't do this.'

She comforted him but felt sure of her decision. 'We need not divorce, at least not straight away. We can continue to live in the house together, but I want you to move into the study. From now on, I will sleep alone.'

It was a crushing disappointment, but Mary found she was more upset about giving up the idea of having a child than about the end of her marriage. She wasn't angry with Jacques; she believed he had done his best to stop drinking and simply could not manage. She still cared what happened to him but she no longer loved him as a wife should.

Just a month after her father's death, Mary took her mother to a doctor, hoping to set her mind at rest about some unusual pains she claimed to be experiencing. Instead, the doctor diagnosed cancer, and a struggle began that consumed Mary for most of 1934. She was in constant pain from her back and still grieving for her father, and for the end of her marriage, when she had to nurse her mother through a painful and inexorable decline.

Wallis wrote offering her sympathies and reporting on the latest news from London:

Thelma Furness has returned to the States for a couple of months and asked me to help entertain the Prince in her absence, but already I find it a chore. He can be exhausting even when one is not his mistress because he needs a woman to help plan his entertainments, his decorative schemes at the Fort, even his ideas for international trade deals! Dear Ernest is being immensely patient about the amount of time the Prince requires of me.

Mary bumped into Thelma at Mona Van der Heyden's cocktail party in New York one February evening, and they greeted each other warmly. Thelma was wearing a flouncy shoulderless ball gown that threatened to slide down and expose her breasts if she moved too suddenly. With her smooth golden skin, shiny black hair and stunning features, she was every bit the Latin temptress.

'Are you missing London?' Mary asked. 'Or is it good to be home?'

'I was born in Switzerland,' Thelma replied, 'and grew up in Buenos Aires, so I'm never quite sure where home is. But I will always love New York. It's more modern than anywhere else. It makes Londoners seem stuck in the past.'

'I like that about them: those ancient buildings and all the traditions they preserve.'

'You would soon get fed up with the ritual in royal circles, believe me.' Thelma leaned in close, speaking confidentially. 'It's quite a bore.'

'I hear Wallis is keeping an eye on the Prince during your absence,' Mary ventured. 'Does he need much looking after?'

Thelma's dark eyes twinkled with mirth. 'I get six phone calls a day as a minimum, all of them about ridiculous details. The way they breed their royals in England seems to make them peculiarly incapable of taking decisions or coping with the modern world.'

'So you came here for a rest?' Mary smiled.

'Something like that.'

They were joined by other guests and the topic of conversation moved on, but Mary snuck a look at Thelma several times during the evening, wondering if she had any idea of the risk she was running by spending so long away from her lover. She was far more beautiful than Wallis; maybe her looks had lulled her into a false sense of security.

~

Wallis wrote of gifts from the Prince: a few pieces of jewellery, money to buy clothes, and a Cairn puppy she referred to as Mr Loo, remarking gloomily: *I do not seem to have a talent for toilet-training dogs and cannot feel any great affection for the messy newcomer.* Ernest also received royal favour: a bolt of cloth in houndstooth-check tweed to be made into a coat by the Prince's tailor, and admittance to the Prince's Masonic lodge, an honour that would be vastly helpful to him in his business affairs. All this generosity, Wallis insisted to Mary, was recompense for the time she spent helping him to manage his social calendar, organising house parties and the like. Meanwhile, she still had to run their home at Bryanston Court. *Keeping up with two men is making me move all the time*, she wrote.

By summer, Mary was hearing gossip at friends' soirées that Wallis was 'the Prince's new girl'. They claimed Thelma had been furious on her return to England to find that her telephone calls were no longer put through the Fort Belvedere switchboard. Mary wrote to Wallis questioning her about this, and received a reply saying that the gossips were, as usual, wrong. Their relationship was entirely innocent: *I think I do amuse him*, she wrote. *I'm the comedy relief, and we like to dance together, but I always have Ernest hanging round my neck, so all is safe.* She added, for emphasis: *The Prince likes my company, but he is certainly not in love with me.*

Mary believed she was telling the truth, even when she heard that Wallis had accompanied the Prince's party for a several-weeks-long holiday in Biarritz, leaving Ernest behind in London. Aunt Bessie was there as chaperone, but Mary couldn't imagine her getting in the way of any budding romance.

When Bessie returned to America in the fall, she telephoned Mary, very concerned about what she had witnessed.

'He follows Wallis like a lapdog,' she said. 'He even has a hangdog expression with those baggy eyes of his. I was appalled by his lack of dignity; this is the man who will one day be King of England.'

'How does Wallis react to the adulation?' Mary asked.

'Hmm . . . You know her as well as I do. She's always happy to accept expensive gifts, and she gives the Prince her undivided attention whenever they're together. But I saw her hide from him one morning when she could not face any more of his childish demands. She slid behind a pergola and covered herself with foliage! It was all I could do to stop myself laughing out loud and giving the game away.'

'Oh dear. Is it not treasonable to refuse the advances of a royal?' Mary felt concerned. Wallis was weaving a complex web.

'I'm worried that my niece is in great danger of ending up without either a husband or a prince. Ernest's pride can surely only take so much battering before he protests in the strongest terms. And you've seen the ruthless way the Prince disposed of Thelma when he had no further use for her.' She paused for effect. 'Wallis must beware or the same fate awaits her – but worse, because at least Thelma has Vanderbilt money to fall back on.'

Mary had mixed feelings after this conversation. Part of her was secretly proud that the girl who had been her best friend for over twenty years had captured the heart of a prince. It was a shame he was not more manly, someone with wit and intelligence; all the same, it was a great adventure.

But poor Ernest must sit through many an evening with the pair, watching the fawning behaviour without being able to criticise. How did you say to a prince, 'Keep your hands off my wife, sir'? Especially when it seemed your wife was encouraging him.

~

In October 1934, Mary's mother finally died, a blessed relief after weeks of confusion induced by the morphine that did little to quell the vicious pains racking her body. Wallis wrote urging Mary to get on the first sailing to Southampton and stay with them as long as she wished so they might look after her. *You helped me after my mother died; please let me return the favour*, she begged.

Although wary after her last visit, Mary yearned to see Wallis and Ernest, and to flee to a life of gaiety that did not involve tending invalids. She sailed on the *Mauretania*, and when she reached Southampton this time she knew exactly how to get the train. She hired her own taxicab from a rank at Waterloo and gave the address – 'Bryanston Court, please' – feeling proud for managing.

It was six thirty, KT hour in the Simpson household, and she was looking forward to a glass of something intoxicating. Normally the babble of conversation could be heard in the hall, but as the maid took her coat and hat, she could just hear a low murmur of voices. She opened the door and there were Wallis, Ernest and the Prince of Wales sitting in a circle by the fire, glasses in hand.

Ernest leapt to his feet and came over to greet her. 'You made it. Well done, my dear.'

Wallis rose and embraced her, then turned to the Prince. 'David, you remember my old schoolfriend Mary, don't you?'

Mary belatedly remembered her curtsey. Should she have done that on entering? And when had Wallis started calling him David?

'Welcome to England,' the Prince said, 'and to our cosy cocktail set.'

Ernest pulled up a chair and fetched her a drink, without asking what she would like. She took a sip and was pleased he had remembered her favourite gin and lemon cocktail.

'Was the crossing very rough?' the Prince asked, drawing on a cigarette. 'October can be a difficult month.'

'I am seasick even in dead calm,' she said. 'The only remedy is gin.'

'Does it not take all the glamour out of drinking in America now they've repealed the Prohibition laws?' Wallis asked. 'You would have loved the 21 Club, David. A doorman checked you out through a peephole before you could get in, and if the barman suspected a police raid, he pressed a button that flipped the bar shelves so the bottles hurtled down a chute.'

While she spoke, the Prince did not take his eyes off her. 'Has this establishment gone out of business now?' he asked Mary.

'Not at all. It still remains, although it's rather easier to gain admittance and they no longer smash the stock.'

The Prince drained his drink and held out his glass towards Ernest. 'Might I have another, old boy? You do mix the perfect martini.'

Ernest started to rise, but Wallis put a restraining hand on the Prince's arm. 'Now, now, David. One is enough. There will be wine with dinner.'

To Mary's amazement, the Prince backed down without a murmur. If only it had been so easy with Jacques!

When dinner was ready, they went through to the dining room, with its huge mirror-topped table. Four places had been set at one end.

'We're having English nursery food,' Wallis announced. 'A dish called shepherd's pie.'

As they ate the meal, the Prince pumped Mary for anecdotes about Wallis's school days, and she told him about the girls at Oldfields getting into trouble for writing to boys, and how Wallis was the first to own up. He chuckled at that, even more so when Mary explained how they used to mock the school motto about gentleness and courtesy.

'Would you courteously pass the salt, Miss Kirk,' Wallis mimicked.

The Prince reached for the salt cellar, accidentally nudging Wallis's glass and causing it to topple over. She jerked her chair back so the wine wouldn't drip onto her gown, and snapped, 'For God's sake, David. Be more careful. I can't stand clumsiness.'

Mary was aghast. How could she speak that way to the heir to the throne? The Prince's face was crestfallen as he tried to mop up the spill with his napkin. Ernest rang the bell for the maid. Mary looked at him, expecting some reaction, but his expression was neutral.

As she lay in the circular bed later that night, reviewing the evening, a thought popped into Mary's head. The way Wallis treated the Prince with a complete lack of deference was similar to the way she used to act with poor Carter Osburn back in the Baltimore days. He too used to hang on her every word; he too was a milksop. Wallis had only indulged him because she liked his car. Perhaps she was only indulging this one because she liked his crown.

Chapter 36

West Sussex, 22 October 1997

USIE LED RACHEL TO A FIRST-FLOOR GUEST bedroom in the west wing of her house. There was a four-poster bed opposite the door, and bay windows on two walls since the room was situated in a corner of the building. The carpet was worn and there were brown patches on the ceiling and flaking paint on the walls, but Rachel thought it would be lovely when redecorated.

'I have absolutely no idea what's in here,' Susie said, lifting the lid of a mahogany chest carved with a Chinese dragon. 'My parents seldom used this room. As a kid, I found the west wing rather spooky.'

The smell that arose was a mixture of faded mothballs, old wood, mustiness and a hint of ancient fabric impregnated with perfume. Rachel leant over and took a deep breath, filling her lungs.

'My favourite smell,' she said. 'The smell of history.'

The garments inside had been folded with layers of tissue paper between them. Susie removed the top layer, and pulled out a ladies' mustard mohair swagger coat, passing it to Rachel with a grimace. Rachel checked the lining and saw it was in good condition. The label read *Forstmann*, an American company.

'It's 1950s. Not my taste but I could try it in the shop,' she said, laying it on the bed.

Next there was a hideous 1960s polyester mini dress with lime green and pink swirls.

'That's definitely one for the charity shop,' Susie giggled, catching Rachel's mock shudder. They put it in a separate pile.

There was a Jackie-Kennedy-style navy-blue suit with cream piping, a belted beige suede jacket, several skirts and pairs of trousers, most from the sixties or seventies, and then Rachel's eye was caught by an exotic floral print on a cornflower-blue background. She pulled out the item: a short-sleeved slim-fitting tunic and, underneath, a matching long, slender skirt. They were exquisite. Inside, the label read *Mainbocher Inc.* in blue capitals.

'Main Bocher was an American designer who was popular in Paris in the 1930s,' she told Susie. 'Wallis Simpson was a fan. When she married the Duke of Windsor, Mainbocher made her wedding dress in a shade that he called "Wallis blue". This outfit is gorgeous. Sure you don't want to keep it?'

Susie snorted, holding the skirt in front of her. 'I could hardly get one leg into this, never mind two.'

'Do you mind if I try it on?' Rachel asked, and Susie waved an arm.

'Be my guest.'

She turned away discreetly as Rachel pulled off the aubergine sheath dress and matching bolero jacket she was wearing and stepped into the Mainbocher. There were covered buttons up the back of the skirt, but although she wrestled with them, frustratingly they would not close over her hips. She was a UK size 8 but this must be at least a size smaller. Nevertheless, she pulled the light-as-air tunic over her head and walked to a full-length mirror to check the effect. It was beautifully cut, skimming the hips, the skirt hem floating around her ankles. What a shame those buttons wouldn't close.

'It looks wonderful on you,' Susie said. 'Maybe you could have it let out.'

As Rachel smoothed her hands over the silky fabric, trying to feel if there was any excess material in the side seams, she realised there was a hidden pocket with something inside. She pulled out a card with old-fashioned cottage-garden roses twisted round an oval frame in which the name *Constance Spry, Florist* was printed. It was a thick, good-quality card, and some words were scribbled in faded blue ink underneath.

'Look at this,' she said, holding it up. She walked over to a lamp and managed to decipher the faded legend: '"Now do you trust us?"' she read. 'Must be some joke from long ago. The owner probably forgot it was there.'

Susie took the card to have a look. 'How strange to come across a note whose significance is long forgotten. Does that often happen?'

'Quite a lot,' Rachel agreed. 'I find old cinema tickets, embroidered handkerchiefs . . . I once found a romantic note addressed to a woman called Julia and signed "from a secret admirer". I was able to return it to her great-niece.'

She slipped off the Mainbocher and got dressed again, then they finished unpacking the trunk and a couple of large cupboards as well. There were plenty of garments Rachel knew she could sell, among them a pale gold duchesse satin ball gown, several floral tea dresses, which were her best-selling items, and a black velvet opera cape. The iron band around her chest loosened a little.

Susie had laid out a rustic loaf, three types of cheese and a green salad for their supper, and she poured them both a glass of red wine.

'Just the one,' Rachel said. She had to drive back later. 'I'm very excited about your Mainbocher dress.' She helped herself to some salad. 'I'm going to look it up when I get back. He made some fabulous outfits for Wallis Simpson and I love the way she dressed.'

'She was a controversial character, though,' Susie said. 'I heard she behaved abominably during the war. She and Edward were sent to the Bahamas for the duration, and seemingly Wallis paid for a New York hairdresser to fly down when she needed her hair done, and she was forever popping up for Fifth Avenue shopping trips. Back in England everyone was on rations and suffering nightly bombardment, so it didn't go down well.'

'Ooh, I imagine not,' Rachel agreed, making a face. She paused. 'Do you think Diana ever met her?'

Susie's expression was wary. 'Why do you ask?'

'I read that she went to Wallis's funeral and I know there was some kind of rapprochement between Wallis and the royal family after Edward died, when she was a harmless old widow in poor health. I just wondered . . .'

Susie hesitated before answering. 'Yes, Diana knew her. Charles introduced them in 1981, during a trip to Paris while they were engaged. By then Wallis had dementia and could barely speak. She lived in a kind of twilight world, behind closed shutters, with nurses coming and going.' She cut a chunk of Brie and placed it on a slice of bread. 'Diana felt terribly sorry for her so she used to drop in if she was visiting Paris. That's what she was like: if anyone was down on their luck, Duch was there for them.'

'Oh my gosh!' Rachel was astonished. 'They kept that well hidden from the press. I'm sure I would remember if it had been reported.'

'You're right. The papers would have had a field day if they knew of a friendship between these two women who both challenged the Windsor dynasty. Can you imagine?' Susie looked gleeful at the thought.

'That's fascinating. I was saying to Alex recently that the two of them would have had a lot to talk about.' Rachel decided to venture the question that appeared to have upset Susie during the interview, watching carefully for a reaction. 'We both thought it odd that Diana chose to visit Villa Windsor the day she died. Do you think it's true that she was considering living there with Dodi?'

'No, never,' Susie replied vehemently. 'She found it a sad place. "It's full of old ghosts," she told me.'

'Perhaps Dodi was trying to persuade her to change her mind?'

'You didn't know her,' Susie said, pushing her plate away without finishing. 'Diana was full of fun, positively bursting with energy – and she had a great line in naughty humour.' She gave a half-smile, clearly remembering some anecdote she wasn't going to share. 'She would never have wanted to live in a museum.'

'What do you think she would have done had she lived?' Rachel asked. 'She was just beginning to be taken seriously for her landmines work. Perhaps she could have gone on to be a UN ambassador or something similar.'

'She would have changed the world,' Susie said firmly. 'I have absolutely no doubt of that.'

Chapter 37

Brighton, 22 October 1997

ON HER RETURN TO BRIGHTON, RACHEL CARRIED Susie's clothes from the car into her flat and laid them over the back of the sofa. She extracted the Mainbocher from the pile and hung it in the doorway on a padded coat hanger, examining the clever cut and impeccable stitching.

She had several fashion reference books, including one with photographs of styles that had appeared in *Vogue* over the years. She looked up Mainbocher in the index, and as she'd expected, there were dozens of entries. She worked her way through, and there, in 1934, was the tunic and skirt – the exact same outfit – being worn by Wallis Simpson herself. She checked the detail of the tendrils in the flower pattern and they were identical. It came from his Eastern-inspired fall collection.

Was there any chance this could be Wallis's dress? she wondered. It was skinny enough. She decided to email Richard and ask his opinion, because if it had belonged to Wallis, Susie would get substantially more at auction than Rachel could charge in the shop.

She booted up the computer and went into her email folder. *Hi Rich*, she typed, *I've just picked up a haul including a Mainbocher from 1934: a Chinese rose-print tunic and matching skirt. My* Vogue *book shows Wallis Simpson wearing it. Do you know anyone at their head office who might be able to tell me if it was hers?*

That night, Rachel tried to ring Alex in Paris to tell him about her day but she kept getting his voicemail. Even at eleven at night, when he must have been in his hotel room, the phone irritatingly went straight to his 'can't take your call' message. She hated going to bed without having spoken to him; it was one of their rules that whenever they were apart they had a bedtime chat. If his phone had run out of charge, he should have called her on the hotel phone. She couldn't ring him because he hadn't mentioned where he was staying.

As soon as she woke the next morning she tried his phone again, and this time he answered, telling her he was rushing to a meeting. She could hear traffic sounds in the background and his footfall on the pavement. 'I was back late and didn't want to wake you,' he said in a tone that wasn't remotely apologetic. She considered telling him she'd found it hard to get to sleep for worrying that something had happened, but it sounded too neurotic. Instead she said, 'Never mind, darling. Have a good day,' before he hung up abruptly as he reached his destination.

Rachel was depressed by the call. Alex seemed to get further away with each day that passed, and she didn't know how to pull him back when he was working such long hours. They needed relaxed, uninterrupted time together but it was hard to see when they were going to get it; next year some time, perhaps.

She tried to cheer herself up by dressing in a favourite outfit: a 1940s dress that had a print of seaweed in shades of pale grey and slate, with hot-pink tropical fish swimming through the fronds. She teamed it with a hot-pink cardigan and peep-toe shoes, ignoring the dark clouds that threatened rain later. The right outfit could usually boost her mood, and this one had special memories because she had been wearing it in Cuba the night she and Alex learned to dance salsa in a rooftop night-club. He picked up the steps faster than her, his hand in the small of her back as they moved to the infectious rhythm of a steel band under a vast starry sky. She made a mental note that they should go dancing in Brighton some time; there were loads of salsa clubs.

Nicola popped by the shop mid morning, wearing a zip-up parka with fur-trimmed hood over jeans and a black and red T-shirt.

'I've brought raisin cookies,' she said, pulling a pack from her oversized handbag. 'Posh ones. Are you hungry?'

'Not for me, thanks,' Rachel said, putting the kettle on. When Nicola removed the parka and sat down, she noticed that her T-shirt was from the Clash's first American tour in 1979. It showed the Statue of Liberty bound in thick ropes.

'Alex has one just like that,' she remarked, then spotted that it was far too big for Nicola. One shoulder had slipped down her arm.

'Yeah, this is his,' Nicola said. 'I borrowed it a couple of months ago and he hasn't asked for it back yet. You won't grass on me, will you?'

Rachel gave a little laugh. 'Chance'd be a fine thing. I hardly see him these days, and when I do, we only seem to argue.'

She decided to confide in Nicola about the latest rows. She had known Alex since college days and might have some useful insight. With any luck she would say that Rachel was over-reacting and that everything would be fine once the filming was over.

Instead, Nicola looked increasingly alarmed as she spoke, and when she finished, said: 'Oh no! I've seen him like this before, but I really believed you two were different.'

Rachel's heart gave a lurch. 'Seen him like what?'

'Getting absorbed in his work, then picking fights with his girlfriend and withdrawing emotionally. He seems to panic whenever a relationship gets serious.' She helped herself to one of the cookies.

Rachel handed her a cup of tea and sat down, feeling sick. 'I'm sure it's partly my fault, because I'm not being supportive enough of his documentary. Everything was perfect until Paris. We hardly ever argued before then.'

Nicola chewed her cookie, brow furrowed. 'He'll never agree to relationship counselling, will he? That's what he needs.'

Rachel couldn't see it. 'Whenever he uses therapists to provide commentaries in one of his programmes, he says they're more screwed up than the rest of us. He thinks they only go into therapy to mask their neuroses.'

'You have to try something. We can't let Alex go through the rest of his life repeating his toxic pattern. He's like the best, most attentive boyfriend ever and girls can't believe their luck until suddenly he switches off the love and withdraws, leaving them high and dry.' Nicola picked up her tea and blew on the surface to cool it.

'So you've seen him do this before?' Rachel knew only the sketchiest details of Alex's love life before she came along. They'd agreed it was unhealthy to pore over the past, and she hadn't been keen to share the lowdown on her own romantic disasters.

'Loads of times,' Nicola said. 'He's even been engaged before. Did you know that?'

Rachel shook her head, stunned. That was something she would have expected him to share, despite the embargo on other details. She reached for a cookie absent-mindedly and started to nibble it.

'Anna was her name,' Nicola said. 'She was devastated when he got cold feet and called it off just weeks before the wedding.'

There was a look on Nicola's face that Rachel couldn't read. Was she enjoying imparting this news? Was she glad things were not entirely rosy between them? Perhaps she was jealous of their happiness at a time when her latest relationship had failed. No, Nicola wasn't like that. She must be misreading her.

'I knew it wasn't going to last with Anna,' Nicola continued, 'because he was cheating on her. It's never a good sign, is it?' She stopped and peered at Rachel. 'Are you OK? You look pale. Sorry, I shouldn't be telling you this right now. Bad timing.'

Rachel hugged herself, stroking the arms of her cardigan. 'I didn't realise Alex was the unfaithful type. I'm allergic to them after my last experience.'

'Oh God, I'm so tactless. Alex is not a compulsive cheater; it's just when a relationship wasn't working in the past, there might have been a slight overlap with the next one. You've got nothing to worry about. I've never seen him so smitten with anyone as he is with you. Truly.'

Nicola was backtracking frantically, trying to smooth over the damage she had caused, but Rachel was silent and withdrawn. She couldn't wait for Nicola to leave so she could be alone.

It was an odd feeling to hear that someone she thought she knew inside out had a callous streak she could never have imagined. There had been a similar coldness when he'd interviewed Susie. Rachel was pretty confident in Alex's love for her, but probably Anna had been confident at the time too. Would Alex be capable of withdrawing his love for no good reason? Could he already have her successor lined up?

~

Back at the flat that evening, Rachel booted up the home computer. She hated herself for what she was about to do, but

Nicola had planted a seed of doubt that she couldn't dispel. She opened Alex's email account, pleased to note it wasn't password-protected; didn't that show he had nothing to hide? She would check anyway, just this once, then forget all about her suspicions. They were unworthy of her.

Amidst the usual junk mails, there were messages from his team about equipment and timings, many of them in a kind of shorthand that meant nothing to her: PAL 700, VHS transfer, burnt-in time code. There were several messages from someone called Pascal, but she quickly worked out that he was one of the researchers in France. Lots of male friends had emailed complaining they hadn't seen him for ages and asking when he could manage 'a swift half', to which he replied that he would call them as soon as he'd proved who'd killed Diana.

And then she noticed that Nicola's name cropped up regularly, every few days. She hesitated before opening one of her mails: *Thanks for picking up the bill last night. You spoil me*, it read. She checked the date and saw it was for the previous Friday, when he had come home late. She opened another mail: *You are the best*, it said, followed by a whole line of kisses, as if Nicola had leant on the X key and held it down with determination. She began to feel uneasy. She read three more emails from Nicola, all of which demonstrated that their Friday evening meetings were a regular occurrence and she and Alex were much closer to each other at the moment than he was to her.

Suddenly she remembered an incident at their New Year's Eve party ten months ago. It was almost 4 a.m. and she was about to head for bed, although a crowd were still partying in the sitting room. She went to the kitchen to get a glass of water but stopped in the doorway when she saw Alex and Nicola standing still with their arms around each other. There was nothing sexual about the hug; it was two friends, both the worse for drink, more or less propping each other up. Rachel had seen them hug before and it hadn't remotely worried her, but this hug lasted a long time. Eventually she cleared her throat dramatically and they jumped apart.

Had she been wrong not to worry about the hug? Could Alex possibly be having an affair with Nicola?

Chapter 38

London, October 1934

THE MORNING AFTER MARY'S ARRIVAL, WALLIS BURST into her bedroom wearing a blue tea gown and flung herself on the bed, just as she used to do in her teens when she stayed over at the Kirk household.

'Did you sleep well, darling?'

'Like the dead.' Mary yawned and stretched. 'I swear, it's marvellous to be here. I've missed you and Ernest.'

'We're simply ecstatic to have you back. Tell me, what do you think of the new addition to our household? The other one, apart from you.' Wallis arranged the tea gown artfully over her legs.

'The Prince of Wales? You seem very informal with him. Why do you call him David?'

'That's what his family call him. He prefers it to Edward.'

'The poor man is clearly smitten. You've made another conquest, Wallie, but doesn't it worry you?'

Wallis gave a secret smile. 'He told me he loves me, and I said not to be so ridiculous.'

'Yet you encourage him by inviting him here? It must be rather awkward for Ernest that he can't relax in his own home without tripping over your lovesick Prince.'

'Ernest and I discussed it and I think he's flattered that the Prince is in love with his wife. What man wouldn't be?' She examined her carefully filed fingernails. 'Anyway, it won't be long before he discards me, just as he discarded Thelma and Freda Dudley Ward before her. I may as well enjoy my day in the sun.'

'You wrote that it was exhausting keeping up with two men, and I could see what you meant last night. Both of them expect you to entertain them. When do *you* ever get to relax?' Mary thought Wallis looked tired, and a little thinner than normal. She always lost weight when she was under pressure.

Wallis sat up, folded her legs beneath her. 'Mama taught me that it is a woman's duty to be entertaining, and I enjoy it! But there are times when there's just not enough of me to go around. This Saturday, for instance, I must help the Prince to host a lunch party at the Fort, while Ernest has gotten it into his head to drive to Bath. I know you enjoy architecture and such like, so I wondered if perhaps you might go with him? Only if you want to . . .'

'I'd love to. The famous Bath of Jane Austen novels. I've always wanted to see it.'

That's why Wallis wanted me here, she thought wryly; to help her juggle her life. But fortunately it suited her to keep Ernest entertained while Wallis pandered to the Prince. It would be fun.

Over breakfast, Wallis suggested to Ernest that he and Mary go to Bath without her.

'Looking after Peter Pan, are you?' he enquired.

Mary turned to Wallis, raising an eyebrow. 'Peter Pan?'

'Because he's never grown up,' Wallis explained with a grin.

Mary was enchanted by the honey-coloured stone terraces of Bath, climbing up from the River Avon. As she and Ernest walked round the Baths, the Pump Room and the Abbey, he clutched a Baedeker but only opened it once to check a date. Everything else he knew.

'I can think of nothing but the characters in Jane Austen's *Persuasion*,' Mary told him. 'The pretentious Sir Walter Elliot and Mrs Clay, the treacherous William Elliot, and the simmering passion between Captain Wentworth and Anne, all played out against this very backdrop. It's a thrill to be here.'

They lunched in a café in the corner of a covered market dating back to the nineteenth century before continuing their exploration.

'I feel as though I am on a movie set,' Mary exclaimed. 'How lucky are the citizens who live in such surroundings.' Her back had begun to ache from all the walking, but the experience was far too magical for her to ask Ernest if they could cut it short.

He had another treat for her on the drive home: as dusk encroached, he turned off the road and into a field.

'Do you recognise this?' he asked, pointing towards some stark black shapes etched against the salmon-pink sky.

'Stonehenge,' Mary breathed. 'Oh my word!'

She got out of the car and walked towards them, feeling her skin prickling.

'The stones are thought to be five thousand years old,' Ernest told her. 'Possibly they were used as an astronomical calendar, but no one can explain how the builders transported such huge blocks without any mechanical aids.'

She laid her hand on one of the stones and imagined all the people who had worshipped at that spot over the millennia, peering out towards the rising or setting sun.

'It's eerie,' she told Ernest, 'and awe-inspiring. Makes me quite giddy.' She slipped her arm through his and shivered. 'Thank you for bringing me. What a special place.'

It was dinner time when they arrived back at Bryanston Court. The maid said Wallis had telephoned to explain she was detained at the Fort and would not be back till the following morning so they should dine without her.

Mary glanced at Ernest, surprised, but his face betrayed no emotion.

Over their meal, she couldn't resist raising the subject. 'It's certainly flattering that Wallie is so essential to the heir to the throne, but I worry that the situation could get out of control. In New York there is already gossip amongst people who have too much time on their hands.'

Ernest swallowed a spoonful of soup before replying. 'I don't care two hoots what the gossips say, but it does feel rather odd when another man buys my wife jewels and clothes. She argues that it is only fair he contributes since she has to attend functions by his side and must have new costumes for each.'

'That's one way of looking at it, I suppose.'

'I'd much rather pay myself but the business is still recovering from the Crash.' He looked at her pointedly. 'You know Wallis and her insecurities over money better than I do.'

Mary nodded. She well remembered Wallis's anguish every time she had to beg Uncle Sol for a handout.

'So if she can feel a little more secure having a wealthy prince to subsidise her extravagant shopping habits until my income picks up again, I suppose I must accept whatever is whispered of me.' He finished his soup and, seeing that Mary had also finished, rang for the maid to bring the fish course.

Only when the maid had left the room again did Mary reply. 'It must be lonely for you when she stays over at the Fort.' She was shocked that Wallis would do such a thing. Was there a chaperone present? What would she do if the lovesick Prince wandered into her room in the night?

'First time it has happened. I suppose she thought it was acceptable since I have you for company.' He took a forkful of fish, staring into the middle distance, before changing the subject.

Chapter 39

London, November 1934

WALLIS'S COCKTAIL HOURS WERE RENOWNED BY now, and so popular she often had to refuse those who called to invite themselves so she could keep the numbers around twenty. She made the drinks herself in a silver shaker, and was skilled at pouring the correct proportions by eye.

Mary stood back and watched her hostessing. Wallis made sure she conversed with everyone, remembering to ask after children, ailing parents and new business ventures. The guests revolved around her like planets round the sun.

'I declare you are the most popular hostess in London,' Mary complimented her when she came to the bar for a refill.

'Only because they hope to bump into the Prince of Wales,' Wallis confided. 'You see them enter the room and glance around, then a shadow of disappointment crosses their faces if he is not here.'

This was true of a new guest one evening, a German diplomat by the name of Joachim von Ribbentrop, who did not attempt to hide his chagrin.

'Mrs Simpson, I had it on good authority that the Prince of Wales was a fixture in your drawing room. Is he going to arrive later?'

Wallis smiled as she handed him a gin martini with two olives. 'He has an official engagement this afternoon. You picked the wrong day to grace us with your presence.'

'I was very much hoping to see him. Perhaps another time.'

'As long as you promise not to discuss politics all evening. I don't want to hear about workers' housing and the evils of Judaism in my KT hour.' She turned to Mary. 'May I introduce my old schoolfriend, Mrs Mary Raffray? I want you two to talk about entirely frivolous subjects,' she instructed, before crossing the room to greet a newcomer, leaving them alone together.

Mary took against von Ribbentrop on sight. His forehead was too high, taking almost half the height of his face, and beneath it his eyes were too close together, too calculating.

'Do you live in London, Mrs Raffray?' he asked.

'No, I'm here for a visit, to bask in the glow of Wallis's glittering social circle.'

He didn't smile. 'And how long do you plan to stay?'

The question was delivered rudely, but Mary assumed the directness was a German quirk. 'Until they throw me out. How long that will be, I have no idea. What brings *you* to London, Mr Ribbentrop?'

While they'd been talking, he'd kept gazing over her shoulder, his eyes roaming the room as if looking for someone more worthy of his attention, but now he fixed his stare on her. 'I work for Herr Hitler, and travel wherever he asks me to.'

'How fascinating! What kind of a man is he?' Mary asked.

Von Ribbentrop smiled. 'He is a genius who will save our country. We are very lucky to have him. If you will excuse me, I see a friend I must talk to. Enjoy your evening, Mrs Raffray.'

He walked off, leaving Mary to gawp at the rudeness.

'How long have you known Ribbentrop?' she asked Wallis the following morning.

'I'd only met him once before, at Emerald Cunard's. He's supposed to be some sort of spy. Isn't that glamorous? I find him charming.'

Mary certainly didn't.

Later that day, a huge bouquet of blush-pink roses was delivered for Wallis, and she smiled when she read the card, before tossing it onto the fire. 'Ribbentrop,' she said. 'Aren't they lovely?'

~

One Sunday in late November, Ernest asked over breakfast whether Wallis or Mary would like to visit Petworth with him. Although the house was not open to the public, there was a park by the great landscape designer Capability Brown.

'I'd love to,' Mary said straight away, and both of them turned to Wallis.

'I'd rather have a lazy day,' she said, stretching. 'You two go. Have fun!'

It was clear but cold, and Mary bundled herself in hat, coat and fur muff for the drive over the South Downs, with their glorious views to the silvery streak of sea beyond. As they strolled in the grounds, Ernest explained that they had previously been formal gardens but that in the 1750s Capability Brown had persuaded the owners to opt for a more natural style. He'd introduced an S-shaped lake, great sweeps of grass and winding paths that took advantage of the stunning vistas.

Two red setters came bounding towards them, with glossy coats in a rich shade of rust. Ernest stroked them and they rubbed their heads against his legs. Mary glanced round to look for their owner and saw a woman in tweeds with a scarf tied around her head. As she got closer, she called: 'Don't encourage them. They think you have food.'

There was something familiar about her brown hair, friendly face and very upper-class accent, but Mary couldn't place her.

'Excuse me,' the woman said. 'Aren't you Mary Kirk from Baltimore?'

'Ye-es,' Mary agreed cautiously.

'Eleanor Jessop,' she said. 'We met at Oldfields. I was there from 1913 to 1914.'

'English Eleanor!' Mary exclaimed. 'My goodness, how are you?' She reached out to shake hands. 'Ernest, this is a schoolfriend of Wallie's and mine.'

Ernest shook hands, and Mary explained that he was Wallis's husband.

'You're still in touch with her then?' Eleanor seemed surprised.

'I'm staying with her in London. Ernest and I just came out for a drive.'

Eleanor's eyes flickered from one to the other, clearly curious. 'Can I invite you for tea? My house is a mile down the road, in the direction of East Lavington.'

Mary looked at Ernest, then said, 'I'm getting rather chilly, so tea would be welcome.'

'I assume you came by car. Do you have room for three in the back?' Eleanor indicated the dogs.

Ernest looked uneasy, and Mary could tell he was worried they would scratch the leather seats, but in the event they just made them rather muddy. Eleanor gave directions and they turned up a drive towards a pretty manor house with a circular parking area outside.

'What a glorious house,' Ernest remarked. 'Eighteenth century?'

'Yes. It's been in my husband's family for generations. Do come in.'

Once they were seated in the spacious drawing room in front of a log fire with a grand pillared fireplace, Mary began to thaw. A maid brought a tray of tea and home-baked scones and Mary and Eleanor chatted about Oldfields days, remembering the Miss Nolands, and some of the other girls.

Ernest was gazing round the room. He spotted a portrait of Eleanor with her hair scraped back into a tight bun and wandered over to have a closer look. 'That's terribly good,' he said. 'The artist has captured a clever likeness.'

Eleanor smiled, pleased at the compliment. 'It's by my husband, Ralph Hargreaves. He would be delighted to hear you say that. I'm sorry he's not around this afternoon, but he's off painting somewhere and I won't see him till dusk. Do stay to meet him.'

'Another time, perhaps.' Ernest looked at his watch. 'Wallis is expecting us at six.'

Before they left, Eleanor and Mary swapped addresses and telephone numbers. Mary gave the Bryanston Court ones as well as those in New York.

'If you're in London, come to our cocktail hour,' Ernest offered. 'Six o'clock most evenings.'

Eleanor replied, 'I'm afraid we don't tend to travel to the city, but I would love you to come here for a longer visit. It's so good to see you, Mary.'

In the car on the way back, Mary told Ernest how Wallis used to do an uncanny impersonation of Eleanor's accent, and how they used to pump her for information about the Prince. 'Funny to think of it now,' she laughed.

As soon as they arrived at Bryanston Court, Mary found Wallis. 'Guess who we met? Do you remember English Eleanor?'

'Oh, her,' Wallis said, making a face. 'Is she still dull as dishwater?'

'On the contrary,' Ernest chipped in. 'She's charming, and lives in a beautifully kept manor house of some distinction.'

'Houses. Yawn.' Wallis was tidying her cocktail bar. 'Chop, chop, you two! You've got five minutes to change before Peter Pan arrives to lap up his martini.'

As she walked past the hall table, Mary noticed a new bouquet of blush-pink roses, the exact shade of the ones von Ribbentrop had sent before. She looked but couldn't see a card beside them.

Chapter 40

Brighton, 23 October 1997

*I*N BED THAT NIGHT, RACHEL COULDN'T STOP thinking about Nicola and Alex. Had she misjudged them both? Two years ago, when she had discovered that her previous boyfriend had been unfaithful most of the time they were together, it had seriously dented her faith in her ability to judge character. Now that insecurity came surging back. Were they making a fool of her?

She and Nicola had shared a lot since they'd met at one of her exhibitions. Rachel had bought a pencil drawing of some seashells, which still hung in her bedroom in a pretty driftwood frame. They'd gone for a drink and liked each other enough to build a friendship that rapidly became close. Nicola knew that Rachel had been badly hurt by her errant boyfriend because she'd consoled her during many cocktail-fuelled evenings. She wouldn't be so cruel as to put her through the same thing again, would she?

Rachel realised that she and Nicola hadn't gone out for a drink together in a long while. Their relationship had been strained since the break-in, but even before that it had become a little awkward once Nicola started working in the shop. It could never be the same when Rachel wrote her pay cheque at the end of the month, when she had to ask her to be more careful about keeping all sales noted in a ledger, when she had criticised her as tactfully as she could for not looking smart enough. All of that altered the dynamic from a friendship of equals to one of employer and employee in a way that slightly poisoned the relationship. Rachel had thought she was doing her a favour because Nicola needed the money, but perhaps she resented it on some level.

A thought flashed through her mind: could Nicola even have staged the burglary and made off with the cash? She rejected that straight away. It would be totally out of character, and would have required more capacity for deceit than Nicola possessed. She could not have faked her shocked sobbing as she spoke to the police that morning.

Rachel mulled it over and decided the affair theory didn't make sense either. Nicola and Alex had been friends for over a decade and people didn't suddenly start having an affair after all that time. She was being paranoid. Alex had asked her to marry him, and his nerves the night he proposed had demonstrated how much he wanted it to happen. She knew she should have more confidence in herself, but the nagging doubts clamoured in her head, stopping her getting to sleep.

~

The following morning when Rachel booted up her computer, she found a reply from Richard in her inbox.

I looked up that Mainbocher and found the photo you mentioned of Wallis wearing it. Does your supplier have any connection with her that would explain the provenance? Send me the measurements and I'll ask at Mainbocher head office. They keep a note of all their clients' measurements right back to the 1930s, and usually still have the dummies the clothes were fitted on (you could only expect celebrity clients to come for one or two fittings, so they had tailors' dummies made to their body shapes; still happens now).

She went to measure the Mainbocher dress: bust 32 inches, waist 23, hips 33 – almost the measurements of a boy. No wonder she hadn't been able to fasten it over her own hips. She emailed them to Richard, with a note that read: *Didn't Wallis say 'You can never be too rich or too thin'? It seems she was a woman of her word.*

The post arrived just before she left for the shop, bringing a letter that informed her the application for a credit card had been approved. She clutched the letter to her chest and closed her eyes in gratitude. November's rent would be paid. She had another month's grace.

Chapter 41

Brighton, 24 October 1997

RACHEL HAD THE CLOTHES FROM SUSIE'S HOUSE cleaned and hanging in the shop two days after picking them up, just in time for the weekend trade. She hoped they would mark a change in her fortunes. Richard had emailed that the Van der Heyden purchases would be with her on 11 November, so she noted that in her Filofax, at the same time marking when the first repayments for the new credit card would be due. There was no remaining leeway; if sales hadn't picked up by the end of November, she would have to close the shop.

Next she started flicking through the last few Fridays. Alex always came home late after his weeks away, and she'd thought he was hurrying straight from the train, but instead it seemed he had been meeting Nicola. Was he with her in London today? What were they doing?

She tried to remember when she and Alex had last made love, and worked out it was three weeks ago. And then she thought of something else: she hadn't had a period since then. Could she be pregnant? She cupped a hand over her belly. It would be so wonderful if it were true. She crossed her fingers and made a wish. *Please*, she asked. *Please*.

Alex came home around 9 p.m. that Friday and she handed him a beer, trying to keep her tone light as she asked: 'Did you bump into Nicola today?'

He gave her a quizzical look. 'London's a big place. I've been stuck in the office.'

That wasn't a 'no', Rachel noted. 'Did you find out what she was doing there?' she persisted.

'No idea,' he said, then changed the subject. 'I've spent the day watching the footage we've got so far and the narrative is all over the place. There are loads of questions about the crash we haven't been able to answer.' He ticked them off on his fingers. 'Where is the white car and who was driving it? Why did Henri Paul have such abnormally high levels of carbon monoxide in his blood? Why was there a delay of two hours and ten minutes between the accident and Diana arriving at hospital? Why was her body embalmed and who gave permission for it?'

Rachel hadn't heard about the carbon monoxide – or had she? She wondered if Alex had told her and she hadn't been listening properly. She did know about the embalming: the conspiracy theorists reckoned it was done to prevent news of Diana's pregnancy leaking out, but Rachel didn't buy that. What difference did it make whether Diana was pregnant or not? No baby would have survived the crash. Besides, the friend she was with in Greece two weeks earlier had told the press she couldn't possibly have been expecting because she'd had her period there.

Rachel had calculated that it was five weeks since she herself had last had a period. She wondered whether to tell Alex she was late. In the old days it would have been nice to share the excitement, but now she wasn't sure how he would react. If he was a classic commitment-phobe, as Nicola suggested, it could make him panic even more. She would wait for a moment when he seemed receptive because she desperately wanted him to greet the news with enthusiasm rather than alarm.

'We don't even know what Diana and Dodi were doing in Paris,' Alex continued, and she realised she hadn't been listening to what he'd been saying. 'There was no compelling reason for them to go there and they must have known the paparazzi would be out in force. Why didn't they head straight back to London and the security of Kensington Palace?'

'Paris is the city of romance!' Rachel offered. 'Dodi wanted to propose to her there, just as you did with me.'

'I'm sure there was some other reason . . .' Alex mused, with one eye on the television screen.

'Do you ever dream about Diana?' Rachel asked. 'I keep having dreams in which I'm trying to pull her out of the wrecked car.'

He shook his head. 'I don't remember my dreams, if I have any. Which I doubt. My head is too full of things I have to remember. I make to-do lists in my sleep.'

Rachel went to the kitchen to start dinner, thinking how sad it was that he didn't remember his dreams. It seemed symbolic somehow.

~

The weekend passed without a major argument, just a tetchy moment when she questioned him about some friends who hadn't RSVP'd to the wedding invitation.

'Either call and ask or strike them from the list,' he snapped.

Rachel tried to be conciliatory. 'I know you're busy, but I'm pretty fraught myself, and we can't ask Mum to ring your friends for you. It'll be a waste of money if we assume they're coming and they don't turn up.'

'I still don't understand why it's costing twenty-five quid a head,' he grumbled. 'I'm sure I could have negotiated a better deal.'

'Sorry, darling, would you rather change it to the Wimpy? We could probably get burger and chips for a pound.'

He took a deep breath and blew it out. 'OK, I'll call and find out what the stragglers are up to.'

There was no affection, no loving kindness, just a vast ocean of space between them. She noticed he still hadn't asked anything about her life: how the shop was doing, when her stock from New York was arriving, how she was feeling about the wedding. Nothing.

They curled up on the sofa on Saturday evening and watched an Indiana Jones movie. It was not the film she would have chosen but it was unchallenging and she relished the physical closeness. She hoped it might lead to sex later, only to be disappointed when he fell asleep before the closing credits and could not be roused.

They had Sunday dinner with her family – a stodgy roast she could only pick at – then first thing on Monday morning Alex rushed for a train to London, giving her a perfunctory kiss and calling, 'See you Friday,' on his way out of the door.

She stared after him for several minutes. They were due to get married in eight weeks and he felt like a flatmate rather than a lover – and not a very considerate flatmate at that.

~

On her way to the shop on Monday morning, Rachel stopped at a chemist and bought a pregnancy test. As soon as she had switched off the alarm and hung up her coat, she went to the toilet and peed on the plastic stick, her heart beating hard. *Oh please*, she begged, crossing her fingers as she laid it on the sink.

The instructions said to wait three minutes, but just at that moment she heard the bell ring as an early customer entered.

It was a man who wanted something for his wife's birthday but didn't know what. Rachel questioned him about her age, her tastes, her size and colouring, and recommended a 1930s silk slip trimmed with lace, which could be worn as a nightdress or even a party dress for the daring. She would be pleased to receive it herself, she assured him. Next he couldn't decide between dove grey and buttermilk, and Rachel steered him towards the latter. He paid cash, obviously relieved to have found a speedy solution to the gift problem. She wrapped the slip in multiple sheets of fine tissue and decorated the parcel with silk ribbons so he could simply hand it over.

As soon as he left, she rushed back to check her test: there was no pink line in the window, not even a faint one. Did that mean she wasn't pregnant, or that it had faded because she'd left it too long? There was another test in the kit but she decided to wait till she got home that evening, when she wouldn't be interrupted.

Later that afternoon a regular customer, a woman in her forties, popped in and produced a carrier bag, which she laid on the counter.

'I wondered if you might be interested in a Schiaparelli jacket? It was love at first sight when I bought it about ten years ago, but I have to face the fact that my size-eight years are over.'

It was bold pink silk, with blue circus horses dancing all over, and four buttons in the shape of acrobats bending backwards. Rachel recognised it straight away. 'That's from her 1938 "Circus" collection. I absolutely love it.'

Nipped at the waist, it had a peplum and bracelet sleeves. She looked at the label and could tell it was genuine. No one could have imitated that print or those extraordinary buttons.

She began to check inside and out for imperfections that would decrease the value. Just at that moment she felt a sharp cramp in her womb and a warmth between her legs. She shifted her weight slightly and another cramp came. Her eyes filled with tears and she screwed them shut and turned away, knowing instantly what it meant.

'Are you all right?' the customer asked.

'Yes, fine.' She took a deep breath. 'I'm happy to display your jacket in the shop, at a price we agree, then I'll give you fifty per cent of whatever it sells for.'

'I was hoping you would buy it from me today, for cash,' the woman said, not meeting her eye. She clearly needed the money.

Rachel was torn. The jacket was a historic piece, exactly the kind of item she loved to stock. 'How much did you have in mind?'

'I thought about five hundred pounds? I checked on the Internet and one sold in America for almost a thousand dollars last year.'

Rachel was sure she was right, but she simply couldn't raise that kind of cash. It broke her heart to miss the chance, but paying bills had to be her priority. 'Sorry, I can't help you,' she said.

As soon as the customer left, Rachel turned the sign on the door to *Closed* and rushed into the bathroom. No need for another pregnancy test. She sat on the toilet, leant her head in her hands and stayed still for a long time.

Chapter 42

Fort Belvedere, 6 December 1934

ARY WROTE TO ELEANOR THE MORNING AFTER their encounter, thanking her for the tea and for allowing them to thaw their bones in front of her fire. *I would very much like to see you again before my return to the States. Is it possible to catch a train to your part of the world?* It would be nice to cultivate a friendship of her own in England, since all the friends she'd made to date were primarily Wallis's.

The reply came by return. Eleanor said she was welcome any time and that there was a train from Victoria station to Pulborough. If she asked the stationmaster to telephone when she arrived, her husband would come and collect her.

Wallis was bemused when Mary mentioned she was planning to visit Eleanor. 'I didn't realise you were close. Well, it can't be this weekend because David has invited you to Fort Belvedere. I'm glad you're getting to visit him in his lair. It's the only place he can be himself.'

On Friday evening, Ernest, Mary and Wallis drove to the Fort, which was near the village of Sunningdale, just west of London. As they pulled up the drive, Mary exclaimed, 'Oh my! It's a proper castle.' There were crenellated walls and a turret with a flag flying from the top.

'It's not actually a castle,' Ernest corrected her. 'It's a Gothic Revival country house built in the 1820s. The architect was Jeffry Wyatville, who was also responsible for the redesign of Windsor Castle.'

Wallis had removed her headscarf and was smoothing her hair into place. 'David's father gave it to him five years ago and he's been remodelling it ever since. He's added a swimming pool and tennis courts, a steam room and loads of bathrooms, so almost every guest room has its own bathroom. He's very keen on that.'

The Prince came out onto the steps to greet them and a host of servants arrived to collect their bags. 'Welcome to my abode,' he said. Mary bobbed a curtsey, noticing that Wallis didn't bother. 'Let me show you to your rooms.'

'David, the staff can do that,' Wallis told him. 'Why don't you go and mix the drinks?'

'You're the cocktail expert,' the Prince argued. 'I would enjoy showing Mary and Ernest upstairs.'

Wallis gave in, and as they walked through the hall and up the grand staircase, the Prince pointed out his redecoration schemes, identified ancestors in portraits, invited them to stop and admire the view from a window at the curve of the stairs. He's proud of this place, Mary realised. That's why he wanted to show us.

Her room was large and light-filled, with bay windows and a book-lined wall. Ernest was next door and Wallis had two rooms at the end of the corridor, not far from the Prince's own bedroom. It all felt peculiar to Mary, and she kept glancing at each of the participants in the *ménage à trois*. Ernest was poker-faced, Wallis had switched into her 'entertainer' mode, being very gay and funny, while the Prince was like an eager child who desperately wanted them to like his house and enjoy his hospitality.

Mary dressed for dinner then came down to the drawing room. Ernest was in white tie, but the other men were less formally attired, while the Prince wore his kilt.

'We're very relaxed here,' he told her when he saw her looking around the room. 'There are no rules.'

'I wouldn't say that,' Wallis chipped in. 'I can think of a few. No food fights in the dining room because it's just been repainted; no repeating of tedious anecdotes we've all heard before . . .'

'And no sleeping with anyone to whom you are actually married,' another guest chipped in, to general merriment.

Mary was introduced to the rest of the party: Lord and Lady Brownlow, the Buists, Guy Trundle and his wife Melosine, Sybil Colefax, Jack Aird, all of them well-known members of society. She talked to Sybil Colefax about her interior design business, and enjoyed hearing about the work she had done at the Fort, but at the same time she kept half an eye on Wallis as she served cocktails, for all the world as if it were her own drawing room.

'I rearranged the furniture in here,' Wallis told her. 'Now the chairs are grouped to take advantage of the view, and there's more space to mingle.'

'You have a good eye,' the Prince complimented her, then added: 'The left one.'

It was a feeble joke, but Wallis laughed out loud, and the Prince beamed with pleasure.

Over dinner, Wallis sat by the Prince's side and kept her attention fixed on him. Even with others watching she chided him to wipe soup from his lip, and to put his cutlery down between mouthfuls of veal. She's like his mother, not his lover, Mary thought. He could have any woman he wanted; why choose Wallis? She wasn't beautiful or rich, but perhaps he realised he would need someone of strong character to back him once he was on the throne.

After dinner, they danced to records played on the Prince's gramophone, and Mary watched, thinking how well Wallis and the Prince moved together. She was miming playfully to 'It Ain't No Fault of Mine', and the Prince quipped, 'Knowing you, Wallis, I expect it probably was.'

Ernest asked Mary to dance to 'My Baby Just Cares for Me', and she glided into his arms. Any stranger witnessing the scene would assume they were two married couples, she thought: Mary and Ernest, Wallis and David.

'We've had a wonderful idea,' the Prince announced. 'Let's all go skiing in February in Kitzbühel. Will you join us, Mrs Raffray?'

'I'm afraid a Paris taxi driver put paid to the possibility of me ever skiing,' Mary replied. 'Besides, I must get back to the States by Christmas.' She had promised to join her sister Anne and family. Although she was enjoying her time in London, she was keen not to outstay her welcome and give Wallis any reason to think of her as the house pest again.

'How about you, Ernest?' The Prince turned to him.

'I'll be at work,' Ernest replied.

'Never mind,' the Prince said, obviously satisfied with this response. 'I'll look after Wallis and try to bring her back in one piece. You don't mind, do you, old chap?'

Ernest smiled benignly. 'Of course not.'

When they went to bed, Mary couldn't sleep. She went to the bathroom around one in the morning and couldn't help noticing a slit of light under Wallis's door. Did she have a visitor? If so, which one?

She tiptoed down the corridor, listened for a moment and, not hearing any voices, tapped lightly on Wallis's door. There was no reply. She tapped again, then whispered, 'Wallie?' Still no reply. Finally she opened the door, just a crack, and peeked inside. The bed was empty. Wallis was nowhere to be seen.

Mary closed the door and glanced towards the Prince's suite. A dim light was burning and she fancied she heard a murmur of voices.

Not wanting to be caught there, she rushed back to her own room and leapt into bed, heart pounding. Surely Wallis was not going to bed with the Prince? That would be madness. Perhaps she had just visited his room to help him with something. But a married woman should not be in another man's bedroom at one in the morning for any reason.

Poor Ernest, she thought. He really does not deserve any of this.

Chapter 43

West Sussex, December 1934

A FEW DAYS AFTER THEIR RETURN TO LONDON, Mary set out to catch a train to Pulborough. It was a tiny station, with just two platforms, one of them shaded by an awning, and a stationmaster sitting in a brick office who was happy to telephone her hosts and offered her a cup of tea while she waited.

Twenty minutes later, an open-topped motorcar pulled up and a very tall man wearing a long scarf leapt out. 'Ralph Hargreaves,' he said. 'And you must be Mrs Raffray.'

She shook his hand, saying, 'How do you do,' and was taken aback when he stood staring at her.

'Is something wrong?' she asked.

'No.' He shook himself. 'It's just that you are so very beautiful. Gosh, that must sound as though I am trying to seduce you. Please forgive me.' He grinned. 'I don't know if my wife mentioned that I am an artist? I specialise in portraiture, and you have the loveliest face, with those merry eyes and pretty mouth . . . There I go again.'

Mary laughed. 'That is quite the nicest greeting I've had in a long while. Thank you.'

She got into the passenger seat and was amused to note that there were smears of paint on the legs of Ralph's trousers and one sleeve of his jacket.

'Have you ever had your portrait painted?' he asked, and she said no, she had never known an artist before.

'We must discuss it,' he insisted, and as he drove, he kept shooting her sidelong glances, as if trying to decide the best angle from which to paint her.

Eleanor greeted her and they sat in the cosy drawing room, picking up the threads of conversation where they had left off, the dogs sniffing hopefully at their clothing. In another week Eleanor's two teenage sons would be home from Eton for the Christmas holidays and she was dying to see them; she asked where Mary would spend Christmas, and Mary found herself telling Eleanor about the end of her marriage.

'I still love Jacques. I will always care for him, but I've realised that it is impossible to cure someone who has a drink problem.'

Eleanor agreed, but said, 'I'm sorry for it, though. He is losing a wonderful wife.'

Mary laughed. 'I must come here to be flattered more often. You and your husband are terribly good at it.'

'How is Wallis?' Eleanor asked, pouring more tea. 'Is she happy?'

Mary hesitated. 'I think so. Why do you ask?'

Eleanor mused. 'She always had the air of a person who was searching for something more and would not be satisfied with an ordinary life. But you know her better; perhaps I am mistaken.'

'She is a complicated character,' Mary agreed.

'Mr Simpson did not seem the type of husband I would have imagined her with . . .'

Mary twisted her mouth to one side before answering. 'He's solid and clever and a good man. Wallis might seem frightfully confident and gregarious but underneath she gets anxious and Ernest anchors her. He's the security she never had as a young girl.'

Eleanor was surprised by this. 'But she strikes me as so independent! I heard she spent a year in China on her own.'

'Not quite on her own. She was staying with a couple, Mr and Mrs Herman Rogers. She has an extraordinary number of friends.'

'And now that she is one of the Prince of Wales's set, I imagine she has more than ever.'

Mary could tell Eleanor was fishing for information. It was tempting to blurt out what she knew, to get another woman's perspective on the complex situation Wallis had gotten herself into, but loyalty stopped her. Loyalty to Wallis or to Ernest? She wasn't sure.

'She and Ernest are very close to the Prince,' she replied. 'He's a lonely character and they've taken him under their wing. Ernest talks to him endlessly about history and politics and they seem to see eye to eye.'

'Is that so?' Eleanor replied, her gaze searching Mary's face. 'How lovely for them.'

On her return to London two days later, Mary found Wallis in the drawing room wearing a beautiful Chinese-patterned dress in a blue fabric printed with roses.

'Is that new? It's divine!' Mary approached for a closer look and saw that it was in fact a tunic worn over a slender ankle-length skirt.

'Do you like it? It's from Mainbocher's fall collection. A thank-you from the Prince for helping with his entertaining.'

'That's very kind of him.' Mary tried to catch her eye, to give her a knowing look, but Wallis turned to reposition an ornament on the mantelpiece.

'How was your stay with English Eleanor?' Wallis imitated her accent.

Mary spoke with enthusiasm. 'It was fun. There's no ceremony, no dressing for dinner, no silver service. Their dogs run amok through the house and her artist husband wears paint-spattered clothing. I like them both.'

'Only a few more days till you sail. How will I manage without you?' Wallis asked, sounding plaintive.

'Perhaps you shouldn't take on so much,' Mary advised, choosing her words with care. 'It's easy to over-commit yourself then find you have obligations you can't fulfil.'

Wallis gave her a sharp look. 'Darling Mary, who knows me better than I know myself: how would you advise that I divest myself of obligations without hurting a certain person's feelings?'

'You need to draw a clear line and not step over it.'

'That's just the problem, though: where exactly to draw the line.'

'Perhaps you need to draw it behind you and take a step back,' Mary suggested, wondering yet again what Wallis had been doing in the Prince's bedroom.

Wallis frowned, then glanced at the clock. 'Don't you want to change? It's almost six.'

'I suppose I had better, so you don't completely outshine me in that stunning outfit.' She kissed Wallis on the cheek. 'I *do* understand,' she whispered, with a sympathetic look.

On the way to her bedroom, Mary heard the doorbell ring and hovered to see if it was an early guest. Instead, she watched the maid take delivery of yet another huge bunch of blush-pink roses. Wallis came to the drawing-room door, plucked the card from the bouquet, read it, then folded it in half and stuck it in her pocket.

She's up to something, Mary thought. But surely not with *Ribbentrop*.

Chapter 44

Brighton, 11 November 1997

HE VAN DER HEYDEN CLOTHES ARRIVED AT LAST and Rachel was beside herself with excitement as she unpacked them. They had been professionally cleaned for the auction so didn't have that musty antique smell she was addicted to, but she marvelled at the top-quality seamstressing: the hidden darts and secret pockets, the hand-stitching and ingenious details. Best of all was the Molyneux crystal beaded dress, but she tucked that away to be secreted in her wardrobe at home.

In a spark of inspiration she called the local paper and asked if they might be interested in running a feature about the collection. They sent a journalist round, and when he saw the quality of the gowns he immediately agreed to write a piece if Rachel would model some of them while standing on the pavement outside the shop. As free advertising, it couldn't have been better.

Rachel knew a fair bit about the era and was able to talk knowledgeably to the journalist. 'American society in the 1920s consisted of families who had made millions in business: the Rockefellers from oil, the du Ponts from gunpowder, the Vanderbilts from shipping and railroads, and the Van der

Heydens from diamonds. Their daughters enjoyed unprecedented freedom in what was known as the Jazz Age. While it would have been considered shocking for their grandmothers to show so much as a hint of their ankles, these girls showed knees and a whole lot more when dancing the Charleston in their flapper dresses.'

The journalist held up his hand, asking her to slow down while he scribbled in shorthand. 'Do you mean sexual freedom?'

Typical journalist, Rachel thought. 'Absolutely! A decade earlier an unmarried woman couldn't be in the company of a man who was not a family member without a chaperone present, but in the 1920s they were out riding in men's cars, drinking bootleg liquor in speakeasies, spending a fortune on racy clothes and dancing up a storm. *The Great Gatsby* was the autobiography of the era.' Rachel loved *Gatsby*; she had read it dozens of times and could recite whole sections by heart.

'Do you know anything about the Van der Heyden girls in particular? Any scandals?'

Rachel smiled. 'Mona was said to have had an affair with a black musician who played at the Cotton Club. And Doris's husband sued her for divorce in 1927 at a time when divorce was still considered scandalous. It seems she was sleeping with his business partner.'

The day the article appeared, Rachel sold the Chanel dancing dress and the Vionnet crêpe gown, as well as several strands of the coloured pearls. Takings were the best they had been for months, and she emailed Richard that evening to thank him.

When he replied, he had other news: *The measurements you sent were Wallis Simpson's and Mainbocher think the dress must be hers, but if you want to get the best price, you'll need to find out how your supplier came to have it in his or her possession. Is there a story?*

Rachel rang Susie and told her the news, asking: 'Do you have any idea how it came to be in the wooden chest in your west wing?'

'I've been thinking about it and I would rather you just sold it in Forgotten Dreams,' Susie replied immediately. 'I don't want the publicity an auction might entail.'

Rachel was mystified. 'But we could be talking thousands if it was Wallis's, and maybe a hundred if I sell it in the shop.'

'I've made up my mind. Sorry.'

It seemed peculiar, since Susie was always saying how short of money she was.

'I've sold a few other items,' Rachel told her. 'Do you want me to put a cheque in the post?'

'I'd prefer cash,' Susie replied. 'Let's keep the bank manager's grubby paws off it. I'll come to the shop when I'm next in Brighton.'

~

By late November, the North Laines were glittering with Christmas decorations, every shop displaying gift ideas in its windows: crystal healing sessions, electric guitars, hand-crafted garden sculptures, a set of essential oils in a hemp basket. Rachel created her own display of period gifts, from fine kid gloves in the palest cream to the art deco flapper-girl lamp and the Van der Heyden pearls. She decorated a miniature Christmas tree with festoons of the pearls and bought some old-fashioned wrapping paper and tissue flowers to offer a gift-wrap service. At last the shop was beginning to look as enticing as it had before the break-in.

There was less than a month to go before the wedding, and although her mum had taken care of most details, Rachel had to collect the marriage licence, buy plain rose-gold wedding bands for the pair of them and choose the accessories to go with her Molyneux dress. She decided on simple crystal-and-pearl earrings, a pair of pearl T-bar shoes with dainty heels, a crystal and ivory-feathered fascinator and a chiffon wrap to throw round her shoulders. When she tried on the whole outfit in front of the bedroom mirror, she felt a thrill of anticipation, but it was almost immediately tempered by the memory of Alex's lack of enthusiasm.

'Shall I order white tie for you?' she had asked him. 'It's an evening wedding so that would be best.'

'Whatever you think,' he'd replied.

'Just over three weeks to go,' she'd said, hoping for some romantic comment, just a scrap of reassurance.

'Scary,' he said, then there was a pause in which he clearly realised she was expecting more. 'Scary but good, of course.'

She had decided not to confront him about his distant behaviour. Creating a drama when he was so stressed about his TV programme would only drive him further away, but all the same it was hard.

During week nights when he was in Paris, she looked through the slides Wendy had lent her and decided there were too many good shots to select just one. Instead she had sixty printed up and bought a leather-bound album for them. She spent many hours arranging the pictures in roughly chronological order, juxtaposing funny and touching ones to make a narrative of his childhood up to the age of twelve, when the photos stopped abruptly, presumably after his mother's death.

Seeing him as a child, with his cheeky grin and outgoing nature clearly already in place, made her feel a pang of love. If they ever had a child, she hoped he or she would turn out just like that little boy – but without the hard edges of the man.

Chapter 45

Brighton, 2 December 1997

SUSIE CALLED BY THE SHOP ONE EVENING JUST AS Rachel was closing up. 'I wondered if you had that cash for me?' she asked.

Rachel looked in the till and there wasn't quite enough. 'Walk down the road to the bank with me and I'll withdraw the rest,' she suggested. 'Have you been Christmas shopping?'

'Just a spot of business,' Susie said, looking round. 'I like your shop. It's like a brothel in a 1920s film starring Greta Garbo.'

Rachel smiled. 'Oh dear, those films always have tragic endings.'

It was a relief when the cash machine disgorged the money she needed to pay Susie, something it would not have done before the newspaper feature on the Van der Heyden clothes boosted trade.

'Do you fancy a drink?' Susie asked. 'I could do with one.'

Her car was parked near the beach, so she suggested they went to a seafront bar, one of the ones that were packed with customers on summer evenings, when they spilled out, glasses in hand, onto the stony beach. Now the awning flapped noisily in the wind and there was only one barman on duty serving a handful of customers. The front wall was glass, with a view to the sea, but at six o'clock it was already so dark Rachel couldn't pick out the West Pier.

She was wearing a dark green Jacquard evening coat that she loved, but it wasn't quite warm enough for the icy weather. She kept it huddled around her as they ordered gin and tonics and a dish of olives, and chose a corner table next to a radiator.

'The thing about the Mainbocher,' Susie began, as if continuing their previous conversation, 'is that it's not mine to sell. I'm not sure why it was in the house.'

'Wallis isn't around to say that it wasn't a gift. It's in your possession so I'm sure we could get around that,' Rachel countered.

Susie continued as if she hadn't heard. 'Besides, you must be very busy with your wedding coming up. Just a couple of weeks to go, isn't it?'

Rachel persevered. 'I have a friend who arranges auctions. I'd give it to him so it would be no trouble. Do you have any idea if one of your ancestors knew Wallis? Or mixed in her social circle?'

'I think my grandmother was at school with her in Baltimore, but she didn't like her much – said she found her stand-offish.'

Rachel was intrigued. 'That's interesting. Did she tell you anything else? Did she socialise with Wallis in the 1930s when she was in London?'

'No, I'm sure she didn't. I would have heard about it.' Susie seemed keen to change the subject. 'What are you wearing for the big day?' she asked.

Rachel described the Molyneux dress that Richard had loaned her, and how excited she was to wear it.

'Are *you* engaged?' she asked, noticing a large diamond solitaire glinting on the ring finger of Susie's left hand.

She looked down. 'No, this is a family ring. My love life is unbelievably complicated. I've always been the independent type, and for the last five years I've been seeing a man just like me who lives in Cornwall. Trouble is, I find I want more than a weekend lover, but he won't move and I won't leave my estate, so we are stuck in an impasse.'

'That's hard,' Rachel sympathised. 'I've been in a relationship like that.'

'It gets worse,' Susie continued. 'I hired a private detective to tail him – I've been meeting the detective this afternoon – and he told me my boyfriend has another lover during the week.'

Rachel snorted in disbelief. 'You did *what*?'

Susie grinned self-deprecatingly. 'It's crazy, because it was hideously expensive when I'm supposed to be saving money. But at least I know how the land lies.'

'What are you going to do about it?' Rachel knew she would never hire a detective to check up on Alex, no matter what.

'That's just it: nothing probably. So it was a complete waste of money.' She drained her glass and signalled to the barman to bring them two more drinks, although Rachel was only halfway down her first.

'Why not talk to him about it?'

'God, no! I'm far too proud to let him find out I had him tailed.' She laughed. 'It's my little extravagance and now I'll have to tighten the purse strings again.'

Someone walked into the bar and a blast of icy air hit them. Rachel rubbed her arms. The barman brought their drinks and Susie gulped hers thirstily.

'So why not let me sell the Mainbocher at auction and get some of the money back?' Rachel persevered.

Susie gave a deep sigh. 'I've got my reasons.' She sounded a little tipsy. 'But I can't possibly tell you when you have a TV producer boyfriend who makes documentaries about . . . about stuff like this.'

'I promise I won't breathe a word of it to Alex if you don't want me to.' Rachel was mystified. 'You can trust me, Susie.'

'It's just that I don't want anyone looking into my family's association with Wallis Simpson.' She gazed towards the blacked-out beach and seemed to be considering her words.

'So there *is* an association?' Rachel asked.

'It's not what you think. She was no friend of the family. In fact she stole something from us. Diana was trying to get it back for me when she . . . when she died.' Susie's voice tailed off, her face a mask of misery.

'Wallis stole something? What was it?' Rachel was spell-bound.

'Nothing especially valuable to anyone else: just a painting by my grandfather.'

'But *why* did she steal it?'

'That's a long story.' Susie shook her head. 'The point is that I asked Diana to go to the Villa Windsor and try to persuade them to give it to me. Until I phoned, she had been planning to fly straight to London so she could see her boys the next day.' Her face appealed for understanding. 'But it was my grandma's hundredth birthday and it would have been the best present ever if I could have got her painting back. Duch, bless her, would do a favour for anyone, so she agreed they would spend the night at Dodi's flat in Paris and bring the painting to London with her in the morning. Without me, they would both still be alive.'

Her eyes filled with tears that started to spill down her cheeks. Rachel put an arm round her. 'That doesn't make it your fault,' she said. 'It was the fault of a drunk driver.'

'Perhaps, perhaps not, but that's how the media would see it. I keep imagining the world's press arriving on my doorstep.

Can you imagine the headlines? "She's to blame" they would say alongside my picture. The coverage of Diana's death has been so hysterical, I'm sure that's what would happen.' Susie wiped her tears with the back of her hand, smearing watery mascara across her cheekbone.

'First of all,' Rachel said, 'there's no reason for it to come out in the press. Secondly, if by some fluke it did, they would write about Diana making a selfless gesture to help a friend. That's more the tone of the coverage. As far as the media are concerned, she's a saint.'

Susie pulled a paper napkin from a dispenser and blew her nose into it. 'It's too unpredictable. I can't take the risk. They might even turn up at Grandma's nursing home. The paparazzi can be scum.'

Rachel was puzzling over Susie's revelation. 'Are you sure the painting was the only reason Diana went to Paris? I heard that Dodi picked up a ring from a jeweller's near the Ritz that day, which his father thinks he was going to give her as an engagement ring. And I believe she might have been given some kind of bracelet while she was at the Villa Windsor.' She described the platinum heart with a J on one side and XVII on the other, telling Susie that Diana wasn't wearing it in pictures before going to the Villa Windsor, only after. It was still nestled in the zip pocket of her purse because she hadn't decided what else to do with it, but she didn't show Susie in case she asked awkward questions about how Rachel came to have it.

'Who do you think gave it to her?' Susie asked, dabbing at her eyes.

Rachel shrugged. 'I don't know. We can't find out any more about it. But you mustn't blame yourself. That's a horrible burden to bear.' She glanced at Susie's empty glass. 'Can I get you another drink?'

Susie shook her head. 'No, I'd better not. I'm driving. I'll help you with yours though.' Rachel hadn't even started her second drink so Susie poured half of it into her own glass and took a slurp.

'Are you sure you're OK to drive?'

'On two G and Ts? Course I am. I can tell you're a townie; everyone drink-drives in the country.'

As they walked up to Susie's Land Rover, which was parked in one of the bays along the seafront, Rachel wondered if she should try to talk her out of driving, but sensed she wouldn't pay any attention.

'Thanks for listening,' Susie said as she got into the driver's seat. 'You're the first person I've told about all this.' She gave a loud sniff, put her keys in the ignition and threw her handbag onto the passenger seat. 'And you're right: I can see it's irrational to blame myself for Diana dying. It's just that I miss her so terribly.'

She pulled her door shut, and as she drove off, Rachel could see that she was crying again.

Chapter 46

New York, April 1935

I N THE SPRING OF 1935, AS FRESH NEW LEAVES
unfurled on the trees in Washington Square, Mary and
Jacques' separation became real: they divided their possessions
and moved out of their lovely home into rented apartments
nearby. She had expected to be ostracised by many of their
social circle when the marital breakdown was announced, but
most friends proved supportive. They still invited her to gatherings, often pairing her with single men of their acquaintance,
which she found awkward and embarrassing. She and Jacques
had not filed for divorce and remained on friendly terms;
around once a week she invited him for dinner, worried that
he was not eating properly.

She loved the bohemian atmosphere of the Village, where
artists and writers frequented former speakeasies and every
block seemed to have a jazz club or a tiny theatre. Her new
apartment was on the fourth floor of a brownstone on Bleecker
Street, a few streets back from Washington Square, where she
could sit on her fire escape and watch the world go by. The
area was always busy until late.

She wrote regularly to Wallis and tried to read between the
lines of her replies to find out how she was balancing her

complicated relationships with the two men in her life. It was always the Prince she wrote about, Mary noticed; Ernest seldom got a mention. It seemed he was acting as chaperone so that Wallis could spend weekends at Fort Belvedere without the British press becoming curious about her. No one outside the Prince's crowd would read anything into it when the list of guests in the Court Circular included 'Mr and Mrs Simpson'. Not a breath of insinuation appeared in the British papers, although the US ones often ran stories about 'the Prince of Wales and his American friend Mrs Simpson'.

Mary was overjoyed when Ernest wrote to say he would be spending two months in New York on business that summer and hoped to see her. She replied that she was entirely at his disposal and asked if Wallis would be accompanying him. She already knew the answer before it arrived: Wallis would be spending the summer with the Prince. He had invited her to stay at a villa in Cannes, but the party included no Aunt Bessie to lend respectability and Mary knew there was bound to be talk. It was as if Wallis had ceased to care about her reputation, or that of her husband.

Ernest arrived in New York on a scorching day in late July 1935, and Mary went to meet him at the pier. He walked down the gangway looking tanned from the crossing, and more relaxed than she had seen him in a while, almost as if he were arriving for a holiday.

'You catch us in a heatwave,' Mary greeted him from beneath a white parasol. 'Blue skies and long sunny days. What a shame you must go to the office.'

'I'll try to finish early,' he replied. 'It's always pleasant to stroll by the waterfront on a summer evening, watching the ferries chug past.'

'Will you see Dorothea and your girls? They must be quite grown up now.'

He opened the door of a taxicab and took her arm as she stepped up. 'Audrey is thirteen, and I will certainly see her as often as I can, but Cynthia is a grown woman of twenty-one and I seldom hear from her.'

Mary remembered that Cynthia was not his daughter, but the child of Dorothea's first marriage.

'I hope you will call on me whenever you have a free evening,' she said. 'I consider it my responsibility to ensure you do not get lonely. Would you like to start by coming for dinner this evening?'

'Indeed.' He smiled. 'I can think of nothing I would enjoy more.'

Mary got her cook to prepare American dishes that she knew Ernest liked: Creole shrimp, Maryland fried chicken, corn bread and grits served with greens. She invited two other couples, and the talk was of new buildings in the city. Ernest looked forward to exploring the Chrysler Building and the Empire State Building, which he had only seen from the outside, and Mary said she would like to visit them too. 'I love the curves of the art deco style; they make sharp corners seem old-fashioned.'

When she and Ernest had a moment to themselves, the conversation turned to Wallis, and Mary asked if her life was as frenetic as it had been six months earlier when she was in London.

'If anything, more so,' Ernest replied, his face giving nothing away. 'Peter Pan makes quite extraordinary demands and rarely allows her time on her own. I bow automatically when I come through my own front door, assuming he will be there, as he almost invariably is.'

'I do worry about the British press getting hold of the story and turning you both into figures of mockery. Is Wallis not concerned about that?'

Ernest shrugged. 'We barely have time to discuss it. I can't remember the last time I spent an evening with my wife. Sometimes I can see that she finds the Prince's attentions onerous, but you and I know that she enjoys the prestige of her position, so it's a subtle balancing act. She does get very tired of having to be constantly "switched on".'

Mary wanted to ask him how he felt, but Ernest's manner did not invite personal questions. He must remember that she had tried to talk him out of pursuing Wallis all those years ago, so she would probably be the last person in whom he would confide.

~

The friendship they had enjoyed in London quickly resumed. Ernest had time on his hands, and so did Mary. She fell into the habit of calling at his Battery Park office in the late afternoon so they could stroll along the esplanade with views out to the bay. In the evenings, they dined together, went to friends' parties or to concerts, and at weekends they chose a district to visit, either to explore the city's ever-changing architecture or to browse in an art gallery. Ernest was rather traditional in his artistic tastes, keen on Turner, Rembrandt and Gainsborough, while Mary adored the modern American art at the Whitney Museum round the corner from her apartment.

'I don't know what they are supposed to *be*,' Ernest complained of abstract paintings.

'Think rather of how they make you *feel*,' Mary urged. 'Oh, I do like finding a subject on which I know more than you. What a rarity!'

She often slipped her arm through his as they walked, and knew they must appear as a married couple. She liked the feeling. Ernest never pulled away, but seemed content to stroll companionably, their stream of conversation never running dry.

One summer evening, after they had finished dinner at her apartment, they sat on chairs pulled out to the fire escape, drinking Scotch and soda from highball glasses and trying to catch a breath of breeze. The maid was inside, clearing the dining room. The street below was bathed in the yellow glow of street lamps, and the chatter of passers-by rose through the air mixed with the sound of horns floating out of a club two doors down.

Ernest had removed his jacket and tie and rolled up his sleeves, and as she spoke, Mary touched his bare arm. She was on her third Scotch and the heat plus the unaccustomed quantity of alcohol loosened her tongue.

'Did you see the story in the *New York Times* today about Wallis and the Prince in a Cannes nightclub?' she asked, knowing he must have. He always read the *Times*.

'Apparently they danced a rumba,' he said, his tone flat.

Mary took a gulp of her drink, running the next words through her mind before saying them aloud. 'If you want to save your marriage, I believe you are going to have to fight for her.'

'How does one fight the heir to the throne of one's country?' he asked. There was a silence, then he said quietly: 'Besides, I'm not entirely sure I do want to fight for her.'

Mary got goose bumps on her arms, despite the heat. 'Really?' she whispered. 'But you adore Wallis.'

'Our marriage has not been entirely harmonious of late. We live quite separate existences. If the Prince wants to marry her, I have decided I shall not stand in his way.'

Mary felt her heart beat faster. 'It won't come to that, will it? Wallis told me the Prince will have to marry someone who can provide him with an heir.'

'It's six months since you saw them together.' He turned to face Mary. 'In that time, Peter Pan has become more obsessive than ever. He follows her constantly, happy only when he has her full attention. I don't think he will let her go, even if she wanted him to. It's a rum state of affairs.' He put his drink down and suddenly took her hand in his. 'You and I have so much in common, Mary,' he said, his voice full of emotion. 'Sometimes I rather think I married the wrong girl.'

They gazed at each other for a long moment, and Mary thought she might faint. When Ernest leant over to kiss her on the lips, she did not draw away.

This is wrong, she thought. I must stop this. But his kisses were exquisite, irresistible.

The maid interrupted them by coming towards the window to say, 'Excuse me, ma'am, but is it all right if I turn in?' She slept in a small room on a lower floor.

'Of course it is,' Mary replied, her cheeks burning. 'I'll see you in the morning.'

They waited until they heard the front door close, then Ernest suggested, 'Shall we go inside to sit in front of your fan? It must be cooler than out here.'

It was an excuse, of course. As soon as they were side by side on the drawing-room sofa, he began to kiss her again, and she responded with all the months and years of unspent passion that had built up inside her. She realised she had never stopped loving Ernest. She had made a good fist of being his friend, but deep down he had always been the husband of her dreams.

Their kissing inevitably led to lovemaking: first an undig-nified scramble on the sofa, then Ernest carried the fan to the bedroom and made love to her on her bed as the air blew over their bare skin. He was only the second man Mary had ever made love with, and she was astonished by the difference between him and Jacques. Ernest showered her with kisses on her neck, her arms, her breasts, stroked his hand up her spine over and over, combed his fingers through her hair. She felt self-conscious about the roundness of her belly and the plumpness of her thighs, but he buried his head in them and breathed her scent, sighing deeply. When he was inside her, she felt whole and complete as a woman. There were no thoughts; only sensations.

Afterwards, as he slept with his head on her breast, she was exhilarated. She touched his hair, felt the texture, smelling the light perfume of his hair oil. It felt right, as though this was how it was always meant to be.

Ernest hurried off at five in the morning, before her maid returned, and Mary lay awake, reliving the night and trying to justify her actions. Wallis did not seem to want Ernest any more; she had set her sights on the Prince and had neglected her husband for too long. Ernest deserved to be happy and not the object of others' pity as they whispered about him being a cuckold. And she, Mary, deserved some happiness too. She had loved Ernest long before Wallis met him. By rights he should have been her husband all along.

But even as she listed these self-justifications, deep down she knew that making love with her best friend's husband was wrong. What if Ernest felt the need to purge his soul in confession? Wallis would never forgive her. Mary was the person she trusted more than any other. They were sisters who had chosen each other, and this was the worst possible betrayal.

The following evening, she arrived at Ernest's office at the hour he finished work, fully intending to tell him that their lapse of the previous evening must never be repeated, but he spoke first.

'Last night was glorious,' he told her, squeezing her arm against him. 'You made me a very happy man. But I fear the consequences if Wallis were to hear of it.'

'Me too,' Mary breathed in relief.

'And yet all day I could not help myself thinking about you, and hoping with all my heart that you will let me make love to you again.'

Mary felt her insides turn to liquid and she blushed fiercely.

'Would you agree to us enjoying our summer together, knowing that in the fall I must return to London, to my wife? I know it is a lot to ask.' He stopped to look Mary square in the eye.

'Yes. I agree,' she said. She simply couldn't help herself.

'Who knows if I will still have a wife by this autumn in anything but name,' he said, stroking her face gently. 'It appears to me that what happens next will be in the lap of the gods.'

Chapter 47

New York, October 1935

MARY COULDN'T STOP CRYING AS THE TUGS PULLED Ernest's ship away from the pier and out into the fast-flowing East River. She stood and watched as it disappeared towards the ocean, already missing him with a great ache in her soul. They had agreed she could write care of his London office, and as soon as she got home she began a letter, telling him how empty her life was without him and how much she hoped they could be together soon. She reread it, then tore it up and wrote another, a chatty letter about the new Hemingway book she had just started, *Green Hills of Africa*, which was about the author's travels on that continent.

I do wish I could travel more, she confided. *I've never even been to the West Coast of America, and the only European cities I know are London and Paris. One day I should love to visit Rome and Venice.*

As soon as Ernest arrived in England, he mailed her a letter several pages long that he had written on the ship. He wrote with great charm, describing the quirks of the other passengers, the food served in first class, the dolphins that followed them one day, cavorting in the ship's wake as if showing off to entertain the passengers. There was no word of love, no hopes for the future, but he closed by saying: *My warmest thanks for making the summer so joyous. You are always in my thoughts.*

Mary hugged herself. The sentiments were lovely but she yearned to hear his voice. If only she could pick up the telephone and ring him. For now, letters would have to suffice.

Wallis wrote from London with amusing stories of life in the Prince's circle. The Duchess of York, wife to David's brother Bertie, had walked into the room while Wallis was doing an impression of her, and as a result had refused ever to meet her again.

David and I call her 'Cookie', she wrote, *because she has the common air – and the plumpness – of a member of the kitchen staff who samples too many of her own wares.* She told Mary that the Prince continued to buy her jewellery, including some 'pretty nice stones', but that when she begged him to give her an evening's peace from time to time, asking him to consider her position with Ernest, he turned a deaf ear. *It puts me under the most enormous strain,* she wrote. *Ernest is an angel but he does get cross that he must do without a wife. We've had fearful rows about it. But David is a child, who never thinks of the consequences of his actions.*

Such sentiments pricked Mary's conscience. She had betrayed this friend who trusted her implicitly. If only Wallis was in love with the Prince, Mary could feel there was some justification for her betrayal, some possibility of a happy outcome – but it was clear she was not. She liked the fact that he was rich as mud, she loved the expensive clothes and jewels he paid for and the generous allowance he now gave her, she liked the fact that everyone in London wanted to be her friend – but she was paying a very high price for it all.

~

Just after the New Year of 1936, Ernest returned to New York for a two-week visit, and straight away he and Mary were lovers again. He spent every evening with her, slept every night in her house, woke up with her every morning. They were running the risk that her maid and cook might gossip to friends and word would get out. Mary gave them bonuses with their wages in the hope that it would encourage them to hold their tongues – but, she thought in a devil-may-care moment, hang the consequences if not. His visit was so brief that she couldn't bear to miss out on a second of it. She loved the easy intimacy of listening to him hum while shaving, of chatting about the newspaper head-lines over breakfast, of remembering that he liked devilled kidneys and asking the cook to prepare them for him.

'Come to London in the spring,' he suggested on his depar-ture. 'Wallis would love to see you.'

They looked at each other, and Mary felt stricken. Here in New York she could pretend Ernest was hers, but in London there would be no such luxury. She would not be able to kiss him when she wished, or straighten his tie or brush lint from his jacket, because that would be Wallis's role. Would she be capable of dissembling? Would Wallis sense the charged atmos-phere between them? She was very sharp about other people's affairs.

Just three days after Ernest left New York, Mary was wakened by her maid bringing a tray of tea with the morning paper. As soon as the drapes were opened, she saw the front-page head-line: King George V had died. That meant the Prince of Wales must now become king.

Mary was gripped with anxiety. Surely Wallis would not be able to continue her current relationship with the King of England? He would be forced to find someone younger, someone who could sit beside him as queen. And if Wallis were no longer occupied with the Prince, she would no doubt turn her attention to her long-neglected husband. It was an unmitigated disaster.

Mary rose, pulled on her tea gown and hurried to her writing desk to compose separate letters to Wallis and Ernest. She asked Wallis to offer her condolences to the Prince, and wondered when he would ascend to the throne. She was largely ignorant of royal protocol. Would it mean they had less time together? Was Wallis sad about this? To Ernest she wrote asking, *What now? Where does this leave us?*

She gave her maid the letters, asking her to mail them immediately, then she paced her apartment trying to imagine the ramifications. No matter how she looked at it, no good could come of the situation.

~

David's accession as Edward VIII was proclaimed from the balcony at St James's Palace the day after his father's death, Wallis wrote in reply.

> *There was a fanfare of gun salutes and trumpets playing the national anthem and the Garter King of Arms proclaiming in solemn tones while soldiers marched around. David is quiet and sad, as you would expect. Already he must spend hours each day on some mysterious red dispatch boxes containing notice of affairs of state. He does not enjoy it and I have to nag him to finish . . . My own company is even more in demand than before, with society hostesses clamouring to swear undying friendship, but I do not flatter myself that it has anything to do with whatever small charms I may possess.*

She did not address the question of where the accession might leave her, and Mary guessed she was as much in the dark as the rest of them. The letter finished: *I hope he will be a modern king, who will update many of the ancient, outmoded customs of the institution he was born into. He could be a great monarch for this new era.*

Ernest wrote with some startling news in February, his tone matter-of-fact and the content anything but:

The new King invited me to dine at York House last night. Wallis would not be there, he told me, so I decided this was the occasion on which we must clarify our mutual positions. Perhaps he had the same idea. I took my friend Bernie Rickatson-Hatt with me, as a witness of sorts. During the meal, conversation was all perfectly general, about politics and such like, but over the brandy and cigars I broached the subject on all our minds by asking about the King's intentions towards my wife. 'Do you plan to marry her?' I asked, straight out. The King rose from his chair and said, 'Do you really think I could be crowned without Wallis by my side?' There was some toing and froing after which I said that if he would promise to look after her, then I was prepared to end my marriage.

Mary's first emotion was jubilation: Ernest would be free and they could be together. But almost immediately, this was tempered by doubts: what would Wallis say? Mary sensed she would be furious to have her fate decided by these two men without them so much as consulting her.

The next letter she received from Wallis did not mention it. *Are you still planning to visit in spring?* she asked. *I'm dying to see you. I must be in Paris in the last week of March for some dress fittings, but why not come at the very end of the month?*

It was going to be excruciating to see Wallis and Ernest together, but Mary reasoned that if she met him on his own first, it might be easier to come to terms with the situation, so she booked a crossing that arrived on 24 March. He met her at Waterloo, giving her a warm hug and a tender kiss before taking her arm to lead her to his car.

'It's wonderful to see you,' he breathed, holding her hand and gazing at her. 'I wish we could be together tonight, but I fear the servants at Bryanston Court would not prove as biddable as yours in Manhattan. One of them would be bound to let the cat out of the bag.'

'I don't mind,' she said, although she was secretly disappointed. She longed to hold him in her arms, and had hoped he might visit her in the circular guest bed once the servants were asleep. But he was a gentleman of principle and would not be unfaithful to his wife in her own home.

During Wallis's absence they dined together, drank whisky – for which Mary had developed a taste – and talked every evening. Predictably, the subject often turned to Wallis and the King.

'She doesn't know of my conversation with Peter Pan,' Ernest said. 'There is a complication in that, as head of the Church of England, he is not supposed to marry a divorcee. But I am sure he will find a way around it.'

'What about an heir?'

Ernest shrugged. 'To be frank, I think it is the least of his concerns. He just wants to be with Wallis. If they don't have children, the succession will pass to his brother Bertie, and then to Bertie's elder daughter Lilibet.'

'Is that what Wallis wants? Have you asked her?'

Ernest shook his head. 'I told you: we never see each other on our own. She is the queen of London society and seldom spends an evening at Bryanston Court. There is no more KT hour here, because she mixes her KTs at York House. A lot has changed since your last visit.'

Wallis arrived back in London on Saturday the 28th and swept into the drawing room in a haze of expensive perfume, stopping short when she saw Mary. 'What a surprise! You're here already. I was expecting you next week.'

'Hello, Wallie.' Mary rose to embrace her. 'I got a cheap first-class berth on an earlier sailing. Of course I'd forgotten all about your trip to Paris. You look divine. Is that new?'

Wallis was wearing a blue wool suit with chalk stripes and a matching trilby. It could have been a man's office wear but for the tiny waist, the padded shoulders, the long slim skirt and the jaunty angle of the hat.

'Charles Creed. I do like his tailoring.' Wallis smoothed her skirt.

'And that's a stunning brooch.' Three diamond-studded feathers curled out of a gold crown. 'A gift from the King, perhaps?'

'The Prince of Wales feathers,' Wallis agreed. 'I guess I should stop wearing it now he's been promoted to the top job.' She flung herself into a chair, removed her hat and kicked off her shoes. 'Oh Mary, I hope you have brought your Baltimore common sense with you, because I am in a complete tizzy. My entire life is unmanageable. You *will* tell me what to do, won't you?'

'You might not like the answer,' Mary teased.

Wallis rang the bell set into the wall by her chair, and when a maid came she said, 'Two martinis, please,' and sighed heavily. 'Thank God for alcohol. I swear it's my only refuge.'

She looked utterly worn out, and Mary felt a surge of compassion. 'You need a vacation. Can't you go away somewhere without the King, and have some time alone to contemplate your situation?'

'He wouldn't let me. It was all I could do to stop him following me to Paris this week.'

Mary gave her a rueful smile. 'Do you remember saying to me once that you weren't lovable; that I was the lovable one of the pair of us? Well, it seems you've found someone who will love you to the ends of the earth and back.'

'It's not love.' Wallis shook her head wearily. 'It's need. It's obsession. He says he can't live without me. He begs me to marry him twenty times a day and won't take no for an answer.'

'Do *you* love *him*?' Mary scarcely dared ask, because the answer meant so much to her. It could change the entire course of her life, either setting Ernest free or keeping him from her for ever.

Wallis didn't answer straight away. The maid came in with their drinks, picked up Wallis's shoes and hat, straightened some cushions and left again.

Wallis took a sip of her martini, then put it down on the table. 'I care about him a lot,' she said. 'But at the end of the day, I'm not sure if that's enough.'

Chapter 48

Brighton, 13 December 1997

BY MID DECEMBER, CHRISTMAS TRADE HAD GOT so busy in Forgotten Dreams that Rachel called Nicola and asked if she could come and help. On her own, she spent so long gift-wrapping purchases that customers had to queue to pay and she had no time to chat or offer advice. She felt a little uneasy around Nicola since finding the emails and realising she was meeting Alex on Friday evenings, but there was no one else she could ask.

She eyed Nicola critically as she walked in and hung her parka on a hook.

'How's things?' she asked.

'Could be worse,' Nicola said, sounding a bit flat. 'I'm looking forward to your wedding.'

'Have you found something to wear for it?' Rachel asked. 'You would suit that fifties silk dress.' She picked it off a rail to show Nicola. It had a structured bust that would give her fabulous cleavage, and the silvery colour with a subtle blue-green floral pattern would look great with her dark colouring.

'It's gorgeous, but I can't possibly afford it.'

'Try it on! Borrow it if you like,' Rachel offered. 'You seem tired. Did you go out last night?' she asked, testing. Alex hadn't arrived home till after ten and had been non-committal when she asked where he'd been.

'I had a quick drink with a friend,' Nicola said. Her back was to Rachel.

'Anyone I know?'

'I don't think so.' She was refolding some cardigans, tidying the shelf on which they were displayed. 'We were talking about Diana. My friend says she had to have a virginity test before she got married. Do you think that could be true?'

Rachel frowned. 'A hymen test? I wouldn't have thought so. There's no infallible method of testing virginity.'

'Diana had to be pure as a nun,' Nicola continued. 'Charles had to find someone young and innocent enough to be unravaged by masculine appendage.'

'What a quaint phrase. Are you suggesting I should do this hymen test before my wedding?' Rachel asked. 'Because I'm afraid I've been ravaged by more masculine appendages than I can count.'

'Do you mean Alex wasn't the first?' Nicola pretended shock. 'Does he know?'

'Feel free to tell him when you see him,' Rachel replied. 'I'd hate for him to enter matrimony under false pretences.'

A customer came in to browse, then another, and soon Forgotten Dreams was teeming with Christmas shoppers. There was a queue for the curtained changing cubicle and the till rang with a gratifying regularity. Rachel and Nicola went out for lunch separately, and it was mid afternoon before there was a lull.

'Did you know that a Catholic priest gave Diana the last rites?' Nicola said, as if she'd been thinking about the subject since their earlier conversation broke off. 'He was based near the hospital so they called him in the middle of the night when they couldn't restart her heart. He sat with her for around four hours until Kensington Palace staff arrived on the first flight from London to prepare her body.'

'How do you know all this stuff?' Rachel asked, sure it must have come from Alex.

'Oh, just reading, conversation . . . you know.' Nicola waved an arm to indicate she had absorbed information from the universe. 'I found that quite moving. Diana wasn't Catholic, but I think she'd have appreciated it.'

The image of the Princess in the oxygen mask came back to Rachel. 'She was dead. She wouldn't have heard any of it.'

'I don't know.' Nicola shrugged. 'They say hearing is the last sense to go. Maybe the ritualistic sound of the words would have been comforting.'

Certainly more comforting than flashbulbs going off in your face, Rachel mused with a shiver.

~

Back at the flat, Alex was on the telephone and just gave a brief wave to acknowledge her arrival. Rachel kicked off her heels and went to the kitchen to pour herself a large vodka and tonic. She held the first taste in her mouth, savouring the alcohol, then let it slide down her throat, warming and soothing. Her stockinged feet were sore from standing all day in what Alex would call 'silly shoes', so she gave them a rub while praying that it would be a peaceful evening. These last few days before their wedding should be a time of love and closeness rather than suspicion and irritability.

There was nothing she felt like eating in the fridge, so she delved into a drawer and pulled out a handful of takeaway menus. The Chinese and pizza ones were rejected straight away, leaving Indian or Thai. She was keen on the Thai hot and sour soup known as *tom yam* and decided to have it with prawns.

Through in the sitting room she placed the menu in front of Alex, a question in her expression. Still listening to someone on the end of the phone, he glanced at the menu and put a tick beside the green chicken curry. She used her mobile phone to place the order. When the first vodka was finished, she poured another and could feel the buzz as it went to her head. She wasn't drunk: just mellow, chilled out. When she heard Alex finish his call, she took him a bottle of beer, clinking her glass against it in a wordless toast.

'Twenty minutes for food, they said. How was your day?'

'Busy,' he replied. 'I have to go up to London tomorrow, then over to Paris on Monday, just for a few hours.'

'Oh no!' Rachel cried. 'Not again.'

'It's important,' he insisted. 'My researcher has managed to get a gardener at Villa Windsor to agree to talk about Diana. It has to be off-camera and he doesn't want to be identified, but he was there when she visited and can tell us about it. But it can only be on Monday, which is his day off. The following week he's going on leave for Christmas, and it will be too late after that because the programme will be edited. Don't worry. I'll fly back Monday night.'

'I was hoping we could spend a peaceful weekend together.' Rachel felt herself sway slightly and sat down. She was a lightweight when it came to alcohol and didn't want Alex to guess she was on her second drink. 'Never mind.'

Something caught her eye: Alex had left a television industry magazine on the coffee table and the front cover showed a well-known actress wearing a lilac evening gown. She picked it up. The dress was a halter-neck, and it was worn with matching elbow-length gloves. It was her Lucien Lelong, the one that had been in the shop window. There couldn't be another. She looked at the date on the magazine and saw it was a couple of weeks old.

'Alex, that's one of the dresses that was stolen from my shop!'

He glanced at the magazine. 'Are you sure? Couldn't it be another one the same?'

She flicked through to read the story inside, which was about a 1920s drama currently being shot by Gazelle Films, the company whose intern had approached her back in October. There were some black-and-white shots accompanying the story and Rachel picked out a satin coat with a black velvet collar and cuffs and a deep border trim that had also been hers. There was no question.

'These are definitely mine. It's too much of a coincidence. I'm calling the police,' she said, reaching for the phone.

'Hang on a minute,' Alex said, taking the magazine from her, running his eyes over the story. 'I know Ben, the head of Gazelle Films. Let me give him a ring. We can ask him where he got the costumes and give him a chance to explain. If you get the police involved, they might confiscate his entire ward-robe and it will hold up filming. Maybe he'll make you an offer instead.'

'I can't do that,' Rachel argued, shocked that he would suggest it. 'I'd be breaking the law. I reported these as stolen, and accepting a backhander not to mention that they've turned up again would be a criminal offence.'

'Why are you always so squeaky clean?' Alex scoffed. 'Ben will be furious with me if his filming's delayed and he hears I could have prevented it. Try to think of my point of view for a change.'

Rachel felt her temper rising. 'What do you mean, "for a change"? I do nothing but try to understand your point of view, but I notice it's never reciprocated. You've been totally unsupportive while I've been struggling to rescue my business.'

'That's not true. I offered to help financially but you turned me down flat.'

Rachel continued: 'That magazine is two weeks old. You knew that dress, you must have seen it dozens of times in my window, yet you didn't think to point it out.'

'I'm sorry, I don't have a photographic memory of your stock. I'm a man, remember?'

Rachel couldn't stop now she had started: 'We haven't talked properly for ages, and you've been grumpy and horrid to me for weeks.'

Alex shifted away from her, folded his arms. 'If anything has come between us recently, it's your attitude to my programme. How do you think I feel when you dismiss it as opportunist and sensational? Is that what you secretly think of all my work? That I jump on bandwagons and rush out populist nonsense? I've found your opinions really hurtful, to be frank.'

'I'm sorry if that's how it's come across.' She frowned. She couldn't think straight. How had he switched the argument away from her burglary?

'It's OK. I'll survive.' His tone was sarcastic.

'Perhaps I should be more supportive, but you should support me too. You never ask how the business is doing.'

'That's because I have faith in you. You're good at your job. I know your new stock is selling well because Nicola told me.' His expression was unemotional.

'When did you see Nicola?' Jealousy buzzed in her chest and she took a swig of vodka.

'I had a drink with her last night when I got off the train. That's allowed, isn't it?' He eyed her defiantly.

'I knew it!' Rachel cried. 'Why did she lie to me about it? I asked her who she'd been out with and she said it was a friend I didn't know. Is there something I should be told about?'

Alex was irritated. 'Oh for God's sake, don't be pathetic. I've got no idea why she didn't tell you. You'd have to ask her.'

'You're talking to her more than you talk to me, it seems.'

'Perhaps that's because she's not on my case the whole time. She's interested in what I'm doing, not constantly looking for things to criticise.' She saw his glance flicker to his notebook, as if he had just remembered something. Even now she didn't have his full attention.

The conversation wasn't going the way Rachel wanted, but she pressed on. 'There are all kinds of things in my life you know nothing about.'

Alex took a swig of beer. 'OK, tell me,' he said, without warmth.

It came out in a rush: 'I thought I was pregnant but it turns out I'm not.'

'How long did you think you were pregnant?' he asked, showing no emotion.

'Just a few days. I wanted to tell you but you were too busy. Then my period came, over a week late.'

Alex nodded, as if that confirmed something. 'So you're hormonal and you're clearly drunk. What do you want me to do about it?'

Suddenly Rachel felt a wave of anger well up inside her. 'Just sod off to Paris!' she yelled. 'What do I care anyway?'

She stormed out of the room and threw herself face-down on the bed, waiting for Alex to come after her. He didn't appear. She heard the doorbell ring as the takeaway was delivered, but he didn't call her and, childishly, she didn't want to be the one to back down. She wasn't hungry anyway.

At first there was no sound from the sitting room, then she heard a murmur of voices as he switched the TV on.

After a while she fell asleep, fully clothed, star-fished across the bed. She woke around 3 a.m. to find that Alex had covered himself with a blanket on the sofa and was out for the count.

Chapter 49

Brighton, 14 December 1997

RACHEL OPENED HER EYES FEELING PARCHED AND noticed a cup of tea by the bed with a note propped against it. The argument of the previous evening came back to her and she felt ashamed of losing her temper.

Sorry to leave unfinished business, the note read, *but I'm catching an early train so I can have the whole day in the edit suite. Ring you tonight.* There was no animal cartoon; that meant Alex was still cross.

She took a sip of tea but it was stone cold. The clock read 10.30 a.m. He must have left ages ago.

Rachel picked up the phone and dialled. It was time to deal with this situation.

'It's me,' she said when Nicola answered. 'Are you free for a drink tonight?'

'OK.' The voice was sleepy. 'What's up?'

'Seven o'clock at the cocktail bar near the Pavilion,' Rachel said. 'Mojitos are on me.'

Next she phoned the police and told them that some of her stolen stock was being used in a film shoot. Whatever Alex thought, that was the only sensible option.

At 6.45 p.m. Rachel set off for the bar, wearing a warm olive-green wool suit with a brown fur collar, and ribbed brown tights with lace-up ankle boots. She pulled on the green velvet turban Alex had given her and her Jacquard coat with a brown fur muff.

One thing she loved about Brighton was that you could walk more or less everywhere. Although it was Sunday night, the streets were busy with revellers spilling out of pubs and clubs, and the sounds of salsa, hard rock and country merged into an undulating wave of sound. The wind had picked up and a black plastic bag flew past at head height before draping itself around a Christmas tree covered in multicoloured fairy lights. She hadn't planned what she would say to Nicola; all she wanted was the truth.

The bar she had suggested was just a block away from the domed Indian-style Pavilion that had formerly been a royal residence, and its decor was in Mughal style, with wall paint-ings, canopied sofas and tiled tabletops.

Nicola arrived late and flustered. 'I lost my keys,' she muttered by way of explanation as she flopped down onto the low sofa.

Rachel had already ordered a jug of mojito, and she stirred it with a twizzle stick then poured a tumbler for Nicola.

'How's your art?' she asked. 'I haven't asked in ages. Are you putting together another exhibition?'

Nicola looked downcast. 'I'm at a crossroads. I had to give up the studio because it was too hard to find the rent on top of that for the flat.'

'You should have said!' Rachel exclaimed. But what could she have done? She couldn't afford to employ Nicola in the shop any more than she already did.

'It's crazy to rent a studio when I'm not earning anything from my work. I've brought everything back to the flat and will work from there – until I become the next Paula Rego, that is.'

Rachel poured her own drink then raised her glass. 'Here's to you becoming Paula Rego,' she said. 'I hope it's just round the corner.'

'We should be toasting your wedding,' Nicola replied. 'Only four days to go.'

Rachel grunted, took a sip of her drink. 'If it happens . . . Alex and I are still arguing constantly. I wondered if he said anything to you when you saw him on Friday?'

Nicola coloured, caught out in her lie. 'He told you?'

'Yes.' Rachel furrowed her brow with what she hoped was a sympathetic expression. 'Why didn't *you* tell me? I've been aware for ages that you and Alex were meeting on Friday evenings. I'm just surprised by the secrecy.' She held her breath. Was this the moment when Nicola would confess to an affair and shatter all her dreams for the future?

Nicola chewed her thumbnail and didn't answer for what seemed an impossibly long time, then she gave a massive sigh. 'I've been having a bad time lately and Alex is helping me to get through it.'

Rachel was dumbfounded. 'Do you mean because of giving up the studio?'

'I suppose that's part of it . . . And I was devastated about being responsible for your break-in. But it's mostly about Tony. I didn't tell you because I knew you would disapprove, but I've been an idiot and chased after him. Alex tried to talk me out of it, but I went to one of the band's gigs in London and turned up at the stage door. Needless to say, I got what I deserved when he treated me like a groupie.' She was mumbling, clearly ashamed.

'What did he do?' Rachel frowned. Why would Nicola make herself so vulnerable? Did she have no self-respect?

'I can't talk about it.' She dug in the pocket of her parka and pulled out a pack of ten Silk Cut and a box of Swan Vestas.

'I've even started smoking again, after three years off. What an idiot!' She extracted a cigarette and lit it, her cheeks hollowing as she sucked in smoke.

Rachel bit back a retort. She hated smoking, hated to get the smell on her clothes.

'I told Alex what happened, and he's been explaining to me the way men like Tony think.' Rachel noticed Nicola's eyes light up when she was talking about Alex. 'He put it very clearly: if a salesman is trying to sell you something and he keeps lowering the price, you'll get the impression there's something wrong with it.' She took a determined gulp of her mojito then a drag on her cigarette, as if seeking salvation in their mood-altering chemicals.

Rachel nodded sympathetically. 'That analogy works to an extent, but you're not dodgy goods; you just picked a dodgy guy. We've all been there.'

'Yeah, but when you found out your last one was cheating on you, you dumped him straight away. You're a strong person, but I'm so pitiful I can't even move on.' She turned her head and blew the smoke away from Rachel.

Rachel hated to think of Tony getting away with his appalling behaviour. 'I'm glad you could talk to Alex about it; really I am. You two go back a long way. I'm just hurt you didn't feel you could tell me.'

Nicola tapped her ash into the ashtray. 'You're so confident, with your amazing style, you would never understand why I was being such a doormat. I just don't want to be alone any more. I'm sick of it. And Alex has been lovely. He called every few days to check I was surviving and he met me on his way home on Friday evenings. Talking to him kept me sane.'

Rachel remembered Nicola's odd reaction to the news of their engagement. Was she jealous of their happiness? Or worried that once Alex was married he would have less time for her? 'I'm not as confident as you think,' she confided. 'You made me question our relationship when you told me that he used to run away when things got serious. It's been a tricky few months and he's not been a great partner by any means.'

Immediately Nicola leapt to his defence. 'It's no wonder he's single-minded about this documentary: it will pull in more viewers than any other he's made. He needs to strike a careful balance so that he pleases everyone from the Diana groupies to the conspiracy theorists while still being true to himself. It sounds to me as if he's doing an incredible job.'

The kernel of suspicion that had been festering in Rachel's mind came to the fore. 'Tell me,' she asked, scrutinising Nicola's face. 'Did anything ever happen between the two of you romantically?'

Nicola blushed and looked away. 'Not really . . . Back at college when we shared a flat for a while, we occasionally slept together.'

Rachel sat back on the sofa, stunned. Neither of them had mentioned it. She might have had a no-analysis-of-exes pact with Alex, but he should have told her that.

Nicola hurried to clarify. 'It was usually just if we were blind drunk and neither of us had anyone else. I mean, it probably only happened a handful of times.'

'I'm amazed I didn't know.' Rachel couldn't picture them together; best not to try.

'I don't think Alex even remembers. If he does, he gives no hint of it.'

Rachel saw hurt flickering in Nicola's eyes. 'Did you mind that it was casual, or were you hoping it would turn into something more?'

Nicola shook her head as if trying to expunge the memory. 'I loved him. He broke my heart badly, but he doesn't know because I never told him. I managed to settle for friendship, and it's fine now. Honestly it is.'

'I'm sorry,' Rachel rubbed her knee affectionately. 'I know how much he values your friendship. He would be devastated to think he had hurt you.'

'You won't say anything . . .'

'I would never breathe a word.'

She watched as Nicola ground her cigarette into the ashtray, ashamed that she had been such a bad friend. She'd been judgemental about Tony, judgemental about Alex's documentary. Somehow the mojitos had given her a clarity she'd been lacking before. She apologised to Nicola for her sanctimonious attitude and they talked till closing time: about the film company who were using her stolen clothes, about the difficulties of working together, and about men and sex and the innate trickiness of relationships. It was a proper heart-to-heart that reaffirmed all the reasons why they had become close in the first place.

Rachel was looking forward to calling Alex when she got home and telling him about her evening, but he had left a message saying he was going to bed and that he would catch up with her the following evening when he returned from Paris.

Chapter 50

London, 28 March 1936

MARY DREADED SEEING ERNEST AND WALLIS together. Would some subconscious look or gesture betray the fact that she and Ernest were lovers? Would she squirm with jealousy as he embraced her oldest friend?

She need not have worried because they were bickering as soon as Ernest came in the front door, neither caring that Mary was in earshot.

'Why didn't you let me know Mary had arrived early?' Wallis snapped. 'I've made plans for the weekend and it's too late to ask hostesses to change their table arrangements to include her.'

'I shall entertain Mary if you are not available,' he said. 'I don't see the problem.'

'The problem is that you are expected at the Wigrams' this evening at seven thirty prompt. Are we to leave Mary to dine on her own?'

'I don't mind at all,' Mary interjected, but neither was listening.

'I would rather have my teeth pulled than go to the Wigrams'. I can picture the scene now: you drooling over Peter Pan at the far end of the table, while everyone else gossips discreetly with their neighbours and casts pitying glances in my direction. I'm not going, Wallis.'

Mary had never heard Ernest speak in anger before. He was invariably mild-mannered and accommodating. Wallis's eyes flashed with anger. She walked towards him, fist clenched as if she might strike him.

'Your king requires you to attend,' she hissed, 'so you will attend.'

Ernest gave a harsh laugh. 'Now you speak for him? How convenient. Tell His Majesty that I am indisposed, or whatever falsehood you care to invent.'

He turned and left the room. Wallis gave Mary a quick glance then followed him, and Mary heard the argument continue in the hallway then behind their closed bedroom door. She was glad Ernest was standing up for himself, and wondered if he was doing so because of her presence.

His defiance won the day and Wallis left alone, wearing a ravishing ruby and diamond necklace and matching bracelet, set off by a simple black satin dress. Ernest and Mary ate a quiet supper together.

'I'm sorry you had to witness that,' he said. 'The atmosphere between my wife and me has been fractious for some time. I often spend the night at the Guards' Club if she is home, solely to avoid such confrontations.'

'I had no idea things were so bad.' Mary risked placing her hand on his, after first checking the dining-room door was closed. 'It must be intolerable.'

'It certainly can't continue much longer,' he agreed. 'One way or another, something has to give.'

~

Wallis returned the following day with news that they had all – including Mary – been invited to Windsor Castle the following weekend. The King would like to show them around.

Mary glanced at Ernest before replying. 'I should very much like to see the castle.' More than the architecture, she was eager to observe the relationship between Wallis and the King, and to see how they behaved when Ernest was around. She wanted some clue as to the direction things were heading.

'If Mary wants to go, then I will come too,' Ernest agreed, making it clear from his tone that that was the only reason for his acquiescence.

The three of them drove to Windsor on Saturday morning, arriving in time for luncheon. Footmen hurried to open the car doors and collect their luggage, while Mary stood back to gawp at the sheer size of the building, hardly noticing the light shower of rain.

Ernest joined her. 'William the Conqueror chose to position a castle here sometime around 1080. The location on a cliff made it the only defensible position along the Thames.'

'Is it really so old?' Mary was surprised. She'd thought buildings from that era would be in ruins.

'It has been much changed and modernised over the years, notably by Georges III and IV in the early nineteenth century. Much of the current appearance dates from then.'

Wallis was already heading inside. 'Don't dawdle, you two,' she called. 'Your king awaits.'

As soon as they entered, Mary was stunned into silence by the grandeur. Never-ending corridors and impossibly high ceilings were covered in ornate wood carvings and positively dripping with gilt. Huge oil portraits lined the walls, and the carpet underfoot was sumptuous. A footman opened the door to a reception room so vast that Mary's entire Manhattan apartment would have fitted comfortably inside. Gold and crystal chandeliers hung from the ceiling, and the furniture looked priceless. The King was standing by a window at the far end; he beckoned them over.

'Rotten weather,' he said. 'I'd been hoping to take the dogs for a walk. Perhaps it will let up later.'

Wallis hurried over and kissed him on the cheek, then slid her arm through his, whispering something in his ear. Ernest bowed and Mary curtseyed.

'Welcome,' he said. 'I'm glad you could join us. One rather rattles around this place on one's own. Wallis thought you might be interested in the art collection.'

'Indeed I am, Your Majesty,' Ernest replied.

'Are you fond of art, Mrs Raffray?' asked the King.

'Very much so,' she replied, sneaking a glance at Ernest, giving him a quick smile as she thought of their trips to galleries the previous summer.

Pre-lunch drinks were brought and they sat round the gigantic fireplace. Mary kept glancing about, wondering when the other guests would arrive. It was only when they walked through to the vast dining room and sat at one end of the table that she realised it was just to be the four of them. How very odd.

She felt shy talking to the King, but Wallis kept the conversation flowing and was not afraid to touch on controversial topics.

'I hear the international committee has come to its senses and Berlin is to be allowed to keep its Olympics after all,' she began. 'It would have been lunacy to move it at this late stage, as no other city would have the infrastructure in place. I'm sure the Germans will do an excellent job.'

'Indeed, they are exemplary when it comes to planning and building,' the King agreed. 'Herr Hitler knows how to motivate workers and get everyone performing at their best.'

Ernest cleared his throat. 'I believe the controversy was over the exclusion of athletes of the Jewish persuasion from the Games. It is my understanding that the Reich has backed down, but I will be most surprised if they have any Jews in the German team. This is not a good time to be Jewish in that country.'

'They have the right to rebalance their population,' the King argued. 'The percentage of Jewish to Aryan citizens had got quite out of hand. At least Hitler has been fair in allowing Jewish citizens the right to move overseas, to countries where they will be welcomed.'

Mary had read criticism of the harshness of Hitler's policies in the US press and she ventured to comment. 'It seems hard that Jewish families must leave behind their homes and possessions. I hear even the wealthiest are able to take very little.'

'Von Ribbentrop assures us that the policies are strict but fair,' Wallis said. 'Doesn't he, darling?' She smiled at the King.

Mary was astonished that she would call him 'darling' in front of Ernest. Was it a slip of the tongue? And when had Wallis's political views become so hard-line? She wondered if someone had been influencing her. Perhaps von Ribbentrop?

Ernest concentrated on his soup and the conversation moved along.

After luncheon, the King signalled to one of his waiting staff, who brought a bolt of cloth balanced across his arms.

'A gift for you, Mrs Raffray,' he said.

Mary stared, speechless. The fine wool cloth was patterned in vivid shades of violet, warm pink and apricot, and it felt soft to the touch. 'Oh my . . .' she began.

'It comes from India. I thought it would complement your spectacular hair colour. Wallis tells me her dressmaker can turn it into any style of your choice.'

'Your Majesty, I'm overwhelmed,' she said. 'That is extraordinarily generous of you.'

'Not at all.' He smiled, pleased with the reaction. 'Any friend of Wallis's is also a friend of mine. Now, who would like to come to the screening room to watch the Grand National?'

The annual horse race had taken place just over a week earlier, but he had a copy of the Movietone footage for them to watch. They were led down a corridor and up a flight of stairs to a room with velvet seats arranged in four rows in front of a screen. Mary watched with fascination as a servant lifted a reel of film and slotted it into the projector, feeding the end of the film through onto another reel. There were lots of crackling noises, then a jerky image appeared of horses and their trainers milling around the starting gate.

The King talked them through the whole thing, explaining the riders' strategies, describing the degree of difficulty of each fence, and giving a short biography of the winning jockey, Fulke Walwyn.

'An amateur, you know. Ex-army man from the 9th Lancers. Look at that finish! He took it by twelve lengths. I wish I'd had money on him. Odds of 10/1.'

'Darling, you hardly need the money.' Wallis patted his arm.

Mary glanced at Ernest but he did not flinch.

After the screening, the King asked if they would like to see some art. 'We've got Rembrandt, Rubens, Van Dyck, Gainsborough . . .' He turned to Mary. 'What is your taste in art, Mrs Raffray?'

She gave Ernest a quick grin. 'I'm partial to modern American art, but I do love portraiture as well. Those Rembrandt portraits where you feel as though the subject could step out of the painting and engage you in conversation – they are sublime.'

The King came to walk alongside her and Wallis stood on his other side, leaving Ernest trailing. 'In that case, I must show you Rembrandt's portrait of his mother. I'm sure you'll like it.'

Wallis objected: 'David, perhaps we should leave Ernest and Mary to wander on their own, rather than give them the formal tour. I can guarantee they are trustworthy.'

Mary felt her cheeks redden. If only she knew.

Wallis smiled at her. 'You weren't thinking of slipping off with a Rembrandt under one arm, were you?'

'It crossed my mind,' Mary quipped, 'but then I noticed those guards with rifles at the front door.'

'We'll be fine on our own,' Ernest interrupted. 'Don't let us detain you.'

Mary was relieved once they were alone. The foursome was too peculiar for words: Wallis with her forced gaiety, Ernest silent and glowering, the King seemingly oblivious to any heightened atmosphere, and herself racked with guilt.

It felt as if they were two separate couples already, since Wallis spoke to the King with the intimacy of a wife. If Wallis and Ernest divorced and Wallis married the King, might Mary marry Ernest? Could they all be friends in future?

Why had they been invited this weekend? Was it a test to see whether the relationships could slide gently into a new configuration that suited all concerned?

Mary comforted herself with this thought during the remainder of the visit. Mary and Ernest; Wallis and David. Perhaps that was the way it was meant to be.

Chapter 51

London, April 1936

BACK AT BRYANSTON COURT, THEY SLIPPED INTO a pattern of Wallis and Mary spending the days together – shopping, having luncheon, getting their hair done, meeting friends. Mary decided to have the King's bolt of cloth made into a tunic and skirt, similar to Wallis's Mainbocher outfit, as the loose shape would be flattering on her less-than-svelte figure.

'I hope Mr Bocher doesn't find out we are copying one of his designs, or I will be on the outs,' Wallis remarked, but she was happy to lend her original to the dressmaker while they cut the pattern.

At some point each evening Wallis slipped off to see the King, decked out in one of the magnificent necklaces or bracelets or brooches he had given her, leaving Mary to dine with Ernest. It suited Mary perfectly, because she enjoyed the company of both on their own, but found it awkward when they were in the same room.

Mary's fortieth birthday came around on 20 April, and it was arranged that Wallis would take her for luncheon at the Ritz, while Ernest would provide the evening entertainment. As the waiter led them to their table, Mary noticed that several diners turned to look at Wallis, and she waved in greeting to one group. She was clearly well known in London. Once they were seated, she ordered two glasses of champagne.

'Such a perfect afternoon drink,' she said. 'You never get too high on champagne. Here's to you, Mary. I hope you have a wonderful decade.'

Mary was carrying a gift Wallis had given her earlier: a brown kid-leather handbag with a V-shaped tortoiseshell clasp. It made her feel sophisticated, and she kept stroking it as they chatted, enjoying the scent of new leather.

'How is Ernest?' Wallis asked. 'Do you think he is terribly upset about the Situation?' That had become their new short-hand.

Mary wrinkled her nose. 'You know Ernest: he doesn't discuss his feelings.'

'Has he not said anything to you? Nothing at all?'

Mary shook her head. 'I guess he is leaving you to make up your mind. If you want to be with the King of England, he probably feels he can't stop you.'

Wallis spoke wistfully. 'I wish he had put his foot down two years ago. Some men would have, but Ernest positively reveres the monarchy.'

'And you don't revere your king?' Mary grinned wickedly.

Wallis snorted while taking a sip of her champagne, and raised a napkin to her face, laughing and choking at the same time. 'Look what you made me do!' she giggled. 'The bubbles went up my nose.'

As they walked out of the hotel two hours later, there was a sound like gunfire, and bright lights flashed. Mary grabbed Wallis's arm, afraid they were being shot at by some maniac.

'Don't worry,' Wallis told her. 'They're photographers. Look straight ahead and keep walking.'

They got into a taxicab, the cameras still flashing and making loud cracking sounds.

'Does that often happen?' Mary asked, flustered. 'How did they know you were there?'

'One of the other diners must have telephoned them. It's tedious that the papers are starting to report on my movements. "The King's friend Mrs Simpson had luncheon at the Ritz" – that's what it will say. Who cares?'

'I always knew you would be famous for something, Wallie, but I don't think either of us would have guessed this.'

That evening Ernest told Mary to dress formally because he had a surprise in store. They took a taxicab across town to Covent Garden and he led her into the grand foyer of the Royal Opera House.

'I hope you will enjoy the opera.' He smiled. 'It is a passion of mine.'

He had reserved a box, and as they went up the grand staircase they passed Wallis's friend Emerald Cunard, who looked from one to the other with surprise.

'Wallis is busy this evening,' Mary explained, 'and Ernest offered to treat me since it is my birthday. I'm rather a heathen when it comes to opera, so I hope he will explain everything as we go along.'

'How lovely! Do enjoy yourselves,' Emerald gushed. Her eyes glittered above her sharp nose and port-wine lipstick.

After they moved on, Ernest whispered to Mary behind his programme: 'I'm not usually one for gossip, but I hear Mrs Cunard is in love with the Opera House's director, Sir Thomas Beecham. The situation is quite hopeless as he will not leave his wife.'

'Ernest!' she mock-rebuked. 'I shall have to revise my entire opinion of you.'

They fell silent as soon as the orchestra struck up, lost from the first moment in the magnificent music of Puccini's *La Bohème*.

~

Next morning, Mary sat in her tea gown to pen notes to both Ernest and Wallis, thanking them for making her birthday so special. To Wallis she wrote that she would always treasure the handbag, which was quite the most stylish she had ever owned. *How clever of you to choose one that will match virtually any outfit, and with a classic style that will never date.*

To Ernest she wrote:

My darling, I was so full of emotion last night that I felt I would explode all over the hallowed carpets of the Opera House. Sadness for the doomed love of Rodolfo and Mimi. Elation at the sublime glory of the music. Contentment to be by your side, our arms touching. Frustration that I cannot put my arms around you and kiss you freely. Anxiety at the precariousness of our situation. Worry that at any moment Wallis will guess how much I love you and long for you to be mine. But despite all this, I can think of no better way to celebrate my birthday. I thank you from the bottom of my heart for making it such a memorable occasion. Yours always, Mary.

She addressed one envelope to Ernest at his office and the other to Wallis at Fort Belvedere, where she was spending the next two days. Then she stopped and looked at the two envelopes for a moment, as an idea came into her head. She couldn't, could she? Her stomach clenched tight as a fist, and she could hear the blood coursing round her brain. It was the impulse of a moment. Wicked. Wrong.

And yet perhaps it would work. Perhaps it would resolve the terrible impasse in which the four of them found themselves.

She put the letter to Ernest into the Fort Belvedere envelope and the letter to Wallis in the other. Then, before she could change her mind, she called the maid and asked her to mail them as quickly as possible.

Chapter 52

Brighton, 15 December 1997

RACHEL TRIED TO RING ALEX WHEN SHE WOKE ON Monday morning but got his answer machine, so she assumed he was on the plane to Paris. It was hard not having spoken to him since their argument on Saturday, not having had a chance to make peace, but she was buoyed by her confessional evening with Nicola. It was good to hear that Alex had been kind to his old friend in her hour of need, but it made it even more upsetting that he had not been kind to her during the same period. Maybe he thought she was strong enough and didn't need support, but he could have shown more interest in her struggle to keep the shop afloat.

She hoped he might try to call her, but wasn't concerned when there was no word because she would see him that evening. She was curious to hear how the interview at Villa Windsor had gone. Was she correct in her theory that Diana had got the platinum heart bracelet there? Would the gardener tell Alex about the painting Diana had gone to fetch for Susie?

The police called to say that Gazelle Films had acquired many of their costumes from a dealer in the East End of London, who appeared to have acquired them from someone else they were trying to track down. They asked if she would go to their set to look through all the costumes and identify which were hers. She told them she couldn't close the shop but asked them to email the images; she could identify them that way.

When she got back that evening, she turned on her computer. It was a rather elderly IBM, with a slow connection speed, and took over an hour to download more than fifty photographs sent from Gazelle Films. When they finally came through, she identified fourteen of the costumes as hers. She emailed her police contact to tell him and said she would be happy to come to some deal that would not halt their filming. *Let them make me an offer*, she wrote, thinking gleefully that it would no doubt be a good one since she had them over a barrel.

There was still no sign of Alex. She checked flight times and found out that the last flight from Paris did not land till 11.30 p.m., so it might be well after midnight when he got home. She decided not to wait up.

She fell asleep quickly, but something woke her at 3 a.m. and she patted the bed beside her. There was no Alex. 'Are you back?' she called out to the empty flat, then, getting no answer, she drifted off to sleep again.

When Alex hadn't turned up by nine on Tuesday morning, she began to worry. Even if he had missed the last plane the night before, he could have caught the first morning one and should have been back by now. She rang his mobile, but it was switched off and would not even let her leave a message. Her anxiety mounting, she rang his cameraman, Kenny.

'Have you heard from Alex?' she asked.

'Not a word,' he replied. 'I was expecting him to ring and update me, but I haven't heard since Sunday. I'll call the rest of the team and ring you back if anyone knows anything.'

'Thanks, Kenny.' Rachel's heart was beating faster now. This was out of character. She rang Nicola next.

'I don't suppose you've heard from Alex? He's gone AWOL in Paris.' She explained the circumstances.

'I hope he hasn't been in an accident.'

Rachel could feel panic starting to take hold and wished Nicola hadn't suggested that. 'I doubt it. Maybe he missed the plane and his mobile has run out of charge. Is there any chance you could open the shop while I wait in for him?'

'Course I will,' Nicola agreed straight away, clearly delighted that Rachel trusted her.

Next Rachel rang Alex's father, reasoning that if there had been an accident, the French authorities would have contacted him as next of kin.

'I haven't spoken to him all week,' he told her. 'He's probably got some lead in his crazy conspiracy theory and gone off to investigate without realising everyone will be worried.'

That reminded Rachel about the visit to Villa Windsor, which had been the reason for his journey. She booted up the computer to check Alex's email account, and found a message from his French researcher, Pascal, setting up the meeting with the gardener, whose name was John Sturkey.

She emailed Pascal, asking if he knew where Alex was, then stared at the screen as she waited for a reply. She had a bad feeling about this. It wasn't like Alex to lose touch for so long. Five interminable minutes later, an email popped up from Pascal saying that Alex had not arrived for the meeting with the gardener the previous day and had not been in touch since Sunday.

Where had he been for the last twenty-four hours? Rachel ran through all the possibilities in her head: he had been in an accident and was unconscious in hospital somewhere, either in Paris or London; he was on a delayed flight back and would arrive at any moment; he'd been attacked in Paris by one of the paparazzi he was investigating; or maybe her suspicion that he was having an affair had been right all along and she'd just got the wrong woman. Paranoia set in. Maybe he had spent the night with his mistress and was still there, planning how he was going to tell her that the wedding was off.

He must be in Paris, she decided; if he'd missed his flight on Monday morning, he would have gone to work at the edit suite and Kenny would know. How did you report a missing person in France? She searched the Internet for the website of the British Embassy in Paris and found a number to call for anyone who was concerned about a British national.

They answered quickly and sounded reassuringly efficient, taking down Alex's details and promising to get back to her once they had made enquiries. This was something they dealt with every day. There were procedures.

Rachel felt sick with nerves. She began sweeping the flat's wooden floors, all the while going over the possible scenarios in her head. Was he injured? Would he be back in time for their wedding?

Half an hour later, the phone rang and she rushed to it, stubbing her toe on the coffee table.

'Miss Wainwright?' a voice said. 'I'm calling with news of Alexander Greene. I'm afraid he was arrested in Paris yesterday morning and is being held in police custody.'

She nearly dropped the phone. That possibility had never crossed her mind. 'Arrested? Why?'

'He's accused of stealing a piece of jewellery from the Alma Tunnel the night Princess Diana died. I'm afraid they are taking rather a dim view.'

'Oh Jesus!' That stupid heart! Why hadn't he returned it when they went to the police station the day after the crash? She should have listened to her instincts; she'd known it would cause trouble.

'We'll make sure he has legal representation and will be in touch when there is any further news.'

Rachel made her decision in an instant. 'I'm coming to Paris. Where is he being held?'

The consular official tried to talk her out of it, saying she wouldn't be allowed to see him and she should let the legal process run its course.

'I'm coming,' she said firmly. 'Please will you give me the address?'

It was the Criminal Brigade headquarters, she was told, the building on quai des Orfèvres where they had been before. She went to the bedroom to pack an overnight bag, being sure to check that the platinum heart was still zipped in the pocket of her purse.

Chapter 53

London, 21 April 1936

WHAT HAVE I DONE? MARY LAY CURLED ON THE BED at Bryanston Court, her mind racing, trying to predict the repercussions of her intemperate action. Ernest must never suspect that she had switched the letters deliberately. Wallis was bound to be cross at first, but surely she would realise that the most sensible thing for all four of them was for Ernest and her to divorce? She must see that. There could be no turning back.

It was tempting to run and hide: perhaps flee to France to visit Aunt Minnie or sail back to the States and let Wallis and Ernest sort out this mess for themselves – but that would be the coward's route. She had to stay and defend herself if necessary. She had to remind Ernest how much better a wife she would make than Wallis.

When he came home that evening, nothing was mentioned so it was clear the letter had not reached him in the afternoon post. Ernest had developed a taste for crime novels of late, and over dinner he recommended that Mary read the Hercule Poirot novels of Agatha Christie.

'I have a formula for uncovering the murderer in the early chapters,' he said. 'It is usually a family member, whichever one is instantly ruled out of the enquiry because he or she has a rock-solid alibi.'

Mary was dubious. 'I don't like to read about violence and bloodshed. I'm too squeamish.'

'There's no violence,' he laughed. 'The stories are brainteasers. They possess no literary value but I find them relaxing.'

'Perhaps you can recommend one in that case, and I'll see if I can guess the murderer.'

The following morning, Mary was too anxious to eat breakfast. She felt sick whenever she thought of Wallis at Fort Belvedere opening her letter to Ernest and scanning the contents. Would she race straight back to Bryanston Court to confront her? Or wait until she had planned to return anyway?

Mary sat down to try and read the book Ernest had lent her, *Murder on the Orient Express*, but it did nothing to calm her nerves. Instead she began to rehearse the arguments she would use when Wallis got home, hoping against hope that she would understand, perhaps even be relieved that the decision had been made for her.

She had dozed off, lying on top of her bedcover, when she was woken by the sound of the front door banging and Wallis's voice in the hall.

'Where is she?' she was asking the maid.

Mary sat up and adjusted her dress just as Wallis burst into her room, the letter in her hand.

'What on earth is this?' she shouted. 'A love letter from you to Ernest? You make me *laugh*.'

Mary had to pretend shock. 'But I wrote to thank you for the handbag . . .' she said, her voice trailing off.

'Yes, and you wrote to thank Ernest for taking you to the opera, and guess what?' She threw the letter on the bed and Mary glanced at it then clasped a hand to her mouth.

'Did you think I didn't guess that you're in love with my husband? Your eyes follow him round the room like some lovesick ingénue. It's pathetic in a woman of forty.'

Mary was shaking, but she screwed up her courage to answer back. 'You can't blame us for having an affair when you spend all your time with the King, and treat poor Ernest with shocking disrespect.'

Wallis took a step forward and slapped Mary's face with all her strength. Mary's head snapped back and her eyes watered.

'You're actually having an affair, are you? You utter *bitch*!' Wallis spat out the words. 'I trusted you, even knowing how you felt about Ernest, because we've been through so much together. "Mary will never betray me," I thought. What kind of fool was I?'

Mary pressed the palm of her hand against her cheek to ease the stinging sensation and tried to introduce a note of reason. 'Wallie, this makes sense for all four of us. The King wants to marry you, and Ernest has told him he will divorce you, so why can't Ernest and I be together? I thought you must have that in mind when you invited us to Windsor Castle for that peculiar foursome.'

Wallis's face paled. 'What do you mean, Ernest has told David he will divorce me? Don't lie.'

'They had dinner together back in February. Bernie Rickatson-Hatt was there too. The King said he could not take the throne without you by his side and Ernest said he would release you so long as the King promised to take care of you. Ask them if you don't believe me.'

Wallis marched to the window. 'How dare they!' She twirled round. 'And how dare you not tell me before now? I will never forgive you for this, Mary. Never.'

'I wish you would calm down, then you'll see this is for the best.'

'Best for whom? For you and Ernest with your dirty little secret? How long has the affair been going on, as a matter of interest?'

Mary blushed.

'No, don't tell me.' Wallis stared at her with contempt. 'It was last summer when he was in New York, wasn't it?'

Mary started to feel indignant. 'Yes, while you were traipsing around the South of France with the Prince. All the American papers were reporting it. "Mrs Simpson danced a rumba with the Prince of Wales": how do you think that made Ernest feel?'

Wallis slammed open the wardrobe door and began flinging Mary's gowns onto the bed. Mary leapt to her feet.

'What are you—'

'I want you out of here. Take your things and leave. Now!'

She swept an arm along the dressing table, so Mary's hairbrush, lipstick and powder compact crashed to the floor. Mary caught hold of her arm and for a moment it seemed they might start a physical fight, both of them trembling with emotion. Suddenly Mary felt defiant. Anger welled up from deep within: a long-held grudge over years of slights, years of being treated as the understudy, years of enduring Wallis's fundamental selfishness.

'You only ever think of yourself,' she hissed. 'Me, me, me.'

Wallis broke away from her grip. 'Get out of my house. If you are not gone in five minutes, I will call the police.' She swept from the room, and Mary heard her bedroom door slam.

There was nothing for it. She pulled out her trunk and began to throw her clothes in, any old how. She lifted the gowns from their hangers in one big armful and thrust them inside, not bothering about crushing them; piled cosmetics into her vanity case; collected her passport and books from a drawer. In not much more than five minutes she had packed everything she had arrived with. Then she called the maid to ask the doorman of the apartment block to come and carry her trunk and hail a taxicab. There was silence from behind Wallis's door.

Mary glanced in the mirror and saw that her left cheek was puce, and there was a scratch by her eye where one of Wallis's rings had caught her. No time to worry about that now.

As she hurried out of the flat, she noticed another huge bouquet of blush-pink roses sitting on the hall table. They had just been delivered, and the little envelope containing the card was still with them. On the spur of the moment, she grabbed it. Wallis had secrets; she was the mistress of subterfuge, and perhaps this card would prove it.

Down on the pavement, the porter was loading her belongings into a taxicab.

'Where to, ma'am?' the driver asked.

She had no idea. 'Just drive,' she said. 'I'll let you know when I decide.'

They headed down Edgware Road, past Marble Arch and into Park Lane. About halfway down, there was a new art deco hotel called the Dorchester. Mary had often admired it in passing, and now she asked the driver to pull into the forecourt while she went inside to enquire if they had a room. The lobby was very smart and she did not like to imagine how much the room would cost, but they had one available so she took it. A porter brought her trunk inside on his trolley and took it to a bedroom on the first floor.

'Where can I make a telephone call?' she asked.

The porter escorted her to the operator's room and she gave the number of Ernest's office, then was shown to a chair in a discreet booth in reception where she could take the call once it was connected.

'I've done the stupidest thing,' she told him when he came on the line, and she explained the 'mix-up' over the letters.

'Wallis is hopping mad and has thrown me out of the apartment, so I've taken a room at the Dorchester for tonight.'

Ernest seemed to take it in his stride. 'Yes, I received your note to her this morning. Don't worry. She would have found out about us sooner or later. It's probably best if you lie low for a while and I'll try to make her see reason.'

Secretly Mary had hoped he would say 'I'll be right there'; might even have taken her for dinner that evening in the hotel restaurant. It was time for him to declare his hand. But he made no such offer.

'I have another apology to make,' she continued. 'I had no idea Wallis didn't know about your conversation with the King concerning her. I'm afraid I let it slip.'

Ernest sighed. 'How did she take it?'

'Not very well, as you can imagine.'

'I'll talk to her tonight – if she's there – and call you from the office in the morning. What room number are you?'

Mary told him. He said goodbye in a businesslike fashion and then hung up, without a word of affection or comfort. Of course, he was in the office. Perhaps his colleagues could over-hear.

She sat there a moment longer, feeling more alone than she had ever felt in her life. All her acquaintances in London were Wallis's friends; all would take Wallis's side. She would have to leave town before Wallis blackened her name. Ernest was kidding himself if he thought she would calm down. Mary had never seen her in such a rage.

Back in her room, she remembered the card she had snatched in the hallway. She dug it out of her handbag and opened it. *See you in Berlin*, it read, signed with the initial J. Had von Ribbentrop invited Wallis over there? Mary had been hoping for something incriminating, proof perhaps that Wallis was having an affair with him, but that wasn't much to go on. She

333

stuffed it back in her bag, then sat at the dressing table and began writing a letter to her sister Anne on Dorchester note-paper: *I am on the outs with Wallis and will book a berth on the next sailing. May I visit you on my return?*

Then she threw down the pen and burst into tears. Why should she leave London? Why should Wallis always get what she wanted? She remembered the way as a fifteen-year-old Wallis had swooped in and grabbed the elder and better-looking of the two Tabb brothers, then didn't want him once she had him. That was her all over; she hadn't changed.

Wallis didn't love Ernest – she didn't know the meaning of the word – but Mary did truly love him and knew she was good for him. I should stay and fight for him, she thought. It was scary to think of fighting with Wallis, but it was the right thing to do.

As soon as she made this decision, Mary felt stronger. Now she just needed to decide where she would stay. She had some money from her parents' estate, and a small allowance from Jackie, but apartment rentals in London were bound to be expensive and she did not know how to go about looking for one. She would need Ernest's help.

She made some notes on another sheet of hotel paper, figuring out how much she could afford to pay in rental, making a stab at the cost of electricity, a telephone line, one maid and the weekly groceries. When she got hungry, she ordered a club sandwich from room service, and asked them to bring her a whisky and soda as well.

Later in the evening, she rang for another large whisky.

Chapter 54

London, 22 April 1936

ERNEST TELEPHONED AT NINE THIRTY THE NEXT morning, and a bellhop came to fetch Mary to take the call.

'Let's not talk on the phone,' she said. 'Can you join me for lunch at the Dorchester? I have some practical matters I must discuss with you.'

He arrived looking as if he hadn't slept much, and was shocked when he saw Mary's face, still a livid red colour.

'Did Wallis do that?' he asked. 'It looks painful. I'm so sorry, my dear.'

'It's hardly your fault,' she replied with a wan smile.

They chose a discreet table in the corner of the dining room, and as they sat down, he patted Mary on the shoulder.

'This must be rotten for you.'

'I'm sure last night was rotten for you as well,' she sympathised.

He cocked his head. 'For some reason Wallis doesn't blame me. She thinks you are an evil temptress who led me astray and I am the innocent victim of your wiles. I denied it, of course, but that is how she chooses to view it.'

'What is she going to do?'

'She wants you on the next ship to New York and asked me to promise never to see you again. Of course, I told her I could make no such promise.' He pursed his lips.

It wasn't exactly the reassurance Mary had been hoping for, but it would have to do.

'In fact, I've decided I want to stay in London,' she said, 'and I need your help to find an apartment. Just a small one. I have my own money.'

'Of course I'll help,' he said, 'but I wonder if it might not be sensible for you to leave town for a while. Until the fuss dies down.'

'I'm not a coward, Ernest. Wallis doesn't scare me.'

'That's not what I'm thinking of . . .' He paused, as if deciding whether to tell her something. She waited.

'You must keep this to yourself, but last week I had a meeting with a senior Conservative politician, Winston Churchill. He told me they are all terribly concerned about the King's desire to marry Wallis. He said it would be constitutionally impossible since she is a divorcee, and that the British people would never accept her as queen. They want me to refuse to give her a divorce so that such a marriage cannot happen.'

Mary's spirits plummeted.

'I told him that I have already promised the King I will stand aside, and he asked that I refuse to honour that promise in the interests of my country and its monarchy. So you see, I am in rather a bind.' He reached across to take Mary's hand.

'They have no right to ask you that,' she objected. 'Governments can't tell you whom to marry or divorce.'

'Of course not. Churchill's a good chap and he accepted that it's a rum do. The truth is, we both have a feeling the King will push the issue himself and that will force the government's hand. But you understand that this is a matter of historic importance and I am keen that neither you nor I are cast as villains.'

Mary saw what he meant. If he left Wallis now, she would run straight into the King's arms and Ernest would be blamed for damaging the institution of the monarchy; *she* would be blamed.

'How long must we wait?' she asked.

'As long as it takes,' was the unsatisfactory answer.

They ate Dover sole for luncheon accompanied by a rather good French wine, while Ernest suggested areas of London in which they might search for an apartment for her.

'Will you visit me in my new home?' she asked, contemplating the long days and nights ahead when she would not dare venture out in society.

'Whenever Wallis is with the King, I will come to you,' he promised.

That distressed Mary: yet again her fate was to be determined by the whims of her erstwhile friend. She swallowed hard, not wishing to quarrel with Ernest.

He continued: 'I may not find the right apartment straight away, especially as I have promised to accompany Wallis to Fort Belvedere this weekend, but I hope I shall find something next week.'

Despair threatened to engulf Mary at the thought of him visiting the Fort. She took a deep breath to control herself. Ernest needed one of the women in his life to be even-tempered, and it would have to be her.

'In that case,' she said, 'I will ask Eleanor if I might spend the weekend with them. She is the only friend I have in this country who is beyond the reach of Wallis's tentacles.'

Suddenly they were interrupted by a plump woman Mary vaguely recognised, who stood right next to their table and jabbed Ernest in the shoulder. He rose to his feet and gave a slight bow.

'Mrs Campbell.'

'*Mister* Simpson,' she replied in an accusatory tone. 'I had your wife on the telephone in tears yesterday. Yes, tears, sir. She says you have taken her oldest friend as your mistress, and I suppose this' – she pointed at Mary – 'is the guilty party. How could you, sir? Poor dear Wallis.'

Before Mary could say a word, Ernest replied in icy tones: 'Mrs Campbell, you are not in full possession of the facts and nor should you be since you mean nothing to me, or to my wife. Please desist from repeating such rumours or you will be hearing from my lawyer.'

Mrs Campbell scuttled away, muttering about his rudeness, and he sat down again, smoothing the napkin on his lap. Mary looked at him with fresh eyes. She had never heard him be impolite to a lady before and had thought it alien to his nature, but he had done it to defend her, to defend both of them, and that was comforting.

Chapter 55

Paris, 16 December 1997

AS SHE SAT ON THE TRAIN TO GATWICK AIRPORT, Rachel tried to formulate a plan. Surely when the police saw that the platinum heart was so tiny – not even a complete piece of jewellery but a bit ripped off Diana's bracelet in the collision – they would not press charges? It was insignificant. They must see that. She wondered if they might at last find out who had given Diana the bracelet and what the engravings signified. Life had been so busy that it had not been at the forefront of her mind, but now her curiosity returned.

Poor Alex must regret that he had ever picked it up. What must he be thinking, stuck in a cell and not even able to make phone calls? A criminal record would affect his entire life, all for a spur-of-the-moment decision. Her heart ached for him.

At the airport, she went first to the British Airways desk, where they told her that all their Paris flights for the day were booked up. She tried Air France next, and they didn't have a seat till evening. Fog earlier in the day had meant some flights being rerouted, so they were all in the wrong places now. The counter assistant gave her the telephone number of Eurostar and she managed to secure a seat on their 12.20 service that reached Gare du Nord around four in the afternoon.

She caught an express train to Victoria station only to find the District and Circle underground lines were not running so she had to zigzag between Tube stations, out of breath and panting. It was as if the world was conspiring against her. At Waterloo, she caught the Paris train with minutes to spare and slumped in the seat, heart thumping.

For the first part of the journey she watched the countryside flit past, trying to calm down and think logically about what she should do next. She was dressed smartly, in a belted slate-grey wool dress under her green Jacquard coat, and she'd brought her black Chanel bag; appearances were important when dealing with police. She planned the words in her head, rehearsing them in schoolgirl French in case there were no English trans-lators available.

Once the train emerged at Calais, into weather that was much sunnier than it had been in Brighton, she took out her make-up bag and began to apply her make-up carefully, to the fascination of a little girl sitting across the aisle. Highlighter, concealer, blusher and eyeliner, all painted on with fine-bristled brushes, followed by mascara and lipstick. She smiled and the girl hid behind her mother's shoulder.

At Gare du Nord she changed some English money into francs and caught a taxi to the Criminal Brigade headquarters on quai des Orfèvres. So much depended on what she said next: Alex's future, their wedding, the children they might one day have . . . She felt tight with nerves but at the same time utterly determined.

'*Mon fiancé est ici,*' she told the policeman at the front desk. '*Alex Greene. S'il vous plaît, pourrais-je parler à quelqu'un? C'est très important.*'

340

She was asked to sit down, and she waited twenty-three interminable minutes, measured by the ticking of a large clock on the wall, before a short bespectacled man emerged through some glass doors and headed towards her.

'Mademoiselle Wainwright? Can I help you?'

Fortunately he spoke English. Rachel explained that her fiancé was being held there, that she had information relating to the case, and that she needed to talk to someone urgently.

'Come back tomorrow morning,' he said, glancing at the clock. 'No one can see you today.'

'Could I talk to Alex?' she asked, but was told that was not possible.

'How about his lawyer?' she persisted. 'Could you tell me who is representing him?'

He sighed, implying in a brief gesture that this was a huge waste of his time, but got up and disappeared through the glass doors. When he came back a few minutes later, he handed her a card with a name and a telephone number: M. Belmont.

On the pavement outside, Rachel took out her mobile phone. It was five thirty and she could see office workers piling onto the pavements, heading for home or for their evening assignations, while Alex sat in his tiny cell, unaware that she knew his whereabouts and was trying to help. She wasn't sure what code to dial when using a mobile in France and had to try a couple of times before she heard the phone ring and a woman's voice answer.

'*Puis-je parler à M. Belmont?*' Rachel asked. '*Je suis la fiancée de Alex Greene, un de ses clients.*'

She knew her spoken French was terrible. The receptionist had to ask her to repeat herself twice before she understood, then she said, '*Un moment.*'

'Miss Wainwright?' A man's voice came on the line. His English had only a trace of an accent. 'Belmont speaking.'

She explained that she had come to Paris to help Alex, that she had brought with her the item he was accused of stealing.

'You had better come to my office,' he said, and gave her the address.

~

'I understand you and Alex were planning to get married on Thursday,' Monsieur Belmont said as he invited her to sit. Rachel's heart sank at his choice of tense. 'I'm afraid we won't know until tomorrow afternoon whether they plan to release him and, if so, whether he will be allowed to leave the country.'

Rachel took the platinum heart from her purse and put it on the desk. 'Look! This is all about a tiny piece of metal that fell off a bracelet. It's nothing!'

Monsieur Belmont picked it up and turned it over, reading the inscription. 'Not quite nothing. To the police, it is theft, and interfering with a crime scene.'

'How did they even find out?' Rachel asked. 'I thought there was no CCTV in the tunnel?'

'Yes, but eleven photographers each took dozens of pictures of the scene. The police confiscated their film, processed it and pieced together what everyone in that tunnel was doing during the critical period. Several pictures show Alex picking up the heart. He was arrested at passport control at Charles de Gaulle yesterday morning.'

Poor Alex. He must have got a terrible shock. That explained why he hadn't been able to phone and warn her.

'He's not a souvenir hunter,' she insisted. 'He wasn't going to try and sell it or anything. It's just a mistake.'

'A very unfortunate mistake. If he had handed it to the Criminal Brigade the next day, he would no doubt have been in the clear.'

Rachel made a decision. She had to get Alex out of jail. 'It wasn't his fault,' she said. 'He gave the heart to me for safe keeping. I was supposed to return it, but I wasn't sure who to give it to and then I forgot all about it. I'm sure Alex thought I returned it ages ago.'

Monsieur Belmont frowned, tapped his pen on the desk. 'That is not the story he told me.'

'Of course not. He wouldn't want to implicate me, but I'm telling you the truth.' She met his eyes, trying not to blink.

The lawyer thought for a moment, watching her. 'If we tell this version of events to the police, you might be charged with receiving stolen goods and I'm not sure it would help Alex much. Let me think about it.'

'What sort of sentence could he face if he's found guilty?' Rachel's stomach gurgled loudly and she folded her arms across her waist.

'Nine months to a year perhaps. But I'm hoping it won't come to that.'

A year! She felt close to tears. 'Can I come to the station with you tomorrow to see him?'

'No, I'm afraid not. However, I will take this object, and I'll point out to the police investigators that neither of you had any interest in making money from it. The fact that it was not handed in was an oversight. If you give me your telephone number, I'll call you as soon as I know the conclusion.'

Rachel gave her mobile number, then asked, 'What are his chances?'

The lawyer tapped his pen again. 'I am not a gambling man, Miss Wainwright. There are politics involved. A British royal died on French soil and the eyes of the world are watching our investigation, so it must be seen to be thorough, with every detail accounted for. And here . . .' He dangled the heart between his thumb and forefinger. 'Here we have a detail.'

Chapter 56

Paris, 16 December 1997

RACHEL WAS TOO STRESSED TO THINK ABOUT negotiating the Métro system and then walking the streets of Paris looking for a hotel, so she hailed a taxi and gave the name of the boutique hotel where she and Alex had stayed in August. They had a room available so she handed over her credit card, hoping against hope that there was enough left before she reached her credit limit. Fortunately the transaction went through.

Upstairs, she flopped onto the satin-cushion-covered bed to make some phone calls: first to Nicola, asking her to mind the shop the following day, then to Kenny, and to both her mother and Alex's father.

'I'll fly out this evening,' Alex's father said straight away. 'Where is he being held?'

'There's no need,' Rachel assured him. 'They might release him tomorrow afternoon, and they won't let us see him in the meantime.'

'I'm not happy that he only has a state-appointed lawyer. If I make some calls I could get someone top-notch on the case in the morning. It might make all the difference. We can't risk a conviction.'

That was a tempting idea. Monsieur Belmont's office had been utilitarian rather than plush. On the other hand, he had seemed perfectly competent. 'It's up to you, of course,' Rachel said, 'but I think the time to get a new lawyer would be if he is not released tomorrow.'

'What if they ask for bail before they release him? I'll stay by the phone all day and have my bank details ready.'

Rachel was touched by his obvious anxiety. She wondered if Alex knew how much his dad cared about him. She didn't think so.

When she had made her calls, she ventured out in search of food. What were they feeding Alex in custody? *Garde à vue*, the French called it: 'keep to see'. Would he have a room to himself, or might he be sharing a cell with real criminals? She imagined a tiny room with bunk beds and a toilet in one corner. He would cope for one more night, but she couldn't begin to imagine his despair if he was sent to a French prison to await trial. Her heart ached for him. If only she could think of some story convincing enough to get him freed straight away.

And what about her? If Monsieur Belmont told the police that she had kept the heart they might decide to arrest her for receiving stolen goods. She and Alex could both end up in prison. How would that affect their future together?

She stopped outside a busy street-corner bistro with specials scrawled illegibly on a blackboard and candle wax dribbling down empty green wine bottles. The waiter showed her to a cramped table near the back, where she ordered a croque monsieur and a glass of *vin rouge*.

It was strange to think that only a few days earlier she had been having doubts about Alex. Now that he was in trouble, her feelings were crystal clear. She loved him and would do whatever it took to get him out of jail. If he were charged, she would perjure herself to try and get him released. She would go to the newspapers, protest on French television, appeal to their MP. One way or another, she wouldn't rest until Alex was free. She missed him – sarcasm, snappiness and all.

Chapter 57

West Sussex, April 1936

ELEANOR AND RALPH WERE DELIGHTED TO WELCOME Mary to their home, and as they sat with drinks on a terrace in their pretty garden, looking out over the lawn, Mary told them the story of her and Wallis, Jackie and Ernest.

'The truth is I've been in love with Ernest since we first met back in 1924,' she confessed, 'but it all got into a terrible muddle. We were both married to other people at the time, then Wallis came along and ensnared him.' She sniffed, determined not to cry. 'His first marriage broke up because of her. But once she had married him, she set her cap at the Prince of Wales. Then my marriage to Jackie broke up – and now it's all a hopeless mess.'

Eleanor was sympathetic. 'The first day I saw you and Ernest at Petworth, I assumed you were a couple. You're so easy and natural together, so interested in what the other has to say. I am sure it's all going to work out. I have an instinct about it.'

'But if Wallis can't marry the King, then I can't marry Ernest. We are bound up in some infernal maze and I can't see how we will ever untangle ourselves.' She could not tell them about Ernest's conversation with Winston Churchill, but they already knew that the King was not allowed to marry a divorcee.

'Why can't she just be his damn mistress?' Ralph suggested. 'English kings have always married some fecund young aristocrat to produce an heir and a spare, and taken the women they love as mistresses. It's a system that's worked since time immemorial.'

'Wallis will want more security,' Mary predicted. 'Having oodles of money is important to her, and so is her social standing.'

Ralph lit a cigarette, narrowing his eyes against the smoke. 'Mistresses can have both of those. The King could settle an allowance on her in perpetuity. I can't see what all the fuss is about.'

If only it were that simple, Mary thought. Wallis wanted the King and she also wanted the respectability of having a husband waiting at home – and what Wallis wanted she tended to get. Besides, Ernest had not asked Mary to marry him; he had never even told her he loved her. She knew he *liked* her, but would he want to remarry as soon as he was free of his current marriage?

'You must let me paint you while you are here,' Ralph suggested. 'There's an expression on your face right now that I would dearly love to capture.'

They agreed she would extend her stay till Ernest found her an apartment, and that work on the painting would begin the next morning.

~

Ernest telephoned from the office on Monday morning, and when Mary asked how his weekend at Fort Belvedere had gone he said, 'Miserable. Wallis was louder and more demanding than ever, bossing the King around in the most demeaning way. When she noticed that the strap of her shoe had come undone she ordered him to get down on hands and knees to fasten it, in front of all the other guests. Personally, I suspect she unfastened it herself to facilitate her little show of power.'

'Did she ask if you had been in touch with me?' Mary ventured.

'She did, and I'm afraid I had to tell her you were visiting the Hargreaveses. You are likely to hear from her.'

Mary laughed hoarsely. 'Who knows? She might want to apologise for slapping me. I doubt it somehow.'

Ernest cleared his throat, then changed the subject to talk about some apartments he was viewing on her behalf.

Thoughts of Wallis were never far from Mary's mind. Her initial distress was turning to fury when she thought about being slapped and unceremoniously evicted. *You'll regret it*, she told Wallis in her head. *No one else will stand by you the way I have.* She felt guilty, too: of course she should not have gone to bed with her friend's husband – but that friend had long since ceased being a wife to him.

When a letter arrived from Wallis the following day, it was full of vitriol.

You are a snake in the grass. I have always been loyal to you and yet you skulk around behind my back, behaving with cunning and deceit. I see now that I read your character wrong from the beginning, and that you were always jealous of me. Whatever I had, you wanted. You used me to gain access to the social circles in which I move, knowing that my friends would never accept you on your own merits because you are dull *and your conversation* tedious.

The letter finished: *Be very clear about this: you will never truly have Ernest. His love for me will always be greater than whatever transient feelings he might currently entertain for you.*

Mary replied the same day, venting her anger on the page:

Far from being jealous of you, I have always felt pity for you. Poor Wallis whose mother does not have much money, poor Wallis whose first marriage was such a disaster, poor Wallis with no family to support her . . . I gave selflessly and you used me for your own ends, right the way through our friendship. Jacques always said I should beware because you were not loyal, and I knew in my heart it was true. You are the most selfish person in the world, only interested in other people for what they can do for you. I will never feel pity for you again. Whatever happens next, you have brought it on yourself.

Back and forth the letters went, each of them raking up old history and trying to inflict the maximum hurt. Fury energised Mary. As soon as a new letter arrived, she rushed to the writing desk, bursting to reply. In one note she hurled the accusation that Wallis had been sleeping with von Ribbentrop as well as the Prince, and in her reply Wallis called her 'ignorant and pathetic'.

After a week of this, Ernest rang and begged her to desist.

'Wallis is suffering terribly from her stomach ulcers and I'm sure it's been brought on by the stress of your correspondence. Whatever her next letter says, please will you ignore it? You be the civilised one.'

It stuck in Mary's craw to let Wallis have the last word, but she was mollified when Ernest promised he would visit her at the Hargreaveses' the following weekend. She was yearning to see him.

She wrote to Buckie instead:

I don't know when Wallis turned into such a hard-nosed bitch. I look back through her life and wonder: was it in China, where she learned habits no lady should know? While here in London I have watched her bewitch a king she can barely stand the sight of, seduce a Nazi spy, and behave with callous disregard for the feelings of Ernest, who is a man of impeccable moral fibre. He still speaks up for her despite all she has heaped on his doorstep, for reasons I cannot fathom.

A reply arrived from Buckie saying she was delighted to hear that Mary had fallen out with her childhood friend. *Wallis has always been entirely self-centred*, she wrote. *It used to break Mother's heart to watch how she controlled you like a puppet, but you never could see it yourself.* She continued: *Over here the newspapers report on her intimacy with the King and only just stop short of calling her a whore, but there is nothing about the Nazi spy. Do tell more.*

Mary clutched the letter to her chest. Despite the hospitality shown her by the Hargreaveses, and the sittings for her portrait that kept her busy each day, she was starting to feel very homesick for America and her true family. London was going to be a lonely and friendless place on her return.

~

When Ernest's car pulled up in front of the Hargreaveses' house, Mary rushed outside, flung her arms around him and kissed him full on the mouth.

'I can't tell you how much I've missed you,' she breathed, inhaling the reassuring scent of him.

He pulled away, embarrassed by her show of affection in front of their hosts, who were standing on the steps. Mary knew that both were discreet and supportive of their situation. She slipped her arm through Ernest's as she introduced him to Ralph. He greeted Eleanor with a handshake.

'We've put Ernest in the room next to yours,' Eleanor told Mary. 'Why don't you take him up and we'll meet for cocktails in the drawing room when you are ready.'

Mary led him upstairs, chatting excitedly about the portrait Ralph was painting and the news from her sister back home and how generous her hosts were being. She was gabbling out of the sheer joy of seeing him.

Once they were in his room, Ernest put his arms round her and kissed her properly, making her giddy with desire.

'I have news for you,' he said. 'As of today, you are the tenant of an apartment at Albion Gate in Hyde Park. It has three bedrooms and two bathrooms, and looks out over the park. I'm sure you'll like it.'

'Isn't that rather close to Bryanston Court?' she asked, wary of bumping into Wallis in the butcher's shop or the greengrocer's.

'Five minutes away. But you'll find she is never there. I attended a dinner with her and the King yesterday and told them it was the last time I was prepared to perform the role of chaperone. It's humiliating and I can't bear it. They will have to think of some other solution.'

'Gosh! How did they take that?' Mary asked.

Ernest grimaced. 'The King and I had rather a difficult talk in private. He pressed me again to divorce Wallis, to which I replied that I was not standing in her way. It's her who does not want to divorce me. He said he would talk to her, so I suspect the situation will accelerate now. He is a most impetuous man.' He shook his head, his expression disapproving.

'Are they going away for the summer?'

'Of course. They'll be off to the South of France at the end of June and we can have some peace.'

That was reassuring, although privately Mary still found it infuriating that her future happiness depended on the woman she felt such hatred for. She had not one ounce of sympathy when Ernest described Wallis bent double in agony because of her ulcers, unable to drink alcohol or eat anything but milk puddings.

Good! she thought, although she murmured sympathetic noises.

'I brought your dress,' Ernest told her, handing over a brown paper parcel. 'The dressmaker sent it. I have paid her for it as well.'

'Thank you,' Mary said. 'That's kind of you.' She knew she would never wear it now. Any pleasure she might have taken in the King's gift had been soured by the bitterness of her fight with Wallis.

They had cocktails, then dinner, and later in the evening Ernest asked Ralph if he might see the portrait of Mary.

'Of course,' Ralph agreed. 'I'd be delighted.'

'That's not fair!' Mary protested. She had not been allowed to view it herself, because Ralph said he did not like his subjects to influence him as he worked.

Mary sat chatting with Eleanor while Ernest followed Ralph to his studio across a yard behind the kitchen. They were gone some half an hour, and when they returned, Ernest had a soft look in his eyes.

'Do you like it?' Mary asked. 'I hope I don't look hideous.'

Ralph followed him into the room, beaming. 'Ernest has offered to buy it, so I suppose he must think it's not too bad.'

Ernest crossed the room and put his arm round Mary's shoulder, kissing her on the cheek. 'It's beautiful,' he said, his voice hoarse with emotion.

Chapter 58

London, May 1936

MARY LIKED THE APARTMENT IN ALBION GATE. IT was compact, with rather small bedrooms, but double doors between the drawing room and dining room could be thrown back to create one large sunny area lined with windows overlooking Hyde Park. She furnished it simply but comfortably with items from Heal's. She was not planning on entertaining anyone there except Ernest, and she wanted it to feel like a home from home, a place where he could relax.

Several times a week he came for dinner and to spend the night, but Wallis was clearly not happy with this arrangement because she swiftly reinstated KT hour at Bryanston Court and insisted Ernest must attend. Some evenings she held impromptu dinners too, and he would have to sneak out to the hall and telephone Mary to say he could not join her that evening. It made her blood boil: she knew Wallis was simply flexing her muscle and detaining him to spite her, but she was in the role of mistress and had no right to complain, so she bit her tongue and never said a cross word to Ernest; she wanted him to see her as an easy-going, good-natured woman with whom he could enjoy a contented life. She just had to count the days until Wallis and the King set off for their summer holiday.

Mary had not been in touch with any of Wallis's set but imagined they would all share Mrs Campbell's reaction. Wallis would have poured poison into their ears about how her old friend had betrayed her – and everyone wanted to stay on the right side of the King's lover. One evening Mary and Ernest ventured out to a show at the Theatre Royal, Drury Lane, a musical called *Rise and Shine*, but Mary spent the entire time looking over her shoulder, convinced that people were talking about them and blaming them for upsetting 'poor Wallis'. It was a lonely period. Many days she saw no one but her maid.

When Ernest spent the evening at Albion Gate, they often discussed what might happen between Wallis and the King. There were many possible outcomes, each with their own set of repercussions.

'I swear I could not bear to curtsey to her,' Mary said. 'If she becomes queen we shall have to keep well away from anywhere we might encounter her.'

'I spoke with Mr Churchill again,' Ernest told her. 'He seems to accept that the King will not back down from his desire to marry Wallis, so they are taking soundings in the Commonwealth to see what the reaction would be. One possibility is a morganatic marriage.' Mary hadn't heard that term before, so he explained: 'It would mean that Wallis could be his wife but would not have a title or any claim to royal estates. In the unlikely event they had children, their offspring would not inherit. It was traditional in the past when people of unequal social status married.'

'It sounds like an ideal solution, so long as it saves me from curtseying.' Mary shivered at the thought.

'Yes,' Ernest agreed, 'but so far Wallis has not accepted the King's proposal and the strain is making her ill. She barely eats and I've never seen her so thin. I've told her to consult a doctor but she refuses.'

He has no idea how much I detest her, Mary realised. It was better that way. When she thought back over their twenty-five-year friendship, she could not remember one selfless thing Wallis had done for her. When her father had died she had merely scribbled a quick letter of condolence, and she had not come to visit while Mary was nursing her mother through her final illness. By contrast Mary had spent days in Washington comforting the distraught Wallis when Alice died.

Wallis knew about her miscarriages now but had never seemed to appreciate how devastating they had been for Mary. She did not know that Jacques had infected her with syphilis, because Mary had never trusted her not to turn it into an amusing anecdote to entertain dinner guests.

Looking back, she could recall no happy memories from their friendship, only her obedient slotting into the role Wallis had allotted: that of the adoring old friend who would do anything for her. Well, not any more. Never again.

~

When Ernest told her that the King and Wallis had invited him to a house party at Blenheim Palace at the end of June, Mary was incensed.

'I thought you were no longer going to act as chaperone for them,' she said, swallowing her annoyance. 'Did you change your mind?'

He poured himself two fingers of Scotch and raised the bottle. 'One for you, dear?'

'Yes, please.'

'Wallis said they want to talk to me about the Situation, so I decided I had best go. Besides, Blenheim is an extraordinary house by Sir John Vanbrugh and Nicholas Hawksmoor; it's about as good as it gets in baroque architecture.'

Mary didn't reply but held out her hand for the drink.

Mistaking her silence for disappointment that she could not see it too, Ernest added: 'I'll ask if I can take you to visit one day. It's quite spectacular.'

All weekend while he was away, Mary was on tenterhooks. She took a parasol and wandered round Hyde Park for hours on end, watching young lovers strolling, children playing with their nursemaids or governesses, gentlemen riding on horseback. Her fate was being determined by three people in a house of architectural significance and it seemed desperately unfair that she was not allowed to represent herself. They wouldn't see it as being about her, though. It was about Wallis; always about bloody Wallis.

She wasn't sure if she would see Ernest on the Sunday night, but he arrived about seven in the evening looking grey and careworn. She poured him a whisky and let him sit down and tell her what had happened in his own time, although she was fit to burst with curiosity.

'It is decided,' he said, looking at her so gravely that she felt sure he was about to say he was returning to Wallis to save his marriage. She could feel her whole body trembling.

'I am to divorce Wallis this summer,' he continued. 'She wants to name you as co-respondent, but I told her that if she pressed that point I would dig my heels in. Instead we will hire a girl to spend the night in a hotel with me – perfectly innocently, of course – then bribe a chambermaid to come in the morning and witness us in bed together. Then Wallis will be able to divorce me on grounds of my adultery, without a stain on her character.'

It took all of Mary's willpower to maintain her composure. Why should Ernest take the blame? It simply wasn't fair. But at the same time, she wanted to sing with joy that he would be free and Wallis would be out of their lives.

'I wouldn't care if I were named,' she said. 'Wallis has told all of London society that I am a marriage wrecker, so why bother to hire some other girl? Besides,' she added coyly, 'I don't like the idea of you having another girl in your bed.'

'I admit it will be rather awkward, but I don't want you to be compromised.'

Mary thought she had been continually compromised since the day she first met Bessiewallis Warfield at summer camp, but she didn't say as much. 'I'll come with you to the hotel,' she said. 'I insist.'

~

Ernest booked a room at the Hotel de Paris in Bray for Tuesday 21 July. He knew the place because the Guards, with whom he had fought during the war, had their annual passing-out parade there. He told Mary that they often hosted shows by cabaret artistes, and there were pleasant walks by the River Thames. All the arrangements were in hand, he assured her.

Ernest took the day off work and they drove down in the afternoon. When they signed the register at reception, Ernest gave Mary's name as 'Buttercup Kennedy' and she had to stifle a nervous giggle. They had a drink in the bar, strolled in the hotel's pretty grounds and fed the swans on the river with pieces of a bread roll Ernest had procured from the restaurant. After dinner they retired to their room – a rather lovely one with a huge bed – and made love.

'I might as well commit the adultery I am to be accused of.' Ernest smiled as he unfastened the buttons of her dress.

'In that case, am I ever glad I didn't let you come with a strange girl!' Mary rejoined.

At 7.30 in the morning, there was a knock on the door and a chambermaid opened it and looked in. 'Breakfast is served, sir' – she looked pointedly at Mary – 'and madam.' As she laid out their toast and tea on a little table, Mary got the sense she did this kind of thing all the time and did not approve.

After breakfast they drove back to London, to the apartment at Albion Gate. The doorman handed Ernest an official-looking letter and he tore it open as they walked up the stairs.

'Good grief, Wallis is a fast worker,' he said. 'This is a letter from her solicitor saying that she is suing me for divorce. She also wants me to move out of Bryanston Court forthwith. Any chance I can stay with you, my dear? You wouldn't put a chap out on the streets, would you?'

Mary couldn't wait until they were inside her front door. She grabbed him by the collar and pulled him towards her for a passionate kiss.

~

In early July, Wallis accompanied the King to the royal estate of Balmoral in Scotland, then they headed off for a cruise of the Greek islands on a yacht called the *Nahlin*. Mary hoped for a couple of months' respite now they were out of town. She and Ernest began touring the countryside at weekends, exploring Cotswold villages and sailing on the Norfolk Broads.

Her sister Anne wrote, sending them articles from the American press about the *Nahlin* cruise. Their authors were confident that Wallis was the King's mistress, despite the presence of several other guests. One paper printed a photograph of Wallis touching the King's hand, which seemed to provide the proof. *All the press say he plans to wed her*, Anne wrote. *It's hot news out here.*

'How come the British press still hasn't cottoned on?' Mary asked Ernest. 'Their editors must read the American papers.'

'Of course they know,' he explained, 'but there's a tradition of not criticising the monarch. It's simply not done.'

'You Brits are so quaint,' Mary teased. 'What century do you live in?'

'At least none of the stories have mentioned you,' he said. 'I want to protect you if I possibly can.'

The divorce hearing was set for 27 October; all being well, they would get the decree nisi in April 1937. *Perhaps Ernest and I can be married in the summer*, Mary daydreamed. She was still not divorced from Jacques, but she had written to him telling him that she was in love with Ernest, and he had replied wishing them happiness and saying he would give her a divorce just as soon as she wanted. *You two are a good match*, he wrote, *and I am glad you will be together. Give Ernest my warmest regards.*

Wallis sent postcards for Ernest from stopping points on their cruise, full of gossip about the other passengers, particularly Lady Diana Cooper, who was, she said, 'a hoot'. But she complained that the weather was too hot and it barely got any cooler at night. There was no mention of Mary in any of the cards, although they were addressed to her apartment in Albion Gate. She was tempted to tear them up, but didn't. There seemed no need. They were heading towards the resolution she wanted, after all.

~

In August, Ralph Hargreaves wrote to Ernest checking that he had received the portrait of Mary, which, he said, had been delivered to Bryanston Court over a month earlier. He hoped they were both pleased with it and hinted very delicately that the fee was due.

The painting had completely slipped their minds, with all the drama of the divorce occupying them that summer. Ernest went to speak to the doorman at Bryanston Court but was told that Wallis had changed the locks and instructed him not to let her husband enter the apartment under any circumstances. 'I'm sorry, sir,' he said, hanging his head.

'I'll have to ask Wallis for it on her return,' Ernest told Mary. He posted a cheque to Ralph with a note apologising for the delay.

~

In mid September, soon after she got back to London, Wallis telephoned Ernest at his office and invited him for dinner at the Savoy.

'Dinner!' Mary exclaimed, unable to hide her irritation. 'Might that not be counted as collusion?' If a judge thought that Ernest and Wallis had colluded over their divorce, he could refuse to grant it.

'We will make sure no one hears of it,' Ernest said. 'I need to ask her to return your portrait, and there are a few other practical matters we must agree upon.'

Once more, Mary had to bite her tongue, even fastening his cufflinks and straightening his bow tie as he got ready to dine with her nemesis. All evening she waited in a chair by the window, sipping whisky and watching for the taxicab to draw up outside that would signal Ernest's return.

It was after midnight when he came in and slumped in the chair adjoining hers, reaching out across the gap to take her hand.

'Well?' she asked, her tongue thick from booze.

'Wallis has never ceased to surprise me in all the years I've known her,' he began. 'You'll never guess the latest. She wants to cancel the divorce and for us to give our marriage another chance.'

Mary pulled her hand away. 'She wants *what?*' It was a struggle not to hurl her glass across the room. What an evil, calculating *bitch*! This was Wallis's attempt to show Mary that she could never truly possess Ernest, just as she had written in her letter. 'What did you reply?'

Ernest sounded weary and sad. 'I told her that all the nice things about our marriage have been spoiled and I do not want to be tied for life to someone I cannot live with.'

Mary frowned. She wished he had told Wallis that he loved *her* now – loved her more than he had ever loved anyone else. But that was not Ernest's nature. He found it hard to speak of emotion. As she grew to know him better, Mary was learning to judge him by his actions rather than his words.

'Bad news about the painting,' he continued. 'She simply refuses to hand it over. I'm afraid you are *persona non grata* as far as she's concerned.'

'She's probably using it for knife-throwing practice,' Mary said, then a bitchy thought came into her head. 'When the King gets bored of her, she can run off and join a circus.'

'And she told me you have a dress of hers. She would like it returned.'

Mary shook her head, mystified. 'I don't know what she's talking about.' She didn't have anything of Wallis's. She must be mistaken.

Chapter 59

Paris, 17 December 1997

NEXT MORNING, RACHEL WAS WOKEN BY HER PHONE ringing. She looked at the screen: 9.45 a.m. She had meant to get up earlier. It was Monsieur Belmont.

'I've seen Alex and he was delighted to hear you have come to Paris. The police are still holding him, though, and I'm not expecting further news till the end of the day. Where are you staying?'

She told him the name of the hotel.

'I'll keep you informed,' he said and hung up brusquely, as though he had a hundred more pressing matters to deal with.

Rachel stretched. That meant she had a day to kick her heels, and straight away she knew what she was going to do. She got directions from the hotel receptionist and set off on the Métro to Porte Maillot, then crossed into the Bois de Boulogne. A road snaked through the woods, with closely packed bare-branched trees on either side. The sky was pale blue, with a shimmering white sun making frost sparkle on the grass.

The Villa Windsor was a three-storey pale-stone building with black balcony railings, surrounded by a high wrought-iron fence and a border of slender trees. To Rachel, it did not have the appearance of a royal palace, despite the pillared entrance and tall, narrow windows. The garden was too small and lacking in privacy, the architecture too square and unadorned.

Rachel knew that Alex had tried and failed to get an interview with the manager, so she thought it best not to ring the bell set into a pillar by the gates. Instead she walked round the perimeter, hoping she might spot a gardener at work, but there was no sign of anyone, no lights in any windows. She positioned herself on the other side of the road with a view of the driveway and waited.

Around 1.30 p.m., a white van drew up and its driver rang the bell. A man with short silver hair appeared and opened the electronic gates, whereupon the van drove in and parked outside the front door. Rachel wandered over to watch from just outside the gate as they carried some large cardboard boxes from the house and loaded them into the van.

When they had finished, the driver signed a docket and drove off. Rachel hurried up the drive before the gates swung closed.

'*Je cherche Monsieur John Sturkey. Est-il ici?*'

'*C'est moi,*' the man replied.

Thank God, Rachel thought. That made things easier. 'Do you speak English?' she asked.

'Yes,' he replied. 'I'm from Devon, so I'm pretty fluent.' She could hear a slight Devonian twang in his accent.

'My name is Rachel Wainwright,' she said, 'and I work with Alex Greene. He was supposed to meet you on Monday? He is very sorry to have missed that appointment. He asked me to come and talk to you today. Is that possible?'

The man looked her up and down, considering. 'Why not?' he replied. 'Alex will pay me the money we agreed? And my name will not be mentioned in his programme?'

'That's right,' she said. 'He just wants information.'

'OK. Let's go inside a moment.'

Rachel held her breath in excitement as she walked up the front steps. This was the former home of the Duke and Duchess of Windsor, Wallis and Edward, who had lived here after the war, and who had both died here, him in 1972 and her in 1986. She was walking on a floor they used to tread.

John Sturkey led her into a tall marble entrance hall with a curving staircase up one side. A flag with the royal standard flew from a balcony overhead. Piles of cardboard boxes stood around, each one plastered with printed notices and customs forms.

'The furniture and house contents were to be auctioned this autumn, but Monsieur Al-Fayed has postponed the sale,' John Sturkey told Rachel. 'In the circumstances.'

She managed to glance into some of the public rooms on the ground floor: a study lined with now-empty bookshelves, the walls painted brick red; a spectacular chandelier in a vast room lined with windows that overlooked the garden; another room with a red carpet and black and gold Chinese lacquer on the walls. In her mind's eye she could see Wallis, with the bouffant hair and heavy jewellery of her later years, holding court at the head of a dining table, while Edward watched with an affectionate smile.

John Sturkey led her to the kitchen, where there was a vast black range down one wall. 'I have some rubbish to burn out the back, but if you come with me we can talk at the same time.'

'That's fine,' Rachel agreed. 'It's very good of you to see me. I promise it won't take long.'

'Perhaps you could give me a hand? It's this pile here.'

In the entrance to a scullery just off the kitchen there was a heap of broken furniture, ripped cardboard boxes, and various odds and ends. She helped to carry them out of the back door to a corner of the grounds where a brazier was burning with an orangey-red glow and a smell of woodsmoke. The kitten heels of her suede boots sank into the muddy grass.

John Sturkey broke a leg off one chair and used it to stir the ashes before poking it down amongst them. Flames began to lick up the sides.

'How long have you been working here?' she asked.

'Since 1970,' he said. 'A long time.' His face was ruddy, as you would expect from someone who worked outdoors, but he was a fit, wiry man with a youthful air. He wore a blue ribbed fisherman's jumper and thick black leather gloves. 'I came over to Paris after falling in love with a French woman and was lucky enough to get this job.'

'It must have been fascinating working for the Duke and Duchess. What were they like?'

He stood on the seat of the wooden chair and ripped the remaining legs off. 'They were generous employers. I got on with both of them. The Duke liked to chat to me about gardening, and the Duchess would trust me to walk her pugs in the park. She didn't trust many, mind, but I have a love of dogs and she knew they'd be safe.'

'I suppose you saw lots of celebrities coming and going over the years,' Rachel probed.

'Of course,' he said. 'The Duke and Duchess loved to entertain. I've seen movie stars, politicians, musicians: all the high and mighty passed through these doors.' He fed the remaining chair legs into the brazier.

'The final years of the Duchess's life must have been very sad, in contrast to those glamorous times.' She watched his face and could see as he replied that he had genuinely cared about her.

'They were tragic. She never recovered from the Duke's death. She was lost without him, like a little bird. I mean, she was thin as a stick anyway, but after he'd gone she faded away till she was hardly there.'

'Do you think he was the love of her life?' It was a silly question. How would their gardener know? She was just wondering out loud.

John Sturkey put some pieces of cardboard onto the fire and it flared up, flames spilling over the edges. 'They argued a lot, but they were used to each other. By the time I met them, they were set in their ways, joined at the hip if you like.' He nodded, a distant look in his eyes.

'I know Alex wanted to ask you about Princess Diana's visits here. Did you ever meet her?'

'Course I did!' he said. 'Loads of times. When she visited the Duchess, she always brought food hampers from Fortnum and Mason and the staff got to share them. The Dundee cake was my favourite.'

'Did she spend long with the Duchess?'

'Usually about half an hour. The Duchess couldn't talk any more by her last years. She was bedridden and blind, a frail creature who was easily alarmed, but the Princess would sit by the bed holding her hand and give her a hug, all skin and bone as she was.'

He fed more fractured pieces of wood into the brazier, where the flames devoured them with a crackling sound. Rachel welcomed the heat; it was a nippy afternoon and the damp chill was seeping into her bones and up through the soles of her boots. She splayed her gloveless fingers towards the fire to warm them.

'Did you ever speak to Diana yourself?'

'I did, yes. She always remembered my name, and would wave to me: "Hello, John!"' He demonstrated her wave and raised his voice a few notches. '"How's the garden? Are the roses early this year?" That kind of thing.'

'Did you see her when she came in August?'

'Yes, and I still get a lump in my throat when I think about it.' He looked Rachel in the eye. 'If only they had stayed here instead of going into the city. Their driver had given the photographers the slip, so no one followed them here. They'd have been safe.'

Rachel had brought a magazine picture of Diana wearing the bracelet on that last day of her life, and she pulled it out to show him. 'Did you happen to notice if she was wearing this bracelet?'

He glanced at it quickly and nodded. 'Aye, that's the one I gave her.'

'*You* gave it to her?' Rachel didn't understand.

'See this old dressing table here?' He kicked at a decrepit piece from which the drawers had been removed. It looked as though it had once been rococo style. 'When I carried it down from the Duchess's bedroom, a funny thing happened. I must have pressed against some kind of secret switch in the coving and a tiny drawer came shooting out. You'd never have found it if you didn't know about it. Anyway, that bracelet was inside. I'd just discovered it when Diana and Dodi arrived. He went into the office, and on the spur of the moment I thought I'd give it to Diana. It seemed the right thing to do.'

'That was a nice gesture. What did you say as you handed it over?'

He gave a little laugh and shook his head. 'I wanted to tell her that I thought it was incredibly kind the way she'd visited the Duchess over the years, and that I admired the work she was doing on landmines and AIDS and so forth. All those words were in my head but I was a tongue-tied idiot. She was much prettier up close than I'd imagined, and all I managed to say was, "This is for you," and I thrust it into her hand.'

Rachel smiled sympathetically. She could imagine Diana would have that effect.

John continued: 'She slipped it on her wrist straight away and said thank you, it was very pretty and she would treasure it. Then Dodi called her into the office and that was that. But she gave me a special wave and called "thank you" again when they were leaving.'

Rachel wondered whether Diana had even noticed the engravings; it didn't sound like it. 'The heart had a Roman number seventeen and an initial J engraved on it. Did they mean anything to you?'

He shrugged and shook his head. 'No idea. I'm sure the Duchess took one helluva lot of secrets to the grave with her.' He stopped and glanced at her. 'Pardon my French.'

She smiled. 'I'm the last person to mind swearing.' She watched as he stirred the brazier, causing the flames to leap into the air. 'Is it true that Diana and Dodi met an interior designer here because they were thinking of refurbishing the house and living in it?'

'No, I read that in some of the papers, but it's rubbish. Diana told me she could never live here. It's too melancholy. Besides, look.' He gestured towards the garden's perimeter. 'It's not private enough. The photographers would be camped out there 24/7.'

'So why did they come?' The crucial question. Did he know about the painting?

'She was having a look at some of the furniture. We'd laid aside a few pieces she liked and she was considering buying them privately.'

That was good news. Susie would be delighted to hear she hadn't just come about her painting. Perhaps she would stop blaming herself.

'What kind of pieces?' she asked.

'Let me think.' He paused, summoning the images from memory. 'There was a carved chest from the bedroom, a chandelier, a bureau from the Duchess's study, a fancy silver candelabra with lots of leaves twined up the candlesticks . . .' He motioned the twining leaves with his gloved fingers. 'And there was a painting she wanted for a friend.'

Rachel leapt back as the breeze blew the flames in her direction. 'What kind of painting?'

'Just a portrait. I don't know who it was. Diana found it straight away amongst the other works.' Some flames flickered towards him but he ignored them, clearly a past master at handling fires. 'She was going to pick it up on the way to the airport the next day because she said it was needed in a hurry. I was planning to clean and package it for her – but then, of course . . .' He added some torn dustsheets to the brazier and pushed them down with a stick, his expression grim.

That would explain why Diana and Dodi had only spent half an hour in the house, Rachel thought.

'What happened to all the items she earmarked?' If the painting was still there, perhaps she could agree some kind of private deal, just as Diana had been planning.

'We're putting them into storage till the auction can go ahead. That van you saw was picking up a load. It's strange seeing the old place so empty, but once we finish the clear-out Mr Al-Fayed will replace everything with replicas so it's like a museum.'

'I suppose that painting will go to auction as well?' Perhaps it had gone already. She held her breath.

He shook his head. 'The auctioneers didn't want it because it was an amateur artist and no one knows who the subject is. The Duchess never hung it on her walls, not as long as I've been here anyroad. It's been hidden away in a cupboard so it's all musty and faded.'

Rachel could barely contain her impatience. 'Is it still here?'

Her tone made him curious. 'Why do I get the impression you know something about it?'

There was nothing for it: she explained that she knew the artist's granddaughter, Susie Hargreaves, who was very keen to reclaim it and give it as a hundredth birthday present to the artist's wife.

He nodded. 'That's the name Diana said: Hargreaves. I'm sure it's in a pile that was going to be disposed of. See that scullery we were in before? Go and have a look there. I can't leave the fire unattended.'

Rachel hurried across the grass, cursing her stupid spindly heels, which were picking up tufts of grass. She realised she didn't know exactly what she was looking for but hoped she would recognise it when she saw it.

The scullery was as large as her sitting room and filled with piles of miscellaneous objects: striped deckchairs, wooden tea chests, an ancient vacuum cleaner and a cracked ceramic sink. It smelled of decay. Rachel realised she didn't even know how big the painting was; if it was a miniature, she had no hope of finding it. She remembered the picture on the wall behind Susie's head when Alex did the interview and guessed it might be a similar size – about four feet tall, three across. She found a stack of paintings by a wall, and as she began to flick through them, a large spider scuttled across the floor.

There were no portraits in that pile so she stepped further into the room. A slight scuffling sound in the corner made her jump. She looked in that direction, hoping it was a mouse rather than a rat, and that was when she saw the back of a painting around the size she was looking for. She climbed over some boxes to reach it, and when she turned it round, she was stunned by the image on the front: an extraordinarily beautiful woman in a low-cut emerald-green dress.

The light was dim so she carried it to the back door to have a proper look. The woman had auburn hair that was parted in the centre and flat on top, with neat curls at the sides. Her lips were painted ruby red, but it was the green eyes that drew you in and held you. She was smiling, looking directly at the viewer, as if inviting them to share a joke. There was a signature in the corner: *R. Hargreaves, '36*. No wonder his wife wanted it back. It was beautiful.

As Rachel carried the painting outside and walked towards John Sturkey, she was trying to decide how to play this. Should she offer him money, and if so, how much? She knew Susie couldn't afford to reimburse her.

He looked up when he saw her coming. 'That's the one. So you know the Hargreaveses, do you? I reckon you should take it to them. If you'd been a day or two later, chances are I'd have burned it. Some things are meant to be.'

Rachel was thrilled. 'Are you sure? I would love to. I can't tell you how happy she'll be.'

'It was one of the Princess's last wishes, if you like, so I'm glad I can help you carry it out. Fetch me that roll of tape from the kitchen table and I'll wrap it up for you.'

He folded two large sheets of cardboard around the painting so it wouldn't get damaged on the journey and, when he had finished taping it, said, 'You didn't come about the TV programme, did you? It was the painting all along.' He gave her a knowing look. 'Does that mean Alex won't pay me the fee?'

Rachel had no idea how much had been agreed but decided she would cover it herself if need be. 'He will. I promise. He's my fiancé, so I'll make him.'

John Sturkey laughed. 'Great. He's got my details. Soon as he can: tell him it's for the wife's Christmas present.'

Rachel shook his hand. 'Is that the woman you came to Paris for?'

'The one and only,' he said. 'Love of my life, she is.'

'I hope you both have a lovely Christmas.'

She hurried round the corner of the house, holding the painting in front of her. Her coat was covered with cobwebs and dust from the scullery, but she would worry about that later.

There was a button to open the Villa's gates, and she waited for them to ease apart with a mechanical hum, then slid out through the gap and hurried down the road through the woods. Her arms were already aching from the weight of the painting and the awkward way she had to hold it, as if in a wide hug.

Chapter 60

London, September 1936

MARY'S ONLY NEWS OF WALLIS CAME FROM THE weekly letters she addressed to Ernest at Albion Gate. He handed them over as soon as he read them so she knew there were no secrets between them.

I have begged Peter Pan to let me go, Wallis wrote:

and he replied that if I leave him he will cut his throat with a hunting knife . . . What kind of man-child have I lumbered myself with? I don't understand how this came about. If I wake in the night, sometimes I imagine that I am at home in Bryanston Court and hear your footsteps coming down the corridor, the Evening Standard *tucked under your arm. Darling Ernest, I can't believe such a thing can have happened to two people who got on so well.*

Ernest's only reaction was a grunt. Mary's was fury, which she disguised by clattering her chair as she rose from the table. 'If she genuinely wants to escape the King, she could just leave. The world is big enough for her to lose herself.'

Ernest folded his linen table napkin precisely. 'She has thought of that, but the King says he will find her wherever she goes. Besides, she knows I can't afford to support her in the grand style to which she has grown accustomed.'

'I don't see why you should support her at all,' Mary muttered.

'Indeed.' Ernest rose from the table and went to prepare for the office.

Mary picked up the letter to check the address: Felixstowe. That was where the divorce hearing was to be held. For the second time in her life, Wallis would become resident somewhere just long enough for her case to be heard at a local court. The coronation was scheduled for May 1937, and the King hoped to marry Wallis beforehand, after the issuing of the decree nisi in April. Mary wished she could snap her fingers and it would be over and done with. The waiting and worrying that something might go wrong was horrid.

In her next letter, Wallis sounded in a low, penitent mood, but still she blamed everyone but herself for her predicament. *The US press has done untold harm in every direction besides printing wicked lies . . . Last time I went out I was followed everywhere by cameramen.* Towards the end of the letter she wrote: *I am sorry about Mary, I am sorry for myself, I am sorry for the King.*

It's a bit late for sorry, Mary thought, not believing Wallis for a moment. She had taken the jewellery, taken the clothes, gone on the cruises. Complaining now was like a whore accepting the money then saying to her client, 'Sorry, but I'd rather not go to bed with you.'

None of these thoughts did she voice to Ernest. She was the civilised one, the calm one, the woman with whom he could enjoy a peaceful life. It was hard to maintain sometimes, but she was determined.

Wallis wrote that on the day of the October hearing, there was a rabble of photographers outside the court, pushing and shoving, their cameras held high above their heads to get the shot.

The noise of their flashbulbs was like a shoot-out in some Western corral. I had to be rescued by two burly police officers who took my elbows in their hands and more or less lifted me into the courthouse, smashing a couple of cameras with their truncheons along the way . . . After that, the court proceedings took precisely fourteen minutes. Dear Buttercup Kennedy was blamed for everything and our case awarded with costs . . . I suppose this was what we agreed, Ernest, but I feel such a weight of sadness that I cannot move from my chair. I must dine with Peter Pan tonight and he will expect me to celebrate, but I feel more alone than I have ever felt in my life.

No doubt that was true, Mary thought, but all she could feel was joy that Ernest was one step closer to being free of Wallis's clutches.

They dined that evening with Ernest's sister Maud, and she shared Mary's pleasure that Wallis would be out of their lives. She had never warmed to her.

'You are mistaken in your belief that she has poisoned London society against you,' Maud told Mary when the men had retired for cigars and brandy in the library. 'I think you'll find that lots of people who used to lick Wallis's boots are now saying they hardly knew her. Only the other day I heard Emerald Cunard claim she had met her "only once or twice" and did not take to her.'

Mary laughed at this. 'Emerald positively fawned over her at the Bryanston Court KT hours. How the worm has turned!'

She felt emboldened enough by this conversation to accept a few invitations, and found there was a tacit acceptance that Ernest had behaved with patriotism and correctness in doing as his King commanded. Ernest's lawyer told him that Wallis had produced Mary's love letter to him in the divorce court in a last-ditch attempt to blacken her name, but no one remarked on it. She and Ernest were seen as the innocent parties in the fiasco and Wallis was the she-devil who was harming the monarchy.

Wallis wrote to Ernest that she was too scared to stay in the Regent's Park house the King had bought for her. *Every mail delivery brings poison-pen letters, calling me harlot and Jezebel (although few of them spell it correctly). And last Sunday, while I was dining out, a brick was thrown through the front window. I can no longer have my hair done or go shopping in case some maniac leaps out to shoot or stab me. I'm pretty flattened out by the world in general.*

On 1 December, after the Bishop of Bradford spoke directly against Wallis and the King, the British press finally jumped on the story. Ernest's friend Bernie Rickatson-Hatts telephoned to say that the *Times* was preparing to publish an attack on Wallis's character, so Ernest dutifully rang Fort Belvedere to warn her. Mary overheard his side of the conversation.

'There's nothing I can do. It's not just the *Times* . . . I can ask around. Perhaps you could stay with some friends in the north of England . . . No, I quite see . . . When do you plan to go? . . . And who will drive? . . . Perhaps that is wisest.'

He came off the phone and glanced at Mary. 'She's hysterical. She thinks she will be killed if she stays in England, so she's fleeing to France.'

Mary's first thought was that it was not far enough. 'Will she stay with her friends, Katherine and Herman Rogers?'

'I imagine so. It's all very hush-hush because she doesn't want the press tailing them. Peter Pan is distraught but admits he can't protect her if she stays.'

'When is she going?'

'Tomorrow.' He mused for a moment. 'She said the damnedest thing: seemingly the King has told Prime Minister Baldwin that if all else fails, he will abdicate rather than lose her.'

Mary was astonished. 'What, he would leave the throne entirely? Become a commoner? That's the *last* thing Wallis would want.'

To risk all in seducing a king only to win him but in the process cause him to lose his throne: it sounded to Mary like one of those traditional fairy stories in which pride led to a fall, or greed led to penury.

Ernest regarded her with a serious expression. 'As a patriotic Englishman, I cannot allow this to happen. I will write to Mr Baldwin this evening.'

'Saying what?' Mary felt fear prickling her skin.

'Two things: that I know Wallis will withdraw from the situation if she is given a chance; and that if my country requires it, I will claim there was collusion over our divorce and therefore we cannot be awarded a decree nisi next April.'

Tears filled Mary's eyes and she covered her face with her hands, turning away so Ernest would not see her cry.

'I'm sorry, my dear.' He looped his arm round her waist from behind. 'But this concerns a centuries-old institution that is worth more than the happiness of a few individuals. We must make a sacrifice if called upon.'

She watched him write his letter and did not try to stop him, but the blood felt like razor blades in her veins.

~

Ernest's offer was not accepted by the prime minister, and a week later, on the evening of 11 December, he and Mary tuned their radio set to the BBC to hear the King broadcast to his subjects. The familiar voice was calm and the words moving as he explained that he was handing over the crown to his brother George with immediate effect and quitting public affairs altogether: 'I have found it impossible to carry the heavy burden of responsibility and to discharge my duties as King as I would wish to do without the help and support of the woman I love.'

Mary and Ernest exchanged glances, shocked that it had come to this.

'I guess Wallie has gotten herself into the history books,' Mary remarked. 'Somewhere between Helen of Troy and Attila the Hun.'

Chapter 61

Fairford, Connecticut, 15 November 1937

MARY STOOD ON A PIER ON NEW YORK'S EAST RIVER, waiting for Ernest to arrive on a crossing from Southampton. She had been in the States since September, because she had to spend six weeks in Reno obtaining her divorce from Jackie. Now the legal paperwork was ready and all the arrangements had been made for her forthcoming wedding to Ernest.

He had never actually asked her to marry him. There was no proposal on bended knee, but once his divorce from Wallis came through in April, he had announced in a matter-of-fact tone that November would be a good month for them to get married, and she had said, 'Yes, that's fine.' Their conversations had been about practicalities; he seemed to have assumed they would be married one day, and she was glad she had not pressed him on the matter before.

She missed Ernest terribly during their two months' separation, with a dull ache she carried around. She also had an irrational fear that Wallis would try to stop their marriage out of spite. If there was a legal technicality, some final spanner she could throw in the works to prevent Mary and Ernest finding happiness, then she would almost certainly do it.

Wallis had married David the previous June at a ceremony in a French chateau. Mary was secretly pleased to hear that few of their sycophants turned up, and none of the British royal family. Herman Rogers gave her away, Cecil Beaton took the photographs, and Wallis wore a Mainbocher dress of 'Wallis blue', a colour he had invented for her, but the high society she had hoped to woo found themselves unavoidably otherwise engaged on 3 June.

They honeymooned in Austria, at Schloss Wasserleonburg, yet even from there, during what should have been the most romantic time of her life, Wallis wrote to Ernest saying how much she missed him: *I think of us so much, though I try not to. I'd love to hear from you if you feel like telling me a bit.*

Mary read that letter in utter disbelief. He's not yours any more, she growled. Leave him alone!

The new Duke and Duchess of Windsor, as they had been styled, would receive a generous allowance from the Crown, and could live their lives as they pleased, but they were no longer allowed to return to England without the new King's permission. That made sense to Mary: King George could not have his brother, the erstwhile pin-up boy, barging in to interfere whenever he felt so inclined. They had settled in Paris, which meant Mary had no fear of bumping into them when she accepted a dinner invitation or Ernest booked theatre tickets. Now she just had to get her own wedding out of the way and she could erase Wallis from her mind for ever. At the grand old age of forty-one, she would finally be with the man she had loved for the last thirteen years, the man with whom she hoped to grow old.

Ernest waved as he walked down the gangplank, a smile lighting up his face. He ran the last few steps and ducked under a rope barrier to throw his arms around her and hold her tight.

~

Mary and Ernest stayed at the Waldorf while making the final preparations for their wedding. Every time they stepped outside the hotel, they ran the gauntlet of photographers with exploding flashbulbs, all of them shouting questions about Wallis and Edward.

'Are you in touch with the Duke and Duchess of Windsor?' 'Does Wallis mind that she didn't get an HRH title?' 'Does Ernest feel responsible for the abdication?'

'No comment,' Mary called every time, with a cheery wave.

Ernest was keen to outwit the press, determined there would be no photographs of their wedding in the newspapers, so instead of a New York location they chose the Fairfield Lawn Country Club in Connecticut, not far from Mary's sister Buckie's home. Two limousines picked them up from the Waldorf on the morning of 19 November – women in one, men in the other – and they drove north for almost two hours. Mary kept turning to check they weren't being followed, but it seemed the photographers outside the hotel had not leapt into their cars fast enough to tail them.

The country club facilities were basic, with uncomfortable folding chairs and tiny tables covered in worn white linen, a few displays of orchids and mimosa doing little to make it seem matrimonial, but none of that mattered to Mary. She and Ernest were wed in front of the fireplace by a justice of the peace, who stumbled over his lines because he had never married anyone before. Mary's heart was full as she repeated the words – 'for better for worse, for richer for poorer, in sickness and in health'. She was determined that she would live by them and do all in her power to make her new husband happy.

~

They sailed back from America on the *Queen Mary*, a luxurious ship that had only made her maiden voyage the previous year.

That winter, all of London society clamoured to entertain them, but Mary and Ernest gravitated towards the literary set, becoming good friends of Mr and Mrs Sacheverell Sitwell, as well as the opera and ballet crowd whom they met at Covent Garden. Mary remained wary of the Americans who had been at the core of Wallis's KT clique, although they all sent wedding presents and effusive congratulations.

At weekends, they sometimes visited friends in the country, including Eleanor and Ralph. Wallis still refused to return Ralph's portrait of Mary; it seemed she'd had it transported to France among the rest of her personal possessions. Ralph sent her a lawyer's letter demanding its return but was ignored, and the legal complications of filing a suit overseas stopped him pursuing it further.

'I can't believe Wallis and Edward went to meet Hitler last October.' Eleanor shook her head. 'What were they thinking?'

'They were trying to make themselves feel they still have some importance in the world,' Mary replied. 'He was the only leader who offered them a state visit. It does seem naïve in the extreme.'

'Rather more than naïvety,' Eleanor continued. 'I think there might be ambition behind it. It's well known that both are fascist sympathisers, and I hear it's now common knowledge' – she glanced across the room to where Ralph and Ernest were engrossed in a conversation of their own – 'that Wallis had an affair with von Ribbentrop.'

Mary nodded. 'I always suspected it because of the regular deliveries of roses. Who told you?'

Eleanor lowered her voice. 'I heard it at Nancy Astor's, and I believe it's all the talk round London. The story goes that Constance Spry, the florist, told another customer that von Ribbentrop asked for exactly seventeen roses in each bouquet he sent Wallis because that's the number of times they went to bed together.'

Mary thought back to the unusually large bunches: she had never counted, but there could easily have been seventeen blooms in each. 'She always hid the cards that came with the bouquets, but I stole one and it read "See you in Berlin". They must have been planning their visit all along.'

'Will you two never be reconciled?' Eleanor gave her a searching look. 'You were close for so long.'

Mary shook her head vehemently. 'She has been hateful towards me. Simply hateful. I will never forgive her.'

~

In the spring of 1938, a long-held dream of Mary's came true when Ernest took her to Italy on a belated honeymoon. They walked round the antiquities in Rome, toured the museums of Florence and glided in a gondola down Venice's Grand Canal. It was remarkable how much they were in tune, Mary thought. They paused before the same paintings, admired the same church interiors, invariably agreed with each other's opinions. Theirs was a meeting of minds, as well as a marriage of great passion.

On their return, they bought a house in Holland Park, a spacious home with plenty of room for entertaining, and hired an interior designer to furnish and decorate it. It would not be ready for several months, so they stayed in Albion Gate in the meantime, and it was there, in early April 1939, that Mary woke one morning feeling terribly sick. She spent the day throwing up, her new Scottie dog Diana curled on the bed beside her.

'It must have been those cocktails at the Sitwells' last night,' she told Ernest. 'I lost count of how many I drank.'

When the sickness continued the following day, and the one after, Ernest insisted on calling a doctor.

'I'm going to take a blood test, Mrs Simpson,' the doctor said, after asking a battery of questions. 'There's no cause for alarm. I'll visit you in a few days when I have the results.'

Mary couldn't help worrying that there was something dreadfully wrong; perhaps she had damaged an internal organ with all the alcohol she had been imbibing. She didn't think she was an alcoholic, not like Jacques, but she and Ernest enjoyed a quiet tipple at home every evening, and when they were out somewhere it was only polite to join in with the general merriment.

'I have some news for you,' the doctor said on his return. Ernest leant forward in his chair, looking grave, and Mary crossed her fingers tightly.

'It seems,' the doctor continued, 'that you are pregnant.'

'Pregnant?' she gasped, and her mouth fell open in shock as she looked at Ernest, who seemed equally stunned. 'But I'm forty-two; I'll be forty-three in a couple of months.'

The doctor nodded. 'We will have extra check-ups during the pregnancy because of your age. I expect your obstetrician will deliver the baby early by Caesarean section, so as not to risk your health in the final weeks.'

'How far gone is the pregnancy?' she asked, still not daring to believe it. 'I lost three babies before twelve weeks, so I don't want to . . .'

The doctor flicked through his diary, counting. 'You are thirteen weeks pregnant as of today,' he announced. 'There could still be a risk so I suggest you take it easy. The baby is due in October.'

Mary looked at Ernest again, scared to rejoice too soon. He leapt from his chair to put an arm round her and kiss her, clearly ecstatic. It's not the same for him, she thought; he has a daughter already. There was no way his excitement could be any match for hers. She had wanted a baby for decades but had long ago given up hope. This was a miracle, a gift from God. She had never in her wildest dreams thought she could be so lucky.

~

I hear you are to have an addition to the family, Wallis wrote to Ernest that summer. *How very irresponsible of Mary! You'd think she'd have been more careful at her age. Still, at least she no longer has a figure to lose.*

Mary laughed out loud when she read the letter. Clearly Wallis was riled that she was giving Ernest something – a son, they hoped – that she, Wallis, had never been able to.

Soon after this, she received a telephone call from Gladys Scanlon, Wallis's old friend, asking when the child was due and when she and Ernest were moving into their new house in Holland Park. Mary could tell she was on a spying mission. Wallis had clearly ordered her to find out.

None of her business, she thought, and was deliberately vague in her answers.

Chapter 62

Paris, 17 December 1997

WHEN RACHEL EMERGED FROM THE MÉTRO IN central Paris, her phone began to beep with messages. She rested the painting on the pavement to check them, hoping there might be news of Alex. Nicola and her mother had both texted, and there were several missed calls from Alex's dad, but no word from Monsieur Belmont. She realised she hadn't been getting a signal in the Bois de Boulogne.

Back in her hotel room, she propped the painting against the wall, took off her filthy coat and mud-caked boots and massaged her aching arms. Her neck was sore from the strain of the awkward position she'd had to adopt as she staggered along, leaning back slightly to counterbalance the painting's weight.

She flopped on the bed to reply to her messages. Nicola wanted to know the price of a dress in the shop and to see if there was any news; her mother wondered what time they hoped to arrive back; and Alex's dad was clearly getting anxious. It was almost 5 p.m.; surely the police must decide soon whether they were going to charge Alex? She sent texts to all three of them, then stripped off and had a shower, taking her mobile into the bathroom so she would hear if it rang.

She had just stepped out of the shower when she heard the room phone ringing and rushed in her towel to answer it. 'Someone here to see you,' the receptionist said. Rachel guessed it must be Monsieur Belmont. She pulled on her dress, although her skin was still damp, and hurried downstairs barefoot. Instead, to her amazement, there was Alex, grinning at her, with two days' growth of beard, filthy clothes and lank, greasy hair. She threw herself into his arms, so relieved she almost cried.

'Does this mean you're not being charged?' she asked, between kisses.

'Unfortunately, no. I won't hear about charges for a couple of weeks. But I'm out, and I'm allowed to fly home and get married.' He squeezed her tight. 'God, it's good to see you.'

Rachel led him upstairs to her room. She felt like having sex straight away, but he held back. 'Can I shower first? I've got the smell of jail all over me: like a mixture of body odour and rancid cooking oil.'

'OK. I'll call to let your dad know you're out.'

'You told Dad about it?' He frowned.

'Yes, and he's been sitting by the phone all day ready to fork out bail if need be. What's more, he didn't once say you were an idiot for hanging onto the heart.'

'Really?' Alex looked surprised but pleased. 'Perhaps I should ring him then.'

Rachel listened as he spoke to his dad. The tone was matter-of-fact rather than emotional, but he said thank you more than once. That was good.

She saw him looking at the large cardboard parcel. 'What's that?' he mouthed.

'A painting,' she said when he came off the phone. 'And we have to figure out a way to get it home, so I'm glad you're here to help.'

'Do you mind if we stay tonight and go back in the morning?' he asked. 'I could do with a breather.'

'OK,' Rachel agreed. 'I'll book the tickets.'

While Alex hummed to himself in the shower, she got the receptionist to give her the numbers of British Airways, Air France and Eurostar, and rang each of them in turn. The flights first thing in the morning were all booked up, presumably by businesspeople with early meetings. Eurostar had seats on their nine o'clock train, but it didn't get into London till 12.30 p.m. and she remembered the trouble she'd had crossing the city the day before. There was a flight that arrived in Gatwick about the same time, so Rachel booked two seats on it.

'Shall I keep the beard or lose it?' Alex called from the bathroom.

'Keep it for tonight.' It would be interesting to make love with him looking a bit rough. 'Lose it for the wedding, though.'

'You're the boss.'

～

It was late evening when they staggered out, arm in arm, to the bistro Rachel had found the night before. They ordered a bottle of Bordeaux and big bowls of boeuf bourguignon, and over the meal, Rachel described her meeting with John Sturkey and what he had told her about Diana and Dodi's visit.

'That's interesting,' Alex nodded, wolfing down his food. 'Makes sense now.'

'Good,' she said, 'because I told him you would pay the fee you agreed.'

He laughed good-naturedly. 'Do I have to pay you for conducting the interview?'

'I'll let you buy me dinner,' she conceded.

In answer to her questions, he described his shock on being detained at the airport then driven off in a police van.

'It was very civilised,' he said. 'Three meals a day, a room of my own, clean sheets on the bed. It was a police holding cell rather than prison, so I was on my own the entire time except when they were questioning me. The worst bit was the first day, when I couldn't phone you.'

Suddenly he looked sad and vulnerable, and she knew he was remembering the cross words they'd exchanged last time they'd spoken.

'What did you do to pass the time?' He was such an active person, she couldn't imagine him trapped in an enclosed space without his phone or computer.

He gave a little laugh. 'You'll be glad to hear I've written my speech for the wedding.'

'Good. So it wasn't a complete waste of time.'

He took her chin gently in his hand and squeezed her lips into a moue. 'I did a lot of thinking as well. About what a shit I've been recently. About the fact that I don't know why you put up with me. I'm sorry, Rachel. I don't deserve you.'

She looked into his eyes, and realised how hard it was for him to open up like this. On the surface he was confident, articulate, self-possessed; he didn't usually let anyone see his vulnerability – not even her.

'I'm serious,' he continued, as if worried she did not believe him. 'I cried like a baby when I heard you had come to Paris to help me. I'd thought you might send the heart by FedEx or something; I never imagined you would actually come over. Monsieur Belmont told me about your gallant attempts to lie for me as well. You are amazing.'

Rachel clutched his wrist. 'I've been awful too. You were right about me having an obnoxious, snotty attitude to the whole Diana thing.'

'I know where you were coming from,' he said. 'The media reaction has been totally over the top. I interviewed a psychologist about the public mourning that followed the crash and he told me they're already calling it "Diana Syndrome". He said people have been arguing about it. Some think it was a positive change in the British national character that allowed those with repressed grief to bring it out into the open; others believe it was a kind of mass hysteria, like the Salem witch trials. I just can't believe that we, of all people, fell out over it.'

'Me neither.'

'You have to understand that us folk who work in TV are sensitive creative types, but we're also gamblers. There's a fair amount of money involved so the stakes are high and it makes for a stressful working environment. But next time I get obsessed with a programme to this extent, you have my full permission to shove me under a cold shower.'

He was clearly anxious for her to understand so that there would be no remaining issues between them. Rachel thought she had never loved him more.

Chapter 63

Paris, 18 December 1997

NEXT MORNING THEY WOKE EARLY AND RACHEL leaned over to kiss Alex, saying, 'Happy wedding day, darling.' They ate a room-service breakfast of croissants and cherry jam while getting ready to leave.

'Do we have time to stop at the Alma Tunnel on the way?' Rachel asked. She had an urge to go back there for the first time since the early hours of 31 August.

'Plenty of time,' he said. 'It's only an hour on the RER to the airport.'

It was awkward because Alex was carrying the painting, while she had both of their travel bags and her handbag. They got off the Métro at Alma-Marceau station and walked to the road above the underpass, where there was still a mass of floral tributes and notes in various languages – French, English, Italian, Japanese and many more – along with poems and drawings left in Diana's memory. Alex propped the painting against a wall and Rachel put the bags down beside it.

'Do you think her death was murder?' she asked as she read the messages. 'What's your conclusion?'

'I just don't know.' He pulled up the collar of his 1940s leather flying jacket, a gift Rachel had given him from the shop. 'There are still a lot of unanswered questions.'

Rachel glanced at him, and something about his tone made her suspect he knew more than he was going to tell her.

'That's where I'll have to leave it in the programme. Perhaps other facts will emerge over time.'

Rachel peered over the parapet at the cars whizzing past into the tunnel below. Suddenly she had a flashback to the explosions of cameras around the wrecked Mercedes, and she shivered. 'If she had died in a landmine accident, it would at least have had some meaning.'

Alex put his arm around her. 'Life is random. It's the connections we make that have meaning.'

They stood for a moment longer, then he glanced at his watch. 'Come on. We've got a wedding to attend.'

~

As soon as they walked into the departures terminal at Charles de Gaulle airport, Rachel knew they were in trouble. Over the tannoy, there was an announcement that mentioned 'Gatwick' then the words '*retardé*' and '*brouillard*'. A moment later, it was repeated in English: their flight was delayed due to fog.

Rachel could have kicked herself. The flights on Tuesday had been affected by fog. Why had she not considered it might be an issue today? Her heart began to beat faster.

Alex hurried to the airline help desk, with Rachel following close behind. He spoke in French, telling the woman behind the counter that they had to get to England because they were getting married at five that afternoon.

The woman checked her monitor and called her supervisor across. All the London airports were closed at the present time; the nearest one still open was East Midlands.

'That's Nottingham. How quickly could we get from Nottingham to Brighton?' Rachel asked, feeling a clutch of panic.

'It's possible in four hours if the trains are in our favour . . .' Alex looked dubious. 'Or we could grab a taxi, but I think that would take longer.'

'Train is our best chance.'

They got seats on the East Midlands plane and boarded, then sat on the runway, the minutes ticking away. There was an announcement about waiting for clearance for take-off. Alex and Rachel kept recalculating.

'If we get to Nottingham by one, there's still a chance,' he said. 'We wouldn't have time to get changed but we could dash straight to the registry office as we are.' He texted Kenny saying that if they didn't make it, he should direct guests straight to the restaurant.

Rachel looked down. Her grey wool dress was smart enough but not a patch on the Molyneux; she'd cleaned her boots as best she could and brushed down her coat, but they still looked grubby. Her palms were sweaty. She thought of all the money her parents had spent on the wedding car, the flowers, the invitations, the photographer . . .

It was the best part of half an hour later when the plane finally nosed into the air above Paris.

'Apologies for the delay,' the captain announced over the intercom. 'Our new arrival time at East Midlands will be one thirty.'

'Sod it. We're not getting married today.' Alex shrugged, then called over the air hostess. 'Could we have a bottle of champagne, please?'

Once Rachel accepted that they couldn't make it and the wedding wasn't happening, she felt the tension ease, like warm syrup trickling through her veins. It wasn't the end of the world; the sky hadn't fallen in.

'Here's to *not* getting married!' they toasted each other, to the bemusement of passengers in the seats round about.

Chapter 64

London, spring 1939

*I*T WOULD HAVE BEEN A TIME OF PERFECT contentment for Mary as she felt the child grow in her belly had it not been for her anxiety about the steady trickle of alarming news from the Continent. Hitler's army had annexed Austria the previous year, and had taken part of Czechoslovakia not long after. Almost every day it seemed there was more evidence of his greed for territory, and amongst their friends, all were convinced that war was coming.

Mary tried to ignore the news, worried that her anxiety might affect their baby, but sometimes she couldn't stop herself.

'Do you think Hitler will attack London?' she asked Ernest. 'Will we be safe here?'

'I'll stock up on sandbags and anti-aircraft guns,' he joked, but Mary could not raise a chuckle. How would she protect her child against bombardment from the air?

'Should we move to New York?' she asked. 'You could run the business from there, as you did before.'

'I am a reservist,' Ernest told her, 'since I served in the last war. Besides, shipping will be crucial for keeping the country supplied with raw materials, so I must stay and do my duty. We will find a place where you and Junior are out of harm's way.'

On 2 September, when he heard that Hitler's troops had invaded Poland, Ernest decided they must leave town immediately in case German bombers made a pre-emptive strike on London. They loaded the car and drove to the home of some friends who lived near Ipswich, and that was where they were at 11.15 the following morning when Prime Minister Chamberlain made his chilling radio broadcast confirming that Britain and Germany were at war.

Mary burst into tears, and Ernest put his arms around her. 'We are the lucky ones,' he said. 'At least we don't have a son being sent off to fight.'

He had already arranged everything for the birth of their child. Mary was booked into a Surrey nursing home on 17 October. Ernest would stay in the hotel next door and commute to work in London each day. They had hired builders to construct an air-raid shelter under their house and planned to return once it was ready.

But just three weeks after the start of the war, on 26 September, Mary woke in the early hours with a cramping sensation in her belly. She reached around the bump and felt wetness between her legs.

'Ernest!' she screamed.

He switched on the light and realised that her waters had broken, soaking the mattress. Panic rose in her throat, making it impossible for her to speak, but Ernest took charge. A local doctor came and advised that he should get her to the nursing home as soon as possible. Ernest rang ahead so Mr Gilliat was pre-warned, and they set off into the night.

All the street lights were switched off in case of German bombers, so the roads were pitch black. Signs had been painted over so they would not help enemy invaders, but fortunately Ernest knew the way. Mary lay on the back seat, propped up on cushions with a towel wedged between her legs, praying that the baby would not come before they got to the nursing home.

Ernest spoke calmly and quietly – 'Be strong, darling; not much further to go' – and something about his authoritative tone made her trust him. She and the baby would be fine; he would make sure of it.

When they arrived, Mary was taken straight to surgery and the baby was delivered soon afterwards: a healthy boy weighing five pounds eleven ounces, who looked the spitting image of his father, with tufts of golden-blonde hair, a round face and calm eyes. Mary couldn't stop sobbing as she kissed his tiny fingers and toes.

As soon as Ernest was allowed into the room, she said, 'Come and meet your son.'

He cupped his hand around the downy head, and for the first time in all the years she had known him, Mary saw the glint of tears in his eyes.

'Hello, little man,' he said, his voice tender. 'Welcome to the world.'

~

Mary and Ernest called their baby Ernest Henry Child Simpson, but he was soon known to all as Whistlebinkie, an endearment coined by Mary because he was so unbelievably small and cute.

They hired a nanny, but Mary preferred to keep him close during the day, rocking him in his bassinet and feeding him from the bottle Nanny made up. She loved the way he gazed at her with his boss eyes and the experimental noises he made as he discovered his vocal cords.

'Have you noticed how puzzled he looks when he hiccups?' she asked Ernest. 'It makes me laugh every time.'

On 11 January, Whistlebinkie was christened at the Guards Chapel, wearing a long embroidered christening gown that was a Simpson family heirloom. The font was decorated with spring flowers and the baby waved his arms as if conducting an orchestra and beamed at the parson as he was sprinkled with holy water. Back home in Holland Park, Mary and Ernest entertained dozens of guests with glasses of champagne in their newly decorated drawing room, which had apricot walls, a chartreuse-green carpet and huge gold-framed mirrors.

'What do you reckon?' Mary asked Georgia Sitwell. 'I fear we may accidentally have hired a colour-blind designer.'

'It's lovely,' Georgia reassured her. 'Very . . . warm.'

Four months into the war, without any sign of German aerial bombardment, Londoners were beginning to wonder if the danger had been exaggerated, and many of those who had left town ventured back. Life went on more or less as normal apart from the rationing of petrol, bacon, butter and sugar.

There was one benefit to the war as far as Mary was concerned, which was that Wallis's letters did not arrive so often. The blue envelopes with their loopy handwriting always put her in a foul mood, even before she read the contents.

In January 1940, Wallis wrote to Ernest: *We should both love to live in England again but the royal family will not see us. They refuse to allocate a suitable house for our use, so we have no choice but to remain in France for the duration.*

'Thank goodness!' Mary breathed. She did not want that woman in the same country as her and her family.

Wallis wrote that she had volunteered for the French Red Cross and was busy delivering plasma, bandages and cigarettes to hospitals in eastern France, while Peter Pan was working for the British Military Mission. She felt aggrieved that the British had not found her a role that would use her talents and contacts, but her offer had been turned down. She added that she missed Ernest and was sad about the way things had turned out. *Some day, I dream that you and I will grow old together once all this nonsense is out of the way.*

Mary ripped that letter in half and threw it in the fire. 'This nonsense' presumably meant their marriages to other people. She felt more secure in her position now that she had given Ernest a son and heir, but in her less confident moments she wondered if he secretly hankered after Wallis. If not, why maintain a correspondence with her?

Most of the time she was too busy to worry. Ernest was an attentive husband and there was certainly no doubting his devotion to Whistlebinkie. Every evening when he got home from the office, he would lean over the bassinet and kiss those soft curls that smelled of soap, milk and that delicious baby fragrance, before turning to Mary and asking, 'How was your day, dear? Shall I pour you a little tipple?'

~

When spring arrived in London, announced by the dazzling yellow flowers of a forsythia bush in their garden, Mary was feeling under the weather. She had not managed to lose her baby weight, and if she walked any distance she felt giddy and sick. She was tired most of the time, often needing a catnap in the afternoon, and her breasts were sore although the milk had long since dried up.

'I think you should see a doctor,' Ernest suggested. 'Perhaps he will prescribe a tonic.'

Their doctor did a full examination, taking Mary's blood pressure and drawing some blood for tests, looking in her eyes and mouth, taking her pulse and asking lots of questions.

'Perhaps I should check your breasts, since you say they hurt,' he mumbled, seeming embarrassed.

Mary stripped off her blouse and lay back on the surgery's daybed. The doctor unfastened her bra and began to knead her breasts. She winced when it hurt in a couple of places and he nodded as if that confirmed something.

'I'd like you to see a specialist. I'll make a phone call and set it up.'

Mary guessed she must have some kind of infection in the milk ducts. The nanny had told her it could be mastitis; that would explain the tenderness and her overwhelming tiredness.

Nothing prepared her for the shock when Sir Launcelot Barrington-Ward finished his examination at his prestigious Harley Street surgery, called Ernest in from the waiting room, and told them both, 'I'm afraid there is a tumour in the left side.'

'Do you mean cancer?' Mary asked, then words failed her. She remembered her mother's agonising death from cancer and went rigid with fear. She couldn't go through that. She wasn't strong enough.

'It's early days, so removal of the breast should get rid of it. I would like to operate as soon as possible.'

Ernest began to ask about practicalities in his calm, businesslike voice: who would perform the surgery, how long would it take to recover, were there any follow-up treatments, what were the statistical probabilities?

Mary watched him talking but didn't take in any of the words. She cupped a hand around her left breast, the one that was soon to be lopped off like dead wood. She didn't mind for herself, but she was heartbroken for Ernest. It felt as if she would no longer be a complete woman; as if she would be less of a wife.

Chapter 65

London, April 1940

MARY RECOVERED QUICKLY FROM THE PHYSICAL side of the operation, but the mental side was harder. Although she was given special pads to fill the left side of her brassiere, she felt deformed and hideous. She would not let Ernest see the jagged dark red scar with criss-cross marks from the stitches. She couldn't bear to look at it herself.

Sir Launcelot assured Ernest that the operation had been a complete success. Tests on the excised breast tissue showed the cancer had been contained, so Mary was expected to make a full recovery. She was back at home in Holland Park by the end of April, in time to hear Whistlebinkie utter his first recognisable word: 'Dada'.

'You may think he's talking about you, Ernest,' Mary joked feebly, 'but I think he is a budding art historian and is commenting on the avant-garde movement of Marcel Duchamp.'

'I'm sure you're right, my dear. We have clearly produced a genius.'

They both laughed as they watched their genius son try to stuff his entire left hand into his mouth.

Mary could spend hours sitting on the floor watching him play. When he sat on her lap, he was fascinated by her necklaces and loved to pull the clip earrings from her earlobes. He was a contented little chap, entirely caught up in the moment, and she wished she could be the same but it was hard to shake off her depression following the operation.

The news from Europe only increased her gloom: during April, Hitler's troops had invaded Denmark and Norway, then, on 10 May, came the invasion of Luxembourg, Belgium, the Netherlands and France. Soon it looked as though there would be German troops on the Channel coast, and the thought petrified her.

Mary and Ernest spent a weekend with Eleanor and Ralph at the end of May, and were stunned into horrified silence to hear from their radio set of the surrender of King Leopold of Belgium and the evacuation of Dunkirk, as British troops were hastily brought home to avoid annihilation by the Germans.

'I hear they are blaming the Duke of Windsor for leaking plans concerning the defence of Belgium to the Germans,' Ralph said. 'Did you read that story in the *Times*, Ernest?'

'I did,' he agreed, 'but in wartime you can't believe everything you read.'

'I wouldn't put it past him,' Mary commented. 'I don't think he would deliberately betray his country, but he is rather naïve and – let's be frank – not terribly clever. I can image some wily von Ribbentrop type tricking him into imparting secret knowledge if they flattered him enough.'

Ernest didn't comment; he was more discreet than her, but she knew he shared her views of the former King's lack of intellect.

'I don't know what to do,' Mary confided in Eleanor once they had left the men to their brandy and cigars. 'I don't feel my baby is safe in London with the Germans getting ever closer, but Ernest has to be there. We have talked about sending the boy to America, but I can't bear it. He's too little. He wouldn't recognise me when he saw me again.'

'He's welcome to stay here,' Eleanor offered. 'We're not close to any targets the Germans might choose to aim at.'

'Are you serious?' Mary hugged her, overcome with relief. 'I would love him to be here. His nanny would come too, so I hope you would have no trouble, and you are close enough that I could visit every weekend.'

'That's settled then. And if it means I get to see you every weekend, all the better.'

~

The Holland Park house felt vast and empty without Whistlebinkie's gurgles and cries echoing in the hallway. When she entered a room, Mary kept looking round for him before remembering he wasn't there. She telephoned every day and asked Eleanor to hold the receiver to his ear as she cooed down the phone. He always sounded happy; it was Mary who was miserable. For nine months her son had given a reason and purpose to her existence, and now he was gone she was empty and low.

When the Local Defence Volunteers movement was hastily set up by the War Office to organise security around vulnerable areas, Ernest was appointed a deputy group leader. That meant he had drills every evening and on Saturdays and Sundays as well. During weekdays he worked with the Admiralty, who had taken over his shipping business and were using it to help keep essential imports arriving. The days were long and Mary knew she had to find something to keep her occupied or else she would go mad. In June, she signed up for the Red Cross and was immediately sent on two courses: 'First Aid' and 'Decontamination after Gas Attacks'.

It was tiring but good to feel that she might be some use to her adopted country.

Still the occasional letter got through from Wallis. She and David had fled northern France in the dead of night when the Germans invaded, going first to their house in Biarritz and then to the Ritz Hotel in Madrid. *Mr Churchill wants us to return to England*, she wrote, *but David insists he will not do so unless I am granted an HRH title. As for myself, I care little, although it seems odd that as his wife I cannot share his form of address.*

She has gone mad, Mary thought. Who would even think of such a thing in wartime, when the country faced imminent invasion? She was careful never to criticise Wallis in front of Ernest, though. She didn't want to risk hearing him defend her.

Through June the news was uniformly dreadful and Mary's anxiety mushroomed: Italy declared war on Britain; German troops marched into Paris; and then France surrendered, agreeing to become a German 'zone of occupation'. French commander General Weygand predicted: 'In three weeks England will have her neck wrung like a chicken.'

Ernest's sister Maud came for dinner, and over a meal of rabbit stew with carrots and boiled potatoes, she asked Ernest, 'Don't you think you should send the child to New York? The Germans could be here at any moment.'

Ernest mumbled something indistinct, so Mary replied for him. 'We considered that, but he seems safe enough with our friends in the country.'

Maud looked alarmed. 'What if they start rounding up Jews and sending them to camps, as I hear they are doing across Europe? Surely you can't take that risk?'

Mary stared at Maud, then at Ernest, uncomprehending. 'Do you have Jewish blood? Simpson is not a Jewish name.'

Ernest sighed heavily. 'I saw no reason to alarm you,' he said, 'but as Maud has brought it up, I should tell you that our family were Jewish in the nineteenth century, when we had the surname Solomon. My father changed the name when he emigrated to New York in 1873 and set up his shipping firm.'

Mary could hardly breathe. All of a sudden she had visions of her baby in the arms of a Nazi in those high-topped leather boots. 'They will check the records. They'll find out,' she said in panic. 'You must come to New York, both of you. And your children, Maud. We must all go. I'll find somewhere for us to stay.'

Ernest looked down at his hands. 'I'm not going,' he told her in a tone that she knew brooked no discussion. 'I must stay and help my country, but I will understand if you want to take Whistlebinkie there for the duration of the war.'

Mary looked at him, aghast. She could not leave him alone in London, this man she had loved for so long. And yet she could not risk her precious, innocent son being taken captive. If the Germans were coming across the Channel, she had to get him to America – but she must stay with her husband. The answer was as clear as it was unbearably cruel.

'With any luck the war will be over in months,' Maud said, in a tone that made it plain she did not believe it.

Mary considered asking her sister Buckie to have Whistlebinkie, but she had no spare rooms, while Anne was too far away in Chicago. When by chance an invitation arrived from her old school friend Renée du Pont, inviting them to her luxurious Manhattan house, it seemed the only solution. Mary and Ernest talked long into the night. He tried to persuade her she must go too, but she had made up her mind and would not reconsider.

On 8 July, Ernest and Mary travelled to Holyhead with Whistlebinkie and his nanny and escorted them to their cabin on a passenger ship bound for New York. When the hooter sounded for all those who were not travelling to leave the ship, Mary gave her baby one last cuddle and kissed his tiny lips, then turned to walk away. She couldn't cry, but every part of her body was shaking with grief. The pain was more appalling than she could ever have imagined.

As the gangplank was raised and the ship moved out into the Irish Sea, Ernest put his arm round her and gripped her tightly, as if he feared that otherwise she might leap into the water and swim after it.

Chapter 66

London, September 1940

*A*IR RAIDS ON THE CAPITAL BEGAN ON 7 SEPTEMBER 1940. As fires raged across London, Mary knew she had done the right thing in sending her son away, but two months on, she still missed him with an excruciating pain. It felt as if she had been viciously stabbed, and seeing another baby in the street caused the knife to twist. *Children are safer in the country,* the hoardings proclaimed, but her precious little part-Jewish boy was safest of all in America now that invasion seemed imminent.

The bombers came every night for two months and Mary worked flat out in the first-aid station at Lancaster Road baths, where she had been posted after passing her courses: cleaning, disinfecting and bandaging flesh wounds, putting temporary splints on broken limbs, applying sterile gauze and bandages sprayed with tannic acid to burns. She had feared she might be squeamish, but when there was a patient in pain before her, she forgot her own feelings and did what she could. She worked late into the night and crawled home to sleep in the dawn, so she and Ernest were seldom there at the same time. A couple of days a week she took a picnic lunch to his office and sat there to eat with him, just so they had an hour alone together.

There hadn't been any letters from Wallis for a long while, but they read in the newspapers that she and David had been shipped off to the Bahamas, where he had been appointed governor.

'Do you think it's true that she is pro-Nazi, as the papers are saying?' Mary asked Ernest over lunch one day.

He pursed his lips. 'Peter Pan may well be, but I rather credited Wallis with more intelligence. Who knows what influences she has been subject to in Europe since her marriage? Their new friends hardly seem salubrious.'

'She was friends with von Ribbentrop back in 1935, was she not?' Mary spoke tentatively. She wasn't sure if Ernest had heard the rumours of their affair.

He laughed. 'I wouldn't say friends exactly.'

'But he sent her all those flowers . . .'

'Ah yes, the seventeen roses. Did she never tell you the story behind them?' He took a bite of his Spam sandwich.

Mary was all ears as she waited for him to continue.

'We met von Ribbentrop at Emerald Cunard's one evening. We were all playing poker and Wallis was on a winning streak. She played quite ruthlessly, as you will remember.' Mary smiled agreement. 'Anyway, she won rather a lot of money from von Ribbentrop, and when he opened his wallet to pay her, he found that he was seventeen pounds short of the total. He apologised and promised he would bring the money round to Bryanston Court the following day. Wallis said: "But how can we trust the word of you Germans? Look how quick you were to break the Treaty of Versailles."'

Mary snorted with laughter. 'Oh, that's *so* Wallis! How did he react?'

Ernest grinned. 'He was ruffled at first, not sure how seriously to take her. I think he was about to launch into a lecture about the punitive nature of the terms of Versailles, but everyone else was laughing so he joined in. And he proved that Germans do have a sense of humour, contrary to the common belief, because he started sending her those bouquets of seventeen roses.'

'I don't know why she didn't tell me,' Mary exclaimed. 'What an amusing story!'

Ernest nodded. 'It was at first, but it became rather embarrassing when the rumour spread that they were having an affair. I think Ribbentrop would have been happy to go to bed with her, because next he sent her a bracelet with the number seventeen engraved on a heart-shaped charm. She was worried Peter Pan would hear the stories so she hid that bracelet and I never once saw her wear it.'

'So there was no affair?' Mary still wasn't convinced.

Ernest finished his sandwich. 'To tell you the truth, Wallis was never terribly keen on that side of things. She loved to flirt but it was mostly promise and no action. I doubt Peter Pan got a hand below her waist before they were married, and probably not often since then.' He winked. 'Take it from one who knows.'

That conversation buoyed Mary enormously. She remembered Wallis saying, 'Don't let them go south of the Mason–Dixon line,' during her marriage to Win. Had she never developed a taste for sexual relations afterwards? Personally, Mary had always adored that side of things.

~

The winter of 1940–41 brought almost nightly bombardments in London, but if anything the people grew more defiant. 'We can take it!' the injured patients at Lancaster Gate baths told each other. 'Hitler will never win because we will never surrender.'

Mary took some teasing that America had not entered the war. 'Are you the only one they're sending, love? Oh well, you might not be able to fly a Spitfire but at least you're a beauty.'

Ernest and Mary began to hold cocktail parties on Friday evenings for any friends who were in town. They were lively affairs with plentiful alcohol, and guests often ended up dancing to the jazz records Mary had brought over from the States. If the air-raid siren sounded, everyone grabbed a bottle and the party continued downstairs in the shelter. It was good to catch up with old friends and forget about the war for a few hours, and if they got tight, they could sleep it off the next morning.

'Do you ever hear from Wallis?' Georgia Sitwell asked Mary one night. 'Is she happy in the Bahamas?'

'I don't know how she could be happy married to that nervous, difficult man,' Mary replied.

Georgia shrugged. 'She went to great lengths to win him, so she must have seen something beyond a crown.'

'Truth be told, she never intended to marry him. Events just got out of control and she couldn't back down.' Mary managed to stop herself from adding, 'Serves her right.'

The only subject she could not discuss with anyone was her baby son. Letters arrived every couple of weeks, and Mary fell apart with grief each time. Once there was a photograph showing him walking with Nanny holding his hands, and the reminder of all the stages of his growth that she was missing was insufferable. At least he looked plump and happy in the picture; that was her only comfort.

Chapter 67

Brighton, 18 December 1997

RACHEL AND ALEX ARRIVED IN BRIGHTON JUST after 6 p.m., by which time the registry office had closed and their wedding guests were enjoying a glass of champagne in the Bonne Auberge. A cheer went up as they walked in, hauling their luggage and a large, unwieldy parcel, and that set the mood for an evening full of laughter. All Rachel's favourite people were in the room, and she darted from one to the next, chatting and hugging and quaffing champagne.

'We're going to reschedule the registry office for next spring,' she told the guests. 'I'll send out fresh invites as soon as I have a date.'

The 1930s wedding cake was splendid, as was her bouquet of lilies of the valley, which Nicola had collected from the florist's. She looked beautiful in her fifties silk dress, and Rachel noticed that Richard seemed to be spending a lot of time at her table.

'Nicola's single,' she whispered discreetly, and he gave her a grin and a thumbs-up.

At the renamed 'Not-the-Wedding-After-Party' two days later, Rachel noticed Nicola and Richard sitting amongst the coats in her bedroom, talking earnestly. She went to rescue some quiche from the oven, to top up glasses and socialise, and when she next looked, they were still in the same spot, still talking.

'I can't believe you never introduced us before. He's gorgeous!' Nicola whispered when she came to the kitchen to refill their glasses.

Rachel was delighted. 'I'm glad to see you two are getting on. He's not your usual type.'

'Why not?' Nicola's face fell.

'Because he's a nice guy.'

Nicola beamed and did a little dance, elbows pumping, hips wiggling.

~

On the evening of Monday 22 December, Rachel and Alex drove to West Sussex to visit Susie Hargreaves. Rachel had telephoned the day after they got back from Paris to say she had a Christmas present for her.

Susie sounded surprised and a bit embarrassed. 'You have? I'm sorry, I didn't think to . . . I haven't bought any presents this year . . .'

'Don't worry. I didn't pay for this. And it's more for your grandmother than for you. I got it in Paris. Can Alex and I bring it down?'

There was a pause while Susie processed this. 'My grandmother? It's not . . . It couldn't be the painting, could it?'

'Indeed it is!'

There was a long pause, so long that Rachel called, 'Hello? Are you still there?' into the phone; then she realised that Susie was in tears.

'I'm sorry,' Rachel chuckled. 'I must stop making you cry.'

As soon as she closed the shop, she drove to collect Alex from the flat then they set off towards Susie's home, chatting along the way about Nicola and Richard, and some other unlikely pairings that had been established at the Saturday-night party. It had continued till the following morning, when Rachel had got up to find guests sprawled across sofas and chairs like a scene from a Toulouse-Lautrec bordello painting.

They pulled into Susie's driveway at 7.30 p.m. and she came out to greet them wearing long brown leather boots and a green Barbour jacket. 'Follow me.' She waved, her car keys dangling. 'I'm going to take you to meet Grandma.'

She climbed into her Land Rover and set off down the drive, taking a right turn at the end. Rachel followed for about two miles along country lanes before Susie took a left into a courtyard with a sign announcing *Laurel Grove Care Home*.

They got out of the car and Alex carried the painting as they followed Susie inside. She had to sign them in at reception, then they were buzzed through to a crimson-carpeted corridor with a number of rooms leading off. She stopped at one and tapped on the door, calling, 'Grandma? It's me.'

Rachel saw a frail, spindly woman in a chair by the window. Her shoulders were hunched and her chin rested on her breastbone as if her neck had collapsed in some degenerative process of age. Her hair was snow white and wispy like baby hair, and the hand she extended was curved in a claw shape.

'This is my grandmother, Eleanor.' Susie introduced them. Alex rested the painting against a wall to come forward and shake her hand.

As well as a bed, there was a bookcase in the room and several shelves of trinkets, a wardrobe, and a door that Rachel could see led to an en suite. Susie brought some extra chairs from the corridor outside, one more than they needed, and arranged them in a semicircle round Eleanor.

'These kind people have brought something for you,' Susie said, and Alex lifted the painting and placed it on the spare chair just two feet in front of Eleanor. Rachel had cleaned off the cobwebs and mildew, and polished the wooden frame. There was a tear in the canvas backing that would have to be mended, but otherwise it wasn't in bad shape.

Eleanor clasped her hands beneath her chin and gazed at the painting in silence for quite some time, too emotional to speak.

'Wasn't she beautiful?' she said at last, her voice croaky with age, her accent that of an aristocrat from a bygone era. 'That's my friend Mary.' She shook her head slightly. 'I never thought I'd see her again. Ralph would be so pleased.'

'I think Alex and Rachel would like to hear the story of the painting,' Susie prompted. 'If you feel up to it.'

'Oh yes, I'd love to. This brings back a time before the war, a time when we were all happy.' As she spoke, she didn't take her eyes off the painting, as if drinking in every detail: the curve of Mary's hand on her lap, the pearl earrings, the vivacious eyes and warm smile.

Eleanor began by explaining what Rachel already knew: that in 1912 she had attended the same school in Baltimore as Wallis Warfield and her best friend Mary Kirk. 'They were a riot!' she explained. 'Everyone gravitated towards them because of their irreverent humour. Mary was the more open character while Wallis was difficult to get close to. She was secretive about her home life, and it was only decades later that Mary told me she was ashamed that her father had died and her mother was not very well off. Isn't it silly how we worry about such things as children?'

She told them that she had lost touch with the two girls after she left the school, but bumped into Mary at Petworth one day in the mid 1930s.

'By that time it was well known in society circles that Wallis and the Prince of Wales were an item, and it was clear that Mary was in love with Wallis's husband Ernest. I so hoped they would end up together.' She paused, recollecting. 'When Wallis heard of Mary and Ernest's affair, they had a furious row and Mary came to stay with us for a while, to lie low. That's when Ralph painted her.' She gestured at the painting. 'But he made the idiotic mistake of sending it to Wallis and Ernest's address and Wallis kidnapped it. That was in 1936, and she held onto it for the next fifty years, until her death.'

'Why did she want it?' Rachel asked, glancing at the painting again.

'Pure spite,' Eleanor replied. 'She couldn't bear it that Mary was the prettier of the two, the even-tempered one and, eventually, the one who got Ernest. Wallis liked to be best at everything. She needed to win.'

Susie chipped in. 'When Diana told me that she was visiting Villa Windsor, I asked her to keep an eye out for the painting. Of course, there was always a chance Wallis had destroyed it.'

'I was sure she wouldn't have,' Eleanor insisted. 'Mary was the closest friend Wallis ever had, and this picture captures her to a T. It's got her personality in the paint.'

Susie took up the story again. 'The Duchess was bedridden with dementia by the time Diana met her, so she wasn't able to tell her about the painting's whereabouts. Her affairs were being managed by a lawyer, who wouldn't hear of anything being removed from the house. Then, after the Duchess died, her will left the bulk of her wealth to the Louis Pasteur Institute, so things became even more complicated.' She reached over to hold her grandma's hand. 'When Mohamed Al-Fayed moved in to restore the house, I wrote to him about the painting but of course I couldn't prove it belonged to us – it didn't, in fact, because Ernest Simpson had paid for it. Al-Fayed's secretary was very polite but suggested we bid for it at the auction of contents. I almost gave up at that point because I knew I wouldn't be able to afford the kind of prices it might reach.'

'I could never forget that picture.' Eleanor had a distant look in her eyes, and Rachel wondered what memories it was conjuring for her. 'Ralph died five years ago and it made me think about it even more. We have many of his other portraits in the house, but this was always his best.'

'Did Wallis and Mary ever make up their argument?' Rachel asked.

'I doubt it.' The old woman shook her head. 'Mary was furious, simply furious. You see, Wallis wouldn't let go of Ernest even once she was married to the Duke. She wrote him letters saying how much she missed him, how good life had been when they were together and how she wished things had worked out differently. She even told him that it was her dream they would end up together again one day. Ernest showed the letters to Mary, thinking honesty was the best policy, but they made her incandescent with rage. You can imagine!'

'He should have told Wallis to stop writing,' Alex said. 'He should have put his foot down.'

Eleanor nodded. 'I agree, but that's not the kind of man he was.'

All of them had angled their seats to look at the portrait as they talked. 'Were Mary and Ernest happy?' Rachel asked.

'I never saw a couple happier,' the old woman breathed. 'They had a baby called Ernest Henry. His father's name.'

'I know Ernest Simpson is dead, but is Mary still alive?' Rachel asked.

'Oh no, dear.' Eleanor gave a little laugh. 'I'm the last of that era. We were all born in the nineteenth century and now we're at the end of the twentieth. It makes me feel ancient to think of it.' She tapped Susie on the hand. 'Do you think you could fetch something from my cupboard? The brown leather handbag on the top shelf.'

Susie rose to her feet and opened the cupboard. Rachel noticed that there weren't many clothes inside; maybe ten dresses. She supposed you didn't need many when you reached the age of a hundred.

Susie passed the bag to her grandmother. It was a stylish clutch bag with a tortoiseshell clasp, and Rachel tried to guess what era it was from. Possibly the 1930s. Her guess was soon confirmed.

'Wallis gave that to Mary for her fortieth birthday back in 1936, two days before the huge argument when they fell out with each other. Of course, Mary didn't want it after that, so she gave it to me, but I never used it. It seemed unlucky somehow. Now I just keep photographs inside.'

She opened the clasp, sorted through a handful of dog-eared black-and-white pictures and passed one to Rachel. There was Ernest Simpson, instantly recognisable with his slicked dark hair and moustache, alongside a smiling Mary, who was cradling a baby wearing a christening robe.

Rachel's eye was caught by something else in the pile of photos: the edge of a Constance Spry business card with its oval illustration of old-fashioned roses. She pointed to it. 'Did Susie tell you I found a Mainbocher dress at the house that appears to have been Wallis's?'

Eleanor nodded. 'That's right. It was in a parcel from Mary's dressmaker. She'd been copying it. I only found it years later and the original was far too small for me, but I wore the copy for quite some time. It had lovely colours: pink, purple and apricot.'

Rachel continued: 'I ask because there was a florist's card just like that in the pocket of Wallis's dress. It read, "Now do you trust us?" I guess we'll never know what it meant.'

Eleanor pulled the Constance Spry card from her piles of photographs and passed it over. In what looked like the same handwriting was the message *See you in Berlin*. Rachel looked at her questioningly.

'Joachim von Ribbentrop,' Eleanor explained. 'He and Wallis were having an affair. Mary wasn't sure if it was true, but I was. This card came with a bouquet he sent Wallis in 1936, the year before she and Edward met Hitler in Berlin. It proves they'd been planning the visit well before the abdication.'

Alex looked at Rachel as he made the connection. 'A bracelet was found at the Duchess of Windsor's house with a heart charm on it that had a J engraved on one side and the Roman numerals XVII on the other.'

'That would be from him.' Eleanor nodded. 'He used to send her bouquets of seventeen roses, supposedly because that was the number of times they slept together. Ernest thought it was to do with a gambling debt, but she would hardly have told him the truth, would she?' She shook her head in disgust. 'Ribbentrop pursued her relentlessly to get to Edward. The two of them were completely in his pocket. I've always thought some secret cabinet papers will be released, or some Nazi documents unearthed, to prove they actually helped the German war effort. Maybe not in my lifetime, but probably in yours.'

Alex glanced at Rachel. 'That sounds like my next project. Perhaps I'll do some digging. Gentle, non-obsessive digging.'

Chapter 68

London, April 1941

'I'LL TELL YOU ONE GOOD THING ABOUT THIS WAR,' Mary quipped to another first-aider at the baths. 'I've lost almost a stone on rations. I call it the Hitler Diet.'

'I've lost a bit too,' her friend replied, pulling at her loose waistband. 'My weakness used to be toast and jam, but I can't stand these National Loaves, and there's no sugar to waste on jam.'

'You look peaky, Mary,' someone chipped in. 'Have you been burning the candle?'

'We have a bit,' Mary said. 'I must try to get more sleep. Are you listening, Luftwaffe?' She tilted her head and called up to the sky.

Being in close contact with so many different people, she picked up lots of colds, sore throats and ticklish coughs, but fortunately Ernest appeared to have a strong constitution because he never caught them from her. She sniffled and hacked her way through the winter on her own.

Grey, overcast weather turned almost overnight to spring. Mary walked out one sunny morning and smelled greenness in the air, felt warmth on her face. Two pigeons made her laugh by copulating on the pavement right in front of her:

the female spread her tail feathers and the male jumped on top for all of five seconds before flying off. 'Poor thing,' Mary soothed. 'He was a cad.'

She was on her way to an appointment with Sir Launcelot Barrington-Ward for her six-monthly check-up. She was not remotely concerned as she had passed the last one with flying colours, so had told Ernest he need not take time off work.

'How long have you had that cough?' Sir Launcelot asked, moving his stethoscope around her chest.

'On and off all winter,' Mary said, and explained about her first-aid work.

'You've lost a lot of weight,' he commented. 'Have you been having night sweats?'

'Only if the Jerries drop a bomb too close,' she answered. 'Why?'

'I'd like to run a few tests,' he said, then, seeing the alarm on her face, added, 'Just to be on the safe side.'

That afternoon she had all manner of tests and X-rays, and when another doctor was brought in to examine her as well, she began to get anxious.

'Can you at least tell me what you're looking for?' she asked.

'Perhaps we should get Ernest to come,' Sir Launcelot replied. 'Do you want to telephone him?'

'No, I want you to tell me what you suspect. I can take it.'

And that was when Sir Launcelot told her they thought the cancer had spread to her lungs, and they wanted to operate urgently.

~

Ernest was by Mary's side, holding her hand, when she came round from the lung operation, and she knew from his face that the news was not good. He had never been good at dissembling. One moment she had been a wife and mother with two or three decades in front of her; the next, the rug was pulled from under her feet. She made a decision then and there not to weep and wail, but to make the best of it. It was wartime; everyone was suffering.

'How long have I got?' she asked when Sir Launcelot came to check on her.

'Goodness, it's not a case of that,' he assured her. 'We've taken out all we can, and once you've recovered from the operation, we're going to start you on a course of radiotherapy. It can be very successful at clearing up any remaining cancer cells. You'll come to the hospital every day for three weeks and the procedure will only take an hour. Be positive, Mrs Simpson. Look to the future.'

The radiotherapy was horrid, like fire on raw skin, and left her chest with thickened red burns that kept her from sleeping at night. Mary had fresh sympathy for all the burns victims she had treated at the first-aid station, with their weeping, oozing wounds. How had they been so uncomplaining?

'As soon as I finish radiotherapy, I want to go and see Whistlebinkie,' she begged Ernest. 'Can you get me to America?'

He hesitated. 'It will be tricky. There are German U-boats patrolling the Atlantic, so passenger shipping has come to a halt.'

'I need to see my boy,' she said firmly. 'You'll find a way; I know you'll find a way.'

Ernest asked at the Admiralty without success, while with every day that passed, Mary felt herself get weaker. By June it was hard to walk any distance because of her shortness of breath. She spent most of her time on the daybed in the drawing room writing letters to her sisters and composing her will. She didn't tell many friends of her illness because she didn't want them to feel awkward and struggle to find platitudes. She and

Ernest seldom discussed it either; they talked about practicalities, such as hiring a live-in nurse. Mary tried to stay positive, but with every day her yearning to see Whistlebinkie grew more intense, till she could think of nothing else.

It was the end of June, just after Hitler's troops had invaded Russia, when Ernest came home with news.

'How do you feel about flying?' he asked. 'Winston Churchill heard of our plight and has offered you a place on a clipper flying to New York, and a return flight four weeks later.'

Mary's stomach lurched. She had been up in a plane with Jacques once and it had made her very sick, but she would grab any chance to see her boy.

'It's very kind of him, but why should Winston Churchill concern himself with me?' she asked. 'I imagine he's terribly busy right now.'

Ernest cleared his throat. 'I think it's felt that I behaved honourably over the divorce from Wallis, and that they owe me a favour. I wish I could accompany you, but it's impossible.' He looked stricken. 'You will come back, won't you?'

'Oh Ernest. Of course I will. How could you ever doubt it?' She caught his hand, pulled him down to her level and kissed him tenderly.

Chapter 69

New York, July 1941

MARY COULDN'T BELIEVE HOW HUGE HER SON HAD grown in little over a year. He would be two in September, but she thought he looked at least three or four as he ran across the hotel lobby to where she sat in a wheelchair pushed by her nurse. He stopped just before he reached her and stared in awe.

'This is your mama,' the nanny told him, lifting him onto Mary's lap.

She hugged him, burying her face in his blonde curls, then drew back to look at him. He was even more like Ernest than before, with his chubby face and serious dark eyes. He touched her face with a hand that still had a bracelet of fat round the wrist, then he spotted her pearl earring and pulled it off.

''Allo, Mama,' he said, and it was one of the most precious moments of her life.

'You are such a big boy,' she said, 'I can't call you Whistlebinkie any more. I'm going to call you Henry.' She had never felt comfortable calling him Ernest; that was her husband's name.

They stayed in a suite in the Waldorf while Mary consulted a New York doctor who had been recommended by Renée du Pont: a handsome man in his thirties called Dr Hofstead who did a lot of research into cancer. After reading her case notes, he advised that she take a new drug made from apricot kernels, which he said had been very successful in fighting her type of the disease. It might make her nauseous, he warned, but she was delighted to try his new approach, and optimistically referred to the prescription he gave as her 'lucky pills'.

They visited Buckie in Massachusetts and spent a glorious week catching up. Mary sat on the porch watching as Henry charged around the garden, endlessly cheerful, finding entertainment in every rock and blade of grass. She kept a bowl by her side into which she threw up discreetly, so her little boy wouldn't notice.

'Buckie, don't you think he's the smartest child that ever was born?' she cooed.

'He's certainly sweet as pie,' her sister agreed, 'and such a contented little man, despite the disruptions in his life. I do wish you could stay here instead of going back to a war zone. The Blitz sounds horrific.'

Mary smiled. 'You would be surprised to see how cheerful we all are in London. The British will fight to the last. And I am cheerful too, because when you have a husband like mine, life is good.'

'But your illness . . .' Buckie grimaced. 'I can't help worrying when I think of poor Mama.'

'Medicine has advanced a lot since then. My lucky pills weren't available when Mama was ill, but I have faith in Dr Hofstead. He's a whizz – and rather easy on the eye,' Mary twinkled.

Back in New York, there was another appointment with Dr Hofstead, who was pleased with her early response to the drug, and visits to Renée du Pont and to Jacques and his new, much younger wife. The rest of the time Mary spent with her son, getting to know and love him more with every day that passed. It felt like a miracle that she and Ernest had created him. By the time she was two weeks into her stay, she knew there was no way she would be able to leave him there. It was impossible. The pain would kill her.

And yet she had to go back to London because she missed Ernest so terribly. Every time she read of another bombing raid she was petrified for him. She needed both of her men together. At least the threat of imminent German invasion had passed after the RAF's victory in the air war. Hitler seemed to have turned his attention to Russia; perhaps he wouldn't bother to conquer Britain. That hope made up her mind.

She rang the RAF telephone number in New York to ask if she could bring two more passengers on the return trip, one of them rather small. There was a nerve-racking overnight wait before they got back to her and said they had received permission to transport her son and his nanny so long as her son sat on a grown-up's lap and didn't cause any trouble.

'Henry, we're going on an adventure,' she told him. 'We're going to fly like a bird in the sky, and we're going home to see your daddy.'

'Da-dee,' he repeated with a big toothy grin, although he couldn't possibly remember him.

~

Ernest got special permission to meet their flight on the airfield, and he came running up the steps of the plane, swooping Henry into his arms and kissing Mary on the lips. She was so worn out from the journey that he called for a stretcher and took her straight by ambulance to a house he had rented for them in the Wiltshire countryside. The staff from their Holland

Park house were already there, and the nurse tucked her up in bed and made her comfortable.

The day after her arrival, Sir Launcelot came to examine her. She showed him the lucky pills she had been given in New York and he nodded sagely and said he had heard of them and so long as the side effects were not intolerable she should continue to take them. He did not think she would benefit from further radiotherapy, he said, but he administered a vitamin shot that would give her more pep.

'Will I need to come to hospital?' she asked. She was feeling so frail, it was hard to imagine how she would get there.

'I suggest you stay here and enjoy spending time with your son,' he replied.

She caught his eye and saw a look that alarmed her: profound compassion. She nearly fell apart as the truth dawned on her, then she remembered her vow: it was wartime and she was going to be brave.

As soon as Sir Launcelot left, Mary asked the nurse to wheel her in a bath chair to watch Henry playing in the garden. He was busy running his toy train along a wall at the edge of the terrace, but when he saw her, he came running for a hug.

She held him tight, breathing in his scent, and wanted to hold him longer but he broke away. His lunchtime sandwich lay unfinished on a picnic table and he fetched it and pushed it to her lips, saying, 'Eat up, Mama, eat up.' She nibbled a little but her throat was too tight to swallow.

It was a struggle to hold back the tidal wave of grief that she was not going to be part of this little boy's future. Other people would read stories to him, teach him to play sports, help him choose a career. Others would watch as he opened his presents on Christmas morning, or when he dressed in uniform for his first day of school. Others would comfort him when he fell ill; it couldn't be her. And none of them would love him as much as she did. He was going to lose so much.

~

The pain got worse. Instead of being concentrated in her chest, it moved to her bones, which ached with a deep, grinding sensation. The nurse gave her morphine injections but she hated the way they left her fuzzy-headed; during the day she tried to manage with codeine pills, even though they were less effective.

She looked at Ernest's face one night and realised how much he had aged in the last year. His hair and moustache were streaked with grey and his cheeks had subsided, giving him a jowly appearance, but he was still a handsome man. I wonder if he knows I am dying, Mary thought, or has he not accepted it? Typical Ernest with his English stiff upper lip; he would never raise the subject but carried on as if everything was normal and Mary was just a tad under the weather.

'Where will you send Henry to school?' she asked. 'Eleanor wrote to me of a very good prep school near them called Westbourne House. He could be a boarder there but Eleanor and Ralph would keep an eye on him. They would invite him for tea every weekend if you were not able to visit.'

'I'll look into it.' He nodded. 'That's kind of them.'

'And make sure he reads. I want him to love books.'

'I will. Of course I will.'

She wanted her son to think of her, but not in a sad way. There were plenty of photographs, but suddenly she thought of the painting Wallis had hijacked.

'Do you think my portrait is still in Wallis's Paris house? What will the Nazis do with it?'

Ernest cleared his throat. 'I hear there has been an agreement that their house is not to be touched by Hitler's troops. It has special protection.'

Mary was incredulous. 'They are dropping bombs on civilians in London yet going out of their way to protect Wallis's possessions? And you tell me she and David were not in bed with the Nazis?' She closed her eyes, too exhausted to argue. Yet again Wallis got special treatment.

'After the war, will you try to get the painting back? That's how I want Henry to remember me. Not like this.' She looked down at her shrunken arms, which were black with bruising from injections.

Ernest coughed into his handkerchief and held it over his face for a few moments before he could reply.

Chapter 70

Brighton, 23 December, 1997

TWO DAYS BEFORE CHRISTMAS, ALEX WENT TO London to show the commissioning editor what was known as an 'offline edit' of the programme. He was worried the channel would ask for bits of footage he didn't have when there was no time or budget left for a major reshoot.

'They'll probably want a nice neat ending that wraps up all the mysteries, and I'll have to convince them it's not possible.' Questions had to be left floating in the air that might or might not be answered at some point in the future.

Rachel got an email from Gazelle Films offering her a substantial sum of money in return for the use of her clothes – easily enough to pay off her overdraft and credit-card loan. It meant the shop was safe. She closed her eyes in silent gratitude, the months of worry finally at an end. If only Alex could have good news too, the day would be perfect. Whenever she had a spare moment, she wondered how he was faring.

Late afternoon, he called from the train. 'They love it! They completely understand the need for open-endedness. They even asked if I'll make another Diana programme next year, about her private humanitarian work: the hospital visits, the regular phone calls to people with terminal illnesses, the flowers and gifts she sent to sick children, the letters to the bereaved. I've amassed loads of material already. There was a lot the public never knew about while she was alive.'

'Brilliant!' Rachel cheered. 'I'm proud of you. You've become television's go-to Diana man.'

'Darling, I have a confession to make,' he said. 'With everything that's been going on, I haven't had time to get you a Christmas present. Is there anything you want and I'll hunt it down tomorrow?'

'A Schiaparelli jacket,' she replied, deadpan.

'OK. Any serious suggestions?'

'That *is* serious.' Her cash-strapped customer had come back that very day, saying she had been unable to find anyone else to buy it, and Rachel had snapped it up.

'Oh God, what have I let myself in for?'

She told him about all the time-pressed husbands she was selling last-minute Christmas gifts to, and added, 'But yours is by far the most expensive.'

~

On Christmas morning, Alex was moved beyond words when he opened the photo album of his childhood. They sat in bed going through it, Rachel wearing the Schiaparelli jacket and Alex with a Christmas ribbon tied round his head. The memories flooded back as he told her the stories behind the photographs.

'Mum loved clothes, just like you. I remember being so proud when we walked down the street because people would gawp at her . . .' He turned the page. 'I caught that fish in the Lake District but Dad had to kill it for me because I was too squeamish . . .' Another page: 'Did you know I was my school swimming champion at the age of ten?'

He couldn't remember some of the scenes but was touched to see evidence of his mother's obvious love for him. 'You just gave me my childhood back,' he told Rachel.

'Speaking of which . . .' she said. 'Susie rang yesterday to say her grandma is not keeping that painting the two of us lugged all the way back from Paris. She's having a print made for herself then sending the original to Mary and Ernest's son, who lives in Israel.'

'That seems fitting, I suppose. How old is he?'

Rachel did a quick calculation. 'He must be in his late fifties.'

'He'll love it. It's a gift full of history – like the one you gave me.'

Rachel had also given him a biography of Wallis Simpson, and after breakfast, before starting to read it, he looked up von Ribbentrop in the index. 'The seventeen roses are mentioned here,' he said, and read out a passage from the book: '"Von Ribbentrop was sent to London with a brief to infiltrate and influence upper-class society. He began an affair with Wallis and reported every conversation he had with her directly to the Führer, who took a special interest, even acquiring film footage of her that he watched at his Obersalzburg hunting lodge."'

Rachel frowned. 'I'm not sure I buy the theory that Ribbentrop bought her seventeen flowers because they'd slept together seventeen times. Why stop at seventeen? If he was seducing her to get to Edward, it would at least have been gallant to pretend he wanted to reach number eighteen. And if the affair was over, why still send her flowers and engrave a bracelet with that number? Besides, in the heat of passion, who counts?'

Alex agreed with her. 'Wallis became a hate figure after the abdication and I think there's been a lot of misogyny in the way she's been written about ever since. Lustful traitorous predator or the most misunderstood woman in history? I want to make a documentary that addresses that question.'

~

They visited Rachel's family on Boxing Day, and Alex's on the 27th, then on Sunday the 28th they planned to have a lazy day before going back to work. They ate breakfast in bed, then Alex went to boot up the computer and check his emails while Rachel was in the shower.

'Oh my God!' she heard him shout, then seconds later the bathroom door burst open.

'What is it?' For a moment she feared bad news, but he was grinning from ear to ear.

'I had an email from Monsieur Belmont back on Christmas Eve. I hadn't checked my mails since then. Get this: the French police aren't pressing charges against me because they don't think the bracelet was Diana's. They sent photos of the heart to her family and her butler, and word came back that none of them recognised it.' He punched the air in triumph.

'Of course they didn't!' Rachel shrieked. 'That's wonderful news.'

He furrowed his brow. 'They must be able to see that she was wearing it in photos taken earlier in the day. I wonder if they don't want the added complication of prosecuting me over such a tiny piece of metal, when the investigation is already so multifaceted. Whatever the reason, it's something of a relief not to face a year in jail.'

'I would have rescued you,' Rachel said. 'And we could have gone on the run. It would have been exciting. But it's probably better this way.'

Chapter 71

Wiltshire, September 1941

ARY WATCHED FROM HER BED ON 28 SEPTEMBER as they celebrated Henry's second birthday. Ernest had bought him a model railway track, complete with signal box, station and a couple of trains, and he got down on the floor to show him how to slot the pieces together, how to change the signal to let a train pass. Ernest made 'woo-woo' noises and Henry copied him. As she lay there, propped up on pillows, Mary thought she had never loved them more. She was filled with so much love, it made her feel as if she were floating.

There was no way she could avoid taking morphine now, as pain rampaged through her body, stamping on the nerve endings, hammering on her skull and brutally kicking her spine. She needed an oxygen mask to hand for when she couldn't catch her breath. The nanny brought Henry to her room for short visits, when he gave her a flower or one of his paintings or sang her a little song he had learned.

'Thank you, darling,' she whispered. 'Mama is very proud of her funny little man.'

She knew she would have to let go of him soon – give him a last-ever hug and kiss, then slip away.

Sometimes she was unable to open her eyes because of the pain and exhaustion, but she could still hear life going on around her. There were moments when she was overwhelmed with sorrow at all she was leaving behind. They had a future she would not be part of. It was too cruel.

She slept for longer periods and had complicated dreams in which people from her past appeared. Wallis was often there, a dark presence she did not trust. They were at a party and Wallis beckoned her across the room, but in the dream Mary didn't want to go; another time they were rowing on a lake and there was something about the familiar face with those penetrating eyes that made her wary. When she awoke, it was a relief to hear Ernest breathing in bed alongside her.

On the night of 1 October, he stayed awake stroking her hair as waves of pain ebbed and flowed. Her eyes were shut most of the time as she kept very still, trying to breathe through the agony. She was aware of the nurse coming to check on her at one point, and when the door closed, she opened her eyelids to see apricot sky through a crack in the curtains. Another new day.

'Are you there?' she whispered to Ernest.

'Yes, darling,' he replied straight away.

There was a question she had been meaning to ask him, a very important question, and now was the time.

'Promise me you won't go back to Wallis once I'm gone,' she said, gasping for breath between the words.

She heard a sob. Ernest was crying. That was odd: he never cried.

'How could you even think it?' he said through his tears. 'I loved you long before I met Wallis. You must know that, Mary. In my heart it was only ever you.'

'Oh,' she said. She was surprised, but it made her happy, like a warm, comforting glow.

That was the last word she uttered. Her rattly breathing grew easier as she slipped into a coma, from which she would never wake.

Chapter 72

Brighton, 28 December 1997

*A*S ALEX SAT READING HIS BIOGRAPHY OF WALLIS
that evening, Rachel made an attempt to tidy the flat,
putting away Christmas presents and sweeping the pine needles
from under the tree. The sheets of cardboard John Sturkey had
wrapped the painting in were stacked in the hall, and as Rachel
lifted them to carry them down to the bins, something slipped
to the floor: a faded blue envelope with large loopy writing on
the outside.

She picked it up and saw it was addressed to *Mrs Mary
Simpson, 11 Upper Phillimore Gardens, London W8*, and that the
stamp on the corner was from the Bahamas. Peering inside,
she saw some sheets of blue notepaper covered in handwriting.
Where had it come from? She remembered the rip in the
canvas at the back of the painting; it must have been hidden
in there and had fallen out during the journey.

The pages were disintegrating at the folds, so Rachel took
great care as she pulled them out and laid them on the floor,
arranging them in order. At the top of the first page, there was
a W with a crown on top. It had to be Wallis. The date was
4 October 1941.

My dear Mary,

I hear on the international grapevine that you have cancer, so perhaps it is time for us to bury the hatchet – and not in each other's backs. We've been through too much over the years to let a man come between us. Don't forget we're the sisters who chose each other. You and I are family.

Do you ever look back and wish we could have been satisfied with ordinary lives? Perhaps me married to Carter Osburn and you with Prosser Tabb? We could have had luncheon at the Baltimore Country Club and discussed the latest fashions in Fuechsl's. Frankly, the very thought makes me yawn, and I imagine it does you too.

I hope we can meet again at the end of this ridiculous, unnecessary war. Hitler never wanted to fight the Brits, you know. He's got the greatest respect for them, but that treacherous Mr Churchill and his clique forced him into it. Britain can never expect to win. They should sue for peace before any more lives are lost and they will find the Germans to be reasonable people. Von Ribbentrop assures me that the Führer has no desire to change the English way of life, although he teases that he would reinstate David as king with me by his side. Wouldn't we have a gay time? I fancy getting my hands on the Crown Jewels and staging a coronation. You could be my chief lady-in-waiting!

Joking aside, can I buy you lunch at the Savoy as soon as peace is declared? In the meantime, don't let Ernest bore you to death with his architecture lectures.

All my love, W.

It sounded as though Wallis had been in touch with von Ribbentrop during wartime, which was almost certainly illegal. Rachel looked at the front of the envelope again and saw there was no postmark. The letter had never been sent. Had Wallis thought better of it, or was there another reason?

'Does it mention Mary Kirk in that biography you're reading?' she called through to Alex.

He looked up. 'Yes. There's loads about her.'

'I don't suppose it says when she died, does it?'

He flicked through the pages: 'Second of October 1941,' he said. 'Why do you ask?'

Historical Afterword

THE STORY OF WALLIS WARFIELD AND HER LONG-TIME friend Mary Kirk fascinated me when I first read of it. Decades-old female friendships are complex and go through many different phases, as theirs seems to have done. I stuck to the main facts in writing about them, but I imagined events from Mary's point of view: what did it feel like to be her? In this, I was greatly assisted by a tip-off from Anne Sebba in her excellent 2012 biography of Wallis entitled *That Woman*. She wrote in her endnotes of a self-published biography of Mary produced by her sister Anne Kirk Cooke and niece Elizabeth Lightfoot, entitled *The Other Mrs Simpson*. It took a while to track down a copy, and it's not in any sense a conventional biography, but it reproduces Mary's letters home from London, and thus let me hear Mary's voice and catch a glimpse of her joyful, generous nature.

The ending of my novel is also true: Mary died of cancer at the age of forty-five, leaving behind her beloved Ernest and her two-year-old son Henry (aka Whistlebinkie). In 1943, Ernest was sent to Bombay as a post ordnance officer, overseeing munition supplies, and Henry went to Pennsylvania to stay with a friend of Mary's called Elizabeth Schiller. He returned to Britain after the war, at which point he was sent to boarding school and does not appear to have spent much time with his father. Seven years after Mary's death, Ernest got married again, to Avril Leveson-Gower, described in the press as a 'sports-woman and socialite'; from photographs online I can see a vague resemblance to Mary. I like to think that Mary was Ernest's favourite among his four wives; certainly he wrote to her sister Anne after her death, *How close Mary seems to me all the time – so close in fact that for the most part I do not have any sense that she is gone.*

Wallis continued to write to Ernest until he died in 1958, and he helped her when she was writing her memoir, *The Heart Has Its Reasons* (1956). I have quoted directly in the novel from some of the letters she wrote to him after their separation, and there can be no doubt that she missed him.

In 2003, British papers were released revealing that Wallis and Ernest were subject to Special Branch surveillance from 1935 after King George V requested help from Prime Minister Baldwin because he was alarmed by the amount of money the Prince of Wales was spending on Wallis and concerned they might be blackmailing him. Superintendent Albert Canning was put on the case and he reported on Wallis's pro-German links and stated that she was having an affair with a Mayfair car salesman called Guy Trundle. (There's not a shred of evidence to support this.) From then until after the war, Wallis was under constant surveillance by British security services, as was Edward, even during the brief period he spent on the throne, and the FBI also kept a dossier on the couple. They were both opposed to America entering the war and naïve in their friendships with leading Germans, but it's hard to believe they were knowingly spying for Germany.

The rumours about Wallis having an affair with von Ribbentrop continue to be investigated by biographers today, and several books and TV documentaries explore her Nazi sympathies and those of the Duke, including Andrew Morton's *Seventeen Carnations* (2016). The Constance Spry bouquets delivered to Wallis are variously reported to have been roses or carnations and may in fact have been both. The engraved platinum bracelet is an invention of mine.

Ernest kept his Jewish heritage very quiet, since prejudice against Jews was widespread in Britain in the early twentieth century and it would have adversely affected his business and social standing. His sister Maud only told Henry about it after his father's death, when he was eighteen years old, and as an adult he decided to embrace his Jewish roots and emigrate to Israel, taking the name Aharon Solomons. He fought in the Yom Kippur war as part of the Israeli Defence Force, and became a scuba-diving and free-diving instructor in Eilat (you'll find videos online of him explaining his methods).

A young Mary Kirk (standing third from left) and Wallis Warfield (standing second from right) at the wedding of a friend. © Topham Picturepoint

As a novelist, I like dramatising the lives of famous figures from the past, but it becomes tricky when they are still alive or have close living relatives. At the time of writing it is almost twenty years since the death of Diana, Princess of Wales, but I decided not to make her a character in this novel. Instead, I invented the characters of Alex, Rachel and Susie Hargreaves, and viewed Diana, and the investigation into her death, through their eyes. The reason for Diana and Dodi's twenty-eight-minute visit to Villa Windsor on 30 August 1997 is still not entirely clear but the painting was my invention. Certainly it seems unlikely that Diana would ever have lived there.

I have no evidence that Diana met the Duchess of Windsor, although it's possible. Wallis was said to be very fond of Prince Charles, whom she met in 1971 when he visited her and the Duke in Paris. She came over to Britain for the Duke's funeral in 1972 and spent three days as a guest of the Queen at Buckingham Palace, after which Charles wrote to her. She is said to have considered bequeathing some of her jewellery to his future wife, but in the event this did not happen. Both Charles and Diana attended Wallis's funeral in 1986, at which her remains were placed next to the Duke's in the royal burial ground near Windsor Castle.

Alex's investigation of the crash that killed Princess Diana is only described in my novel between 31 August and Christmas 1997, by which time the conspiracy theorists were just getting started. For the stories of the 'flash before the crash', the search for the Fiat Uno, Diana's premonitions that she would be murdered, the arguments over the carbon monoxide in Henri Paul's blood, the large amount, of money that had been deposited in his bank account, the delays in an ambulance getting Diana to hospital, and many more controversies, there are a number of books available, as well as documentaries that can be found online.

Two programmes were shown on British television in June 1998: one backing the conspiracy theorists and the other, by journalist Martyn Gregory, pointing out the flaws in their arguments. Martyn Gregory's account seems to me the more convincing, but opinion polls at that time indicated that a staggering 85 per cent of the British public believed Diana had been murdered.

The French investigation into the crash did not report until 1999; it concluded that Diana died as a result of an accident caused by Henri Paul driving at high speed while intoxicated. It was followed by Operation Paget in the UK in 2004, an investigation into the various conspiracy theories, and a full judicial inquest, which reported in April 2008 that Diana and Dodi were killed as a result of the gross negligence of Henri Paul, and that the pursuing paparazzi were a contributory factor. For a full account of the crash, you can read the inquest findings online.

The emotional impact of Diana's death was very real. There were dozens of sobbing faces in the crowd outside her funeral, and statistics show that the suicide rate in England and Wales increased by 17 per cent in the four weeks after her death, while documented instances of self-harm rose by 44.3 per cent. However, it would be hard to prove that it signalled a long-term change in the British national character, as some claimed at the time. Was the communal expression of grief valuable for those concerned? Or do some look back on it a little shamefaced now? Certainly it started a trend for massive floral tributes after the deaths of much-loved celebrities, with the north London display for George Michael a recent example.

I agree with the opinion Susie Hargreaves expresses in the novel, that Diana would have gone on to make a valuable contribution to the world. She would probably have had a few more romantic dramas as well. It will be fascinating to see the new perspectives on her all-too-brief life that will undoubtedly emerge around the twentieth anniversary of her death on 31 August 2017.

A transcript of the speech made by Edward VIII when he publicly announced his abdication via radio from Windsor Castle

At long last I am able to say a few words of my own. I have never wanted to withhold anything, but until now it has not been constitutionally possible for me to speak.

A few hours ago I discharged my last duty as King and Emperor, and now that I have been succeeded by my brother, the Duke of York, my first words must be to declare my allegiance to him. This I do with all my heart.

You all know the reasons which have impelled me to renounce the throne. But I want you to understand that in making up my mind I did not forget the country or the empire, which, as Prince of Wales and lately as King, I have for twenty-five years tried to serve.

But you must believe me when I tell you that I have found it impossible to carry the heavy burden of responsibility and to discharge my duties as King as I would wish to do without the help and support of the woman I love.

And I want you to know that the decision I have made has been mine and mine alone. This was a thing I had to judge entirely for myself. The other person most nearly concerned has tried up to the last to persuade me to take a different course.

I have made this, the most serious decision of my life, only upon the single thought of what would, in the end, be best for all.

This decision has been made less difficult to me by the sure knowledge that my brother, with his long training in the public affairs of this country and with his fine qualities, will be able to take my place forthwith without interruption or injury to the life and progress of the empire. And he has one matchless blessing, enjoyed by so many of you, and not bestowed on me – a happy home with his wife and children.

During these hard days I have been comforted by her majesty my mother and by my family. The ministers of the crown, and in particular, Mr Baldwin, the Prime Minister, have always treated me with full consideration. There has never been any constitutional difference between me and them, and between me and Parliament. Bred in the constitutional tradition by my father, I should never have allowed any such issue to arise.

Ever since I was Prince of Wales, and later on when I occupied the throne, I have been treated with the greatest kindness by all classes of the people wherever I have lived or journeyed throughout the empire. For that I am very grateful.

I now quit altogether public affairs and I lay down my burden. It may be some time before I return to my native land, but I shall always follow the fortunes of the British race and empire with profound interest, and if at any time in the future I can be found of service to his majesty in a private station, I shall not fail.

And now, we all have a new King. I wish him and you, his people, happiness and prosperity with all my heart. God bless you all! God save the King!

Edward VIII, 11 December 1936

Notes

Some quotations in this novel have been paraphrased from printed sources, as follows.

Page 8, line 20: 'My grandma used to say, "Never let a man kiss your hand or he'll never marry you." That, and "Never marry a Yankee."'

'"Never marry a Yankee" was one of her fiercer injunctions . . . She also laid down another rule: "Never allow a man to kiss your hand. If you do, he'll never ask you to marry him."' From *The Heart Has Its Reasons*, by The Duchess of Windsor, first published 1956.

Page 15, line 2: 'She told me: "If you step on a puppy's tail, it hurts just as much as if you step on a dog's."'

'"If you step on a puppy's tail," she used to say, "it hurts just as much as if you step on a dog's."' From *The Heart Has Its Reasons*, by The Duchess of Windsor, first published 1956.

Page 87, line 19: 'Mother says that being a successful wife is an "exercise in understanding", and that I must try harder.'

'Being a successful wife is an exercise in understanding.' From *The Heart Has Its Reasons*, by The Duchess of Windsor, first published 1956.

Page 90, line 21: "'Wallie can no more keep from flirting than she can from breathing.'"
'She could no more keep from flirting than from breathing.' From *That Woman*, by Anne Sebba, first published 2012.

Page 144, line 3: "'I'm very fond of him, and he is *kind*, which would be a marked contrast to the last husband.'"
"'I am very fond of him and he is *kind*, which will be a contrast . . .'" From *That Woman*, by Anne Sebba, first published 2012.

Page 145, line 5: 'She wrote of their honeymoon driving through France and Spain, in which Ernest took the role of tour guide, with his impeccable French and his detailed knowledge of the architecture and customs: *like a* Baedeker, *a* Guide Michelin *and an encyclopaedia all wrapped up in a retiring and modest manner.'*
"'a *Baedeker*, a *Guide Michelin* and an encyclopaedia all wrapped up in a retiring and modest manner.'" From *That Woman*, by Anne Sebba, first published 2012.

Page 147, line 19: '*I was much amused to hear the advice she gave him,* Wallis wrote. *She said that, as with explosives, he must handle me with care. He replied that he was well aware of my explosive possibilities and felt sure he was equal to the task.'*
"'Like explosives, she needs to be handled with care." Ernest replied that he was well aware of the explosive content but had no misgivings.' From *The Heart Has Its Reasons*, by The Duchess of Windsor, first published 1956.

Page 174, line 22: '"No one wants to leave Wallis's parties," Mike Scanlon whispered to Mary, "because they have so much pep in them."'

'"Wallis' parties have so much pep no one ever wants to leave," commented one guest.' From *That Woman*, by Anne Sebba, first published 2012.

Page 176, line 31: 'She replied in her best flirtatious style: "Why, sir, you are just a heartbreak to any woman because you flatter her but you can never marry her."'

'In the early days she used to say to him: "You are just a heartbreak to any woman because you can never marry her."' From *That Woman*, by Anne Sebba, first published 2012.

Page 216, line 25: 'Ernest got along marvellously with their host over a shared love of history: *dates and circumstances were flying back and forth across the table like ping-pong balls.*'

'The Prince, like Ernest, fancied himself a lay student of history; in a moment dates and circumstances were flying back and forth across the table like ping-pong balls.' From *The Heart Has Its Reasons*, by The Duchess of Windsor, first published 1956.

Page 218, line 26: 'Mary opened it to find a typed radiogram message: *Wishing you a safe crossing and a speedy return to England. Edward P.*'

'It was a *bon voyage* message, signed Edward P., wishing Ernest and me a safe crossing and a speedy return to England.' From *The Heart Has Its Reasons*, by The Duchess of Windsor, first published 1956.

Page 224, line 28: '*I think I do amuse him*, she wrote. *I'm the comedy relief, and we like to dance together, but I always have Ernest hanging round my neck, so all is safe.*'

"'I'm the comedy relief and we like to dance together but I always have Ernest hanging around my neck so all is safe.'" From *That Woman*, by Anne Sebba, first published 2012.

Page 362, line 6: 'Ernest sounded weary and sad. "I told her that all the nice things about our marriage have been spoiled and I do not want to be tied for life to someone I cannot live with.'"

"'All the nice things are spoiled and I don't want to be tied for life to someone I cannot live with.'" From *That Woman*, by Anne Sebba, first published 2012.

Page 374, line 8: '*If I wake in the night, sometimes I imagine that I am at home in Bryanston Court and hear your footsteps coming down the corridor, the* Evening Standard *tucked under your arm. Darling Ernest, I can't believe such a thing can have happened to two people who got on so well.*'

'I wake up in the night sometimes and think I must be lying on that strange chaise longue and hear your footsteps coming down the passage of the flat and there you are with the *Evening Standard* under your arm. I can't believe that such a thing could have happened to two people who got along so well.' From *That Woman*, by Anne Sebba, first published 2012.

Page 375, line 17: '*The US press has done untold harm in every direction besides printing wicked lies . . . Last time I went out I was followed everywhere by cameramen.* Towards the end of the letter she wrote: *I am sorry about Mary, I am sorry for myself, I am sorry for the King.*'

"'. . . the US press has done <u>untold harm</u> in every direction besides printing wicked lies – I feel small and licked by it all. I shall come back Wednesday afternoon but remain in seclusion as last time I went out I was followed everywhere by cameramen . . . I am sorry about the club ghosts, I am sorry

about Mary – I am sorry for myself. I am sorry for the King."'
From *That Woman*, by Anne Sebba, first published 2012.

Page 376, line 24: "'I think you'll find that lots of people who used to lick Wallis's boots are now saying they hardly knew her. Only the other day I heard Emerald Cunard claim she had met her 'only once or twice' and did not take to her." . . . "She has been hateful towards me. Simply hateful."'

"'Lots of people who used to lick her boots are now saying they hardly knew her . . . Sally (Lally?) Cunard particularly, I'm told. Of course I did not see her. She has been hateful towards me and (I) can't pretend that I'm sorry she has gone."'
From *The Other Mrs Simpson*, by Anne Kirk Cooke and Elizabeth Lightfoot, first published 1977.

Page 377, line 15: '*I'm pretty flattened out by the world in general*'
"'I've been pretty flattened out by the world in general. . ."'
From *That Woman*, by Anne Sebba, first published 2012.

Page 379, line 4: "'I have found it impossible to carry the heavy burden of responsibility and to discharge my duties as King as I would wish to do without the help and support of the woman I love."'
From 1936 abdication speech broadcast on radio.

Page 381, line 11: 'Wallis wrote to Ernest saying how much she missed him: *I think of us so much, though I try not to. I'd love to hear from you if you feel like telling me a bit.*'
"'I think of us so much, though I try not to." She craved news about him. "I wonder so often how you are? How the business is getting on etc. I thought I'd write a few lines to say I'd love to hear from you if you feel like telling me a bit."'
From *That Woman*, by Anne Sebba, first published 2012.

Page 399, line 29: 'Wallis wrote that she had volunteered for the French Red Cross and was busy delivering plasma, bandages and cigarettes to hospitals in eastern France, while Peter Pan was working for the British Military Mission.'

'[She] took a job with the Section Sanitaire Automobile (SSA) of the French Red Cross, delivering plasma, bandages and cigarettes to the hospitals behind the Maginot Line in eastern France.' From *That Woman*, by Anne Sebba, first published 2012.

Page 411, line 14: '"I don't know how she could be happy married to that nervous, difficult man," Mary replied.'

'"I do not envy her her life with that nervous difficult little man."' From *The Other Mrs Simpson*, by Anne Kirk Cooke and Elizabeth Lightfoot, first published 1977.

Page 442, line 8: '*How close Mary seems to me all the time – so close in fact that for the most part I do not have any sense that she is gone.*'

'As to that, it has been an amazing experience to realize how close Mary seems to me all the time – so close in fact that for the most part I do not have any sense that she is gone.' From *The Other Mrs Simpson*, by Anne Kirk Cooke and Elizabeth Lightfoot, first published 1977.

Acknowledgements

My agent, Vivien Green of Sheil Land, has long been fascinated by Wallis Simpson (mainly because of the jewellery, I suspect) and suggested I write about her. Mr Ideas Man Richard Hughes then told me that Princess Diana visited Villa Windsor on the day she died, and the germ of the idea for this novel was born. Huge thanks to both of them for all their inspiration and support.

I changed publishers with this book, which is a nerve-racking process, akin to leaving the family home and taking up residence with another family in the hope they will adopt you. To my immense relief, new editor Sherise Hobbs and marketing supremo Jen Doyle made me feel instantly welcome by taking me for a champagne lunch. Sherise gave top-notch editorial guidance on the text, Jane Selley did a sensitive copy-edit and Katie Green did a forensic proofread. My gratitude to them and to Emily Gowers, Mari Evans, and the rest of the Headline team, who were wonderful from the very start.

Early readers of this novel included the indomitable Karen Sullivan of Orenda Books, who sent me a five-page email of detailed notes and suggestions, despite being officially the busiest person in the universe. Bloggers Lor Bingham and

Abbie Rutherford also made loads of valuable suggestions, as did the brilliant Gaia Banks at Sheil Land and the aforementioned Richard Hughes, while Abby Endler was my American dialogue coach. Thank you all.

A special mention to Zoe Hill at Schlesinger Library Research Services, Harvard for scanning Mary Kirk's letters and finding me a copy of the book by her sister Anne and niece Elizabeth. Catherine Lamb kindly put me in touch with John Peacock, who offered useful fashion advice, and Bettina Hartas Geary, a trained therapist, wrote a fascinating email to me about 'Diana Syndrome'.

The book blogging community have yet again been wonderfully supportive and encouraging in the last year and a special mention goes to Anne Williams, Karen Cocking, Anne Cater, Julie Boon, Kate Atherton, Liz Barnsley, Victoria Goldman, Jess Bickerton, Laura McKeen, Linda Hill, Rachel Gilbey, Sharon Wilden, Emma Crowley, Bronagh McAteer, Rebecca Pugh, Maryline VP, Kaisha Holloway, Magdalena Johansson, Amanda Moran, Emma B, Ana Thom, Jody Hoekstra, Joanne Baird, Louise Wykes, Susan Head and Tina Hartas, as well as the ever-glamorous Tracy Fenton.

A special shout-out to Robert Blenman for buying copies of *The Secret Wife* for virtually everyone he knows, as did my gorgeous sister Fiona Williams. Huge gratitude to Christina Jansen and Jutta Russell for making me look presentable in author photos. For their extraordinarily generous social media support, my warmest thanks to Barbara Doukas, Jan Moran and Simon Kettlewell, as well as author pals Marnie Riches, Louise Beech and Kerry Fisher.

And thanks to Karel Bata for everything.